# BUT FIRST

# YOU

# NEED A

# PLAN

## K. L. ANDERSON

*Leapfrog Press*
*New York and London*

Published in 2022 in the United States by Leapfrog Press Inc.

Leapfrog Press Inc.

www.leapfrogpress.com

Distributed in the United States by
Consortium Book Sales and Distribution
St. Paul, Minnesota 55114

www.cbsd.com

Author portrait: © Nicole Butler
Cover design: James Shannon
Typesetting: Prepress Plus

First Edition

ISBN 978-1-948585-71-2

Library of Congress Cataloging-in-Publication Data

Printed and bound in the United Kingdom

The Forest Stewardship Council® is an international non-governmental organisation that promotes environmentally appropriate, socially beneficial, and economically viable management of the world's forests. To learn more visit www.fsc.org

**LEAPFROG GLOBAL FICTION PRIZE**

K. L. Anderson's *But First You Need a Plan* was judged to be the winner of the 2021 Leapfrog Global Fiction Prize. Judge of the 2021 contest, Ann Hood, said of Anderson's entry:

*I love, love, love the mystery element in the novel. It kept me reading faster and faster, eager to know what happened on that roof! I gasped and nodded in equal measure, proving Flannery O'Connor's advice that a good ending has the reader saying both, "I never saw it coming," and "I knew it all along."*

### Past Winners of the Leapfrog Global Fiction Prize

2022: *Rage and Other Cages* by Aimee LaBrie
2022: *Jellyfish Dreaming* by D. K. McCutchen
2021: *But First You Need a Plan* by K. L. Anderson
2021: *Lost River, 1918* by Faith Shearin
      *My Sister Lives in the Sea* by Faith Shearin
2020: *Amphibians* by Lara Tupper
2019: *Vanishing: Five Stories* by Cai Emmons
2018: *Why No Goodbye?* by Pamela L. Laskin
2017: *Trip Wire: Stories* by Sandra Hunter
2016: *The Quality of Mercy* by Katayoun Medhat
2015: *Report from a Burning Place* by George Looney
2015: *The Solace of Monsters* by Laurie Blauner
2014: *The Lonesome Trials of Johnny Riles* by Gregory Hill
2013: *Going Anywhere* by David Armstrong
2012: *Being Dead in South Carolina* by Jacob White
2012: *Lone Wolves* by John Smelcer
2011: *Dancing at the Gold Monkey* by Allen Learst
2010: *How to Stop Loving Someone* by Joan Connor
2010: *Riding on Duke's Train* by Mick Carlon
2009: *Billie Girl* by Vickie Weaver

These titles can be bought at: https://bookshop.org/shop/leapfrog

# THE AUTHOR

K. L. Anderson has spent most of her life looking for balance between the creative and the analytical, the human and the natural. She has earned degrees in English and Biology, and has worked as an ecologist, wetland scientist, and technical writer and editor. Originally from Chicago, she now lives in Seattle with her husband and son. *But First You Need a Plan* is her first book.

## ACKNOWLEDGMENTS

Thank you to the team at Leapfrog for your guidance, editorial and otherwise, and for giving my manuscript a home: Tobias Steed, Rebecca Cuthbert, Shannon Clinton-Copeland, James Shannon, and Mary Bisbee-Beek. Thank you to Ann Hood – without your enthusiasm this book would never have come to be. I am so grateful to Karen Walag for reading my early drafts and taking this journey with me. You were always there to help me solve problems and to lift me up when I needed it. Thank you to Laurel Choate for your invaluable advice and to Nicole Butler for your generosity. To the many friends, family members, colleagues, and strangers who have nudged me to keep going over the years – every encouraging word matters. I am indebted to you. To Tim Schreiber and Milo Schreiber, thank you for your love and support, for always reminding me to eat, and for tolerating all those weekend hours when I put a closed door between us so I could work. And to my mother, Claudette Anderson, thank you for far too many things to mention here. You really are the nicest person I know.

*For Mom*

# Part I

# CHAPTER 1
## (CASSIE)

A woman fell.

They found her on the sidewalk, checked her vitals, and pronounced her dead. Then they zipped her up in black plastic and carted her away. At some point, I assume, they would have checked her clothing for identification, searched the area around her for... personal effects? A gun? Meanwhile, Danny was unconscious on the roof, blood soaking through his shirt and beginning to pool beneath him. There would have been an ambulance, EMTs, radios, a stretcher. Was it morning by then? Probably.

Hours passed before they called me, before they knew who to call. When the kids asked where their father was, I told them he must have gotten up early for work, while secretly wondering if he'd left us. I started making arrangements, running numbers, deciding how I felt about the prospect of a Danny-less future. The unsuspecting wife, quietly planning for a lesser tragedy. I should have imagined the truth would be worse.

My mother perches on the edge of her chair, reading aloud from a book she impulse-bought at some gift shop. "You must not visualize the injuries of the wounded, because to do so is to invite the same agony upon yourself." Her voice is hushed, like clapping mittens; it matches the tan upholstery of the furniture, the pastel prints on the walls. "Your job is to believe in recovery, focus on the life force inside."

The kids listen to her foolishness, their eyes shining with worry. I'm supposed to protect them, somehow, through visualization or fancy breathing, but all I see is a falling woman. The spread of her arms and the desperate fluttering of her clothes. When forced to give her a face I imagine a more exotic version of me: lustrous green eyes and wiry muscles and high, strong cheekbones. She's a little bit reckless, that girl who stays out all night and carries a gun in her purse because, well, you never know. Her hair I haven't figured out yet, but her nail polish is definitely red. Garish. She's wearing a denim jacket over a floral print dress, light-colored pumps, scuffed at the heels. She meets Danny on the roof. Or they go up together.

On the hospital's first floor, a TV hangs from the ceiling, its volume low, the only authority on outside events we've been too preoccupied to care about. Its purpose is to offer us news, but the broadcast never mentions Danny. What I want is footage from the crime scene, a clear shot of the building where it happened, interviews with eyewitnesses. *I saw her fall. That was my neighbor. She wasn't what you would call nice.* Instead, I see fire. Smoke smeared black across an afternoon sky. Whose news is this? I switch to a different channel, but the images are the same: flames devour a building, a man crosses the street holding a wad of fabric over his nose and mouth. There are words I can't decipher. *Refinery. Revenge. Gaia.* If only someone would extinguish the fire; maybe then they could switch to Danny.

In the meantime, I speculate.

They were on a roof together late at night. They talked about...I don't know what. They argued. She was standing too close to the edge, and when she fired, the recoil of the gun pushed her off balance.

Too clichéd? Then how about this one:

Danny followed her onto the roof to help. She was in trouble, ready to escape. He tried to talk her down but discovered he didn't know how. The woman was resolute, and what's more she found his attempts at heroism annoying, so she let him have a couple in the chest before jumping.

Danny as the hero? Not impossible, but my gut disagrees.

It was the darkest part of the night. Danny didn't need to see the weapon to know it was there. He'd been expecting this, his little bit of trouble suddenly a little bit out of control. It wasn't the first gunshot he'd heard, the first woman he'd seen in the moments before death.

Sometimes, speculation feels nearly the same as panic. The disquiet of pre-truth as the imagination races down unlit passageways, searching for light. Dozens of scenarios, all with the same terrible conclusion.

# CHAPTER 2

We're not Hospital People, Danny and me. Sometimes, though, you make exceptions. The last time we were here, I was giving birth. They said the second child would be easy, but there were hours of excruciating labor, a groggy night afterward, the unpleasant sense that I'd left the baby in a room draped in velvet because it seemed like a better place for her than wherever I was headed. It was my turn to pick a name, which I did with an appropriate mixture of gravity and whimsy. Danny told me he loved the *sound* of Penelope, but when it was time to fill out the paperwork, he wondered out loud if maybe it didn't work better as an idea than an actual name. That maybe, as a person, she sounded like the kind of girl who had eight nannies and dressed like a slut, and why couldn't we just stick to naming our kids after people we knew? Nel was our compromise; a tiny name for a tiny girl. So much smaller than her brother ever was. When we took her home Danny promised me that was it. No more hospitals, ever.

Five years later, here we all are: the entire Irving clan, waiting for news under lights that flicker and glare, cold white tinged with purple. From certain angles, you can almost pluck grief from the air. I imagine ghosts in the rooms, layers of death and recovery. Histories bleached white but never fully erased. What happened, I wonder, to the last rooftop victim that came through here? Which room was his, and what kinds of secrets did he keep from *his* wife?

The kids are so well behaved that I wonder if they're already stricken with whatever stress-induced syndrome they'll be diagnosed with in a few months or years. It makes me uneasy the way they sit, without complaining, in hard chairs that are too big for them. They're adaptable when they're young, Danny likes to say.

*Bricks of soft clay. It's the older ones who get damaged.* He might die, I realize. Their father. Nel is blowing on a pinwheel, trying her hardest to keep it spinning. So much determination on her face, as if her breath is the key to Danny's life. What will I have to tell her, once we find out what happened? That it was all Daddy's fault?

Nearby there is hand-holding, arm rubbing, *I'm so glad you're here*-ing. Danny's best friend Evan is crying. Not just crying but weeping. He's been doing this for hours, like he's having a nervous breakdown, my imagination of what one would look like. He keeps saying *the good ones always have bad luck; it's not fair; the good ones.* Danny's mother Deb clutches a tissue and nods in agreement, her face splotched red. Her husband Bill sits tall-backed with a jittery leg and an arm on her shoulder. *Let's just see what happens. Let's give it some time here.*

My mother flits and flutters around them, placing her palms on her face, on her neck, tracing her collarbones with her fingertips. Eventually she's back at my side, a restless hand straying toward my shoulder. "Dad sends his prayers," she lies.

Her attention turns to the scene spread out before her: the kids and me, our bodies in haphazard sitting positions with a dozen unopened bags of chips at our feet. Distantly, I remember a vending machine, a full row of Cool Ranch Doritos slipping down, spiral after spiral, until it felt like I'd punched a hole in the snacks. My mother tilts her head, furrows her brow, observes us with all the grace of a water buffalo.

"Let's go to the cafeteria," she announces. The kids look up, disoriented and sleepy. They're so fragile right now, breakable versions of the children they were yesterday.

"No thank you," says Nel. "I'm not hungry."

My mother turns to E. "How about you, sweetie?"

"What happens when someone dies? In one of the rooms?"

Her hand finds his arm and squeezes. "No, don't. It isn't..."

"Is there a button that they press? Does like a dead body squad come or something?"

"There's a morgue in the basement," I offer. "It's not on the map they give you, though. I already checked."

"Cassandra!" my mother hisses. "You're not helping."

*But he's a kid who likes facts.* I don't say this, even though it's true.

Both things are: E needs facts and I'm no help and none of my explanations are working. My mother smothers the children in a hug, a sight that makes me crave a bed and a dark room. With a sigh, my head drops to the back of the chair next to me. *Just for a few seconds*, I promise, but my eyelids are made of iron, inches thick and sliding shut with a clang. *Good. Now we'll be safer. We'll start here and build something better.* I hear shuffling, whispers, feet on carpeting. *See? They've already started the renovations.* Inside my fortress I plan out the future: new mattresses and clean sheets, a seven-story house with so many stairways and secret shortcuts that we'll get lost inside and never have to leave. We'll bake little cakes, and leave them on the windowsills, so that the elves and fairies can—

"Cassandra." My mother's voice crackles, a dirty log on a fire. The gates slide open; the pastel room snaps back into focus. The kids and Doritos are gone. My mother is crouched in front of me, her eyes even with mine. Up close, the purple-tinged lighting accentuates the asymmetry in her face, the fault line my father created. Two halves that no longer match. Right side hard, left side soft.

"Listen, sweetie. I'm supposing that maybe it's not the best idea for the kids to be here. What do you think?"

"What else am I supposed to do with them?"

"Let me watch them."

I try to follow her words, understand where they are headed. "But you're also here."

She sighs, shakes her head in that familiar way. "I could take them home with me and see that they get to bed."

I wait.

"Once they're settled in, I'll come back. Your dad will be there if they need anything."

A freezing fog settles over us. Is it the air conditioning, turned up too high? I can't remember what month it is, what time it is. It was hot and then it wasn't. People were talking about the weather. Someone mentioned a cold front. Maybe that's what this is.

My mother can see the formation building behind my eyes, dark clouds skittering and piling on top of other dark clouds. "Honey, be reasonable. I don't know what you think might happen. Eventually you have to come around. Your dad—"

"I'm more comfortable having them here with me."

For a moment the soft side of her face hardens and the two halves match. She gives me a look like she'll go outside and fight me if she needs to, but then I see her stop, close her eyes, do whatever bullshit counting exercise she's taught herself. The left side of her face relaxes and attempts to smile.

"We might need to come up with a trauma plan for them or something."

"I don't know what that is."

She's back to flitting and fluttering, her fingers spread apart and pressing against her neck as if to confirm its existence. "I don't quite know either. But Rosemary Rasmussen helped her sister with one for her kids after their dad had his accident. I told you about that, right?"

We're definitely not Trauma Plan People. My mother knows this. She must.

"Mom."

Her voice is thin, a faint gray line. "As long as they stay safe, okay? Be smart."

# CHAPTER 3

Danny was shot twice. The bullets went into his front and came out his back, leaving a trail of damage behind. Fragments of bone, a collapsed lung, shredded pieces of body. Blood inside and out. Still, the hospital staff pronounces him Very Lucky. There's a good chance they'll be able to stabilize him. Danny seems like a fighter. Sometimes you can tell; the ones who aren't ready to let go. For now, though, they're keeping him unconscious. It will be a day, at least, before we can talk to him.

In the meantime, we search the internet, unearth whatever scraps of information it's willing to offer. For instance: Danny was shot on the roof of a four-story apartment building in the West Milton neighborhood. We ponder this, wondering if four stories is taller than it seems, or if a person could fall from this height and just as easily not die, her fate not decided until the moment of impact.

She remains nameless, faceless, reason-less. The falling woman.

Danny's stepfather, Bill, is certain that they are intentionally withholding her name from the press. "There's more to this investigation than they're letting on. I'm guessing they still haven't found the firearm." He says the word like a man who uses it regularly. *Firearm.* We let it permeate our thoughts, the implications of it, until a new thought settles in that allows a host of new possibilities to bloom. The woman who fell wasn't the shooter at all. There was a third person on the roof, who shot Danny and pushed the woman, then fled the scene. Does this make sense? Does it make us more clear-headed and hopeful? *Three* people on the roof. The gunman/gunwoman still at large.

They all ask the same questions: the police, Danny's parents, my mother. *Do you have any idea why Danny might have been on that roof?*

*Did he tell you where he was going that evening? Was he with anyone?*
*Do you know anyone who lives on South Jefferson Street?*
*Did he call you that night, at any point?*
*Was there any indication that he was having an affair?*
*Where were* you *that night, Mrs. Irving?*

There it is. I'm a suspect. A jealous madwoman who would follow Danny and his mistress up onto a roof, who would shoot my husband, push the woman to her death, leave my kids alone in the middle of the night to do this. Is Danny a suspect, too? We're not Lawyer People. How could we ever afford one, or two, for that matter? Every hour I spend in the hospital is an hour I'm not working. Same for Danny—unconscious Danny who may need weeks to recover. Does insurance cover recovery? Does the shooter pay our medical bills? I don't know how any of it works. Meanwhile, Danny sleeps.

We're not Hold a Grudge People, but this one is going to be tough.

Bill pulls me aside. He has brilliant blue eyes, a face incised with lines, and the slightly bulging, purply nose of a reformed drinker. He's a reformed everything-er. Danny's mother, Deb, likes redemption stories, men who learn restraint through love. Every time I talk about my own father to Danny, he offers up Bill as a comparison. My father and Bill are examples of men who got their shit together. They're proof that people can change, that happy endings are possible.

Bill's voice is rough, like wet gravel. "Listen, Cas. Deb and I want to know who did this." He pauses, leads me by the shoulders into a corner, moves in closer. "Or if Danny did something that you know about and we need to take care of it. I think you get what I'm saying. We understand keeping quiet with the cops and all that, but *we* need the facts. As family. You know we would do anything, whatever we can. But we need time to process. If he doesn't make it…we just need to process here. Dump it all in the hopper and sort through it. Promise me you'll help us do that."

His eyes are blue rockets, ready to launch and take care of business. All I need to do is give the instruction, let him know what needs to be done.

"I honestly don't know anything."

He continues to stare, rockets at the ready. The hands on my shoulders press down in a manner that offers no comfort. Then he nods and closes his eyes, pulls me in for a hug, kisses my head.

"You're always family. Okay? No matter what."

Time passes. I watch Nel and E curl up in their uncomfortable chairs and fall asleep. E's adult namesake, Evan, appears next to me, large and red-faced. Inexplicably, he's changed his clothes in the last few hours, his brown tweed blazer switched out for one in navy blue velour. They came from the estate sale of some eccentric professor, and he's been trying them out, one at a time, with the same pair of tan Carhartts. New attire for his new job, which isn't actually a job at all but some shady pyramid scheme. Network marketing, Evan calls it. The membership fee is a small investment, the opportunities tremendous. All it takes is a little discipline, a desire to spread the word, sell the books and memberships, attend the conventions. Now that Evan has found *The Secret Path to Joy*, a golden future awaits.

He leans in close, his shoulder brushing my cheek. "What did Danny tell you?"

"About what?"

"Any of it. He looked to me like he was about to explode. Do you know what I'm talking about? Just so bottled up, so afraid to live."

Even when I'm not sleep-deprived, Evan's words rarely make sense anymore. I listen to his nonsense, aware that my legs feel like anvils. If I could just detach them from the rest of me I'd be able to float away, be gone forever. My arms lift up, out to the sides, ready for a release that doesn't occur.

"Cas? Are you okay? Cas? Oh, Jesus Christ."

He leads me away, a hand on my elbow. At the end of the hall he pushes a door open and starts down a set of stairs. It's possible that this is an escape, an option I haven't considered yet. Just keep following him, down as many flights as there are to go, underground, into a tunnel under the city, away, away...

The stairwell ends at a second door, which leads us out onto a parking lot. How long has it been since I last stepped outside? It's overcast and windy, much colder than I'm expecting. I hug myself and rub my bare arms, waiting for Evan to offer me his hideous jacket, but he's too busy looking up at the sky to notice me shivering.

"You know, I like living here. I do. The people and all the human energy humming around us all the time. But fuck. Sometimes I just miss seeing stars at night. It's hard to explain."

"I know what stars look like. You don't have to explain."

"Of course. I'm just trying to get my hands around this one the right way." He taps a finger against his cheekbone. "That deep, almost *shining* blackness of an unpolluted sky. And then the stars spread out like infinity." He spreads his arms, inhales deeply. "Sometimes it takes tragedy to reflect, to understand..."

"I don't need a motivational speech right now."

"I know it seems like a battlefield—"

"No, not...what does that even mean?"

Evan's hand finds my shoulder. "I had this dream once, about the stars. Me on some dirty sidewalk somewhere, looking up at the sky and feeling like someone had just knocked the wind out of me, because I knew it was a once-in-a-lifetime moment. Just the *immensity* of it. This particular arrangement of stars on this particular night, their mesmerizing beauty. And I *had* them; for those few minutes they were mine. When they started to fade it was like someone had ripped out my heart and stomped on it. I wanted to forget what I'd seen, because I knew remembering it later would be absolute sadness. Do you understand me? We all have something this wonderful, but it's so overwhelming that we can't figure out a way to keep it."

None of it makes sense, but my eyes burn with tears anyway. Facing into the wind, I hug myself tighter, as though I'm emptying myself in preparation for whatever will come next.

Evan's voice is almost a whisper. "Wasn't Danny that for you? Wasn't he your star-filled sky?" He steps forward and embraces me. "Because I understand what you're feeling now. I really do."

What *am* I feeling? It doesn't seem like a matter of sadness at all, no matter how much Evan goes on about his ridiculous star-filled skies. It's a matter of weight, the pressure from above, the anvil-heavy legs that I can't release, all the parts of me that are made out of matter and stand in the way of me turning into a wisp of air, the freezing fog, creeping along the ground and then vanishing when the sun burns me away.

Evan releases me, steps away, pushes his hair back on his head, where it stays for a few seconds before flopping into his face again. "I think Danny will be fine." He says this matter-of-factly, pulling open his jacket and reaching into a pocket. "I didn't want to do this in front of everyone, but I know you're going to need a little help."

I expect to see an envelope, a check—*here's something for your hardship*—but where would Evan scrape together any money? Instead, he pulls out a green plastic pill bottle and offers it to me.

"What do I want with that? Danny would kill you."

He presses the container into my hand. "It's harmless. All natural, plant-based ingredients. To take the edge off, help you sleep."

"I don't have trouble—"

"They want you to stay up, but you shouldn't have to. What you need to do is find your comfortable spot. Let the world go dark and open yourself to future possibilities. Danny's parents can take the kids. They want to help, so let them. I know it seems hard now, but it's going to get worse before it gets better."

"What do you mean by that?"

He laughs, messily, bringing his hand to his mouth and wiping it across his lips. By the time it drops back at his side, he's crying again, his body shaking as he digs into his jacket a second time and produces a silver flask. I watch him unscrew the cap, tilt his head back, slosh the liquid around like mouthwash before swallowing.

"What the fuck, Evan? Why are you like this? Come on." I hand the pill bottle back to him. "I don't need these."

"Stop being such an obstinate little…just stop." He dumps several pills into his palm. "I'm not talking about sleep. I'm talking about relief: complete, black relief. Open up."

"This is a terrible idea." But I follow his instructions anyway, closing my eyes as he sets a pill on my tongue. It tastes like someone's failed garden, yard waste on the brink of decay. I grab the flask and force it down with a gulp of whiskey.

Evan considers the sky again, like a photographer searching for the best light. The gesture reminds me of something else; a night years before when Danny and I were at his apartment and Evan made a comment that seemed uncomfortably out of place. Danny glanced at me and shrugged while Evan stood at the window, contemplating something on the other side of it with crossed arms. A suggestion, maybe, that there were other places I should know about but never would.

"What do you know?" I ask.

He lifts the flask to his mouth again. "I don't know anything."

"I want to know why—"

"I'm telling you. There's only one answer. It's 'no.'"

"Is Danny about to go to jail? That's what I keep wondering."

"For getting shot?"

"It doesn't feel right."

He shrugs. "You never know, do you? How things might shake out. Danny comes to and then…" He makes a gesture with his hands that reminds me of fireworks.

I want Evan to tell me what I already know. That Danny's the kind who would go on a roof. This wasn't the first roof, the first building.

"How about we all just sit tight and wait for him to wake up and tell us. You have to understand this: I don't know anything."

"What if he doesn't wake up?"

Evan shrugs, and it's the same look, the same gesture, the same everything. What was it that Danny said to him that night? *You never know when to let things die.* I remember walking down the hall past the bedroom and seeing the two of them standing just inside, with the light off, whispering. A flash of paper near their waists, moving quickly out of view when I approached, and Danny's response later, when I asked him: *just a little trouble Evan's been dealing with. You know how he is.*

"Call me if you need anything." Evan presses the pill bottle into my hand and takes off across the parking lot.

Back upstairs, they've made a decision. The kids will go to Deb and Bill's for a home-cooked meal. A few meals. A few nights, if necessary. They'll share a bed in the guest room, stay close to one another. Come to the hospital during the day. We need to get back to our routines, back to our jobs.

"We decided this," says Nel, "so that you can be with Daddy by yourself." At five years old, where does she come up with these ideas, these sentences?

E nods—I guess in agreement—then turns away. He looks just like his dad. What is it they say? Cut from the same cloth? Sure. The same cloth.

Nel takes my hand and leads me to a chair next to Danny's bed. You can't fight against a little hand with a purpose. Earlier in the day, she told me that she doesn't want to be a fairy anymore—that they don't exist—but when I look at her what I see is exactly this: she's light and fluttery with her sweet gestures and ruby lips and impossibly beautiful face. I imagine her pointing a magic wand at my head and commanding it to fall, slowly, until it comes to rest on the mattress next to Danny's shoulder. "Just like home," she says.

Stepping back, Nel tilts her head and smiles. "You have to hold his hand, Mommy, so he knows it's you."

Evan's mystery pill begins to work. I feel my head nod and my eyes close. Nel places my hand on top of Danny's, my fingers resting in the grooves between his. I expect his body to flinch or twitch or whatever it is that unconscious bodies do, but he remains perfectly still. We all presume he'll come back to us, but there are what ifs to consider. They've urged us to consider them. What if I'm asleep when he goes? What if he dies while I'm lying here, holding his hand?

The world has no color, no sounds. The room is empty and its blackness is the texture of satin. Something else was supposed to happen; I waited for it and wanted it and let the kids tape their pictures to the walls and hope for it. We thought we were planning for it but instead we went to bed at night with nothing accomplished and in the morning we did the same things all over again until we found ourselves here, in this empty room.

The blackness, it turns out, isn't black at all. I'm standing on a beach at midday, the sun bright overhead and waves pressing up over the sand, my toes just beyond the water's reach. Danny is next to me, staring into my face with darkly innocent eyes and that perfect jawline. I remember him like this: handsomely disheveled, his jeans and t-shirt faded and snug, his strong arms, the slight furrow to his brow. The quiet kind, the brooding kind.

"Where are we? Where are all the people?"

"Did you come here to meet people?" He smiles. His eyes are clear and attentive.

"No, I…it just seems so empty."

He laughs. "Well, maybe they'll be here later."

The sand is as soft as hope and seemingly brand new, even though I know it's ancient, that eons ago it was rocks and mountains. The beach is wide and flat, unbroken by the signs of man. At its edge a row of palm trees rustles in a breeze that I can't feel. Off in the distance, I see green hills rising up and rolling away. I try to turn around to investigate what's behind me, but my body doesn't move.

"I don't know if you want to look back there," says Danny.

"Why not?"

"Stop fighting. Stay still." His smile is as warm as the sun. It rises up slightly higher on the left side than the right. "I bought you an island."

"We can't afford this."

"Maybe not. But still, you came."

"I don't remember the trip. Was it by boat?"

"We need to talk."

"That's not really…why?"

"Why else would I buy a deserted fucking island?"

The smile is gone. He looks sad, his shoulders rolled slightly forward. Talking's never been his thing. We're not Have a Conversation People. We're Read Each Other's Body Language People, Figure It Out Quietly People, Break the Silence with Sex People. So what does it mean if he wants to talk?

"Okay. Why don't you start by telling me what you did, up on the roof."

"It's a long story. We don't have enough time. The tide is coming in. You'll have to come back if you want to hear it."

"I'll stay here. We can watch the tide come in together."

Danny's face is a gorgeous mix of lines and shadows, like a sculpture. I want him to keep talking so we can stay like this. The two of us, a beach, green hills, everything else forgotten.

Forgotten.

What have I forgotten? It nags at me, the faint picture in my head. A magic wand. A girl with tiny hands and an equally tiny voice. Do I know her? Is she mine? The blackness creeps over her edges. She's so small, it won't take much. But I'll forget about her eventually, won't I? And the other one too. The boy. While Danny and I watch the tide coming in, the blackness will befriend them and carry them away to some other paradise.

Someone is pressing on my shoulder from behind. A man that I can't see is trying to push me off a roof. He thinks I'm her, that other woman. I reach out for Danny's hand. He bought us an island. Danny. We thought we were alone but we're not.

More pressure on my shoulder. *Cassie. Cassie.*

"Wake up."

# CHAPTER 4

Finally, the internet has useful information. The full name of the deceased: Dora MacIntosh, resident of Mapleville, nearly two hundred miles away. There's a picture of a thirtyish woman with brown eyes and brown hair and a painted-on smile that reveals nothing. A stock photo of Dora MacIntosh, M.D., from the Mapleville Family Medicine website.

A doctor? From out of town? This is who Danny was meeting on a roof in the middle of the night?

We look at photographs of the building. 4267 S. Jefferson Street. It's red brick, non-descript, like a hundred other apartments in the city. The numbers above the front door are gold, the seven angled slightly to the right. Why do the pictures make me pause? It's not the building itself, but something about the high curb against the street and the fire hydrant next to it. They remind me of...what? Nothing.

The detectives ask us more questions. They talk to Danny's family, Evan, my parents. Do we know Dora MacIntosh? No, we do not. Did Danny ever mention the name? No, he did not. The conversations are unproductive: the police learn nothing from us and we learn nothing from them. They continue to assure us, however, that they will get to the bottom of it, find the responsible parties. The way they stand up and collect their things, I know they're still gathering evidence, weaving together a story around me and my jealous tendencies, my violent tendencies, my infatuation with roofs.

"I don't see why they don't just wait until the doctors wake him up," says Deb. "Then we'll all find out what happened. Why ask *us* about it?" She looks at me for longer than necessary, rubbing the locket that rests against her chest as if making a wish.

"They need to post an armed guard outside his room," Bill insists. "*Not necessary at this time*? What is that supposed to mean? If Danny saw something he shouldn't have, there's no telling what the wrong person might try to do to him."

Evan stands up. "I'll take care of him. He's my responsibility." He and Bill hug: large, lumbering men who are all limbs clapping backs. Evan looks like he's about to start with the waterworks again, until Bill backs up suddenly, like he's remembering an important obligation, and leaves the room.

Evan turns to me and winks. "What can I do for you, Cas? Do you need me to drive you to work? Pick up the kids?"

"No."

"How did you sleep? Did what I gave you work?"

"Shhh. Not so loud."

I think about the golden sand, Danny's bare feet and rolled up jeans. He invited me there to talk. That was what he said. *We need to talk.*

Danny is awake. He can receive visitors. He can receive me.

The wife should go straight to the hospital, but I head to the Silver Whistle instead. It's a Wednesday night and this is where I go on Wednesdays. After all the waiting around we've done, Danny can do a little waiting of his own. I have friends here, who expect me, on Wednesdays. Back to our routines. Back to our jobs. It's sound advice.

As soon as I step through the door, Cherie runs over and hugs me so hard I nearly tumble backwards. "Why haven't you been answering my texts? Christ. We were all worried sick about you." She's all red hair and maroon lips and fake eyelashes.

"I don't want to talk about it, okay? Can we just…"

She waves a hand at me. "Yeah, sure, of course. Come hang out. Have some fun." I follow her to a table in the corner where a group has already gathered: Julia and Annette and Lori and Julia's cousin Rocky and two guys with shoulder-length hair that we met a few weeks back who pretend that they're twins but clearly aren't. They open up and surround me in noisy, human warmth. *Aw, Cassie, get over here. Come sit next to me and tell me what happened.* The not-twins stare at me awkwardly. *Your husband was shot? That's so messed up.* Annette glares at them and tells them to get lost, puts her arm around my shoulder and hands me a glass of beer. *No, I can't drink. I have to go back to the hospital soon.* Cherie smiles at me from across the table and the scent of someone's perfume rises up, sweet and delicious.

We talk about the usual—*this place is terrible; why do we keep coming here?* Julia and Rocky start a list on the back of a napkin of all the bars we should be going to instead. We laugh about this and about a million other things that shouldn't be funny, and maybe time is passing outside the bar but there's no way for me to tell. It seems like a single instant, stretched out and passed around the table, like the parts of a dream that happen just before waking up. Julia puts Rocky's favorite song on the jukebox and he climbs onto the table and sings. We watch, cheering him on, until Sue the waitress rushes over and threatens to ban him for life.

Another round appears. Someone hands me a drink, which I set down on the table and ignore. It's time to go to the hospital. Just a few more minutes, and my mind will be in the right place, ready to listen to Danny tell me a story about a roof and a woman named Dora MacIntosh.

Cherie picks up my drink and pulls me aside, locking her arm into mine. "It makes me so sad that this happened to you. Like *you* needed this. You were already, you know, below par in the happiness department lately."

"Thanks."

"No really, this whole thing is criminal." She brings her head low and tries to whisper. "I'm not sure if it's *appropriate* to flirt with your favorite bartender when the husband's in a coma, but I won't tell anyone if you do."

I lose track of time. Annette takes Cherie home. Lori leaves. Julia and Rocky play darts with the non-twins. I'm enveloped in a safe murmur, my own voice lost in the din. A young couple at a nearby table tries to explain dating in the modern era to me, that nobody even uses that word anymore. It's more fluid than that: gender, love, commitment. People pair off but keep their options open. When I tell them that I'm thirty and I've been married for ten years, they look at me like I'm a time traveler from the distant past. This isn't where I'm supposed to be, where the wife of a gunshot victim should be.

I stay anyway, say goodbye to Julia and her cousin, watch the non-date finish their drinks and move on. Instead of checking my watch, I make my way over to the bar and slide onto my usual stool. Lee nods without looking up. I follow his movements in the mirror, watching his reflection pour beer and scoop ice and poke a straw into a glass, brow rippled with concentration. I will him to think a funny thought, crack a smile, rub his cheek in that certain way. *Look up look up look up.* Five minutes pass—or is it longer?—before he raises his head, makes eye contact, walks over.

"You're nothing but trouble," he says.

I smile, but something is off. Is it him or me? Have I misread the joke?

"What's up?"

He runs his fingers through his hair. "It's been a long week is all."

"Why? What happened?"

He opens his mouth, then pauses and gives me a strange look. "I guess…never mind. I think your shit might be worse than my shit right now. I'm actually surprised to see you here tonight."

"It's a lot more pleasant here than the places I've been hanging out lately."

"Oh yeah?"

"I like the neon signs. Those rows of bottles lined up in front of the mirror, the way they reflect the light while bad music plays behind me. It feels like, I don't know… going to the prom."

Lee almost smiles but doesn't quite get there. He rubs at the bar with a cloth, erasing a spot that doesn't exist.

"So I guess you and the hubby have a lot to talk about."

I wonder who told him, which one of my friends.

"I haven't talked to him yet." We're both focused on Lee's hand, the cloth, the shining surface beneath it. "He just woke up," I add, wondering what explanation I should be giving instead.

"Well, he has a lot to tell you, I'm guessing."

"We'll see."

Lee steps away to tend to a loud couple at the other end of the bar. How close to closing time is it? I miss Cherie's echoing laugh, her red hair, the human warmth from earlier when time was frozen. *Below par in the happiness department.* What did she mean by that? As I try to work this out, Lee sets a drink in front of me. A vodka tonic, by the looks of it. He places his hands on the bar and waits. I examine his forearms, the tattoo of a dagger on the right one and handwritten words in black ink on the left.

# I didn't come here to

They disappear beneath his shirt sleeve. Behind him, above his head, a hockey game plays out, silently, on a screen. A white team, a red team.

"At the hospital, every time I look at a television, it's the news."

"You'd think people would want a break from that. I mean, considering."

"They take these stories and stretch them out, like they're...I don't know. What do you call that?"

"Desensitization?"

"That too, I guess. For two days, they talked about those explosions, at the oil refinery. The number dead, the number injured. They had to keep showing footage of the smoke to remind us how it looked pouring out of the buildings. Then this panel of experts came on to debate whether it was the oil company's fault or the work of an ecoterrorist group."

"Is this why you're here? To escape the news?"

I stare at my drink, try to finish the phrase written on Lee's arm. Every few days he scrubs it clean and writes a new one. I can never decide how pretentious he is, how brilliant, whether it matters.

# I didn't come here to

It could be anything.

"I can't drink. I have to go."

"Yeah, I know."

"Maybe a ginger ale instead?"

Lee nods at the glass and crosses his arms. "That *is* a ginger ale." His eyes are golden brown, soft and kind. Puppy dog eyes, I always think, although I know the expression means something different. I cross my own arms in response, offer him my best skeptical expression.

He pretends to be offended. "What? You don't believe me?"

Our eyes lock as I pick up the glass and sip from the straw. A moment like this can crush a person. I don't know what to do with anything, where to put anything. How could I, in the midst of all of my disarray?

"Cheers," says Lee. "In case I don't see you for a while."

Maybe I could try to explain it all to him, every emotion I've felt for the last thirty years and where they've gone, what they've done to me. You assume life is linear, but then you find out that the events in it don't always happen in the right order. You discover yourself living out another person's story and wonder what happened to yours, how the fragments of it could be so small that they almost disappear when pulled apart, those fragile moments of near-nothing, before they're reassembled into something you pray is better but never quite is. Leaps forward and backward and forward again and the pieces dropped along the way that you're certain you no longer need but the pain of losing them surprises you anyway. Would Lee understand?

Either way, I guess one vodka tonic won't hurt.

The next morning, they all wonder where I've been. *We were worried. You weren't answering your phone. We thought bad things. After going through the worst with Danny, we couldn't help it.*

I don't see how it matters, since I haven't missed anything. Danny is awake, but still not talking. He is unable to talk.

Let me say this again, for emphasis. *Danny can't speak.*

This is not all that uncommon, they tell us. It won't be permanent.

It shouldn't be.

On a small whiteboard, Danny has communicated this to us, to the doctors, the police: he doesn't remember what happened. All he remembers is a flash. He doesn't recognize the woman who fell, the apartment building where it happened. None of it is familiar.

Over the next several days, Danny's body continues to recover, but not his memory or his ability to speak. Eventually, they release him into my custody. I push him down the hall in a wheelchair, help him into the car, drive him home. The dutiful wife, taking care of her mute, patched-up husband. How much does it cost to rent a wheelchair? We're definitely not Wheelchair People.

There will be months of rehab. He'll be on short-term disability. *Hopefully* short-term. The state has a program, with lots of paper-work. I try not to think about all the bills the state "program" won't cover. About his eligibility once they find out.

Once they find out what?

Good question.

Danny sits in the passenger seat and stares straight ahead. There's nothing worth looking at, but he pretends to anyway. He is no longer a person who talks. He writes notes instead.

## I'M SORRY THIS HAPPENED

"I can't read that right now. I'm driving."

## I'M SORRY I CANT TALK

"Stop being sorry. Start remembering."

# CHAPTER 5
## (DANNY)

The cabin slept six, with room for another couple on the couches, a dozen on the floor in sleeping bags. You could fit twenty people, no problem. Just make sure that everyone brought along some snacks and beer, maybe some firewood. We had to remember to put away the food at night so the critters wouldn't get to it. There wasn't any electricity or running water, which was easier to get used to than you would think. We showered outside in this get-up we called the Contraption. When we showered at all.

I'm not sure why you need to know this, about the raccoons or how many couches there were. I'm just telling a story here, starting at the beginning, with the cabin. With Dora. It's important that you hear it the right way, from me.

It was Dora's parents' place. They had money but you never quite knew how much. Like there must have been a bigger, swankier summer house somewhere else. Lakefront property with a real shower and a working refrigerator and a sleek racing boat tied up to the dock, a place where her parents stayed in July and August when the rest of us were out at the end of the longest, windiest road anyone had ever driven, a road in such bad shape it could hardly be called a road at all. We asked, but Dora wasn't telling. She sure acted like a rich girl; at least that's what it seemed like. But sometimes, with people like her, there was a different reason for it. The parents got it just right and raised their kids to be confident and certain, to believe that everything they wanted had always been theirs.

There was always one. Or two. Maybe three. You could find them. You could wait for them to find you. The girls with earnest plans for the future: college, success, a taller-than-average, compassionate guy who would make a supportive husband. There was a small window during which we were just what they wanted. Guys with no future but the right kind of now. The late-blooming and quickly fading rebellion.

Yeah, you could definitely fit twenty people in that place, and to hear Dora brag about it, there were times when she did. People piled in trucks and trekked all the way up that dangerous road to her little cabin. But that week it was just the six of us. Three couples, if you want to call us that. Transitory, fading. You get the idea. Just a week near the end of July. A few pictures to look at later while we cried about everything we weren't anymore.

The names aren't important. There was Dora. She's the one you're interested in. There was Dora and then there were all of us. If the cabin is still around, you can take a flashlight into one of the upstairs closets, and maybe you'll find our names carved into the wood. I think we did this. I remember doing it.

There was a rhythm back then, a way we all talked. I can't remember it anymore. What any of us said, word for word? There's no way. I'm just paraphrasing, more or less. If I had a recording of us to listen back to, I don't think I could stand it. So yes, all of these conversations are made up, but at the same time, they're not. They're the gist. They're what you need to know.

I remember that Dora was gorgeous, a girl who had just grown up. We had a set of portable speakers with us, and about a hundred batteries so we could listen to music all week. She didn't like what the rest of us picked and kept changing it to these tinkling little pop songs that sounded like they were sung by girls who looked just like her. They were all more or less the same, except somehow the words would be different, and Dora knew them all. She used to dance around in the kitchen, half girl, half woman, singing song after song after song. Just when you thought it was the last one, another one would come on and she'd know that one too. Sometimes she'd take the other girls' hands and they'd all dance around together, laughing and singing and trading these looks like…what were they? Some kind of secret language. We'd pretend we had more important things to do than watch them, but we knew that soon they'd be sweaty and thirsty and come grab the beer cans out of our hands and ask what time we were eating dinner. Those songs—sometimes I'll hear one of them and it stops me cold. All I see is Dora singing along in that little sky blue bikini top, her skin smooth and bronzed, her dark hair falling around her shoulders, messy and sexy.

This is all just to provide a context, you understand. To set the scene, for what happened later. These aren't details you need to dwell on, but in the interest of truth I need to include them. Don't get hung up here, please. It was all a long time ago.

At night it was always so quiet. Up in the bedroom with Dora... once things got going we stopped talking, and even though she sometimes brought her mouth up to my ear like she was about to whisper something, she never did. Either that or she said it so quietly I couldn't hear. Her hair was everywhere: in my face and all over my neck and plastered to my arms. She liked to climb on top and put her hand on my chest and stare straight into my eyes, daring me to look away. I had no choice but to stare back and see that expression on her face—so serious, like she was working out a problem and this was the only way to solve it, by fucking me. This would go on for a while. A minute or two? And then I'd have to speak, ask her if she was doing all right. She'd blink, her eyes would soften, and that sweet little smile would reappear. I'd smile back and think that in the history of man there had to be at least three or four instances when a guy like me ended up with someone like her. At least three or four. She was quiet, all the way up until the end when she'd make a surprised little gasp as if she wasn't expecting it. And then, as we lay there together, sweating, she'd whisper *thank you*, and this just about killed me.

Dora was seventeen and I was twenty. I guess that means it might have technically been illegal. I mean, I'll admit to it without feeling guilty. I think she might have been more grown up than I was and she made sure I knew it. *Don't worry. You're not going to break me. I've done this before.*

Her friends, I can't really say what they were like. They were pretty too, and on their way to other places. We were all okay with this. Like I said, the window was small. In another year or two we wouldn't be kids anymore and "technically illegal" would lead to parents pressing charges. We knew the life stages, and we understood when our peaks would end and we'd head down into our valleys.

You can't fault us for that week in July all those years ago, okay? You can't fault us for remembering it as the best part of an otherwise boring summer.

We made stupid plans, the six of us. In five years we would all come back. There was talk about taking a blood oath. There was a knife out, pressed against a dirty palm.

*Not a* real *blood oath, you freak.*

*Fine, I swear it on this rock, then. This rock as our witness.*

We all looked at the rock and laughed. *Sure. Okay. That rock as our witness.*

*Let's come back in five years, no matter what we're doing. Let's make that promise.*

*Sure. Okay. Five years.*

*Every five years.*

*Like a high school reunion.*

We laughed. We couldn't stop laughing. One of the girls said, *I want to end up with a man who makes me laugh this much. This is exactly how I want it to be.*

*I might still be single in five years. You never know.*

Someone found a notebook and a couple of pens. We wrote each other notes and folded them into squares, promising to read them when we came back. Then we dropped them inside a sandwich bag and sealed it shut. Dora found an old jewelry box in one of the closets and set the baggie inside of it, in that same neat and careful way she did everything.

*It's like a time capsule.*

*We need more than just letters, then. Fill that box up.*

People threw objects to her; beer caps and a bottle of nail polish. A guitar pick. A couple condoms. Whatever we could find.

*It's full. Nothing else fits.*

*Are you really going to bury that?*

*Five years, everyone. We'll come back and dig it up.*

Dora wrote the year on top of the box and set it next to the rock.

One of us got a shovel and dug a hole, and that was that.

Later that evening, Dora came over and sat on my lap and put her arms around my neck. *What did you write to me? Your letter to me. What did it say?*

*Come back in five years and I guess you'll find out.*

*Do you want to know what mine said?*

I placed a finger on her lips and shook my head. Then she took my hand away and pulled my head toward hers and we kissed like it was the end of the world.

At least three or four instances. It can happen.

# CHAPTER 6
## (CASSIE)

We're not getting anywhere.

Nobody knows who Dora MacIntosh is or why she was in town. Nobody has a connection to 4267 S. Jefferson Street or its nineteen residents. Danny is awake but he isn't helping the investigation. He still can't talk, and he's stopped shaving. Half the hair in his beard is gray. He's written a hundred notes that say

*I can't remember what happened. The whole day is missing.*

The doctor says it's shock, that I should read up on PTSD, that our lives have changed for good. Even if Danny talks again, it will never be the same for us. I need a plan, some tools, support.

My mother stops by with dinners, takes the kids to the aquarium, a car show, the library. Danny's mother and Bill host sleepovers, movie nights, answer questions that we can't.

"We looked it up," says E. "There was this one woman who went more than ten years before she could talk again." Bill claps him on the shoulder and tells him that the thing about outliers is that they're not typical; it won't be ten years for Danny.

Inexplicably, Nel learns how to make tea for Danny. She fills the teapot with water and lays a teabag in a cup, then waits for the water to boil. She announces when it's ready, instructs me to pour the water and carry the cup over to Danny.

"It's for his throat," she informs me. "I saw it on TV."
I text Danny.

> Why are you doing this to your
> children?

He throws his phone at the couch and squeaks out his response
with a dry erase marker.

# STOP SENDING TEXTS
# TALK TO ME

> Would you like me to say it out
> loud? That I don't believe you
> can't talk?

Delivered

The way he struggles to his feet and drags himself toward the
door, it's like he's someone's grandfather. We used to mock people
like this. We used to say how pathetic, better to run straight off a
cliff than turn on the autopilot and live in slow motion. But now,
somehow, here we are.

Danny leaves the apartment for a half hour at a time. He gets as
far as he can before the pain becomes so unbearable that he turns
around and shuffles back home. I want to believe in his determination, that somehow he will fix us, just like he used to.

When the kids are with their grandparents, the apartment is
empty and cold. Danny shuffles his way from the living room to
the kitchen, stopping in the hallway to perform a silent inventory
of the pictures on the wall, the ones the kids taped up of all the
places they want to visit. It started when E was in second grade, the
instructions in some kids' magazine that came home in his backpack. *Do you want to travel? Here's an idea! Print or cut out pictures
of places you really want to see, and hang them up on a bulletin board or*

*a blank wall. After you visit one of your special destinations, take down the picture.* Danny and I watched the wall fill up with pictures of places we'd never be able to go, cursing the school, the magazine, the writer who thought this was a good idea. E taped up pictures of mountains and forests and fields of snow. Sites you could never find, even if you tried. More recently, Nel has added her own pictures: roller coasters and butterfly houses and the world's largest candy shop.

In another fifteen years this may be all we have left of the kids—a reminder of what was impossible. Danny must be thinking it too. He turns to me with his mouth slightly open, as though he's preparing to speak. It's the part where he confides in me at last, where he sees the layers of frustration and disappointment on my face and tells me what really happened.

Five seconds pass, ten seconds, before he turns away.

They call it an invisible weight and they're right. It falls, it thunks, it settles itself in my stomach. We're different forever. It never goes back. The rest of our lives is *making it work* and *figuring it out* and *getting past it.*

The green pill bottle Evan gave me is shoved inside the pocket of an old pair of jeans, deep at the bottom of a dresser drawer. I sneak into the bedroom and close the door behind me, then pour the contents into my palm and hesitate. Four left. *All natural* Evan called them, except I know there are plants out there that can kill you. There's no label on the bottle to tell me what mix of nature's chemicals I'm ingesting, but right now this seems like a better option than another restless night spent staring at the ceiling.

In the living room, Danny sits on the couch and holds out his hand to me, pulls me close. My head settles onto his shoulder and I close my eyes, listening to the muffled voices rising up from the apartment beneath us. He smells different, I realize. Like a different person. A dog wouldn't even recognize him. I cry into his sleeve and he rests his head on top of mine.

"I hate the beard."

He taps my knee twice, stops, and taps it twice again. It must be some kind of code, but I'm too drowsy to figure out how to decipher it. As Danny takes my hand, I try to fill in the blanks, insert the words he might have said on a night like this before the accident.

How long does this go on? When do they bring him in for questioning and keep him forever?

The blackness falls, replaced by golden sand, the sun shining overhead. We're at the line between water and land, the waves breaking just out of reach. Danny's face is bright and soft, like watercolors. He's wearing a clean white shirt, and when he smiles his teeth are just as clean, just as white.

"I'm glad you came back. You've been such a miserable bitch lately." He laughs, lightly. "I keep telling you I'm sorry and you never accept my fucking apologies."

"They don't sound sincere."

"They don't *sound* like anything."

"Because you won't talk anymore."

"*Can't* talk."

"Is there a difference? I don't remember the conversations we used to have. What did we talk about?"

"Look, the point is we're here, now. *This* is the conversation you'll remember. Or should we spend our time overanalyzing the situation instead?"

His eyes are bright and clear. They remind me of the deep end of a swimming pool.

"Fine," I say. "Go on."

He turns toward the ocean and raises his arm, palm up, as if offering me the sky. "Do you see all that water out there?"

I turn my head without turning it. The ocean is brilliant, blue and endless. It seems like we should all live underwater, like humans should have figured out how to do this by now.

"When I first came here," Danny says, "I thought it was going to be the moment to end all moments. Like this is what it all comes down to; once you're here, it will all be clear. I mean, people are always talking about finding answers and I always thought what's so great about the answers? It's all just trivia. It doesn't help you…

you know, live. It doesn't tell you what to do. It tells you what you should have done. Do you follow me? Answers don't help when all they tell you is what you should have been instead of who you were.

"But the waves kept lapping at the shore—they were never going to stop—and I got to thinking. Maybe answers wouldn't be such a bad thing. It wouldn't hurt to do a little bit of looking around, and maybe it'd all be bullshit, but then at least I would know that too. I could go back and tell my friends not to bother.

"So I start wondering: why am I the only one here? Aren't there other people who are as curious as me, who want to live in paradise as much as me? And that's when I start thinking what if this is all some kind of a parable, except instead of a scorpion and a hare you have…me? And then I realize that I don't even know which ocean this is, which side of it I'm on."

"You've been here the whole time? This exact spot?"

He holds out his hands, forearms up, like it's a ridiculous question. "I haven't moved, Cassie. Otherwise, how would you find me?"

Somehow, I manage to raise my arm, turn my wrist. Danny presses his palm against mine. We touch without touching.

"I'm kind of…I mean, this is good. Like, I'm happy you would bring me here and tell me about—you know—whatever that just was."

The sun is a presence more than a thing I can necessarily see. But whatever it is, it warms my face. We'll stay here, I decide. We'll be that couple who retires young. Danny's parents will drop off the kids and we'll send them to school, somewhere in town, where the teachers will be barefoot and pass out wooden recorders on the first day of class.

"I almost left you," Danny says. "Twice, I almost left. Why didn't I leave? Was it the kids?"

I stop, try to rewind. It seems like I should have the power to do this, to make Danny say different words. I listen for the white rush of wind, the green rustle of leaves, but all I hear is a cottony, stuffed-up silence, broken by the clear sound of a dog panting. Is that what it is? A tired and thirsty animal? I hit the rewind button again, but nothing happens. The panting continues. What *is* that?

"No, that was me," I say finally. "*I* was the one who almost left. The first time for real, and the second time just in my head because it felt good to think about it." Why am I saying this? Why is this what we're talking about?

"Oh, I get confused about that. Well then how about me? How many times did *I* almost leave *you*?"

"I didn't think... I didn't know. I mean, is this about that night on the roof, because we still haven't—"

"Was it you who shot me? Because I wanted to leave?"

"No! How would I have known you wanted that? Nothing was any different that day. They keep asking me and I can't come up with the answer they want. How could I shoot you if I wasn't there? I don't even know that building, that it even had a roof."

"Every building has a roof, stupid."

"You know what I mean."

"But you do know the building."

"No."

"I think you might."

It's true, isn't it? The street out front. A fire hydrant and a high curb and the eerie yellow of the streetlights. We were moving in a car and it was night and all the colors blurred together as we headed toward a place I didn't know but thought I might want to. Music on the radio. I liked it but didn't like it. The car door opening and the cool night and the concrete so close to my head and warm, even in the dark, that I wanted to lie on it and sleep. It couldn't be the same place, though. Is it even *my* memory?

Whatever the sun is, it must be majestic. The sky a wonder made of nothing but blue. A bird flies by, with wide, floppy wings, low above the sand, looking for treasure in the surf.

I see it again. The heavy door that pushed me off balance and the row of buzzers and the tiles on the floor. Newspaper circulars and a greasy bag with fast food garbage in it. How would I know a place like this? I try again to turn my head, but the muscles in my neck don't flex, or contract, or whatever it is that muscles are supposed to do.

"Danny?"

"Yes, my darling."

"What's behind me?"

Dora MacIntosh was thirty-two. She was a family practice doctor, with patients who didn't love her but mostly appreciated her. She was no-nonsense but had a way of using words that calmed people. Her online obituary provides these facts about her: not married, no kids (thank God). There was a fiancé, though, who was of course devastated but with time he would recover.

Dora MacIntosh.

Dora MacIntosh.

Dora MacIntosh.

No family in town, no conference to attend, no reason to be here. None of her friends knew she was away that weekend, not even the fiancé. It's perplexing. Possibly, it's indicative of foul play. I imagine her being forced into the trunk of a car and then later led up onto a roof at gunpoint. Do these sorts of things actually happen? Dora MacIntosh in a trunk and Danny up on the roof?

Danny up on the roof.

Why would he be there? Did Dora sneak away for the weekend to see him?

Out of nowhere, her brother turns up at the bakery—*Dora MacIntosh's brother*—asking to talk to me after my shift ends. He's tall, dressed like a fisherman, maybe, in a pea coat and a black knit cap. He has big hands, covered in big gloves, dark eyes and thick eyebrows. He doesn't match what I know of her, what I've imagined from her picture and the few things I've read. Looking at the shape and color of his face, it doesn't seem possible that they could be from the same family, but I remember his name from the obituary: Gerry MacIntosh, one of her two surviving brothers.

He talks slowly, considers me in an awkward, halting way, as if there is some quality in me that prevents him from completing his sentences. I imagine a terrifying creature inside of him, punching its way out. There's emptiness in his eyes, pain on his brow. It's the grief, I guess. It seems to erase parts of him, making it nearly impossible for him to hold himself together. This is what he looks like to me; he's collapsing in on himself.

He shows me a picture of her—his favorite picture. So much joy. So full of life. It's a close-up of her face, a gorgeous smiling girl with big eyes and pale lips and a few freckles dotting her nose. She must have been a teenager when it was taken. Gerry tells me they were close as kids. During the winters their family would take ski vacations and they'd race each other down the slopes, and in the summer they'd stay at a little cabin off in the middle of nowhere, with no running water or electricity. Times in between he walked with her to school and fought for her honor and helped her with her homework. Then he left home and they both got so busy with everything that he forgot to keep up. You couldn't even tell that time was passing. He stopped paying attention for what felt like five minutes and this is what happened.

This.

We walk side by side in the cold, slightly out of breath, hands shoved deep in pockets. The sidewalk is salt-white, the sky lifeless gray, like the inside of a rock. It seems too cold to talk, to pick out words from the tight air. Gerry lumbers a bit as he walks. Do his knees hurt? We should stop. We should tell one another goodbye and good luck, but instead we keep moving forward.

"The investigation," he says. "It doesn't seem like they've found out much of anything."

"Nobody has information. Nobody remembers."

"It's hard to believe."

"They might still think it was me, that Danny and this...your sister were having an affair, and I..."

"I don't think that."

"Well, anyway."

"The question seems to be whether Danny pushed her, if this is something he would do."

"I never would have thought so."

"Or whether she jumped. Does it happen that people jump, even though they don't seem like the type? Does anyone really seem like the type?"

"I didn't know Dora existed before this. For me, it seems like she couldn't have. Because even if Danny can't remember what happened that night, shouldn't he be able to remember *her*? I mean if they knew each other?"

Gerry cringes, although the cause is unclear. I imagine twenty different kinds of pain coursing through his body. I want to tell him it will be okay, except I know it won't. There's no way to re-imagine a happy ending for Dora.

It's hard to say how far we walk together. We turn down a residential street, then another one. I lose track of which direction we're facing. North? East?

"She didn't shoot him," Gerry says. "I know this. So then I keep going over it in my head, thinking though all the possibilities. Like if there was some other person involved, how much does that complicate the story? Does this other guy offer them a choice? Either jump or I shoot you." He holds out two fingers like he's pointing a gun. "Dora picks the free fall and Danny picks the other thing: a bullet to the chest."

I shake my head. No, it isn't right. How would a scenario like this happen? Who would even have this fantasy? "Two," I say. "Two bullets."

"Well, whatever it was. It all seems random. One bullet, two bullets. I want to learn a version of the story in which she just happened to be walking down the sidewalk and saw people in trouble and she went up to help."

"And Danny went up to help too. He was like that."

"And this version is the one that makes the most sense. Out of however many possible explanations, this one ends up sticking." He turns to look at me, and so I nod.

"You're right."

Gerry's breathing is heavy and quick, but he keeps moving, like he's forgotten there are other options for his legs and feet. "So you think they didn't know each other, then?" he asks.

"How could they?"

"And you believe Danny?"

"It seems like I would have heard of her."

"No. Not that. I mean this." He lifts his hands and holds them out like he's offering me the air between them. "That he doesn't remember anything from that night. Do you believe this?"

I shake my head, but recite Danny's explanation anyway. Words written on a whiteboard in his handwriting. "There was a flash. It was sudden, like the sun exploding, and it erased everything that came before it. Hours."

"The sun exploding at night? Is this plausible?"

"It was almost morning when the paramedics got to him. I think that's what they told me."

"The coroner said that Dora was..."

I wonder how the sentence is supposed to end, but Gerry lets it trail off into silence. It's been ten or twenty minutes since we've turned a corner, what seems like miles. How far away from the bakery are we? Am I supposed to lead the way back? I glance at a doorway and see a pile of blankets, soft-edged rectangles of cardboard, a vaguely human shape beneath them.

"It's cold out today," says Gerry. "But I didn't know it was *this* cold."

I nod, aware of the pain in my toes and my face. If we stop moving, we'll freeze. At what point does it turn desperate, this aimless stroll with Dora's brother?

"The thing is," I explain, "I'm okay with him forgetting. I can believe in the flash. It just seems like he forgot too much. Like maybe he added on extra and packaged it all up together."

"Two for one," says Gerry.

"It's convenient."

"He might confide in you later."

"We're not...he's not like that."

Gerry exhales. The steam from his breath rises up and disappears. "There was a cabin she loved. A place up in the woods. I mentioned it earlier. She used to invite people up there sometimes. Did Danny ever talk about a place like this? Did he ever show you pictures?"

I think of Danny and Evan in the bedroom doorway with the light off. The flash of paper, Evan's little bit of trouble that I always assumed was really Danny's little bit of trouble. Another one of his harmless secrets. The idea of photographs throws me off. Danny isn't like that. We're not Pictures of Cabins People.

"He isn't sentimental. His brother got into trouble and ran away and Danny had to realign all of his expectations." I expect Gerry to ask me to explain, but he stays quiet, keeps walking, leaves the thought behind. For a while I listen to his breathing, the rumble of an occasional car driving past. It seems dark, late.

Finally, he stops.

"I need to go," I tell him. "It'll be my kids' bedtime soon."

We're in the middle of a block and Gerry is facing the street, looking across to the other side.

"There," he says.

I search for a street sign. The wind has picked up and I can barely open my eyes. Did they say it was supposed to snow? It feels wrong for that. Too cold. But Gerry is checking the sky anyway, the winter gray night. He stares at nothing, the bereaved brother in a strange city. No, not nothing. He seems to be watching, like there might be a person up there, on that roof across—

"Oh…"

It's too dark to read the street numbers, but at this point why would I need to? The building, red brick, lit up by the streetlight. The yellow fire hydrant. The high curb. The row of trees in planting squares. As we cross the street, they all become familiar.

The door to the foyer catches, then gives way. It's heavy enough to knock a person over. The floor is tiled in white and black. There's a row of mailboxes and doorbells. Little white stickers with names handwritten in ink. D'Agostino, Pavaleski, Rashid, Lewis. No, these are not people that I know.

"I checked earlier today." Gerry explains. "There's no way up onto the roof, unless you want to scale the wall. There's a door, but it's padlocked. They must have come through here first. So does that mean someone buzzed them in?"

*The first floor. The apartment in the back.* Why do I know this? The threadbare carpeting and the stain on the wall. A man with a chipped tooth and unkind eyes.

Gerry's body is so large I can't see a clear path to the doorway. Dread settles deep in my chest. This isn't a place I should be. *We need to go. You need to get home.* Who said that? I turn sideways and squeeze past Gerry, grabbing for the door. A gloved hand finds my shoulder.

"You're upset about this. I'm sorry." He steps aside to let me pass, holds the door for me as I head back out into the cold.

"No, it's okay. I just need to…"

That other night was the opposite of this one. It was so hot out the world was spinning. Why would I let someone bring me back here? Without saying goodbye, I head back across the street and down the deserted sidewalk, already on my phone begging to be rescued.

Cherie lectures me as we drive back to my car. "Christ, how far did you walk?"

"He's grieving."

"Yeah. Okay."

"What was I supposed to do?"

She makes a face—narrows her eyes and presses her lips togeth-er—then turns away. We pull in behind my car and sit in silence for about thirty seconds. I wonder what happened to Dora's brother after I left, whether he made it back to…his car? Because what if he just kept walking? I could picture him doing this, so sick from mourning that doesn't realize he's been walking all night until his legs finally collapse and he becomes a heap in some doorway.

Cherie sighs. "Want to go get a drink or something? You look like you're about three minutes away from hypothermia."

"I think I just want to go home and take a hot bath."

"Speaking of which, is Danny still keeping you warm at night? I mean, do all *those* parts still work okay?"

"Seriously, this is not the conversation we're having right now."

"As your best friend, it's my duty to ask the hard questions, find out the hard facts. Shit, it's cold." She reaches for a knob on the dashboard and tries to turn it, even though the heat is already cranked as high as it will go.

"Why don't I just see you another time?"

Cherie takes my hand, flattens it between both of hers, and rubs gently. "Fine. But we really need to talk about why you let a strange man drag you miles away from your car on the coldest day of the year. I mean, I know you're going through some shit, but don't let it turn you stupid."

I shake my head. "You exaggerate."

"Not really."

"Don't tell anyone about this, okay?"

"We gossip because we love. Remember that."

Her embrace is like a blanket, warm and then gone. By the time I'm inside my own car, I'm shivering again. My fingers are so cold it hurts to bend them. Danny is always reminding me to keep hand warmer packets in my car, just in case. Is that what tonight is? An emergency? I rifle through the glove compartment with its mess of old insurance cards and broken sunglasses, grab the first aid kit and pop the lid. A half sheet of paper is tucked inside, a black ink drawing done by one of the kids. But no. This one is too good to be one of theirs. A two-story house with hills in the distance. Round-topped trees covered in apples, a dog curled up and sleeping, an out-of-place rock wall with a waterfall. It takes me a minute to recognize it. He only added the waterfall because I insisted on it. I remember being surprised by how well he could draw; proud, as if I was the one discovering his talents for the first time.

*The sun will rise eventually.*

That's my handwriting at the bottom. He drew the pictures and I wrote the words.

*We can't live on fruit. We'll need some vegetables. A few cows.*

*I guess I could learn how to milk a cow, but don't they kick you? How about avocados?*

*I want a window, the biggest window we can find.*

*I want more stories than this. More rooms.*

*It's a farmhouse, not a castle.*

*Then put them underground, with a secret trap door that it will take me years to find. I just want to know that they're there.*

I wasn't supposed to remember. That was why I drank so much. The night was a shimmery bubble, already floating to the ground, on the verge of disappearing.

Why save the picture, then? Why leave it here to remind myself?

Thirty-five minutes later I'm at The Silver Whistle, walking toward the bar, my body sore from its battle against the cold. Inside, it's warm and nearly empty. I can't remember how we ended up picking this place. It was Lori's idea, or Cherie's. Find a boring bar and make it ours.

Lee sees me and stops mid-stride. Just for a second—unless I'm imagining it—and then keeps walking. What did we decide last time? Did we decide anything?

He's wearing black jeans, a gray shirt, a striped knit cap that would look ridiculous on anyone else. He gives me a look, narrowed eyes that I don't quite know how to interpret but that arrest me anyway. In the span of three minutes, I am warm.

A vodka tonic appears in front of me. And next to it a steaming mug, the string of a tea bag draped over the side.

"Hot tea with a shot of whiskey. You look like you need it."

"Uh…thanks?" It feels like I'm standing inside a hole, waiting for him to pull me out. There is no order between us. Debris surrounds me, unfamiliar objects that have tumbled down from high shelves and shattered at my feet. Does Lee see it too, the mess we've created?

His face is young and old at the same time. He has the beginnings of a beard that somehow never grows in all the way. His forehead is creased, the outside corners of his eyes bracketed by faint lines that radiate out toward his hairline. It makes me want to take a paintbrush and touch up the imperfections, smooth him out and return him to the innocence of childhood. The reason I stay is all of this: the way he stands, the way he wears his pants, the way he moves his arms, the way he looks at me sometimes. His eyes are light brown, speckled with gold, and at the right moments I see myself reflected in them, a surprising, lovely version of me that shines bright, briefly, before vanishing.

"I didn't expect you back here."

I shrug and take a long, careful sip of the tea. Its liquid warmth coats my stomach and then rises up, up, up to a spot just behind my eyes. I think of the kids' dark bedrooms, their slow deep breathing, Danny sitting on the couch watching TV.

"I had other plans tonight, but they were fucked by a stranger."

He lifts my glass and drinks from it. "Fucked by a stranger, huh?" I tell myself to stand up stand up stand up, but it's never worked before so why would it work now?

"We must have walked sixty miles. I still can't feel my toes."

"It sounds biblical."

Gently, he lifts my hand and wipes the bar underneath it, then sets it back down and traces it with his index finger.

"How's the heat in the van?" I ask.

When he leans forward on his elbows across the bar, his eyes are even with mine. He smells of earth and spices and liquid laundry detergent.

"Your face is red. It looks like a sun burn."

"Wind burn." I close my eyes and feel a tear slipping out.

"How's your husband doing?"

I shake my head.

"I guess he had quite a story to tell you, huh? About his escapades on that roof."

I wipe the corner of my eye with my palm. "He can't talk and he doesn't remember anything."

Lee considers this. He mulls it over, staring at my face, trapping me in place. "What do you mean?"

"There was a flash. It stole the entire day from him."

He stands up and crosses his arms. "Wow. That's messed up."

"I guess. Or convenient, maybe."

"So you still don't know what happened to him?"

"Suspended animation."

He smiles, finally lifting me out of my hole. I drink the vodka tonic and he brings me another one, takes the nearly full tea away, goes about the small movements of his job. I sit and drink and watch the way he moves, the perfect fit of his pants, the writing on his wrist:

# Order and disorder are many times the same

We go out to the van so I can sober up before driving home. It's the same excuse as always. This is the way I stumble into the storm. Wind, rain, the rumble in the sky, the depths from which it appears, the lows and highs and completeness of it. I want to escape it, but also to be consumed by it, those few minutes of exhilaration before it passes away. The gentle scatter of rainfall afterward.

When I get home, the house is quiet. Everyone is asleep. I never called, never told anyone I was going to be late. Climbing into bed next to Danny, I make a hundred promises to myself before falling asleep.

Time goes by. Another week. The kids fill the house with their noise, covering up the silence that lies underneath. When they fall asleep it's like stepping off a cliff. I can feel the chisel, the sharp edge carving away, the canyon around me slowly growing larger.

"It's good to see you again," says Danny. "I keep wishing you were here with me, listening to the waves. It's this swish swish swish kind of a sound—so humanizing and harmonious, like this is the way the womb was, maybe."

"Humanizing?"

"And then a big one comes out of nowhere. It's the most violent thing you've ever seen, everything torn up and churning into pieces and sucked out to sea. Destruction and birth and destruction and birth and destruction. The cycle of the ocean. Brilliant."

"How long have you been out here, doing all this thinking?"

"Just since the accident. When was that? I can't remember."

"A month and a half ago, I guess."

"And you've only visited me three times?"

"I'm busy, Danny."

"With that bartender?"

"You don't know about that. It's just...nothing."

"It's the cycle of the fucking ocean, Cassie. Think about that before you say it's nothing."

He's lit up, outlined in gold like some immortal being. Do I look the same? Are we a perfect, glowing pair? I hold out my arms, look down at my feet, but I can't make out features that resemble parts of a human body. I wonder about my insides, whether immortal Danny can look through all the gray and see my pinwheel of emotions: the purple of my desperation, the orange of my guilt, the red of my anger.

"I saw the building, Danny. I went inside."

He smiles. "You wanted to."

"No. I don't know if that's true. It was just to see whether it matched, you know, what I saw last time."

"What you remembered."

"The flash."

"The flash happens later. Much, much later."

"What happens first?"

"Let's stay on the first floor for a while. It might actually be more important than the roof. I don't know. There's an apartment there. I can't remember which one, which number. But you go inside and—"

"Wait. How do I get inside?"

"You're with some people."

"Dora MacIntosh? Do I know her?"

Danny shrugs. "I can't see their faces. I see legs, feet, a silver key ring. Someone unlocks the door and you all head inside."

"Do I want to be there?"

"It's hard to say. It seems like maybe yes. But you're tortured as usual, and so maybe no and yes at the same time. Always a fight in there." He points to his own head, taps on it twice.

"I know what you mean."

"The inside of the apartment looks...looks...there's a carpet, a rug, some kind of scrap remnant thing. And over in the corner..."

He stops, looks off to the side. "I just remembered. I've been meaning to tell you. On the way here I found a rock."

"What? No, you were talking about the apartment. What's in the corner?"

"All of that can wait. This rock is important. I don't want to forget it."

"But—"

"Shhh." He puts a finger up to his mouth. "Listen."

I wait for the sound of the waves but it never comes.

"What happens," says Danny, "is I see this rock and I bend over and pick it up. Somehow, I am compelled to do this. In my hand, it's perfectly smooth. Perfectly small. Are you understanding me? I put it in my pocket, thinking I'll carry it around with me for a while. Use it to keep my fingers busy and all that. I'm walking along, touching the rock, acting like we've found one another, this rock and me. It feels just like fate. But then an instant later I take it out of my pocket and throw it as hard as I can into the ocean. Turns out this is pretty far. A few hundred miles, maybe."

"Nobody can throw a rock that far."

"And yet, here at the ends of the earth, things are different."

"But a few hundred *miles*?"

He shrugs. "Give or take. The exact distance isn't important. What *is* important is the millions of years that my perfectly smooth, perfectly sized stone was out there in the ocean, carried around by water, by the currents, by the vortex of a storm. Sinking and rising and sinking and rising and then finally coming to rest. Then, for a hundred years, not even moving an inch. How many times does this happen? How does the thing ever see the light of day again? Nobody could ever document this, the series of events that cause this rock to end up at my feet on this very beach. How do you contemplate that? Maybe you could try, but would there ever be enough time?"

I feel a shudder pass through me, an understanding. I'm rising, like a rain cloud, swelling with moisture.

"I can see that you get it." Danny continues. "There's not enough time. What choice do you have but to throw it back so that it can be lost at sea for another million years?"

# CHAPTER 7

## (DANNY)

If I'm being completely honest—and I might, if you stick with me long enough—it was more than just a time capsule. We buried more than that.

And if you pressed me, I could tell you everyone's name. The girls—yes I knew them: Dora MacIntosh. Katy Perez. Suzie Gluhova. We called her Suzie Q—I forget why—and she told us she hated it but you never could tell with girls like that. The crossed arms and the hips cocked and the pout. You had to navigate it, you know? Just like a boat down a river filled with rapids. How much was real and how much was for show.

And then there was me, of course. Your hero. I can call myself that, but that wouldn't be too honest. I just happened to be there, at a place where certain events took place. My buddy was there with me too, a guy we called Stitch. He'd been in a motorcycle accident earlier in the summer, and there was a huge, sewn-up gash running up his left leg, and another one near his elbow. He must have had half a spool of surgical thread running through his skin. Probably he was lucky to be alive, but we didn't realize it at the time. Instead we just gave him a dumb nickname.

The third guy was from a different town, a football star, I guess; I didn't know too much about him. He had the long legs and the biceps and a deep voice that made him sound older than he was. Taz Ferris. Probably not his given name, but I never knew for sure.

Did I mention how beautiful it was? How unbelievably serene? Like if someone asked me to create paradise on earth it never would have occurred to me to take a dirty little cabin, a long, dusty road that went on forever, and the insane heat of late July and submit that to the judges. And yet, there it was. There we were. The six of us in paradise.

Who could remember what day of the week it was? Wednesday
or Thursday? Dora was the only one keeping track, I guess because
it was her place and she had to kick us out at the end of the week.
At any rate, we'd been there a while by then. We had our routines:
drinking, fucking, waking up late, eating, heading outside for the
day.

It was early in the afternoon. We'd hiked up to the top of a low
ridge with sandwiches and Suzie's pot brownies. Lunch was over
and we were lit up and laughing, trying to play tic-tac-toe in the
dirt with sticks, except nobody could find the Xs and Os. Taz and
Katy had wandered off, holding hands. They were standing with
their backs to us, looking off at the green hills, and somehow this
was hilarious.

"What do you think they're talking about?" asked Stitch.

"None of your business," said Dora.

"Wait," I said. Time had slowed down and I thought if it stopped
altogether I could hear the forest talking to me. The little creatures
in the dirt, digging around.

"Wait. Shh."

I tapped on the ground and listened for a response. The earth
seemed to be breathing. But before I could get all the way in tune
with it, it was broken by a different sound. A motor, a distant helicopter.

"Wait."

Dora and Suzie started giggling. "What are we waiting for?"

"It was right here." I tapped the ground again.

"Dude. We're all up here." Stitch was waving his arms in wide
circles, which seemed hysterical until I looked over at Taz and Katy,
the way he had his arm around her and was pointing at something
off in the distance. Seeing the two of them together made me sad.
I couldn't tell you why.

"Do you think they really like each other? I mean, like, honest to
God *like* each other?"

"Katy says they cuddle at night. He has a pet name for her, but
she won't tell me."

"What an idiot," said Dora, then covered her mouth and started
laughing again.

"I know," said Suzie. "It's just so...*adorable.*"

Dora put her hand on my arm. "Don't you want to call *me* something? Like Baby? Or Sweetie Pie?" She was giggling, trying to find me with her eyes but not coming anywhere close.

"Dora." There was more after that. It was the start to something. I opened my mouth but nothing came out. I can't remember what I was thinking, what I might have wanted to say.

Taz called out suddenly. "Hey look. Up there. What's that coming down?"

We all peered out across the valley, where the helicopter I'd heard earlier was slowly heading away from us. Was it close or far away? I couldn't tell. The chopped-up rumble of its rotors seemed to be coming from a different part of the sky than the aircraft itself.

I heard Suzie gasp, and a few seconds later I saw them too: three shapes descending from the sky, one of them floating down beneath a Day-Glo orange parachute.

"What are those? Sky divers?"

"In a forest?"

We waited for parachutes to appear above the other two objects, but they continued to fall.

Katy lifted her hands and pressed them against the sides of her face. "Oh my God, what if they're about to…?"

At last, a mass of blue billowed out like a quick-blooming flower, hanging in the air for barely a second or two before crashing into the treeline. The second shape continued to fall until it was gone, out of our range of vision.

"That seemed like it opened too late," said Stitch.

"Shit. What about the other one?"

"Why did the orange one open so much earlier?"

"That one wasn't a person," said Stitch. "It was smaller. I'm guessing it was a package maybe."

"A package of what?"

"I don't know. Whatever the fuck people drop from helicopters. Supplies."

"Why would anyone do that? They'd just get caught in the trees."

"The person jumps into the wilderness and then has to find the supplies. The tent and everything. People pay money to do this."

"But that parachute opened so late." Katy's hands were still plastered to her face, but she'd pulled them down over her mouth, her eyes searching the sky. For what? More jumpers? Another helicopter?

"Should we go somewhere for help?" We all looked at Dora. It was her cabin, her woods. Maybe this was normal.

"I don't know. I've never seen anything like that before." She seemed transfixed, unable to take her eyes off of the spot where the last object had disappeared.

"Was the last one a package too?" asked Katy. "Did anyone notice?"

The truth was that you couldn't be certain of anything, not from that distance and that angle, with the sun in that position and a rewired, earth-listening brain. To me it just seemed like it had been an illusion, a trick of the light and our imaginations, a realistic figment that disintegrated before hitting the ground.

I don't really know how to explain what happened next. Taz filled four or five water bottles and shoved them inside a backpack that was way too big for anyone to want to carry. He was going to try to find the jumpers, find out if they were okay. He had a topographic map, a compass, a sleeping bag in case of…well, in case.

"Shit, Taz. What are you doing? There's no phone reception out here. You won't be able to call anyone for help."

"Don't worry, man. I do this all the time."

He had a first aid kit. Flares. A headlamp. Little packets of dried food. Where did all this stuff come from?

Katy beamed at him as he packed. She was certain of him, of his decision, that his efforts would end up being heroic.

I guess we tried to get him to stop, but I think mostly we let him go. We wanted to see if he would make it back, whether he was just shit-talking the whole wilderness survival thing. Katy insisted on going with him, even after he told her no, never, absolutely not. The two of them headed off together, hand in hand, and I thought it was possible that they would die. We'd drive back down the long road without them and later there would be a search party.

It must have been two o'clock when they left. How long would it take them to walk down into the valley? I mean, did any of us really want to do that math?

Truthfully, I don't know how much we worried. I worry more now, thinking about it. Despite the way it turned out, I still wonder about other ways it might have turned out and whether they would have ended up being better or worse.

That night, we didn't play any of Dora's songs. We didn't drink much, either. You could hear the insects outside. We played cards and Stitch told us stories about people in his family that I'd never heard of before and were probably made up: a great uncle who'd taken up fire breathing as a hobby, a distant cousin who slept in a custom-made coffin, identical twins on his mother's side who were training to be astronauts. He seemed to be filling the silence with words, understanding that we needed them to be there.

We looked at the floor, at the walls, felt the time passing.

"When you were kids, what did you talk about doing the most?" Dora asked.

"We were going to ride motorcycles. Head south and go as far as we could. Live somewhere with long hair and no shirts and, like, be fishermen or hut-builders or something." Stitch looked over at me and I smiled back at him.

"It's true," I said.

"Really? Both of you?"

"All boys have that dream, or one like it. What do girls want to do?"

"Get married," said Suzie, laughing. "I don't get it. I mean, how stupid to think that this would be the happiest thing in our lives."

"Messed up by fairy tales," said Stitch.

"I wanted to jump out of an airplane," said Dora. The room became quiet. "Sky diving. I thought it..." She was staring at her feet. I put my hand on her thigh and rubbed it gently. I don't know if I ever loved her, really, but at that moment I came close.

"Don't worry," said Suzie. "Taz is like a bloodhound. He can find anything."

By the time the sky had gone dark, they still weren't back. It was too early to go to bed, but Dora did anyway, with no explanation. A few minutes later I went up and crawled in next to her, unsure if she wanted me there. Her arms were folded on top of her chest.

"Sometimes," she said, "I just…think the wrong things."

I took a deep breath.

"Like I think up things to be afraid of. I just sit there and imagine them happening, the most terrible outcomes, everything breaking, in flames, suffering. In my head, I practice yelling for help and then waiting for someone to save me and realizing that nobody will. So then I start preparing myself. Fight or flight. Which one do I pick?"

Her voice was someone else's. It was low but steady, like she was reading to me from a book. "Not all the time. I don't want you to get the wrong idea. I appreciate what I have. I understand my good fortune. I'm not one of those girls with all the drama. This is quiet. It's in my head when I should be sleeping, or sometimes when I'm out walking and ten blocks later I realize that I don't remember moving my feet, turning my body. It's like my brain separates from the rest of me."

I wanted to say that I understood, but I also wanted her to stop talking. There were too many words coming out of her mouth and I didn't want to hear them, to be there while she worked through this, when she finally came to the realization that it wasn't anything, that it was just the end of a long day and the darkness and being out where there weren't any computers or TVs to put someone else's ideas into your head.

"The thing is, I think I'm basically a good person, but is that just because I've learned the right behaviors, or is it me? Because those are different. I have—"

"Of course it's you. You're good, Dora. Trust me."

"You don't even know me."

Her body didn't change as she said this. Just the same Zen-like calm; her head, neck, and shoulders at rest, her hands loosely crossed on her chest.

I didn't have anything else to say, so I let the crickets talk to her instead. It was two bodies sharing a room, just like it had always been with Curt. Him on the top and me on the bottom, looking up at the slats that held him suspended above me. He stared at the ceiling and I stared at the bottom of his mattress, and even though I always complained about not getting a turn on the top bunk, I knew this was the right order: ceiling, Curt, me. Ceiling, Curt, me.

Whenever he changed positions, the whole bed would shake, and I'd lie there, trying not to count how many times he rolled from one side to the other. Usually I'd fall asleep before him, but sometimes I'd realize that the bed was still and I could hear his breathing and the night had become peaceful. I'd sit up carefully and nudge myself out of bed and tiptoe down the hall to my parents' room. My dad would be splayed out with his limbs at strange angles and the blankets half kicked off, and my mom would be nearly invisible, just the top of her head and a beautiful mess of black hair poking out the top of the comforter. I wanted to build up a wall around the mound formed by her body, make a soft-lined nest for her to sleep in. Afterward, I'd check the front door and the back door and the windows, making sure they were all locked before heading back to bed.

At that point, we were just people, living. We had our places where we slept at night and these happened to be under the roof of a single house. Just like the four of us that night: me, Dora, Stitch, and Suzie. I wanted to be awake, in case Taz and Katy came back, but I guess I drifted off to sleep right away. I don't know about Dora. For all I know, she might have been awake for hours.

They came back the next morning. Ten or eleven maybe, right at the start of the hottest part of the day. They were covered in sweat but didn't look tired. How was it that they looked? Invigorated, maybe. Hopped up with adrenaline.

"Oh, thank God. Thank God. Thank God." Suzie and Dora went running out the back door, like little dogs greeting their owners.

Katy's eyes were wide. She was smiling so big she looked ready to burst.

"You'll never believe what we found."

You have to realize I'm just at this point retelling a story that someone else told me. I can't say for sure exactly what they saw. I mean, they told us. They had loads of details. But what I think I'm getting at is that people lie. They misconstrue. About events like this, especially. Sometimes you feel like you have to, and later, when you regret it, it's too late to straighten it out.

After they left the cabin, they walked down into the valley. Taz set a compass bearing and they found a river channel and crossed it. You wouldn't think they could find whatever it was that had landed in the forest, but they claimed they did; they used the river to find it. I still don't know how that makes sense, how the two ideas would be related.

"Oh my God," said Katy. "It was so terrible." But her words didn't match her face, the huge smile that twitched slightly at the ends. It was like she was so messed up inside that her muscles didn't know what else to do.

Taz's hands were shaking. He wasn't saying much, just kind of sitting there, hugging his pack, like he was thinking about where he'd hike to next. Katy told the story by herself, occasionally turning to him and asking for confirmation. He'd nod back silently. Watching it made my stomach knot up. Something wasn't right.

"Those people? The ones who jumped?"

I'd like to say we could tell just from her face what she was about to say, but that wouldn't be true.

"They're dead."

Suzie gasped. Dora looked confused. She was looking at Katy's hands instead of her face, watching the way her fingers twisted and rubbed and pulled.

"Wait," said Stitch. "How many people are dead?"

That weird smile on Katy's face was starting to falter. "I think the orange one was carrying supplies, but those other two…"

We stared at her, waiting for more. The sun was almost directly overhead by this time, and it felt like I was turning into one of those paintings that when you get up close are made out of millions of dots. If we would just move to the shade, everything would begin to make sense. But we couldn't move. We looked at Taz and then back at Katy, waiting for her to clarify how *they're dead* didn't mean what we thought it did. There was a context we were missing.

*They're dead, but not really.*

"We found a clearing," Katy said finally. "Maybe that's where they were headed." She looked at Taz, but he was turned away from the rest of us, staring off in the distance.

"But we saw one of the parachutes open."

Katy shook her head. "It was too late."

"You're telling me that two people tried to skydive into a forest and they fucked it up? That was what we saw? Two incompetent jumpers?"

Katy's eyes were huge. She nodded.

"Why would anyone take a parachute into a forest?" Stitch was angry now. He never liked being tricked. "Why wouldn't you just drive?"

"It's a wilderness area, you idiot," said Dora. "We're right on the edge of it. You can't drive any further."

The literal end of the road, I thought to myself. Which seemed funny, but it wasn't the right time for that sort of thing. The girls and Stitch were smothering Katy, who was crying now, a strange, desiccated sobbing that didn't produce any tears. It occurred to me that she was probably dehydrated.

I looked at Taz to see what he thought about all of this. He'd been sitting still for so long that it seemed like he could be made out of molded concrete, his face hard and pale. That's when it finally sunk in what all of us had seen: two people falling to their death.

"I don't get it. Did they just not know what they were doing? One parachute doesn't open, and the other one waits until..."

Katy took a deep breath. The sobbing seemed to have stopped as quickly as it had come on.

"We couldn't think of any way to explain it. Standing there, I mean. Two bodies? In the woods? That fall from the sky? It was all make believe."

Katy's eyes bounced from person to person: Dora, Suzy, Stich, Me. We expected her to laugh at any moment and say *you guys are so gullible. It wasn't anything.* But her hands were shaking; her whole body, really. "This is why I was so impulsive, I guess."

Did she mean there were pictures? She wouldn't, would she?

"I mean, I didn't think. I just looked at the body and assumed that later I would figure everything out. Because what was going through my head at that particular instant was that we were dealing with a terrible accident, and what if we couldn't find our way back or someone moved the bodies before we could drive to a place with phone reception and call the authorities? Who would you even call and what would you say?"

She stopped talking and turned toward Taz, who no longer even seemed to be listening. He was looking off toward a different ridge, a different valley.

"So we decided to take it. It was lying a little ways from her, the woman whose parachute.... I guess she'd been carrying it? I don't know why you would, but..."

"Carrying what?" asked Suzie.

"The woman. She was so young. No older than me. It didn't seem like we were actually...I mean, I couldn't feel my feet. It seemed like we only had about thirty seconds before I would figure out how to use them again and start running away. I don't have any other explanation. It just felt like the thing to do at the time."

I remember listening to all this, blinking, wondering where it was going. Stitch was right. They were setting us up for a practical joke. All we had to do was wait it out and Katy would get to the punch line, which would be that some asshole dropped their garbage into the forest. In a few seconds Taz was going to look back at us and start bellowing out that laugh of his and say *you guys would fall for anything, wouldn't you?*

Katy walked over to Taz and whispered into his ear. Without looking at her, he shifted his body so that she could access his pack.

She turned around holding it in her hands. That thing. Light in color and about a foot and a half long. I tried to study its shape, to place it as a familiar object in the world. The way it curved, gently, and then came to a point, like an animal horn.

"Why would you jump out of a helicopter with this?" Katy asked. She held it carefully, like she was afraid of dropping it.

An animal horn?

I thought it was a joke, that the thing in her hands belonged to her. It was a fake that she'd brought with her. This whole reveal had been orchestrated ahead of time. I remember thinking what a complicated joke it was, what a strange prop it involved.

And then we all moved in for a better look.

Ivory, okay? This is what it was. Polished up to a high shine. Katy was showing it off like it was some model boat she'd put together or something.

"Holy shit," said Dora. "This is crazy."

"What ...?" asked Stitch.

"It's a tusk," Katy said, like she was announcing the sex of a baby. "We're sure of it."

Our brains tried, desperately, to process the information they were receiving, to accept it as fact.

"You mean like from an elephant?"

"Look at it."

"Why is it so small?"

"Maybe it's from a little one. Oh my God. What if they killed a baby elephant for this?"

That's when Katy stood up straight—I swear to God she was at least a foot taller than normal—and gave us this look. Crazy but not crazy—do you know what I mean?

"If someone did that…well then I guess they deserved to die."

*This* was what we buried, just a little ways from our time capsule. Because we didn't know what else to do.

# CHAPTER 8
## (CASSIE)

Danny has started cooking dinners for the family. Chili and hamburgers and casseroles. He stands at the cutting board, painstakingly chopping onions and carrots. He says a PT told him that it's good to use his hands in this way. The more pieces the better. On the whiteboard, he writes numerals:

He draws an arrow from the 1 to the 3.

No good. Thumbs down. An arrow from 1 to 2 is good, thumbs up. An arrow from 2 to 3, also good.

*ORDER* he writes in capital letters, then underlines it.

# ORDER

Thumbs up again. I don't know what this has to do with his hands, what PT he's talking about.

Nel sits next to him with her own whiteboard and practices writing her numbers, drawing arrows that look like Danny's. He writes 1234 and she copies him.

# 1 2 3 4

"Now write how old I am," she says, and Danny writes a 5.

# 5

Nel carefully draws her own lines, her own half circle, her own number 5.

"Now write how old you are."

Danny pauses, then writes a 3 in front of the 5.

# 3 5

E sits on the other end of the couch watching them. He studies the whiteboards, the writing that appears and is then rubbed away. He listens but doesn't say much. I'm trying to look for warning signs, but I can't remember what they are, if I've ever known. He isn't bored or withdrawn or disengaged. Whatever word you want to use for it, he isn't. I hold my breath until Nel says something funny and I see him smile. Danny punches him lightly on the arm and he smiles again.

On the way to the bathroom I notice that Nel has added a new picture to the dream wall. It's a Disney cruise ship, an ad she found in a magazine. She's young enough to keep hoping. What does it say about E that he's stopped adding pictures? Has he lost interest, or is he being realistic, or is he waiting, patiently, for us to come up with the cash for some plane tickets? Could we, if we started saving now? I scan the pictures, looking for the least exotic one. A tropical rainforest. Mountaintops. An African plain. Bora Bora. A boat surrounded by blue ice walls. Where is this one? Hawaii, maybe? It looks so pristine, the sand empty of footprints. No signs of people anywhere. No grass huts or boats. Just the ocean stretching out as far as—

My island. The one Danny bought for me. This is it.

*That changes everything*, I think. But why would it? They've always just been dreams.

I turn around and glance back toward the couch. Danny is with his children, miming laughter while they talk and giggle. I try to document the moment, save it for later. *Here we are in happy times.* Image fade.

I had a plan. I did.

I was going to make little cakes, create a signature line of pastries, open a bakery. Cassie's Little Cakes. Cassie's Cakelets. Something along those lines.

Culinary and Pastry Arts. A ten-week program, with all the white clothes, the hat, the ugly shoes. Tiny flowers made of frosting. Those little white dishes you always see at the cooking store. Little cakes, little pies. Everything little.

My mother bit her lip and pretended to be supportive. *I guess if you think this is what's going to get you somewhere.*

My father looked up from his crossword puzzle and laughed, as if at a private joke. *You might want to see if you're any good first. Maybe get a real job and practice on the weekends.*

Twenty grand for tuition seems like a lot, but all you have to do is save up. It's just a matter of patience, of waiting. Of letting time pass.

Danny fell out of the sky and landed on my lap. He was that kind of a guy. He'd use a dumb pick-up line on you, tell you how beautiful you were, and somehow it wouldn't make you want to throw up. Instead, you'd ask him to take you home and show you what he meant. He'd hold your hand, open doors, tell you he loved pastry chefs, he loved small cakes, whatever. He'd jump onto a table to make the world's shortest toast to his best friend and everyone in the room would clap and beam.

He'd tell you he understood baking because he was also someone who needed to use his hands. It was like…

He'd frown, he'd think. He'd kiss you instead. The unfinished sentences piled up, broken twigs weaved into a nest that became your home.

My mother said *you're too young to get married, don't you think? What about going to school, those little cakes you wanted to make? Or just a regular college?*

My father asked *who is his father?* As if all men of a certain age still participated in the pastime of determining whether other men's children were suitable for marriage.

*He's dead*, I replied. *You don't know him.*

When I turned twenty, Danny threw me a party. I showed up at his apartment and all the furniture was gone. There was a long table stretching across the living room, a stereo blaring music, a kitchen packed with alcohol. I never found out where the furniture went. *Magic*, he told me, and the next time I visited the furniture was back like it had never been moved. Magic was real. Love was magic. Something along those lines.

We had to get married, I told my parents, because I was pregnant.

My mother pressed her hands into her face and turned away, railing at the tabletop. *You're too young for this. What about school?*

I listened to my father call Danny a degenerate. I paid attention to his eyes, his shoulders, his hands, but all I could read from them was that he was going through the motions. *Why did you ever let him lay his hands on you? I told you to go to the community college. I wish you would have listened to me.* This wasn't what he wanted to say to me. His eyes were matte-brown. A finger tapped nervously against his leg. I didn't know him, who he was.

I told Danny that I could paint pictures of the things my parents said, that I knew exactly which colors to pick, what kind of brush strokes I would use, the shapes and lines that would represent them—the abstraction of my parents. *You're like me*, Danny said. *You need to use your hands.* And then he put his hands on me and the room began to rock and spin and it didn't feel like we were on the earth anymore.

I wasn't really pregnant, of course. We weren't Pregnant at Twenty People. But the lie worked; people stopped calling us impulsive, telling us we were too young. We thought we'd tell them the truth later, in a few weeks and then in a few more weeks. My belly was supposed to grow, but it didn't. We thought they'd figure it out, but instead they became uncomfortable. Rooms creaked with embarrassment, backs were stiff, eyes averted, sentences caught on words and ripped open, rolling out onto the floor. *You lost the baby, didn't you?* Deb asked me, finally. Her face was soft and sad, warm eyes, trembling lip. The hope of her first grandchild waning. What else could I do but share her sadness and cry, myself, for what was lost? Danny followed my lead. He was convincing. Bill put a hand on his shoulder and said *you two are young yet. You have plenty of time.*

Word spread. My mother took me into a quiet room and told me about her own failed attempts: the brother I never had, the sister I never had. Maybe there was a genetic reason why it was also happening to me, but she didn't know for sure, just that she understood how I felt. The heartache like no other.

I tried to relate, to empathize with her empathy, but couldn't stretch myself quite that far. So much sadness I'd never known about. *It's okay*, I told her. *At least I still have Danny, right?*

A year later I really was pregnant. A boy came out, just like they told us he would, and Danny named him Evan, after his best friend.

It was years before I learned the details about Danny's family history. A piece here, a piece there. I knew that his brother Curt had run away when they were teenagers, something to do with his father. Whenever Danny started telling the story, his face would turn pale, as though a roiling pain had overtaken him and he was lost inside of it. He would start sinking and I'd watch, unable to help, as a horrible memory pulled him under. He'd close his eyes and turn away, fold his body into a ball and wait for it to pass. All I could do was curl up around him with my head pressed against his back, listening to his breathing as it slowed and stretched out again, thinking about waking up next to him in the morning, turning toward him and seeing him smile.

Eventually I had enough pieces to understand. His father with a broken leg, a simple accident that changed the course of events with no warning. He filled a prescription for pain killers, took them without thinking, without knowing what could happen. Sometimes, addiction is immediate. In some people. The person never goes back.

For a long time they didn't know. A man turned inside out, was how Danny explained it. Resorting to acts that no man should. Curt was saving up his money, getting ready to move out. A desperate father steals his son's cash and all hell breaks loose. Danny wouldn't say much about his brother, except that it seemed like the only time his house wasn't cold was when Curt was around. He remembered lying in bed trying to get warm and how his mother's lips were always blue. But whenever Curt came home Danny could feel the quick heat of his body, spreading across the room.

"You're lucky your family was normal," Danny always said. I tried to explain it to him, how we were but also we weren't. There was that night. That one night, when my father kept telling me I had to be fearless. It was like his brain was caught in a loop, stuck on a single thought that he needed me to understand. *You have to be fearless, Cassie, it's the most important thing. It's the cornerstone of your character.* He looked at me funny; he was put together wrong. I don't know how you can explain it. You watch the scene as it plays out before you, recalculating all of your future outcomes. You go to bed already practicing for the next evening and the one after that, and then in the morning you're afraid to get out of bed, but you do; you walk on bare feet, more softly than you ever have before, back to the same dining room. Only this time it's your real parents again—the ones that you remember—and everyone eats breakfast and carries on with their days, and it's like a page has been ripped out of a book. But you can't forget that you read the page, and so every day you worry, because what if it happens again? It wasn't right, the way I tried to explain it. Danny smiled and laughed lightly. His hands were so gentle.

"That isn't anything. You have to trust me. It's nothing. Think of it as a bad dream that you woke up from and now you're here. Think of yourself as really, really lucky."

My mom's face, yes. It has a hard side and a soft side now. That day must have existed because my parents never really came back from it. Over time, I understood this. But back then Danny's words were peace and I appreciated having them to believe in.

We kept saving for my tuition, but something always came up. A security deposit on a new apartment, a second car, a faster computer. It was about being patient. Waiting. Letting time pass.

It seemed like we should have had more saved but we didn't, and this was okay. The world was rich and wonderful and we were aware of this and of ourselves, embedded inside of it. We weren't beholden to our bank accounts, to rewards we thought we deserved. We didn't negotiate with inequity, look at others and wonder about chance and privilege. We were never Why Not Us People.

Evan proposed to his girlfriend, Jill. Danny was the Best Man. The *best* Best Man. A few weeks before the wedding, he took Evan on a road trip. They were going to meet up with some friends and drive across the country. Or at least as far as they could go in a long weekend. Before he left, Danny took my face into his hands and smiled down at me, told me he was soaking me in to carry me with him.

*I'm going to miss you, Cassie. Where did I ever find you?*

The best man. The best husband.

I never found out exactly where they went on that trip, what they did when they got there. I get it—it was a bachelor party. But it was the same with every trip. There were no stories, no details, no reminiscing later about all the fun they'd had. Instead there were occasional glances, comments that didn't quite make sense, the feeling that I was small and they were big, that the world they occupied was larger than the one I knew.

It's a loose board in the closet. I can't remember how I found it the first time, how I happened to pull down on it hard enough to dislodge it, along with the nailed-on piece of plywood that covered up a hole in the back wall. When I saw the money inside, I thought I'd found the previous tenant's stash: $340, in tens and twenties. How could you forget about this much money? Was it possible that someone had died and left it behind?

But no. No. You think up these explanations and after a few seconds they become preposterous. This was *Danny's* hiding spot. He'd built it to keep what was inside hidden from me.

We're not Snoop in Each Other's Things People, though. We believe in secrets. In private spaces at the back of a closet. These are allowances that we make so that we don't overlap one another so completely that we stop being two different people. We trust and we love and we trust and we love and we trust and…

When I pulled back the board a few months later, the money was gone. I don't know. I've never known. It's a pattern. The money builds up slowly. It's passing time, an exercise in patience. It builds up and then it disappears. And I keep my mouth closed, because we all have to have our secrets.

# CHAPTER 9

The beach is unwavering in its sameness. It's always gorgeous, clean, idyllic. Paradise never falls to darkness.

"You're beautiful in this light," says Danny. "I just stare at you and think how lucky I am."

"That's...thank you."

"Even your desperation is beautiful. I don't think most people would get that."

"Desperation? Come on, Danny. Why do you do this?"

He rubs his chin with the back of his hand, then rests his head on it and smiles.

"I'm thinking about what you told me that one time, about the blank spaces, the pockets of nothing. How when the earthquake takes the building down we'll be saved by all of our mistakes."

Did I say this? It sounds familiar, but I can't quite remember. It's stretched out and slowed down, like a muscle I haven't needed to use in months. I can hear his response, though. *That's bullshit. We're already in the blank spaces.*

No, it wasn't Danny who said this. I'm thinking of a different person, a different conversation. I blink and stare, bring the man in front of me into focus. It's Danny, right? Yes, I'm certain of it. Danny. So then why...?

"You remember this don't you?" he asks.

The words don't come to me, but the night does, bits of it emerging from a fog. Lee got off work early and we stayed in the van for hours. A row of shots lined up next to the sink: a few for now, a few for later. His shirt with its faint odor of laundry detergent was lying on the floor, leaving behind the spicy earth smell of his skin, like exotic mushrooms, strange life forms bursting from the soil. The blanket covering my shoulders was infused with the same essence, only deeper and stronger. I imagined him driving out to the woods every night and wrapping himself in it, lying on the ground in the moonlight.

He had so many shot glasses. So many cupboards, filled with objects, that he would open and then close again. A box of cords and cables. Some magazines stacked neatly in a corner. Stories about how it was a vintage van that he'd fixed up himself, the work that went into it, getting it to look just right. We talked for what felt like hours and laughed about ideas that didn't make sense, and I knew there might never be another night like it. We planned out everything: the apartment in the city and the house in the country, just ridiculous enough to be meaningless, for us to know that it was meaningless.

*Why do you want so many rooms? I'm curious.*

*Secret doors, like I said. Dark staircases that make me hold my breath. I'd like to find a ballroom. A big chandelier. I don't know why.*

The black marker. I wrote something on his left arm, didn't I? He drew pictures. We laughed, and then…?

The rest doesn't quite come back to me. It feels like I told him too much—everything—except what would my "everything" be? I remember being dizzy afterward—too drunk, probably—and understanding for the first time that the outline was solid, the line around my unidentifiable everything. It was black and bold and the completeness of it was a relief. But a few minutes later all I felt was a heart-wrenching emptiness, and I didn't know how you could go from one to the other so quickly. I kept talking, trying to bring us back to a place I was too drunk to recognize. I laughed. Maybe I drank more shots.

What did I say? What was it that made him so angry?

*What did you do? Come on. Tell me what happened. I won't say anything. I promise you. I promise you.*

I remember his face, the way he looked at me like he'd just bitten into a rotten apple. Time passed, a blank space that I can't patch together. I laughed into it, but there was only the rotten apple face, and it made me feel like I was in sixth grade, all the things I did wrong that year, all the times friends would demand to know why I'd done something stupid and I didn't have an answer. I must have said something. I must have tried, but then I remember arguing, his voice raised. *What do you want from me? Why are you here?*

He picked up my dress from the floor and threw it at me, then turned away and reached for his phone. I watched his back, trying to freeze my smile in place, so that when he turned around he would be able to see...well, I wasn't sure exactly. A hand seemed to reach up from beneath me and grab my jaw from the inside. I felt it on my teeth, pulling backward, trying to turn me inside out. I picked up one of the shot glasses and tossed it back, then another. Lee was still talking on the phone and I tried to pick out words as I got dressed. *I don't know, man; I don't trust that guy....Oh yeah? What did she say...No, not anymore...Yeah, okay.*

When I stood up, the floor was sloping to the right, so I leaned to the left to keep myself straight.

Lee tossed his phone on a seat, then turned around to look for his pants. I was staring at the scars on his chest, the soft pink tissue that formed an X, as if someone had opened him up with a knife to cut out his heart and then sewed him closed again. He noticed me watching him.

*What?*

*I think I'm way too drunk to drive home. Also, you're being a dick.*

Is this even the right order, the way it happened? Me standing, swaying, with him so still in comparison, stuck in place, staring at me? Those few seconds of being afraid, of being on edge. No, not a few seconds but all the time, every day, always on edge. And Lee so still, so focused on me, and me feeling like the floor was going to dissolve and I would just sink into it, through it, leak out the bottom.

The van was warm and the mushroom odor rose up from under our feet.

*I wasn't being...I wouldn't care...* The words weren't coming out the way I was saying them. The floor was tipping and rotating and I stepped to the side to avoid disaster.

He moved forward, grabbing my waist to hold me steady. *Careful, sunshine.*

Sunshine. The beach. Unending, never-changing paradise.

This is Danny in front of me now. That night is as impossible as this day.

"You're making me confused, Danny. I'm too many places at once."

"I'm sorry. I thought you weren't coming home that night. You drank so much."

"I don't know how that happened. I didn't mean to."

"Do you remember that he drove you home, in your car? He parked it outside and left it for you. That was nice of him. I wonder how he got home? The bus, do you think?"

"No, I don't remember. I thought he let me drive."

"You woke up on the couch, just before morning."

Of course I did. Tumbled into consciousness with the musty smell still in my nose and a churning sensation in my stomach. I rushed to the bathroom and threw up, but the feeling didn't pass, so I went to the bedroom and undressed while Danny slept. I tried to find him in the dark but all I could make out was a barely discernible shape on the bed and the sound of his slow breathing. I put on clean underwear and an old T-shirt and walked back to the living room, picked up my purse from the floor and stood by the window where the light from the streetlight shone in. I remembered depositing my paycheck and getting out some cash. Twenty for me and the rest for groceries on the way home. We always start out with the best intentions, and then somehow we come home with an almost empty wallet and none of the food we'd planned to eat.

This time it was out of my system. The literal and figurative purge and the sun just starting to come up so everything felt right. I could have my own hiding spot, pick up some shifts at work, go out less. If I put away twenty dollars from every paycheck from here on out, how much would that add up to in a year? I was too tired to do the math, so I went into the kitchen and made toast, quietly eating up the last of the bread and then brushing the crumbs off the table into my hand. When I returned to the bedroom, the orange beginnings of daylight were creeping in through the curtains. Crawling into bed, I could see Danny's rising and falling chest, the soft curves of his eyelids. I could have let the sound of his breathing soothe me to sleep, but instead I rolled onto my back and stared up at the ceiling, imagining it falling down, crushing us in our bed.

"You wanted us to die," said Danny.

"No I didn't. I was tired. It was a metaphor."

"For what?"

"You had that secret hole at the back of the closet. I saw the money come and go. It was like hope and then...what?"

"It's the cycle of the ocean, Cassie. Don't try to change the subject."

"You always had what I wanted. You were the best at everything."

"That's an exaggeration."

"I wanted what you had, but when I finally got there it wasn't there anymore."

"I wish you would have told me this earlier. Maybe then none of this would have happened."

"None of what?" When I sigh, it feels like I'm taking all the world's air into my lungs and then releasing it again. "When are we going to talk about the roof, Danny?"

"Could we just spend some time here first? I bought you this fucking island. It's the least you could do."

# CHAPTER 10

The kids love their Uncle Evan. When he visits for dinner Nel sets the table with the good dishes, the ones my mother gave me as a wedding gift. She hands Evan a juice glass with a picture of a rooster on the side and carefully pours him milk.

"Thank you, my dear. You're wonderful."

After dinner the two Evans play a game on the computer. I can't tell if they're on the same side or different sides, but whenever I walk by and glance at the screen, there's a tiny person running through a maze of elaborate graphics, trying to reach some unspecified destination. Nel stands next to them and watches, laughing.

Evan offers to go with Danny on his nightly walk. "At this rate you're going to be faster than me by the summer." He punches Danny on the arm and Danny flinches. Once again, Evan's eyes are wet and red, and when Danny turns away I wonder if he's crying too. Afterward, they're gone for much longer than usual.

Nel says, "Daddy is walking so far tonight, that's good right?"

"Of course it's good," says E. "It means he's getting better."

"And then he'll be able to talk again."

Is it a statement or a question? E glances in my direction, his gaze bouncing around the room briefly before landing on me, as though by accident. We share a look that I immediately regret.

The kids take their showers and wait up for Danny to return so they can say goodnight. Nel starts chattering about a magic book that makes people happy that Uncle Evan told her about earlier in the evening. "He said he *has* the book and he would show it to me. Do you think it's true, Mommy? Do you think there is such a thing?"

I count to five, slowly, before answering. "All I can say is *I've never seen one before.*"

We watch a program on TV for longer than I'm expecting, until finally the door opens quietly and Danny and Evan walk into the apartment. I look at Evan's coat, wonder which pocket contains whatever it is the two of them were looking at outside, what "little bit of trouble" one or both of them is dealing with this time.

After the kids fall asleep, the three of us sit in the living room, in front of the TV. It's up to Evan and me to keep a conversation going, to decide if we want to have one in the first place.

"Why did you tell Nel about a 'magic' book? Stop brainwashing my family."

"Relax," says Evan. "Just get over yourself for a minute. How about teaching them to acknowledge other points of view? Magic is all a matter of perception, anyway."

I look over at Danny, but he's pretending to be engrossed in the news. Another fire. Another refinery spewing smoke, a spokesman from the oil company calling it the work of Revenge Gaia, the charismatic activist who refutes him, point by point. *How would we get past the security barrier? Why would we want to release that much carbon into the atmosphere?* Danny changes the channel.

"If you get them started young," Evan continues, "think about the possibilities. I'm just saying. Step outside the fence and then look back inside. Withhold judgment for a few minutes and then tell me what you see."

"Don't bring up the book again. I'm serious. If I have to permanently uninvite you from this apartment I will."

Evan lets out a half-laugh and turns toward the TV. "You know, anger only seems like it helps. Really, it cuts off your heart from your brain. You may not think it's possible to become any more miserable than you already are, but you'd be surprised. Until you start reprioritizing—"

"Shut up, Evan. Stop talking."

For the next several minutes, we watch the TV in silence. I can't understand what I'm looking at. A woman is fighting someone who looks exactly like her. Somehow, they have the same face. It's the most ridiculous thing I've ever seen. Why would we waste our time on this?

"The insurance company is challenging the claim," I say. "No payment pending the investigation to determine the responsible party for the injury."

"They can't do that," says Evan.

Danny turns with a flat stare, considering me in the same way a person might consider a blank wall.

"Even if they pay, the deductible alone is—"

Abruptly, Danny stands up and retreats to the bedroom, closing the door behind him. For a few minutes I let myself believe that he's gone to remove the shelf in the closet, to gather up all of the cash he's saved so he can offer it to me.

"He was tired," offers Evan. "We went farther than he usually does."

"Lori got me a job at the restaurant where her sister works. Did Danny tell you? I have two jobs now and he has zero."

"It doesn't need to be like this, Cas. You're on the wrong path is all."

"You have to go now."

"Walk me to my car."

I hesitate, ready to tell him off, then remember that he has something for me. He stands at the door while I put on my coat and shoes, then gestures for me to go first. Once we're outside, he grabs my arm and pulls me down the sidewalk until we reach the end of the block, gives me a little shove as he lets me go.

He presses a green pill bottle into my hand. "You're still not sleeping? This was supposed to be temporary."

His voice is tight, like metal wire. Something must have happened when he was out walking with Danny earlier. How else can I explain his behavior? They've been friends for so long. When they fight it feels like the world is ending.

I put my hand on his arm. "This is going to sound crazy, but there's a beach, an island. I go there and Danny talks to me."

"What in God's name are you talking about?"

"I can see it happening, about to happen. It's slow, yes, but—"

Evan turns away. "I can't listen to any of this right now."

"No, listen. It's this great—"

"Why can't you get your shit together, Cassie? You're supposed to be the one carrying Danny now. He would do anything for you and now that it's your turn all you're giving him is more misery."

"I'm trying, okay? It's not exactly easy."

He looks at me, licks his lips. "You went back to that bartender? I don't even understand how you could. Your husband barely remembers how to walk and you're off screwing the city's lowlife?"

He's crying again. I don't understand how tears can come out of a person so fast. Just watching him, I feel my own eyes start to burn.

"How do you...No. It's nothing. There's nothing."

"After all of this...I mean Danny and I are just barely keeping things straight, and then you go back to that fucking bartender. Why would you do that?"

Evan's sobs are huge and breathless. They radiate throughout his solid, six-foot-four frame.

"I don't get it with all the crying. What's wrong with you?"

He wipes at his face with the back of one hand, and then with the back of the other, wipes both on his coat. "It cleanses, okay. It's like a shower for your soul. God." He looks down the street, as if measuring how far we've walked. "I have low testosterone," he adds. "It's a condition."

I put my hand on his arm again, but he shakes it off. He looks back at me, his face wet and monstrous in the streetlight.

"We're standing here, you and me, and I'm telling you that you have to stop with that piece of shit bartender. The police are still conducting an investigation. How do you think this looks? I thought you were smarter than this, that you could put ideas together logically."

I don't understand how he knows, what he saw that he can accuse me of this. If he'd come into the bar I would have seen him. You can't miss Evan.

"Is this what you and Danny were talking about outside? Because if you told him something that isn't true I need to—"

"Stop. Stop! I don't want to hear it. Stay away from the bartender, and go home and follow Danny's lead and everything will be okay. You can do this. You can save Danny. Promise me you will."

Save Danny? I don't know how to do this, what he even means by it. But Evan is too big, and the only way to get around him is to put my head into his massive chest and hug him, cry with him on the street corner and listen to myself making promises I can't deliver.

The beach is a picture, taped to the wall by a hopeful boy. We're on a tiny piece of land, surrounded by cutout scenery, and as long as we don't move, the island is ours. Beneath my feet the sand feels real. I can hear the ocean. This is where we are happy. A vacation we never took before our kids were born. Danny takes my hand and smiles.

"I'm always so glad to see you. I can stop looking, now that you're here."

"Could we skip the foreplay this time and talk about that night?"

"Of course, whatever you want. It's your island."

"You keep saying that."

He drops my hand and raises his arms in a dramatic sweeping gesture. "It's true!"

I watch him, the spectacle of him. "Tell me about that night."

"It's going to take a while, you realize."

"Then let's start now."

"These things, they're like the breeze. They come in and lift—"

"Shut up and start talking."

He drops his arms. His face turns gray. I look away, across the water, at the horizon line.

"You said it was a ground floor apartment. We're there with some people. One of them has a key and opens the door."

"So at least we know we didn't break in."

"At least. You said there's a rug on the floor, and something in the corner."

"Forget the corner. Instead, let's talk about the table next to the recliner. A little wooden table. Round."

"You're right. There's a recliner. I remember because…"

"Because you don't see them all that often anymore."

"Right. What else? What's on the table?"

Danny takes in a deep breath. I wait for the exhale, but it never comes. I turn toward him.

"What?"

"A gun."

As soon as he says the word I can see it. Silver, shiny and cold-looking, smudged with fingerprints.

"The same one someone used to shoot you?"

Danny shrugs. "Could be."

"Who does it belong to? Is there a person in the recliner? Is anyone home?"

"Yes, but I don't remember the faces. What I see is a woman's leg with a scab on the ankle like she's cut herself shaving. She has shoes that shine, silvery blue, with straps that crisscross their way up her ankles. I notice her shoes."

"You do?"

He nods. "Then I see a man pushing her backwards. Arms that belong to a person whose face I can't see. She's losing her balance and falling into the recliner."

As soon as he describes it, I see it too; it's my own memory. A woman in a tight black dress with silver straps. Solid arms, solid legs, a beautiful face. She's the most gorgeous woman I've ever seen but doesn't know it. If she did, she wouldn't be wasting her time here. Her shoes are strapped on; they shimmer like moonstones. She's standing with a hand on her hip, running the other one through her hair. There's another pair of hands, too. A man's hands, the ones that are pushing her. The look of surprise on the woman's face. The momentary loss of her beauty as she opens her mouth and brings her head to the side and reaches out, trying to break the fall.

"What else, Danny?"

"The gun isn't on the table anymore. A man is holding it, pointing it at someone. A woman is laughing. I don't know why she's laughing."

"The woman with the shoes?"

"No, a different person. It's hard to remember."

"What about the man holding the gun. Do you know who that is?"

"He's blocked out. I can't see his face."

"But it's someone you know."

"Is it? Do we know him?"

On Wednesday, Lori calls to tell me they've found a new place, a new bar with big tables that nobody has discovered yet. And best of all, it's closer. We won't have to drive as far or deal with that crazy intersection out past Vanderbilt Street. "You haven't been out in ages. We miss you."

"I miss you too, but I can't tonight. I have plans at home."

"Just don't forget about us, okay? We're here for you."

A few minutes later, Cherie calls and demands that I put Danny on the phone. "I need to talk some sense into that husband of yours."

"It doesn't have anything to do with Danny. Nel asked me to show her how to bake little cakes. We're having a girls' night."

"Why does it have to be tonight? This is how it starts, Cassie. You give up your last bits of freedom and before you know it it's all over."

"She's excited about it. I can't cancel."

Cherie laughs. "Come on. Don't tell me you're turning into one of those moms?"

"What do you mean?"

"You know."

"No, I don't think so. Be more specific."

"Nothing. Sorry. Just forget it. I should go." Her voice is flat.

"I'll see you another time."

"Fine. Some other time. Fine."

We hang up and I wonder what is happening. I keep looking for stable footing that doesn't seem to exist. I can't even see the ground. I'm supposed to navigate a treacherous landscape—a field full of obstacles—but it's impossible. There are too many. And Danny just sits around. When I'm not home, he's at his computer. At the end of the day, I see the evidence: dirty bowls and coffee mugs and crumbs on the floor. When I ask him what he does all day, he writes down a single word on his whiteboard:

# REHAB

Nel and I make the small cakes. Our girls' night. We make up signs that say

# NO BOYS ALLOWED IN KITCHEN

and Nel giggles as we hang them up. We lay all of the ingredients out on the table: the flour, the sugar, the food coloring, the decorating bags and fifteen different icing nozzles. I catch myself looking in on us, picturing how this would seem to a stranger who happened to observe us. Warmth and happiness and aprons covered with flour.

While we're mixing up the batter, the boys sneak into the kitchen with devious smiles. Nel screams. "No, get out!"

E laughs, "I saw it. I saw what they were doing!" and runs away. Danny tickles Nel and she laughs so hard she can hardly breathe. When he stops, she tells him he has to leave because we're making secret cakes. He comes up from behind me and rests his chin on my shoulder, wraps his arms around my waist. I stand there with a carton of eggs in my hands and close my eyes. It seems like he'll clear his throat and whisper something in my ear, but instead he just hugs me for three or four seconds before letting go.

"Why are the cakes small?" asks Nel.

"I don't know. They're just…"

"Cute?"

"Yes."

"Like a cupcake?"

"Even cuter than that."

We pour the batter into the little baking tins that Danny bought for me a hundred years ago. Twenty-two of them. I don't know why the number. He had a reason that he never told me and I never asked to hear. Instead I counted them and laughed and told him I'd bake him twenty-two cakes.

The oven is warm and the kitchen begins to smell like sweetness and laughter. We let the cakes cool on racks and confer about our favorite colors, our favorite flavors. We both like vanilla. We both like purple. Nel lines up the cooled-down cakes on the counter and we strategize how we're going to decorate them. Then I step back and let Nel go crazy with the frosting.

By the time we let the boys back in, the kitchen is a mess.

Danny holds up his whiteboard.

# SMELLS SO GOOD

"You get to pick whichever one you want, Daddy."

He points to a cake covered in blue frosting with three little white flowers in the middle. Nel shakes her head. He points to a pink one with green polka dots. Nel shakes her head again. They go through this three or four times until he finally picks the one she wants him to have, with the two glops of yellow frosting that are supposed to be fairy wings.

Danny sits at the table with his cake and rubs his hands together. The kids laugh at their father. Danny bites into the cake and rubs his stomach and gives her the thumbs up sign. I imagine again the person outside, looking in on us, how perfect we must seem. I try to stand inside the experience and become a part of it, but my mind drifts away, takes me away, again and again.

It takes a long time to clean up. Danny helps for a while, then starts massaging my shoulders. His face touches my ear, and I hear the faint sound of his breathing. He grabs my hand and squeezes it gently. When I turn around, his wide-eyed stare says *listen* and *please understand*. We've tried this before: speaking without speaking, communicating with our eyes. *Love creates its own language*, he told me once, but I don't hear anything in his exhausted gaze. The tilt of his head, the way he presses his fingertips into my arm. All of it is nothing.

Later, after the kids have drifted off, I climb into bed and listen to Danny fall asleep next to me. After a half hour of staring at the ceiling, I'm back in the living room, sitting on the couch with the remote in my hand but the TV off. I look around and wonder what's missing, where I'm supposed to look for it, where I should be instead.

How much more time passes? Another half hour? I stand up and walk back to the bedroom.

"I'm going to take some cakes to Cherie," I announce to Danny's unmoving body. I wait, long enough to be certain that he really is asleep, before changing my clothes.

***

Cherie isn't home when I drop by. Her roommate, Larry, answers the door, takes a minute to process me, recognize me.

"I thought you all were out getting into trouble," he says, with no inflection in his voice.

"I couldn't tonight." I hold out a shoebox with four cakes inside. "Can you give these to Cherie, tell her they're from me?"

As he reaches for the box, I hesitate.

"Actually..." I open the lid and remove one of the cakes. "I need this one. The rest are for her."

Larry chuckles. "You got hungry coming all the way out here, huh?"

I chuckle back.

***

The drive out to the Silver Whistle from Cherie's place takes about twenty-five minutes. We used to joke about this, that we were so far away from home that nobody would know where to find us. Somehow, though, Evan did. How else would he know about Lee?

A few snowflakes flutter down, twinkling under the streetlights. The sharp, icy shine that covers the landscape reminds me of a different winter night that I can't quite place; one that looked the same but held more hope than this one. The memory hovers in my periphery, and when I'm finally on the verge of bringing it into focus, it escapes me like a sigh.

The parking lot is nearly empty. I spot Lee's van off in the corner, looking unexpectedly sinister in the shadows. I drive past it, making a loop through the lot, checking for familiar cars, engines running, Evan's black Honda. Did he follow me here once? Was that what happened?

I pull into a spot a few rows away from the entrance. The salt crunches under my shoes as I walk across the parking lot. The bar's windows are fogged up, the neon signs muted behind them. At the door, I hesitate, scanning the parking lot once more: the empty cars and crisscrossing tire tracks. That other winter night—was it during high school? Was I somewhere with my friends? The harder I concentrate on it, the more it evades me.

A rush of cold air follows me into the bar. Lee looks up, with no expression on his face. He's having a conversation with a man in a plaid shirt, gesturing with his hands, smiling briefly, nodding. I've seen the man before; he sits by himself, drinks by himself, sometimes watching the TV but more often staring at nothing. In the corner, a few people are playing darts, and at one of the window tables a college-aged guy sits, checking his phone. That's it. Six patrons in all.

I head left, to the end of the bar and onto my usual stool. Lee drops a coaster in front of me.

"Well. This is unexpected."

"Happy birthday." I set the cake on the coaster.

"I don't have a birthday. And if I did it definitely wouldn't be today."

"Well then I guess you don't get to eat this." I pick up the cake and bring it toward my mouth.

Lee catches my wrist. "What I mean is I'm touched you remembered."

My heart stops. Time stops. Nights like this don't count. I feel myself peeling away from reality. The fake me is so thin you can barely see her.

"Fresh-baked," I say.

Lee takes the cake from my hand, rests it in his palm and admires it. "I'm a little confused by this. It's like someone zapped a normal cake with a shrinking ray."

"My daughter calls them fairy cakes."

He eyes me, briefly. "Okay." For one hesitant moment, he runs a hand through his hair, then devours half the cake in one bite.

"But that's not really why I'm here."

Lee looks away, toward the other end of the bar. "No, I guess it's not."

"I'm just wondering. I've been trying to organize...well, just straighten out some things in my head.

"That night in August, when we...when you drove me home.

We went somewhere first, didn't we? You drove me to a...I can't remember. A place. There was a man there. A few people. A pair of shoes. I don't remember what happened there, how I got home. I can't connect the dots."

He stops chewing for a second, then starts again. I watch his mouth move, his hands move, the ripple of muscle where his shirt touches his arm. He told me once that he got the dagger tattoo when he was young and stupid, that his life has basically been living with his own bad decisions. He's like a ball, rocketing forward after being hit by a bat. There's no way to follow it, control it, predict where it will end up. How did I get here? It didn't seem like this is where it was heading, but this is important too. This is part of it, that night.

For a few minutes, we both focus on the cake. With a second bite he finishes it, then takes the towel off his shoulder and cleans up the crumbs, the coaster.

"I was wondering how much of that night you remembered," he says finally.

I fall asleep in the van while I'm waiting. It's late, so late. The night is raw and lifeless, and so cold that I have to crawl inside a sleeping bag to stay warm. When was the last time I did this? The memories are deep, already dissolving. Whenever it was, it wasn't important.

I awake with a start, aware of a dream that's already gone, of clenching my teeth, being forced to stay and fight when what I really wanted to do was run.

I was supposed to be thinking about what to say to Lee, practicing sentences ahead of time. *Everything just seemed so hopeless. I wanted to be different. I wanted too much.* It shouldn't be complicated; it doesn't need to be.

By the time the door slides open, I've forgotten all of it. Lee climbs into the driver's seat and turns on the ignition, fiddles with the controls on the dashboard. If he started driving away with me in the back, where would he take me? What would we become? Pieces of this feel familiar too. Something he said. Something I said. The struggle to remember brings on a wave of nausea. The heat roars through the vents, a dusty burnt maple-y smell.

I'm still wrapped in the sleeping bag when Lee climbs over me and sits to my right. He leans forward with his elbows on his knees and rubs his hands together, turns his head just enough to look at me, smiles, then looks down at the floor. Time passes like this, minutes that feel precious although I can't say why. The white noise of the heater makes me feel quiet and safe. I examine Lee's profile, the shape of his forehead and his nose. He's one of those people who look different from the side—so different that it feels unexpected.

He talks at the floor. "What if someone told you about a curse, if you heard that you might be cursed? Would it make you worry?"

"I don't get it. What kind of a curse?"

Lee shakes his head. "I don't know. It's nothing. Never mind."

We fall back into silence. The heater continues pushing out warm air, reminding me that the engine is running, that I'm ignoring all the warnings I've ever heard about idling vehicles and odorless gases and snow. Are they even true?

"So, I've been having these dreams. About that night."

"That night was fucked up," he says. "It was like…I don't know. I mean, at first it was good."

He clasps his hands together, taps his thumbs, lets more time pass between us.

"I can't decide what you are," he says finally. "I keep trying to come up with a category for you. Where do you fit? That's what I'm wondering."

"Why do I need a category?"

"I need to break this down. Into pieces, you know. Part A, Part B, Part C. Figure out how it all connects. It's complicated."

"No, that's the thing. It's *not* complicated. That's us. We make it complicated when it's not."

He lets out a cold, short laugh. "My God. You don't know a fucking thing. And I mean that only in the most respectful way, of course."

I feel the heat rise, my spine stiffen. *Stand and fight.* I open my mouth, but before any words come out, Lee's hand is on my cheek, unexpectedly warm. He smiles. "Only in the most respectful way," he says again, more gently this time.

"You're kind of an asshole sometimes. You were that night. I remember this. You tried to throw me out but I was too drunk to stand."

His hand drops, into his lap, and he stares at me. "Out of everything, this is what you remember?" It's something about the way he says it. It feels like a lost prize, the last of a hundred chances used up.

"No. We were having fun at first. We were laughing and...there were shots. You were wearing a blue shirt and then you weren't anymore and for a long time we were talking and then we were arguing, but I don't remember why. You called me a judgmental bitch."

"Only in the most respectful way, I'm sure."

"But then you were nice again. You helped me outside and led me to some bushes."

He stands up. "I need a drink. Do you want a drink?"

"No."

He climbs over me again and opens a cupboard door, produces a beer bottle from somewhere, tosses the cap off, then sits back down, this time in a seat facing mine, and takes a long drink. I wonder how much time we have. Ten minutes? Twenty? Before the carbon monoxide makes us fall asleep and disappear?

It comes back to me, what I wanted to say. *The thing is that I wanted too much. I do. I want too much.* Or did I say this once already? Has it already happened?

*Not too much. That's the thing. It seems like it is but it's not. It's the amount that I should have. I know this because every day feels incomplete, no matter what I do. There's always a last piece that isn't there.*

Lee sets his bottle on the floor and reaches into his back pocket. I'm still nervous, I realize, not certain about the order of things, what happens next. It's a pile of cash—tips, I guess, although it seems like a big stack of money for such a slow night. He pulls a drawer open and throws the cash inside.

"Big tips tonight?"

Lee picks up his beer and drinks again. "I told you before. Walter pays me in cash."

"He does? You told me that?"

He rubs his forehead with the palm of his hand, runs it through his hair, exhales. "Fine. What part do you want to know about?

After we got in your car?"

"Why were we arguing?"

"You wouldn't let up, that's why. I don't know what happened. We were rolling along and then…I don't even know how to explain it. You just went into overdrive. Started talking a mile a minute, telling me about your kids, about your son's teacher at school, about some teacher that you had when you were a kid, friends you used to have. It was…I don't know. Like someone uncorked you and… just…this river came spilling out. And then that thing about your dad. The dictionary and the way he held it when he swung it, and how your mom's face split in two, but without really splitting. The way your dad told you to be fearless but you never really knew if you were or not. You told me that eventually your parents were like worn-down stones. Is any of this sounding familiar to you?"

"This is what made you mad?"

"No, of course not. But I have to admit. I started getting worried where your brain was headed. It seemed like any second the whole thing would take a turn and enter some places I wasn't interested in going. I've seen this before. Soon you'd be crying, blaming me, accusing me of ruining your life. If you wanted to deal with your guilt then fine, but I wasn't interested in participating. We're people; we do things. We didn't ruin anything."

"No. No. That's it exactly. I'm the same as you."

Lee sips from his beer, stares at the tops of his knees.

"So then you started in on me. *Where are you from?* You asked me this about three hundred times. *Do you ever go home? What did you do before you came here? What's the story with that scar on your chest? What's the story with that dagger on your arm? What did you do? How bad was it? Are you hiding from somebody?* You were so set on imagining the worst about me.

"I wouldn't answer you, and you couldn't deal with it. 'I'm so tired of all the secrets' you said. 'Why do you guys always have secrets? Just tell me. What did you do? What did you run away from?'"

"I remember this. You had this look on your face like…"

"I was pissed. Yes. You're remembering that right."

"So then I went outside and threw up. In some bushes."

"You were way too drunk to drive home, but you wanted to get in your car, you wanted me to take you home. Only I was drunk too, so I took off in the other direction, away from town, cruising down empty side streets. I didn't know where I was going, or even where you lived, who was going to be up waiting for you. I thought eventually you'd be lucid enough to tell me. Either that or you'd pass out and we'd both fall asleep at the side of the road for a few hours. But instead you kept talking."

I climb into the driver's seat and turn off the ignition. The heat cuts off, leaving silence behind. I stare out the windshield, knowing I'm supposed to remember, that maybe I do remember, I will when I've heard it, and maybe I don't want to hear it.

Behind me, Lee continues talking. "You started making things up. All these stories about me. That 'Lee' sounds like a made-up name. That maybe I'm a fugitive. I ran away because I got in a fight and beat the other guy up so badly he barely survived. He's blind in one eye, disabled for life because of me, and if he ever finds me he'll kill me for what I did.

"I honestly don't know where all this dark shit was coming from. You just kept going, each idea worse than the one before it. Your imagination—I mean, who has an imagination like this? You envisioned my whole life, the questionable things I did to make ends meet. The story about the scar on my chest, so terrible I can never repeat it. The torment that I live with. You described it to me as if I should be feeling it, as if I had done all of these things. Some woman I lived with, the intensity with which I loved her, the way she looked when she told me she was pregnant: all smiles and glowing from the inside out. I promised to be there for her and the baby, but the idea of this was too powerful, the hold it had over me, that I ran away from them too. I kept thinking that each one was the last bad decision I would make, but with me it turned out to be a pattern. It turned out to be me."

"But all that's in the past," I say quietly. It comes to me like an echo. My own voice, bouncing off a distant canyon wall.

"You do remember."

I shake my head, not certain whether he is even looking at me, whether we're even in the same place any longer. It feels like floating; I'm in a huge, stagnant saltwater lake where I can sit, immobile, for the rest of my life. I could tell him to stop and close my eyes, suspend myself forever, let my brain continue to forget.

"I don't get it, why would I do this?"

"I'm not even going to try to psychoanalyze, okay? It was around this time that you finally started slowing down—how do I even describe it? Maybe like someone had unplugged you. You became wistful. You weren't even listening to me when I told you that none of your crazy ideas were true, and after a while it seemed like a waste of breath to even try. We kept driving around and I lost track of where we were, how we got to whatever street it was that we were on. I started to get it through my head that maybe you were Satan. You were Death, in disguise, coming for me. You were looking for a loophole, trying to get a false confession out of me, and once you did you'd change into some terrifying black bird and fly out of the car and I'd be so distracted watching you go that I'd drive into oncoming traffic, and that would be the end of it."

"God. That's terrible."

"I mean, I didn't *really* think this. Of course not. But the night was so hot. Everything was in the wrong order, and I didn't understand what the two of us were doing in the car together, where we were going."

"So you took me to that apartment. The one where Danny was shot. 4267 S. Jefferson."

He pauses. I want to turn around and look at his face, but this feels better. The blackness in front of me, the cold air pushing in around me, cooling me down.

"No, this was a different building. Just a place a guy I know lives. I don't even know why I brought you there. It was a bad idea. I think I just wanted to get out of the car."

"But I saw it. I went there and it looked familiar to me."

"A lot of apartments in this city look just like that."

The tiles on the floor. The ancient wallpaper lining the hallway. Where does the story go next? I try to remember it on my own, but the conversations Lee is relaying to me don't resonate anywhere in my memory. Maybe I *could* have been Death, about to change into a bird. I could have been anyone.

"This guy I know...I shouldn't have taken you there. He's garbage, but I drove us there anyway. I think it was because you wouldn't listen to anything I said. It started to feel like there were nails driving through my forehead. I couldn't deal with it anymore."

The seat starts tilting backwards. The van is ripping open, offering me to the winter sky.

There's a gun on the table. A man pushing a woman with a scab on her leg, making her fall backwards.

"You sat down on the couch next to him. Your dress wasn't even all the way buttoned up and I was pretty sure you weren't wearing any underwear. He asked me who you were, and I just shrugged at him. Somehow, I was sure this was the right thing; I convinced myself that it was. You looked at everyone, into their faces, at their clothes, their feet. The guy I know said something to you—maybe you remember, but I'm not going to repeat it—and you told him to fuck off. That's when it started dawning on me what a terrible idea it was, bringing you there. There was a woman. You started complimenting her shoes, telling her they were the best shoes you'd ever seen. She flashed you a huge smile and lifted up her foot—she was wearing this stiletto that went on forever—and you put your hand one her ankle and told her that you needed shoes just like hers.

"I think that was when you looked over and noticed the gun, on the table. I tried to tell you that it wasn't loaded—it was never loaded—but I don't think you heard me. The guy reached over and picked it up, and then told you to lick the woman's feet. I guess it didn't register that he was talking to you. This is when I started wondering how I was going to get you out of there. I watched him half pointing the gun at you, gesturing toward the woman's shoe. 'Go on. Lick her feet.' You told him to get lost again and after that he really was pointing the gun at you. He had this twisted smile on his face, and the barrel was lined up with your nose, but I don't even think you flinched. You just seemed... fascinated. I thought maybe you thought it was a toy or something. The woman with the shoes told him to get the gun out of your face and then he pointed it at her, and you didn't even take the time to think before you pushed his arm out of the way and asked him what kind of a person aims a gun at people for fun? He started laughing like this was the funniest thing he'd ever heard, but I didn't want to stick around and see what would happen next. The woman with the shoes told me to take you home. The guy gave her a shove and she fell backwards, and you wanted to stay and help her but by this time I was already pulling you out the door."

I hear it, but it seems unreal.

"Did we go on the roof after that?"

"No. We got in the car."

"You drove me home."

"Yeah, I drove you home."

"So then…this has nothing to do with Danny? With Dora McIntosh?"

Finally, I turn around in the seat to look at Lee. He's leaning back, face tilted up toward the ceiling, thin wisps of steam rising from his mouth.

"I don't know who that is," he says. "I don't know what happened to your husband."

I try to swim through the story he's just told me, to lift my head and look back at the water and see the sun reflecting off it neatly and simply, but I can't do it. There is no straight line to follow, no line at all. Because what if he really did shoot Danny? What if none of this is true?

Lee stands up, tosses the empty beer bottle into a box. Why does this break my heart? When he faces me again, there is a look of finality on his face. It feels like the last conversation we will have. I wonder how to say goodbye, if there's a different word you're supposed to use for this, except that this isn't anything. It was never anything. He is nobody, just like Dora.

# CHAPTER 11
## (DANNY)

We were young. We messed up. I mean, that really sums up the whole story—those two sentences. But I guess you want the details anyway.

The last night at the cabin, Dora gave me the formal breakup speech. *I like you, but... This has been great, but... You know I can never forget you, but...* Not like it was a surprise. She said these things are like chapters in a book. You don't know which is your favorite chapter, sometimes even when you get to it; you have to read the whole story to find out. I didn't say much in response, just listened to her talk, her voice barely above a whisper. After a while, I realized she wasn't going to stop, I knew where she was heading. It felt like we were ducking our heads in a basement, just barely missing the ceiling, but sooner or later we'd stand up and it'd smack us. Two people dead in the woods.

*I keep trying to decide if life is precious or not, and I can't. I still don't know how to answer that question.*

We left them there. We were going to leave them there.

*What is our responsibility to another person simply because we're both humans? Do we have one?*

Outside, buried under ground, was an elephant tusk; inexplicable, stolen. Two people dead in the woods. Dora's words floated past me. I focused on the smell of her, the smoothness of her arm against mine, her brown hair spilling onto my shoulder.

I mean, I understood it, even then. She was just trying to find a way to reshape what was wrong into something that looked like it was right. But you can't do that in just a few hours. It takes years, and even then I don't know.

*Think about it for a minute. What happened to us—is it any different from what happens to anyone else?*

It got to the point where I wanted to not have to listen to her anymore, to not have to interject, every now and then, that I was on her side. I wanted to be able, for once, to explain myself to her, but I couldn't figure out how to put what I was thinking into words. It had something to do with all the time we spend deliberating over what's already happened. There's a human urge or something that makes us want to spread the past out on a table in front of us, let it sit in the sun for a while and desiccate and then come back and chew over it some more. What we forget is that it's done; it's over. It's been over for years.

If I'd tried to explain this to Dora, we might have been up all night, so instead I pulled her in for a kiss. She responded like—I don't know how to describe it. I could feel all the delicate parts of her spilling out. She was letting them go and I was squeezing her for more. Being rough usually wasn't my thing, but I figure you're allowed to with a girl after she's just broken up with you. After you've just buried a dead person's dead animal tusk under the ground and watched some guy cut up his hand up with a rock because he goes a little bit crazy, you're allowed.

I don't know what was going through Taz's head, what was up with that rock. What I said before about the knife and the palm and a blood oath—that never happened. What did happen was Taz jammed a rock into the back of his hand and dragged its jagged edge through the skin. By the time we understood what we were seeing, the worst of it was already done. I remember blinking, watching Katy run to him and put her arm on his shoulder, whisper into his ear. Dora got out a first aid kit and bandaged him up like she was already a doctor. I remember how she laid out all the items, the way the paper crinkled as she unwrapped a white square of gauze, the look of concentration as she asked him if he was able to spread his fingers all the way apart.

Afterward, we left the bloody rock there, I guess to mark the site? I don't really know why we did it, but back then, in some fucked-up way, it made sense.

Taz's hand was too swollen for him to drive, so he climbed into the passenger seat of his truck and sat there waiting for Katy to finish hugging the rest of us goodbye. I always wondered if there was more in his backpack that they weren't telling us about, but it was already too late. We'd never see him again. We'd made plans to come back in five years, but I was sure we wouldn't. After you bury secrets as big as ours in the ground, you don't. At that point you turn around and you go forward, away from your mistakes and stupidity, and hope that eventually you'll forget that they ever happened.

No, we didn't keep in touch. We went about doing our own things, and there were plenty of them to do. Stitch shed his nickname when the weather got too cold for shorts and nobody noticed the scar anymore. Back to plain old Evan. I guess I thought maybe I could get through this story without mentioning him by name, but without him there's no way to finish it. Evan Conway. We stayed friends, somehow. We moved up to the city and got an apartment together. We never mentioned Dora, Suzie, any of it. We got new jobs. We made halfhearted plans to take over the world. But I don't know. Did he ever get on the internet late at night too? Those pictures of elephants brought to their knees, their faces so mutilated it just makes you want to spit to get the taste of it out of your mouth. Those piles of tusks that you stare at, doing the math—how many animals? The bonfires to destroy them, which I guess was taking some kind of a stand, but it just seems like more mutilation, more waste. I mean, I've never been all that into saving the Earth, but those pictures; I wish I'd never seen them.

For almost five years, I didn't hear the name Dora MacIntosh. She had become a ghost, like all the others before her. And if you spend your time thinking about ghosts, your life becomes a graveyard.

Somewhere along the way I met the right girl. She was hot as a firecracker, with big, soulful eyes and a smile that you had to coax out of her. The first time we met, the room got brighter and the bass line pounded deeper and it felt like she was reading my mind.

I don't know what it was, how to explain it, but she just had this yearning, this rough-edged desire, and half the time it was for me. Evan told me I was too young to play house but then he met a girl and the same thing happened to him. This is the history of man in a nutshell. We think we'll be the ones to come up with a new way of being men, but it turns out we do exactly the same things as everyone else and live the same way and die the same way until everyone we ever knew, or ever knew us, is gone.

If not for that email, I could end this right here. But instead, she tracked me down. I don't know how. Dora fucking MacIntosh.

She believed in promises. This was what she was emailing to tell us. It was time to go back to the cabin and dig up the time capsule. *The time capsule.*

Evan agreed with her; we had to go back. Sometimes, he said, he dreamt about it. He'd start digging into the dirt where the tusk was buried, but as soon as he got close to it, two human skeletons would run toward him, and that was when he'd look down and realize he was standing over an empty hole in the ground.

"I think Dora must have dug it up. Wouldn't you if it was your cabin? I mean, just to be able to sleep there at night. Otherwise..."

I shrugged. "I haven't thought about it."

He was going to be married in a few weeks. He needed to get this out of his system. He wanted me to go with him. You get the idea. You know how it is. Just for a couple days this time and then back to our lives.

Dora was different than I remembered her. It was hard to pinpoint. Less carefree, you could say, but wasn't that all of us after five years? She was twenty-two by then and possibly more gorgeous than I remembered, although her hair was short and tidy in some trendy-looking style, a single detail that made the entirety of her different. She had finished her first year of medical school, and I told her that it was nice to see her sticking with it. It was something to say. After five years, you have to start somewhere.

"What did you think I was going to do? Become a waitress instead?"

Maybe it was nothing, maybe it was just time filling in around us, but the way she talked, the inflection in her voice; it just felt a little like lemon juice on a cut, you know? When Evan started joking around, asked if we would be staying in the same rooms as last time, Dora crossed her arms and gave him a hard look. It was familiar, a variation on something I'd seen in another lifetime.

"You two are in the small bedroom upstairs. Suzie and I get the bigger one across the hall. Katy and Taz are downstairs."

"Those two are still together?"

"Inseparable." She exhaled in a way that made me think that maybe she found this annoying, but I didn't want to start speculating, reading into anything. I was on a mission to keep it simple, not get wrapped up in all the details, get through the weekend and then go home and forget about it all over again.

"She looks great," Evan noted as we watched her walk away. "I don't remember her being that hot before."

"She was that hot before."

"She was? I can't wait to see Suzie Q."

"Are you going to tell her you're getting married?"

"If it comes up."

The weather was different that year. The first day it rained almost nonstop. We sat around on the musty furniture and talked about how much we hoped Katy and Taz hadn't run into any trouble on the drive. You wouldn't think a conversation about a car ride could go on for that long. Evan and I cracked out some beers to break the ice, but Suzie and Dora told us it was way too early to be drinking. Times had changed, I guess.

Evan got me alone in the kitchen to fill me in on his reading of the situation. Dora was single; he was sure of it. He wasn't sure about Suzie Q. She seemed to be dodging the issue. "I'm guessing she has a boyfriend but she doesn't want me to know about him. What do you think that means?"

"I don't see how any of this matters." All I'd read of the situation was what she'd told us: Suzie was a year out of college with a job that didn't make much sense to me. An analyst. A company that provided services to other companies. She had a job, a thing, a life that had nothing to do with ours.

The girls wanted to see pictures of Cassie. They wanted to size her up, to size me up based on who I'd picked to spend my time with. I don't understand girls and the way they always categorize and rank everything. It's like nothing can just be, on its own. It always has to exist in comparison to a hundred other things.

"How could you not have any pictures of her on your phone? What kind of a shitty husband are you?"

"I remember what she looks like."

Suzie rolled her eyes. "How do you not get it?"

"Oh leave him alone." Dora tapped my knee lightly and smiled. "The word romantic isn't in his lexicon."

Evan shot me a glance, and I knew what he was thinking: is this the way Dora talked now?

It was around dusk when Taz and Katy finally showed up. Katy handed out enormous hugs and acted like we were her best friends in the world. Taz shook our hands—his grip was hard and strong—and we tried not to notice but it was the first thing you were going to look for, right? That scar, weaving its way across the top of his left hand.

"You guys look great," I said, even though they didn't. They had both put on at least ten pounds, and I don't know what it was about Katy. She looked worn out, like someone had hung her out in a field, exposed to the sun and rain for the last five years. But what was *on* them looked great. Taz was wearing these pants, this shirt, these fucking shoes. A big watch with diamonds where the number twelve should have been. Katy had a huge rock on her finger and was going on nonstop with stories about their honeymoon to the Bahamas, their recent trip to Greece, showing us pictures of their house on three acres with a four-car garage. Clean-smelling nighttime skies. You could have all of this at twenty-three, it turned out.

By this time the girls were finally drinking and the mood had lightened up some. Dora was laughing and giving me these looks from the corner of the room, and every so often she'd put a hand on my arm or my waist as she walked by. With no way of calling home it was like stepping backwards in time. I thought after a few more drinks I could believe that all of it was a recording of an event that had happened a long time ago and I'd just never gotten around to watching. Like Dora with her chapters. We were still on page thirty-five and Cassie wouldn't show up until page ninety.

What did we do that first night? What does it matter? We played cards. We drank a lot because there was no other way to get through it. Evan and Suzie vanished into the kitchen and then from the cabin altogether. I opened the back door and saw their dark, groping shapes out on the porch, so I turned around and went upstairs to bed.

I don't know what time it was when Dora came in. The door creaked shut and I woke up.

"Sorry," she whispered. She was a gray shape in the darkness; I could make out the blanket draped around her shoulders. "I can't get in the other room. Stitch and Suzie are…working through some things."

I don't think I said anything, just kind of shifted over as she crawled into bed with me.

"I can trust you, right?" She didn't wait for an answer. Pretty soon it was her shoulder next to mine, the sound of her breathing, the tip of her foot touching my ankle.

I looked up at the ceiling, at the patterns made by the wood planks, the rafters lined up in rows, the way those on opposite sides leaned forward, resting on one another but at the same time holding each other up. The seeming simplicity of it. I wondered what it would be like to build a house by yourself, to put up walls and lay down a floor and slope a roof down over the top of it. It was one of those things. It felt impossible, even though I knew it could be done, that I could learn to do it if I ever felt like it, instead of working on a road crew or digging basements for the rest of my life.

"Hey, I have to tell you something." She grabbed my forearm as if to lead me somewhere.

I closed my eyes and listened for the crickets, but that night the rain was keeping them quiet.

"What is it?" I asked finally.

"Last time we were here, after you guys left..."

I waited, and after a minute or two passed I wondered if she'd fallen asleep. Somehow, I started thinking about that blue bikini top, holding her bare shoulders in my hands and staring down into her eyes. You weren't supposed to come back, and yet somehow here we were.

With a long exhale, she rolled over to face me, her hands tucked underneath her cheek.

"I dug up the time capsule." She paused in the silence. "Do you hate me?"

"If you really want to know, I don't give a shit about that stupid box or what you did with it."

"You know..." She let out a sharp breath. "Some men grow up and become better men. Other men grow hard. Why are you the hard kind? It's like your defense mechanisms are part of your personality now, like every day you're going to war."

"Dora...please. I can't listen to this right now. I'm sure you're right about everything. Now just... tell me about the time capsule."

"Okay, but only because it's so dark in here right now and I can't really see your face."

I closed my eyes and thought if I was lucky I would just drift off and in a few seconds it would be morning.

"I felt so empty after you guys left. Maybe you don't quite know my mindset. It had been such a great summer and it seemed like my life was rushing past me, moving so fast that I couldn't grab onto anything. And then there was this one week and I grabbed onto you. I mean, I know—I understand—but there was something so solid about you. I can't even explain it. It doesn't matter now. Suzie and I had just finished cleaning up and we were sitting on the couch with our cameras, looking through the pictures we'd taken. There was this one of the two of us, you and me. I don't even know when she took it. I couldn't remember when it happened and that's the point. We were sitting on the couch looking at each other, kind of tipped in toward one another with all the parts of our bodies fitting in together, in just...this way. I'm staring at it, at myself, and wanting it, wanting to be her, even though I am her, I *was* her.

You've only just left and I'm envying this, how easy it was and the way we're smiling at each other. And I know there was nothing…I know logic and reason, but I just felt like I needed to read what you wrote to me. Like maybe that would close it all up for me. My own box of…whatever. Selfish, I guess. So I dug it up."

I hear her breathing next to me, panting almost.

"Well, what did it say?"

"See, that's exactly it. You don't even remember. The big things become small things, you know? It all gets pressed down and smoothed over and then shoved inside a little box and tied up with a bow and when you look back all you see are a thousand boxes and a thousand bows and they all look the same; you can't tell them apart anymore. But this is how it's supposed to be; it's good like this. We've decided that, haven't we? Collectively? And I wouldn't say I disagree with it, but still. Life is too long."

I remember wanting to respond to this, because in a crazy way she did sort of make sense, although I couldn't tell you why. Instead, I just kept thinking about the rain and the rafters and how when I was a kid I would lie in bed imagining what it would be like to have the top bunk. Then, one day, Curt came home and told me to switch with him; he was tired of climbing up and down the ladder every night. We moved our bedding without any ceremony—Curt barely even looked at me—and I thought about all the places he'd been that day and how he couldn't wait to get back to them, whatever they were. I didn't know. When he took his clothes off and dropped them on the floor, I smelled smoke, spice, sweat, a slightly bitter odor that I didn't recognize but that made me think of railroad tracks. That first night up in the top bunk I wanted to cry. It was like I was a hole—there was nothing to me at all—and the only way to keep myself together was to rub my fingers along the ceiling and map out the texture of the paint until the feeling passed. And the thing was, these were the good times. It hadn't even gotten bad at that point. I thought maybe I could tell Dora this story so she would know that I was awake and thinking, but what was the point to it? I wouldn't have known where to begin anyway.

"I had a good time that week, too."

I heard Dora sigh and felt her fingers move down my arm until they found my hand and curled around it. They were cold, and I thought the least I could do was warm them up for her.

"I don't even know if I want to *be* a doctor. I don't remember deciding to do this; it was so long ago. It just became part of the plan, and even though I grew up and...oh, I don't know...*evolved*, the future never did. There was only ever one course of events. I had a picture in my head of the house I would live in, these rose bushes I'd have in the garden. A curved stone walkway up to the door. Perfect grass in the backyard. Sunshine. A bedroom with French doors that opened out onto some magnificent backyard. I don't even like roses! I mean, why would I want this stuff?

"Sometimes I think I should be one of those people sitting in a cafe with a book, just reading and letting time pass. Instead of filling my brain with human anatomy, I could fill it with...anything else. Imagine being a magnet for thoughts, having the time to muse and deliberate and become a *complete* adult human."

It sounded so tiring to me. Her quest for completeness. All those million thoughts. By this time her hand was warm, and it felt like mostly I had done my part. The rain was coming down harder and all I really wanted to do was power down until morning.

"I'm sorry, Dora."

She squeezed my hand, and that was it. When I woke up in the morning Dora was gone and the rain had stopped.

# CHAPTER 12
## (CASSIE)

It turns out the police *are* doing their job. An investigation has been taking place, and information begins to bubble to the surface. The police are able to make connections that weren't apparent before.

I remember Detective Raugl from the days after the accident. He's short and compact, with a tiny mouth and a pointy nose and closely cropped hair. Manicured nails. Everything about him tidy and polite.

I expect he's going to ask me about my meeting with Gerry, but he brings up Lee instead. Am I having an affair, he wants to know, with a bartender at the Silver Whistle? He sniffs and looks down, as if the question embarrasses him.

"I…don't. I wouldn't call it that."

"Well what is the nature of your relationship with Mr. Holdorf?"

I try to correct the detective, fill in Lee's real last name, but even as I wonder why I would do this, the name doesn't come to me. Certainly I know it. Certainly.

"We didn't really…it was loose. Just an agreement. No, I don't mean an agreement. Just…it was temporary."

Surely he's seen this before. He must understand how some things, without ever being named, just are.

"For simplicity, let's call it an affair."

I don't answer. He has a notepad, a silver pen that looks too fancy for what we're doing here. It must have been a gift from someone. I imagine this, the explanation that came with it. *I wanted you to have a nice pen for your job.*

"Have you been to his apartment?"

"No, of course not. I told you it was temporary. It wasn't a thing."

He studies me. He seems to be unrolling my face, flattening it, looking for abnormalities, the smallest of tics. I let him take my eyes apart. I stare back at him. I wouldn't even know what to lie about.

"Did your husband know about it? About whatever was occurring between you and the bartender?"

Already I know where this is leading. The trajectory is clear, a rock skipping across a long, still pool.

"I don't think so." It seems like the right answer, except that if Evan knows then Danny could too. The detective sees me think of this. Somehow he can read my thoughts. "Danny would have said something," I explain.

This part feels true. I look at the detective so that he will also see this in my face. He taps the point of his silver pen on the notepad, takes a sip from a coffee cup.

"What I'm having a hard time with is the simple fact that you were having an affair with a man who lived in the building where your husband was shot."

I wait for his words to make sense. They dance, tauntingly, just above my eyes.

"My first thought is that your husband and this man have a reason to meet up that night. Your husband has a reason to be angry with him."

"What? No. Lee didn't live there. I always thought—I mean, I think he lived in that van."

"That's what he told you?"

"Well, you wouldn't want to advertise, right? But he had it all fixed up with a bed and a sink and everything. And he never talked about living anywhere else."

"So this is where you went to…spend time? His van? You drove it somewhere?"

"No, we just stayed in the parking lot of the bar." As the words come out, I realize how they sound. To anyone who wasn't there to understand it.

"You never met up anywhere else?" Detective Raugl fixes his eyes on me. I wonder how many people he questions in a day, how many of them tell lies. How many try to tell the truth but when they do their answers come out sounding wrong anyway.

"Just one time. He took me to a friend's place."

It was a different building; Lee insisted this. But now, with

Detective Raugl sitting across from me, it seems the most obvious of lies. The high curb. The heavy door. The rough, worn carpeting and the lingering smells of somebody's dinner. Grocery store circulars on the floor under the mailboxes.

"When was this?"

"It was hot. August, maybe."

"And who was the friend?"

"I guess 'friend' is the wrong word. It was some guy he knew. He lived in an apartment...I don't know where. I was drunk that night; we drank these shots. Anyway, the guy was kind of insane. He pointed a gun at me."

"You saw a firearm in the apartment?"

It's not possible, is it? That it could be the same gun, the one that shot Danny?

"It's hard to say for sure. I mean this is what...it was over nothing. A pair of shoes. Lee told me the gun was never loaded."

"Okay. And then what happened?"

"No, I mean he told me all this later. The other day. Night. I was trying to remember."

"You blacked out?"

I cringe. "No. Well, I don't know what you would call it. I do have little bits of the night, but Lee helped me fill in the parts that were missing."

Detective Raugl shifts his body, resettles himself into his chair. As the words come out, I watch him hear them, process them, scratch out another few words in his notebook.

"So you're claiming you have no recollection of where the apartment was? Just that you were there?"

"That's right." It sounds bad, it sounds...

"When you say 'filled in the parts that were missing,' how much would that be, approximately? Fifty percent? Seventy-five percent? Ninety percent?"

"I can't really think of it in terms of numbers. I just know that the pieces match. What he told me. It clicked. None of it seemed made up."

"Here's what I'm getting at. You can't say for sure where this apartment building was. You can't say for sure that Lee Holdorf didn't live there. Correct?"

I feel him pushing me, down a road that I've never seen before, that I don't want to exist. "I guess."

"And what you do remember about the night was fed to you by a man with whom you were romantically involved, but whose last name it appears you didn't even know until a few minutes ago."

"Is romantic the right word? I feel like it's not." I speak slowly, try make myself sound confident. I am confident. I remember the shots, laughing. There was a riddle. We solved it together. Right before the argument.

"I don't think he would live in a place like that. It seemed..."

Do I know what kind of a place he would live in? I try to imagine him getting up in the morning, making breakfast, brushing his teeth, opening the blinds. Would he have blinds? Would he be one of those people who leaves them open all the time? Closed all the time?

"You couldn't see him living there, but you could see him living in a van?"

I feel heat rising to my face, my heart beating more quickly. "I guess it doesn't make sense, but this is the truth. I'm telling you everything I know."

"Do you remember Danny saying anything about Dora MacIntosh?"

"You already asked me this."

"I'm asking again in case one of those 'little bits' has come to you since then. Did he ever bring her up, even in passing?"

Dora MacIntosh Dora MacIntosh Dora MacIntosh. Danny knew her, didn't he? That's what this detective has found out; that Danny lied about not knowing her.

"No."

Detective Raugl stares at me, past me. For a few seconds, we're not even in the same room. I can imagine it, where he must be, that he must have some woman in his past. They all do. Danny has Dora, and Detective Raugl has his own ancient passions that haunt him. Something shifts in his countenance and he returns his attention to the notepad. "Let's go back to that night at the apartment building. What was the name of the person you visited—the bartender's friend-is-too-strong-of-a-word with the gun?"

Certainly Lee would have told me, but it's a blank. If I ever knew it, it's lost in the darkness. "I don't know. I can't remember if Lee even introduced us. But I remember what he looked like. He had dark hair—jet black—and a chip out of one of his front teeth. He had these tattoos around his wrists. They looked like bracelets." The details fall out of the darkness. I can see the man's face, his antagonistic smile.

"So Lee brought you there and then afterward you left together."

"He wanted to take me home. Like I said, the guy who lived there was acting unstable, with that gun and everything."

Detective Raugl throws down the pen and folds his arms. He's not wearing a wedding ring. I can't decide between never married and divorced, but either way, I imagine lonely nights. A house that's too big for him. Most of his time spent in one room, where he eats microwaveable meals and thinks about his case files. I imagine decades of this.

"Here's the thing," he says. "The man you've just described is Lee's roommate. So I want you to think how all of this sounds to me, that you somehow didn't know where you were, can't remember, whatever it is."

I open my mouth to speak, and then stop, frozen. "Huh? I don't get what you're saying."

"Lee took you to his own apartment that night."

"But...I don't see how that's possible. He would have told me."

Detective Raugl writes something on his notepad. *Untruthful. Delusional.* I could come up with a whole list of words he might be using to describe me.

Of course it's possible. I should have prepared for this. Lee is a liar too.

When I revisit the beach, it feels urgent. All this time, Danny's been waltzing me through a conversation that doesn't matter. We've been wasting our time.

It's as peaceful as ever, the water as expansive and blue. Danny has been standing here for months, it seems, waiting for me.

"I miss you when you're away," he says.

"I miss you too."

"It gets lonely. There's so much space. I try to write you letters in the stars at night, but I don't think you've been reading them."

"What do they say?"

He shrugs. "It doesn't last. The feeling comes and then it goes, just like the tides. There's a system here. A rhythm. And sometimes the breeze changes direction and there's a certain smell in the air. Soft and fragrant. I'm guessing it's a night-blooming flower. I've never seen one. I didn't know such a thing existed. They have the most incredible life forms here. Plants and animals I've never heard of before. A whole different set than where we're from."

"That apartment. Let's talk about it. I went there once. Did you know that?"

"Of course I did. Isn't this what we've been talking about all along? That night at the apartment, with your bartender."

"He's not mine. Obviously not. He's…"

Danny throws his arms up into the air, like he's releasing a handful of glitter. I wait for it to flutter down on us; sand, glitter, the sun, all of it.

"I'm sorry," he says. "What were we talking about?"

I can barely remember it myself. All I have to do is let go, let it be forgotten, and it will just be the two of us on an empty beach. It seems so easy, the simplest of solutions to a problem we've been trying to solve for weeks.

"Let's go for a walk," I say. "Help me turn around."

"It's exactly the same over there as it is over here. There's no need to go anywhere."

"So we just stand here? We never leave?"

"You're hitting too hard with the metaphor, okay Cas? Just trust me. Please. Like you used to."

Somehow, I squirm my dream body into a position where I can turn around. *Finally*, I think, but what I find is exactly what Danny told me there would be: more sand, more ocean, more trees off in the distance; a mirror image of what's in the other direction. The island goes on forever. It never ends. This is our infinite happiness. Danny's gift to me.

"You see? There was nothing to worry about."

"But…"

"Why does there always have to be something the matter?"

"What if a storm comes? We don't have any shelter."

"Don't worry, we'll figure it out." He steps toward me and grabs me lightly by the arms. When was the last time I saw him like this? The kindness on his face, the certainty in his eyes, the solidness of him.

"But what if I don't come back?"

"Then don't leave."

He pulls me closer and I know we're kissing, but it feels different, like air. He's the air and so am I, and isn't this what I've wanted all along? If I stay, we could have this forever. If I could just stop asking questions, stop wondering. Who wouldn't make this trade?

Behind Danny's head, a photograph flutters down and comes to rest in the sand.

*Stop wondering.*

Trees, a rocky stream. *Why am I wondering about this?*

Danny went away sometimes. *You've got to make time for the boys,* he always said. First there was the road trip before Evan got married, and then there were other times. Day trips, overnight stays, long weekends. Not so often that it ever seemed unusual; two or three times a year, maybe. He had a friend who owned a small cabin in Clearfield. Nothing fancy. Just a place to go sit and think. He talked about a path through the woods that led to a small lake, where he always tried to fish but never caught anything, probably because there weren't any fish there, but that was never the point. It was about the quiet, the slow movement of the sun across the sky, the surface of the water that looked like glass. He'd watch the ducks paddling around and somehow this healed him. He never invited me to go and I never asked. I didn't understand how to deal with whatever had happened in his past except allow him the time away, the glassy lake, the ducks. It seems stupid now. But he always went there around his brother's birthday, and what could I say to that?

He told me it was cheap. It didn't cost anything, except for the gas to get down there and a little money for food, but he never ate much of anything with no easy way to cook. He told me this, but before he went there would be money in his secret hole, and after he left it would always be empty.

I asked to see pictures of it once, and Danny looked confused. "They wouldn't do it justice," he explained. But when he returned from the next trip there were pictures on his phone. Not of the lake or even the cabin, but of some trees, a stream, nothing exciting. It could have been anywhere.

Nothing clicked before. That night in the cold, Gerry MacIntosh mentioned a family cabin "off in the middle of nowhere." Is anything clicking now? Because I wonder, if you pile coincidence on top of coincidence, if you wouldn't come up with a match at some point.

# CHAPTER 13

Evan's apartment is cold and it smells faintly of cabbage. Even when I'm inside with the door closed it doesn't feel like I've left the outside. It's spare, with flat surfaces and hard angles and a few pieces of mismatched tan furniture. Except for the boxes stacked in the corner, he's managed to keep the place tidy; empty more so than uncluttered, and somehow this depresses me. On a sunny day, maybe it's different, but today the world is winter white, winter gray, the sky low and flat and as drab as a metal girder. The only light in the apartment comes in through the windows, and I wonder what the place would look like set on fire, the walls decorated in orange flames.

"Does your heat not work?"

He looks around the room, as if this might help him understand my question. "Oh. I like it better this way." He's wearing a t-shirt and some old work pants. A pair of scuffed up, paint-splattered boots. "I don't really get cold ever."

The walls are empty except for three picture frames, hung together in a cluster opposite the couch. Photographs of his kids: Mia, Denver, and the little one, whose name I can't remember.

Evan hands me a glass of cloudy tap water and sits on one of the low, wide arms of the couch. There aren't any tables, so I place the glass on a windowsill instead. When I look up, Evan's arm is pressed against his face. It looks like he's wiping his brow, but after a few seconds I realize he's crying. Again.

"Stop doing that. It makes me uncomfortable." I turn on a floor lamp in the corner, which emits a dim, whining light.

"I told you, I have testosterone issues. It's not like I want to do this, but when it happens I don't want to stop it. If it's a personal truth coming to the surface, then you need to let it out, no matter the form."

I close my eyes. "I don't even understand you anymore. Listening to you talk, it's like hearing someone vomit up half-digested words."

"It takes time, Cas."

I walk over to the stacks of cardboard boxes and peer into the open one on top. It's filled with books: hardcover, new, identical. *The Secret Path to Joy: A Journey for Our Lifetime.*

Evan stands up and approaches me. "I could give you a deal on that. Because you're basically family."

"Why would I buy a book about joy from the unhappiest person I know? Look at you. You can't stop weeping."

His face is wet and sallow and flesh seems to hang off his cheekbones. He didn't always look like this, did he? "Right now is a tough time, but we'll get through it." He places his hands on my shoulders and looks directly into my eyes. "I'm going to tell you something, because I think it could really help you."

"Stop it. This is creepy."

"Listen, Cassie. There is a very specific set of steps, and you have to follow them exactly like they're written or it doesn't work. Five steps, each one harder than the one before it, and in each life a million complications that put us off the path. But the biggest struggle isn't even staying on the path, it's getting on the path to begin with. That's Step 1. Rethink your Definition of Joy. Let others define it for you, if that's what it takes."

He releases my shoulders and steps back. "There. I've said it. It's a gift from me because I love you and I love Danny and there's so little time—"

"Stop it. Stop talking to me. Why is it so dark in this miserable place?"

I look around for other lamps, but there are just empty surfaces and hard edges and Evan's tortured face. I walk through the rest of the apartment and turn on whatever light switches I can find. The kitchen, the bathroom, the bedroom. I open the top drawer of his dresser and look inside. It's filled with mail, opened and unopened; bills and other things I don't want to see.

"You don't even know what you're looking for," says Evan.

"Those papers that you and Danny look at; whatever it is you're hiding from me."

"I always told him he should trust you but he said it wasn't about trust. It was about giving you the gift of ignorance."

"Fuck you." The place is so small; it can't take long to search it all. I head back into the kitchen and open drawers, cupboards, the pantry.

"And now the two of you, you're just…dissolving. Like pieces of rotted-out wood that have been soaking in water for years. I know how this goes. I could hand you the script."

I look inside pots, bowls, the Crockpot, the freezer. He has one cookbook, covered in a film of grease, which I hold upside-down by the spine and shake, watching two pieces of paper fall to the floor. Recipes, written out by hand.

"He knew Dora MacIntosh, didn't he? Those trips by himself to go fishing? He was going to see Dora."

Evan places his hands on his forehead. "No, he wasn't. These are questions you shouldn't be asking. You're winding yourself up into a mess that shouldn't include you." His body shakes as he resumes his sobbing.

I can feel a shift, a misaligned gear turning and clicking back into place.

"So was he up on the roof to protect her or to kill her?"

Evan grabs my shoulders again, roughly this time. His fingers press in, searching for bone. "How could you think that about Danny? Listen to yourself talking. Everything that comes out of your mouth is poison." He shakes me. It's the same way, I think, that you might shake someone just before pushing her off a roof. "You have to wait until Danny starts talking. Let *him* tell you what happened."

He shoves me and I stumble backwards, hitting the door frame of his bedroom. Where would you hide secrets? Where do other people hide them? All at once, the answer is obvious. I turn and run into the bedroom, locking the door behind me.

Of course they would each have one. They would have helped each other build them, using the same design. I start pulling on the shelves, knocking objects to the floor, looking for a plywood panel like the one in our closet at home. I knock all along the walls, listening for the sound of hollow space, hearing Evan's muffled voice from the living room. It takes a while before I notice the shoebox lying on its side with the lid open, photographs spilling out onto the floor.

I sift through the pictures, looking for… I don't know what. Why would Evan have a photograph that would explain Danny's lies? The pictures are all of his kids, him and Jill, Evan and Danny as teenagers, other people from his past. There's one of him and a woman I don't recognize, with black hair and deep, dark eyes and a look on her face like she knows everything in the world but isn't going to tell anyone. I don't know why this picture stops me, why I should care about this woman. It's not Dora; I know this, but there's still something about it. The brown couch they're sitting on, wood surrounding them. It's not a place I recognize. The woman has her hands out in front of her and her mouth is open slightly, like she's in the middle of telling a story. Evan has an arm around her waist and is leaning in closer for the picture. All I see is arms, legs; Evan's and hers and someone else's who is just out of the frame, sitting on the couch on the other side of the woman. Shoes that I don't necessarily recognize, but that are familiar anyway; the ankle that comes out of them, the leg, the knee. Danny. He is there too, with Evan and the woman, in whatever place this is that I've certainly never heard about before.

I carry the picture out to the living room, where Evan has settled himself onto the couch, his head resting backwards and his knees jutting up and out to the sides.

"Where was this picture taken? Who is this woman?"

He's staring up at the ceiling, all the fire drained from his face. "The past is a complication. We have to work through it. It takes... persistence. The places we were before have a bearing on the places we end up later. The roof. Being shot in the chest. These are the things that take people off the path."

He pulls his head forward. It seems to rest on his shoulders precariously, as if it's only a matter of time before it will roll backward, or off to one side. At last he acknowledges the photograph. He smiles at it, almost laughs. "She's just a person I knew once. Danny and I knew her. We don't anymore."

He closes his eyes and inhales deeply and I wait for the crying to resume. This time I understand it though. Something about the picture, Evan so young, the woman so beautiful, the way his face changes once he remembers her.

Gently, he removes the picture from my hand. "The thing about tragedy is this. It's only a nightmare until you work through it.

Then it's a great gift. You create your own truth, you come up with your own take on the rules. You're in the unique position to write your own book and stand up in front of packed rooms and tell your own secrets. I mean, Danny could, once he's talking again. The possibilities are tremendous."

"What do you mean *Danny* could? He's not...oh, shit. Is that what he's been doing at the computer every day? Working on some project for you? God, Evan, you're like an infection, you're just..."

Evan holds a finger up to his mouth. "Shhh. Listen. Do you know about potential? We all have it, but some of us more than others. Danny, for instance. The unrealized potential there is enormous."

"I don't want to hear this. Just tell me who Dora MacIntosh was. Why was she was up on that roof with Danny?"

"Your bartender, on the other hand. He's not even close. I told this to Danny, but he wasn't listening through all the noise."

I stop. Whatever it is I'm doing, I stop and listen to the low whine of the floor lamp, the sound of Evan's breathing. Why does it sound so loud?

"Evan."

"He seemed pleasant enough when I talked to him, all things considered, but it felt like a dimension was missing. By comparison, Danny is ancient. He comes straight out of eternity."

My stomach churns and rolls. I'm on a boat that's leaning, about to capsize. "You told me you wouldn't tell Danny about him."

"I never said that." Evan rubs his hands together, then smooths them across his head. "The thing is this. And please remember that I love you. Don't forget that as I'm telling you this."

I don't know the person in front of me. Whatever it is he's about to say, it already doesn't make sense.

"Danny went to confront that asshole bartender that night. That's as much as I know. I mean, you can put the pieces together in a pretty straight line between point A and point B and maybe the details stop mattering. I'm telling you this because I consider you family. This secret? What the book says? It's truth. One word of colossal importance to all of us. If we all search for truth, and we all speak truth, the human community elevates itself up. Keep this in mind when I tell you the next part."

He clasps his hands together and rests them in his lap, then looks at me as if he expects me to beg him for whatever is coming next.

"Did you care about him? I mean, really care what was going to happen to him once…once…well. You know."

"None of your fucking business."

"Danny is my best friend."

"Who is Dora MacIntosh?"

"She's the mystery, isn't she? Appearing like she did out of nowhere, somehow ending up on a roof. It's like, I don't know. Magic, I guess. Although I would hope for a better end for magic."

I close my eyes. The whine of the lamp settles between my eyes and turns to liquid noise while Evan continues talking.

"You understand that I had to tell the police what I knew about the bartender, about Danny going there and the line between A and B."

"When?"

"What?"

"When did you tell them this?"

"I can't be sure. A week ago maybe."

"And what about Dora MacIntosh?"

"What about her? I'm not convinced she went up on the roof with the two of them. Hey, it's okay to cry. I won't judge you."

"I'm not crying. It's that lamp. My God, what's wrong with that lamp?"

"I think she was just an innocent bystander. She went up there to try to prevent whatever she thought was about to happen, which makes this so much more of a tragedy, don't you think?"

"But Danny knew her. A long time ago."

Evan closes his eyes, as if what I have just said is so painful that he must retreat into darkness after hearing it spoken aloud. But even closed, his eyes are whining, the room is whining and churning and spinning and we've used up all the air. Why are we breathing so hard, so loudly? *You run out of oxygen, you run out of options.* Who said this? What would it have been about? I take five steps across the room to the lamp, lift it over my head, ready to plunge it through a window. Evan grabs it from behind, pulls it from my hands, sets it back on the floor.

"Cas," he says calmly. "Cassie. Stop." He encircles me with his substantial arms, presses my face into his chest. He smells like the clay my kids play with sometimes. Why would he smell like this?

"I promise you it will get better. You just have to read the book, let yourself be ready for it."

Now I am the one unable to stop sobbing.

# CHAPTER 14
## (DANNY)

By morning the rain had stopped. Outside, the trees were still dripping, but the gray clouds were rolling away and off in the west you could see blue and white, a soft summer sky approaching. There wasn't much conversation during breakfast; we drank our coffee and sat around, waiting for the sun to burn through.

Suzie Q passed around a photograph she'd brought with her, a picture of the six of us, from five years earlier.

"We look so young," said Katy.

"Look at how long Dora's hair was."

"I loved that blue bikini."

"The boys all look so neat and clean-shaven." Dora glanced from Evan to Taz to me with an expression that I couldn't read.

"I never would have thought Danny would be married by now," said Suzie. She gave me a long, slow stare that must have meant something but there's no way I was going to figure it out.

"All right." Evan stood up. "Enough. Where's the shovel?"

Without waiting for an answer, he walked out onto the porch, down the back stairs, off in the direction of the woods.

Dora stood up next. "I was hoping we could have like a...people could get up and talk or something."

"Let's just get it over with," said Taz.

"The shovel's out in the shed," Dora called out as Evan headed back from the woods. She hurried out with a key and a few seconds later the door to the shed swung open and Evan disappeared inside. We heard shuffling, objects dropping. Evan reappeared with a shovel slung over his shoulder and marched back toward the woods.

"We should wait for the others," said Katy.

"Then tell them to get moving."

Dora hesitated. I imagined her coming back inside and laying into us about how much this meant to her, tugging at our arms, pulling us out of our chairs. But instead, she ran off after Evan. I assumed the rest of us would stand up and follow her, but it was like we were stuck in our seats, sitting there dumbly, clutching empty coffee mugs.

"They're not going to find the tusk," Taz announced. "If that's what they're looking for."

If there had been any sounds in the room before he spoke, they were gone now.

Suzie Q frowned. "What?"

"It's not there. Someone dug it up already."

Suzie stood up and tottered slightly, as though she couldn't decide whether to run off into the woods or stick around and listen to the rest of whatever Taz had to say.

"How do you know this?"

"Don't be mad at us." Katy said. Her arms were wrapped across her chest. "It was ours, so we came back for it. Last fall, after we got engaged, right before the snow hit and they closed the road for the season."

Suzie stared, her expression hard and strangely pained. "*You* dug it up?"

"We talked about it a lot first, we did. We tried to consider all the options. And of course we thought of you guys, but in the end it was our responsibility."

Taz shifted slightly. "I never slept very well knowing it was buried up here."

"He used to have dreams," Katy explained. "Ghosts following him around, a baby elephant left to die up on a cliff somewhere. And we were trying to get pregnant, so we thought…"

Suzie reminded me of red-hot metal. Her lips were pressed together and her hands were on her hips. "What were you going to do with it? Sell it?"

Taz rubbed the scar on the back of his hand. Katy shook her head. "No, you don't understand. It's not about owning or selling or profiting. It's about…power. *Experience.* I can't really explain it. People *died* because of that tusk. You have to respect that and harness that. Follow it where it leads you."

"What in God's name are you even talking about?"

"Its value isn't monetary," said Taz. "That's what Katy means."

"We said we'd decide what to do *together*. The six of us."

"What does it matter anyway? Someone dug it up before we even got there. Be mad at them."

Suzie's eyes were like a laser, the way they drilled through me. "Was it you?"

"No."

"Come on," said Taz. "Danny cared the least about it. I don't even think he got within three feet of it that day."

"Well maybe that's why he came back for it. To get rid of it."

"I didn't."

"You guys are all pathetic." Suzie nearly spit the words at us. I didn't understand how an object could do this to people, could fill them with so much anger. We watched her stomp away, out the door and off toward the woods.

"You didn't, did you?" Katy asked me. Her voice was low and kind. She always had that quality about her, which I probably never appreciated enough back then.

I shook my head. "I swear on...whatever you want me to swear on."

"The thing is—it wouldn't be *right* to sell it." Katy was addressing me like I was the one who had demanded an explanation. "If we profit from it, then we're contributors. You wouldn't want to put more product into the market. What we were thinking was that it was our responsibility to keep the ivory safe; to pretend that it didn't exist. To *protect* it."

Just the way that she said it—*our responsibility to keep the ivory safe*—it felt like she had prepared the statement ahead of time. The whole speech, maybe, was rehearsed.

"We wanted to celebrate the animal that died," said Taz. "That was our thinking." His voice was quiet. Dead, almost. He didn't seem like a person who wanted to celebrate anything. He seemed like a person who was closing up shop, picking out his own gravestone.

"And what about those bodies you guys found? Did you celebrate *them*?"

Taz stared down at his lap, still rubbing at his scar. Katy looked away, across the room, at something that didn't exist. Their shoulders and hips and thighs were pressed together like they were…I don't know. Like they wanted to be the same person.

"We didn't take anything lightly. We really thought it over. It was agonizing."

"So you didn't report them to anyone?"

Neither one of them would look at me. The air was thick with their silence. Five years wasn't long enough, I realized. We sat there for an eternity, until finally Taz stood up and somehow managed to push himself forward, out the front door of the cabin, and off to God-knows-where.

"You know, any of us could have reported them," Katy said quietly. "*You* could have."

I was strategizing my own exit when Suzie Q came barreling out of the woods and back into the cabin. "Why are you guys just sitting here?" She plopped down in the chair next to me and crossed her arms in a huff. "I can't deal with this by myself."

"What? Didn't they find the time capsule?" asked Katy. "Because it was there when we—"

"Nobody's fessing up about the tusk. Dora won't admit to digging it up."

"It had to be her. Who else could it have been?"

"She seemed pretty shocked about the whole thing. So either she's a great actress or…" Suzie shrugged. "I don't even care about her ridiculous time capsule, her *emotions*. And what's going on with her and Stitch?"

"Why? What are they doing?"

"Just the way he's looking at her, holding her hand, acting like every dumb thing she says is so *profound*. Then the next thing you know they're heading off together, up to the ridge where we saw the…you know. I suggested maybe all of us should go, but Dora got on that fucking high horse of hers and said she wouldn't be able to *reflect* if too many people were with her. How much do you want to bet she's confessing everything to Stitch?"

"It doesn't matter," said Katy. "I'm tired of caring so much about it."

I guess we all thought it would only be a few minutes before they came back. And then a few more after that, and a few more, until an hour had passed and it was almost noon and we decided it was time to find them. Somehow, we assumed they'd still be up on that ridge, but when we finally made to the top, it was empty.

As we looked out over the valley, I half expected to see the two of them falling from the sky. Evan and Dora this time. In fact, I could imagine it, the way it would look, almost like a hallucination. For a little while there I really had myself convinced we'd never see them again.

We looked for a long time. A couple hours, maybe? It's hard to say. Taz had a compass and a whistle he kept blowing, and afterward he'd call their names and then wait, listening for an answer.

I think we were all wondering the same thing: did they go looking for the bodies?

Suzie was swatting at mosquitoes and her arms and legs were covered in bites and scratches. At some point Taz stopped and asked me to head back to the cabin with her; there was no point in dragging all of us any further. "Dora is such an idiot sometimes," Suzie muttered, but she turned around without complaining,

By the time we got back, it was mid-afternoon. Suzie went to rinse off in the outdoor shower, and I sat on the couch by myself and wondered what would happen if Taz and Katy found the bodies a second time. Would we call the police, finally, and pretend it was the first time we'd ever seen them? Would there even be anything left to find, after five years out in the woods? I was working through all of this in my head when Suzie appeared in front of me, wearing a towel and the sweetest, most devious little smile you've ever seen. Her hair was wet and wavy. I could see drops of water on the wooden floor, a trail of partial footprints heading across the room.

"Danny," she said. "What do you say to a woman dressed only in a towel?"

"This is a riddle?"

She scrunched her hair in her hands, squeezing water out onto the floor. "Come on. What do you say?"

I stared at her for a while before answering, looked her up and down. There's something about bare feet. I don't know what it is.

Wet legs. A washed face.

"I think I stand up and leave the room to give her some privacy."

"But do you say anything before you leave?"

"I say 'you have the smoothest skin I've ever seen.' Even with all the scratches."

She smiled. "What else?"

"You look even better with no makeup on."

"And what else?"

"Whoever gets to see what's under that towel is a lucky man."

She pulled the towel open and bent forward, wrapping it around her hair and then piling it up on her head. And I guess I could have looked away but I didn't.

Suzie put her hands on her hips. "Thank you. Finally. A gentleman." Which wasn't what I felt like, but I wasn't going to argue. For a couple more seconds, we stayed like this: me looking, her letting me. It was the kind of weekend you couldn't explain, even if you tried. And when she turned and walked away, I didn't know which end was up anymore. I pictured her up there waiting for me. I pictured myself going up there and—

Well, you get the idea. The point was that I didn't. The point was that after a few minutes she came back down, dressed in clean clothes and with her hair combed and her makeup reapplied, pretending that nothing had happened.

"Is it too early to start drinking?" she asked.

⸺

At around dusk, Taz and Katy returned with no sign of Dora or Evan.

Katy was apologetic. "I'm sorry, but I couldn't spend another night out there. Not after last time."

Taz nodded. "I'm sure they..." He turned away without finishing the sentence.

Suzie Q threw her arms around Katy and kissed her cheek. "I've decided to forgive you guys. I don't know what was wrong with me. I'm still mad at Dora, though."

"It *is* her cabin," said Katy.

"Yeah, but this was different. This was *ours*. If she dug it up, then…why would she do that?"

"Maybe it wasn't her. Maybe it was someone else?"

"But…I don't even get who that would be."

They kept this up for hours. A hundred meaningless conversations that never went anywhere. And just when you sensed one coming to a close and were hoping for some quiet to balance out the intolerable chatter, they'd bring up that fucking tusk, wondering all over again who dug it up, why anyone would do it, where it was. It seemed so crucial to them, like this was the key to all of our futures: figuring out what happened to that tusk.

Eventually, I got sick of hearing it. Physically sick. I felt my stomach lurch, and all the beer I'd drunk that afternoon just kind of rose up and clung to the base of my throat, so I headed outside for some fresh air, stood on the porch looking out at the darkness. I caught myself wishing for a cyclone to come along and pick up the cabin and everyone in it and send us all miles away. More people falling from the sky, landing in the middle of a different nowhere.

I grabbed a flashlight off the porch and stumbled toward the woods. The shovel was still there, leaning against a tree. A hole in the ground. The little box filled with our junk.

The nausea passed and I sat on the ground next to the box. There was the Ziploc bag with the scraps of paper inside. Was this what we came all this way to read? Was there a point to any of it?

---

Dear Danny,

Thank you for sharing a very special Summer with me.

I will never forget you.

♡ Dara

I read the thing more than once; I don't know why, what I wanted out of it. Whatever it was, I wasn't going to find it.

"Fuck you, Dora," I said, into the trees.

Dora,

Close your eyes and listen
to the sounds of life. When
you open them again. I'll
be gone
          — DFI

I didn't remember writing it or even thinking it, who I must have
been to come up with those words.

The ground was damp, but I stretched out on my back anyway.
Above me, leaves spread out in a pattern that wasn't really a pattern at all but just happenstance. Somehow this got to me: the way
they looked, hanging there, against the blue-black sky. It seemed
okay to fall asleep, pull a Rip Van Winkle and wake up again years
later with the world changed and spend the rest of my life trying
to fit in. But I wasn't sleepy. Everything was disjointed and turned
on its side and there was no way to fix any of it. I thought of my
brother again, the way his eyes glassed over sometimes and it was
like talking to a robot. How I never wanted to be that robot but I
became it anyway. How I couldn't explain this to anyone, not even
Cassie, although with her it seemed like maybe I didn't have to. She
could fill in the sentences on her own and she'd always understand
me.

At some point I went back to the cabin. By this time, Dora and
Evan had returned. Evan told me some story, but I knew him well

enough that I could tell when he was lying. *We got lost. It started getting dark. Dora got so scared. I don't even know how we found our way back. It was kind of like some hand of God shit.* It was all over his face—what had really happened. They were near the cabin when we set off looking for them. They'd kept themselves hidden, listened to us talking, let us leave.

Eventually, we stopped talking about the tusk, but the trip had already ruined me. I started up thinking about it again, this time more than I ever had before. I remembered watching them all that day, the way they held that piece of ivory, passing it around, stroking it like they wanted to make love to it. I closed my eyes and wondered how I would explain it to Cassie if I ever tried. How when I looked at the tusk it felt like an explosion, a battlefield, the outcome of too much of everything. Maybe it felt smooth but when you looked at it for long enough you could tell that it shouldn't be. Nothing was that smooth, that simple. The place it had come from was devastated, gone, ripped apart.

# CHAPTER 15
## (CASSIE)

Our beach is different this time. The ocean, the sand, the palm trees—they're worn out, somehow. I can sense the inevitability of decay around us. Being in paradise is just as futile as being anywhere. Why would we think otherwise? Danny continues to beam at me. All of this futility and he acts as though nothing has changed.

"Do you just stand here? The whole time I'm away, is this where you are?"

"Mostly."

"Doesn't it ever get to be too much?"

"Here? Look around you. I don't think I even understand the question."

"But..."

"Don't be one of those too much of a good thing people, Cas. God, I hate people like that. The malaise. The jadedness. That's not us. We stick with it. We make it work."

I exhale slowly and start counting, from the beginning, whatever that means. One...two...three...four. Above me, the sky feels like a tightly stretched sheet. It has an end somewhere. It must. The ocean too. The sand. A finite number of grains. Of course. They are here to count. Danny and me until the end of time, just counting each day until the sun sets.

"You don't believe me, do you?" asks Danny.

"I'm just tired."

"You don't sleep enough. You stay up too late, or you lie in bed with your eyes open waiting for...I wish I knew what."

"But we used to do that sometimes, at night. Don't you remember? I would ask you questions."

"I always tried to answer in five words or less."

"You'd hold up my hand and count them off on my fingers as

you talked."

"Of course I remember that."

"We don't do that anymore."

"After you asked all your questions and had all your answers I wasn't interesting anymore."

Where is his face? In the place where Danny is supposed to be I see the shape of a man, a suggestion of the features I remember, granular as the sand.

"I don't think it happened that way."

"Why would you? You have your reasons to justify what you do. You rely on them. Otherwise, well... how could you live with yourself?"

"You were in love with Dora MacIntosh."

"A hypothesis. That's all it is."

"But what if all those reasons you were just talking about—if you take them all out and stack them on top of each other—what if they add up to Dora MacIntosh?"

Danny shakes his head. "It's too late now. She's dead."

"Too late for what? That's not even what I'm saying."

"I know exactly what you're saying. You're saying that you're better than me, that Dora deserved to die, and that it's not your fault she did."

"No. Danny..."

"Why do you keep bringing this up? We have this beach now. We have everything we need."

"But...what do you eat? Where do you go to the bathroom?"

"There's no need. My pores absorb salt from the air and that takes care of it. It's a different way of being human. Come find out with me."

"I don't want to keep counting. It's already making me tired."

"Suit yourself."

It seems like I'm supposed to go, but I don't know how. Each time, it's a mystery how I get here, how I leave.

"What are you working on all day, Danny? When you sit at the computer?"

He turns away from me and rubs his face, looks out across the water.

"I guess we find out once it's finished, don't we?"

Did Lee shoot Danny? Is it possible?

That scar on his chest, almost a perfect X, like someone had drawn it there. I can't imagine the situation, the rationale, the explanation.

*It was an accident. It happened a long time ago.* How do you have an accident in the shape of a nearly perfect X?

I try to imagine a conversation he and Danny might have had, the circumstances under which they would have made the slow hike up to the roof together, but I can't place them in the same universe, speaking words to one another. I can't picture either one of them upset enough to shoot, upsetting enough to be shot at. All morning at the bakery I work out this impossible scene in my head, letting it rise, punching it down, starting it over.

When my shift ends, I call the Silver Whistle.

"Is Lee there? I mean, I know he's not usually scheduled until later, but I wanted to—"

"He doesn't work here anymore."

"Oh. Was he...?" The word 'arrested' sticks in my throat. "Did he go somewhere?"

"How am I supposed to know where he is? He quit, okay?" The woman I'm talking to can't give me his phone number or any other personal information.

I wonder what's next, what I'm supposed to want now. *Did you shoot Danny? And then afterward did you pretend like nothing had happened?*

Any minute, he'll call me to explain. He'll track down my number because you can—it's not that hard—and tell me he's in the van, he's driving down a road he's never been on before and the scenery is beautiful, the sky feels like freedom, his eyes are open, his soul is shining. It was time to go and I was the one who made him realize. *Thank you*, he'll say.

*Do you think I'd be good at raising chickens? Or goats?*

*I don't know. What do they eat?*

*We could try different things, trial and error, figure it out.*

*Trial and error. Now you're talking.*

4267 S. Jefferson isn't far by car. Ten minutes at the most. I follow the same route Gerry MacIntosh and I walked together on that strange, cold evening: the few twists at the beginning, the long trek east to the building.

The front door pushes back like it doesn't want me there, then slowly gives way and peels open. I consider the row of doorbells, the list of names that belong to strangers. D'Agostino/Song, Mc-Clean, Rashid/Lewis. There is no Holdorf, a name that still doesn't seem possible. If I think hard enough, certainly my brain will sort through the fuzz of memory and tell me which button to push. Cutler, Pavaleski/Brown. It was on the first floor, wasn't it? 1A? 1B? As I wait and stare, a woman pushes open the inside door. I move aside to let her pass.

"I'm visiting a friend and I can't..."

But in three steps she's gone, uninterested in my reasons for catching the door before it closes behind her.

I walk down the short hallway, reading the number on the first door. 1A. We came in together that night. Lee held me upright, then let me drop to the floor while he reached for his keys and unlocked the door. His keys. He had keys.

How many steps did we take? It could have been two or it could have been a hundred. I remember my right shoulder hitting the doorknob, a strange sunburst of a stain on the wall close to the floor. Right here. This one. 1B.

Is this the way it happened? Danny knocked on the door and then waited for an answer, not even practicing what he was going to say first, because he didn't want to overthink it. Probably he didn't know why he was here but because there were no other options this was where he ended up. He would have knocked louder than this, though. He wouldn't have had to do it a second time, like me.

I don't know the man who answers. He's wearing a gray sweatshirt and a pair of jeans, and his hair is wet and tousled, like he just stepped out of the shower. His eyes are light brown, rimmed in red, and possess a quality that strikes me as familiar. Then I notice the tattoos that encircle his wrists like macramé bracelets.

"What the fuck do you want?" When he talks I see the chipped front tooth, the blackness of his wet hair. He has an unfriendly face. He's always had an unfriendly face.

"You're the roommate. I remember you."

"Not anymore. Nobody's roommate now. The other one moved out. I assume that's who you're looking for."

"But where—"

"Gone."

He moves his head quickly from side to side. I don't understand his face, the haircut. What did they look like before?

"Can I come in?"

"Is that what you want?"

"I guess."

The last time I was here, he threatened me with a gun, but it's different now; I'm sober, it's daytime. He steps aside and gives the door a push. I'm expecting to see the couch, the coffee table. The recliner, the end table with the gun on it, but the furniture has been rearranged. Pieces of it are missing. The carpet remnants are gone and the hardwood glistens. The place smells like a sick mix of chemicals.

"What'd you do with everything?"

"Just fixed the place up a little. On account of my slob of a room-mate moving out."

He sits on the couch and leans forward, his elbows on his knees. It's impossible to imagine what he was doing before I showed up, what he does every day, what he and Lee talked about as they sat around the living room with the TV on, if this was even something they did. I want to ask him to show me Lee's empty room, to check if he left anything behind. Why would I want this?

"Here's what I don't get," he says, waving a finger in the general direction of nothing. "Why let the husband find out? I never understand that."

"I don't think…"

"I've seen this before. You women, you're like this. You can't keep secrets. You go home with that smile, that smug, pleased little look that you all perfect so well. Your hair's all messy, your clothes don't fit right anymore, and you smell like you just crawled out of an armpit. Then later you say *I didn't think he would notice anything*, when we all know that what you wanted all along was for him to notice."

I shake my head. "It's not like that."

"The way I see it is like one of those diagrams. The circle with all the dots? You know what I'm talking about?"

"No."

"The circle. The dots. Come on, baby, don't make me get out a pen and draw it for you. I'm talking about people. The way we cluster together on the line or off the line, where we are in the circle. Most of us want to be off all the way over here." He extends his arm out to the side and wiggles his fingertips. "But there's these fucking annoying dots bouncing around into us and pulling us toward the center. We don't want to be there but you never get it. You keep pulling and pulling. It's like, life would be so much easier without all of you bouncers around. But then again, it wouldn't be anywhere near as fun either, and that's, like, the vice versa of the whole situation, I guess. That's what brings us all the pain."

He smacks his hand on the coffee table, which seems to jump an inch off the floor. I know this can't be possible, but still.

"Sit down." He points to a rickety looking wooden chair a few feet away from me. "It makes me nervous when people stand."

I walk past him, to the recliner, and sit there instead. The chair seems to swallow me up and point me toward the ceiling. The table next to it is empty and smells of lemon wax.

"What happened to your gun?"

He smiles and rubs his hands together. They sound warm and dry, in need of moisturizer.

"That's a good question. What happened to the gun? To which I shrug and say 'what gun?'"

"I saw it on this table. You pointed it at me."

"But I've never seen you before. You see, you have to practice these answers when the cops come around two and three times. *No, sir, I don't know that woman. No, sir, he never mentioned a married woman. We don't talk about things like that, me and Lee. We keep it loose. Nobody gets nosy. No sir, I don't own a gun, but Lee does.*"

The room begins to shift, its square edges dissolving into dangerous shapes. I try to imagine Lee pointing a gun at Danny but find that I don't have the imagination for this, to create pictures of people and weapons, shadows on a rooftop at night.

"I'm not a bouncer, by the way. A bouncing dot. Whatever you called it. I'm way off the line, nowhere near the center."

"You're that little innocent-looking button on the wall that someone presses just to see what'll happen and it turns out it makes the whole place turn to shit. That's what I see when I look at you. So fuck you, Dora."

It's not unlike getting punched in the stomach, hearing her name. *Dora.* So intimate. So light that it could be the sound of raindrops on a leaf. *Dora.*

"Don't call me that. How could you call me that?"

"What, don't you—"

"If anyone is a button on the wall, it's her."

He pauses and looks at me, confused. Then his eyes lift and his mouth stretches out into a smile, if you can call it that. I stare at his chipped front tooth, the way it destroys his whole face.

"Oh, oh, wait. That was *her* name, wasn't it? The one who died. With the wig."

"Wig? What…? You mean you saw Dora that night? With Danny?"

He taps his finger on the arm of his chair and considers me, for far too long. He's a man that once asked me to lick another woman's feet at gunpoint. Why would I come back here?

"One thing I've learned in my life is how to tell when a girl wants something from you. You all have the same look. You think we don't know the difference, but we do. So here's the deal. I'm going to tell you exactly what I told the police a few days ago when they came around looking for Lee. Then you're going to leave and never come back."

A terrible, breathless moment passes before I remember how to speak.

"Fine. Just tell me what you know."

"I'd never seen either of them before. Your husband shows up at the door in the middle of the night. I'm guessing it was about three in the morning, but I'm generally bad with time, so let's say give or take. This man—your husband—had a face that looked like it was made out of rock, his jaw clenched so hard it was like someone had sewed the thing shut. I take it he's mad, but I don't know why or at who. He asks me, 'are you the bartender?'

"Now normally, Lee and I don't mess around in each other's affairs, and I guess I could have sent old Rockface home, but that night I didn't feel like it. Who knows? Maybe I was just curious about the whole thing. So I went and banged on Lee's bedroom door, told him some jerk was looking for him.

"A few minutes later, out stumbles Lee with his hair sticking up in about ten different directions, wearing only a pair of jeans. And about a minute after that, out comes this woman with white-blonde hair, streaked black underneath, that didn't match the rest of her. It was either a botched dye job or one of those wigs girls wear when they want to make themselves look ugly, like that's some kind of power trip for them. She comes along and stands next to Lee and the two of them stare at Rockface, who proceeds to ask Lee the same question he asked me. 'Are you the bartender?' Lee has this look on his face like he's not in the mood to deal with any of it."

"Wait a minute. Dora came out of the bedroom with Lee? But—"

"Do not interrupt me. You want to hear the story, shut up and listen. If not, you can leave right now." His face is hard. I remember this. Him, from that night; despising him.

"Fine. Talk."

"So as I was saying, Rockface asks Lee if he's the bartender, and already you can see Lee's hackles going up, the change in his posture, getting himself set to do whatever the situation requires.

"'What do you want?' Lee says, and the woman does this thing where she puts her hand on his arm like he's some attack dog she's trying to keep calm."

I shake my head, as if this will erase what I've just heard. *No. Not like that.*

"After that the conversation stops. I'm still trying to figure out what's going on, who's mad at who and why this woman's hair is so messed up. They're all in the doorway. Lee and the dude with the locked up jaw are staring at each other and nobody's saying anything and I know what it is—it's the quiet right before the bomb lands and destroys the city. And I'm not saying Lee isn't a halfway decent guy, but his shit is his shit and mine is mine, so I tell him to take it outside. I'm not interested in a nuclear war in my apartment. So they leave. They close the door and walk away. All three of them.

"I had no idea they were going up on the roof. I had no idea Lee had his gun with him. Like I said, it wasn't my shit to care about.

"I didn't hear the gunshots, but then again the TV was on. And then again also, this isn't the quietest neighborhood, not even at

four in the morning or whatever time it was. And on top of that it's
a neighborhood where we all mind our own business.

"I'm not sure how much time passed before Lee came back.
Long enough for me to fall asleep in that chair you're sitting in,
though, because when I woke up Lee was standing in the middle of
the room, staring at me, holding what I can only guess was a warm
firearm in his hand. The man was gone, the woman was gone, and I
seriously thought it might be me next. He just looked a little crazy.
Not crazy crazy, but calm crazy. Which is like always worse, right?

"He told me 'I think I just killed two people.' The way he said
it, it was like the voice you'd use when you're talking to a baby. Not
baby talk, but new-parent soft and soothing, like he could have
been on the radio reading dedications with it or something. That
creepy psychotic voice, and I've got him in my living room standing
in front of me with these dead eyes, holding that fucking gun.

"He points the thing at me and says 'if you say anything about
this you're dead.' Then he leaves and when he comes back later
that day, we don't talk about anything, we don't acknowledge it.
But I know he would do it; kill me while I'm sleeping. I've always
thought this about him.

"Not long after that, he loaded all his stuff in the van and
stopped coming back to the apartment. And no, I'm not upset that
he's gone."

He sits back in his seat and waits for me to…I don't know—
leave? Cry? Beg him for more details? None of it seems right or
real. I must be in one of those places where the truth doesn't exist.
It's a side effect of Evan's mysterious pills. Waking nightmares.
Men with chipped teeth. An apartment washed clean. Dora in a
wig, coming out of Lee's bedroom.

"How did I do?" he asks. "Pretty good right?"

I try to stand, but my body is stuck. The muscles and bones are
gone, leaving only skin and sweat behind.

"No, seriously. How did I do?"

"You said…the part about…I mean, you told the police anyway?
That Lee…"

"Only later, of course. Keep your mouth shut until it makes sense
to talk. After the negotiating's all done."

And then I see it. Danny's flash. The world goes white, erased inward from the edges and then replaced by the dark tunnel of mis-understanding, of picking the wrong card from the deck, the wrong entrée from the menu, the wrong pair of shoes to wear. I see a globe cracked in half, colors spilling out and dissolving into the air, carried away in the clouds like condensation. I see an old wooden table inside a small dining room, my father sitting at one end of it telling me a story I can't understand about people he used to know, friends of his, about diving off bridges and racing go-carts down the steepest street in town and standing in the middle of train tracks, flipping off the conductor before jumping to the side at the last minute. He's showing me a magic trick, one of what seems like hundreds that he knows, and telling me that danger makes you better, it burns out all the fear and replaces it with scar tissue and the best thing in life is to be fearless. He's telling me that the eas-iest way to lose out on life is to have something to lose, something for other people to take. Then I see the broken globe again, empty of colors. My father is hitting my mother in the side of the head with a dictionary, swinging it like a bat that strikes her without a sound, and she falls without a sound, her startled body landing on the dining room rug, braided in muffled brown and white and gray.

There's a newspaper on the table. An empty glass.

I do stand up. Somehow, I manage this. "He didn't tell me. Nei-ther of them told me."

"It all comes around, eventually."

Lee's roommate turns his head slowly as I walk across the room to the door.

"I'm sorry your boyfriend's gone."

"Fuck you."

"No really. He owes me money, that disgusting little prick."

As I step out into the hallway, he calls after me. "Happily ever after, right Dora?"

My knees wobble, but somehow they manage to turn me toward the exit.

"Tell your husband we're good. I got everything. Tell him not to come back."

What does he mean? I hold my breath as I walk through the foyer, past the mailboxes, pulling on the heavy door that sticks and pushes back before releasing me into the cold afternoon. I can't remember what time it is, where I was before coming here. My car is somewhere, isn't it? I drove here, didn't I?

*Tell your husband we're good.*

For a few seconds, I stand on the sidewalk, unsure where to go. It feels like I haven't finished, like I was supposed to go up on the roof and look for clues, to stand where they were and imagine them there together: Danny and Lee and Dora with her soft hand on Lee's arm. Four in the morning on a warm fall night. It's too hazy to see stars, but nobody notices. Nobody is looking up. They have a conversation I can't imagine. They start fighting. Dora steps between them with words I don't want to imagine. Someone pushes her out of the way and she stumbles backward and falls. Lee pushes her and Danny runs after him so he shoots.

Or Danny is the one who pushes her. He pushes her because...? Because...?

Or she falls without anybody noticing. It's dark and hard to see, and after Lee shoots Danny he searches for the blonde woman, calling her name, before thinking to look over the edge, at the sidewalk below.

Or she watches a scene play out that she doesn't want to see and, not really understanding what she's doing, she jumps.

Who is Dora MacIntosh?

*Tell your husband we're good. I got everything.*

If only I'd known what to pay attention to in the days following the accident. Danny was unconscious and Lee was still working at the Silver Whistle. I went there on Wednesday and we had a conversation. After putting my husband in the hospital, he talked to me, acted like nothing was different.

*Did* he act like nothing was different?

There were no cuts or bruises, because I would have noticed. No evidence of a fight. Nothing at all amiss or unusual. Just the same old sweet Lee. Right?

If the roommate's story is true, why wouldn't he have left town sooner? Why would he bother sticking around?

At home, the kids are fighting. When I walk in the door, Nel comes running toward me with a tear-streaked face, telling me that E is breaking all her toys. After a few minutes of trying to make sense out of the commotion, I piece together that E has pulled the head off one of her dolls and cracked a plastic dish from her kitchen set.

"I thought it would be funny," says E. "A headless tea party."

"It's not funny!" Nel breathes through her nose, hard and fast like she's hyperventilating.

"I didn't even break it. All you have to do is stick the head back on."

"You stepped on a teacup. I hate you."

"It was in the middle of the floor. Don't put your toys in such a stupid place."

"Don't call me stupid. Mommy, tell him to stop."

Danny is standing in the corner with a whiteboard hanging on a cord around his neck, a dry erase marker in his hand. The board is blank. One foot is slightly in front of the other, as though his body froze while he was in the act of walking. I look at his face, see him watching us with dead-eyed curiosity, in the same way a person might watch a TV. For now, he's interested, but at any moment he might decide to change the channel.

Nel is crying. E is glaring. Danny is watching, doing nothing.

"I'm sure your brother didn't mean to break the teacup. I'm sure it was an accident." I turn toward the closet to hang up my coat. From behind me comes a soul-piercing shriek. Nel comes running toward me.

"He kicked me!"

"You hit me first."

I wait for Danny to step in and fix our afternoon, but he's motionless in the corner, this mute husband of mine who can only speak with his eyes. They stare, now, not at the children but at me.

Nel runs at E and he pushes her away, a little too hard. She smacks her head on an end table and screams. E's eyes grow wide and I can see the regret, the worry. He runs away, past Danny, who's still in the corner, watching me.

I close my eyes and shake my head. This afternoon can't possibly be real.

"Why are you just standing there?" I yell.

Danny blinks but doesn't move.

*Tell your husband we're good. I got everything.*

I stare at Danny and scream, as loud as I can, as loud as I would if I was jumping off a cliff.

Afterward, everything is quiet.

After the kids go to bed, I tidy up the bathroom. There are puddles of water and dirty clothes on the floor. The toilet hasn't been cleaned. There are hairs in the sink. Danny hasn't done anything all day except sit at the computer and write his silly life-after-tragedy book or whatever it is he's doing. I lie down on the floor and rest my head on a pile of clothes. The tiles are warm beneath me and the fan emits a comforting hum.

*It's going to get worse before it gets better.* Evan was right. *Let everything go dark and empty and open yourself up to future possibilities.* It doesn't mean anything, but sometimes it's not the words themselves that matter but how you say them; what the other person wants to hear.

The bathroom smells like soap and toothpaste and recently drained bathwater. It's not the worst place to be, considering where I've been in the last eight hours. This is the way you reset. You rest, you drift, you let go and wake up somewhere else.

There's a knocking I haven't been expecting. Knock knock knock. Knock knock knock. In threes. Knock knock knock. I raise my head slowly, pull myself up into a sitting position, and open the door. Danny looks down at me: a pair of eyes, a still mouth, an unkempt beard. What happened to the rest of him?

He hands me the whiteboard.

I THINK YOU NEED HELP

I throw the whiteboard in the tub, then shove a wet towel into my face and scream again.

Danny sits on the toilet seat. His left hand opens with a flash of green. There's Evan's pill bottle, resting in his palm, offered up as evidence. His eyes never let up. They stare and stare and stare.

"Open it. Smell them. All natural. From plants."

Danny narrows his eyes, shakes his head, lets me really feel his disappointment.

It used to be his fault, but now, somehow, it's all mine.

# CHAPTER 16
## (DANNY)

The story doesn't get any better from here.

It must have been a couple years before we heard the news that Katy was dead. A car accident. The other driver drunk and reckless. I remember standing in Evan's bedroom when he told me, the careful way he spoke the words and showed me the obituary, then waited for my reaction, as though I might somehow be able to discount the evidence and twist a different conclusion out of it.

*This can't be happening. How is this real?*

*Dora says Taz can't even get out of bed.*

Dora again. I didn't even know she had Evan's phone number, that they'd been in communication since the last trip to the cabin.

By this time, Evan was on workman's comp after an accident left him with two mutilated toes. He joked that his future as a ballerina was over, that he'd have to get rid of his tights. He and Jill were already fighting. I mean not just a good one here and there but picking at each other over every little thing. Evan called it passion, but to me they acted like siblings who had spent too much time under the same roof. So I guess I could see why he would be talking to Dora. I mean she was the kind. She would turn up when you didn't need her to, but for some reason it always felt like you did.

I could imagine Dora kneeling on the floor as she held the phone up to her ear, the way her face would have looked, the way her voice would have sounded. *Katy's gone and I don't know what to do. Please tell me what I should do.*

Evan went to the funeral. He explained to Jill that a childhood friend had died and it felt like one of his hands had been cut off, that the only way to tie off the wound was to make the three-hour drive and send her off properly. Jill said that if he was going to be tying off a wound she'd rather not be part of it, if it was all the same. Which it was. Of course. It was what he was hoping for. Three hours in the car to think and cry and reopen the time capsule in his brain, and head back down that road to be there for Dora. I mean, that's really why he went. For her.

When Evan came back, he was different. It was like his motor had slowed down and he couldn't execute a task without thinking about it for ten or fifteen minutes first. He'd close his eyes sometimes, block all of us out while he tried to catch up.

"It happens so fast," he told me.

"What does?"

He shrugged. "We don't even know. That's how bad it is. *Everything* moves, and we have to train our brains to stay still once in a while."

"I don't know what that means."

"Do you know that Dora doesn't even want to be a doctor?"

"She just likes to talk. Don't let her get inside your head."

"But I think...I think she's the only one who makes sense. I could listen to her all day. Life could have meaning."

He was looking at me like a kid would. Dazzled and confused. Hope and hopelessness all mixed up together. It made me feel bad for him, that he would get pulled this hard into some fantasy.

"I think you need to start working again, get a routine going."

He started crying, put his hands on his head like it had cracked open and he was trying to keep what was inside from spilling out. "Jill's pregnant. I mean, I have...this is...there's no way out now."

"Why would you want out? What would that do for you?"

He closed his eyes and wiped his nose with his hand. "It's just too fast. If I can get a handle on that I think I'll be okay."

We weren't talking about a curse back then. I don't remember the first time one of us used the word, when it finally occurred to us that maybe there was a reason Katy had died so young.

# CHAPTER 17
## (CASSIE)

Sometimes when I'm in the kitchen washing dishes, Danny comes up behind me, turns off the water, and leads me to the bedroom, where we have sex quietly and efficiently. In the silence I'm aware of his concentration, the precision of his movements, the focus of his eyes on a spot somewhere on my forehead, near my hairline. Afterward, as we lie next to each other, I watch him tap his hands on his stomach, thinking about God only knows what.

"You need to get a job," I say.

No answer.

"There are jobs you can do where you don't have to talk. They might even like it better if you're a mute."

No answer.

"How long does this go on?" I listen for sounds. A clock ticking, maybe, except when was the last time anyone had a clock like that? Danny's breathing is all I hear.

## I DON'T UNDERSTAND WHY YOU CHEATED ON ME

he writes on his whiteboard. Frowny face. God, I can't take the frowny faces, the smiling faces, the thumbs up and thumbs down.

"I was lonely." Is this even true? Or was it the money in the closet that kept disappearing, the way the hope would appear but then always vanish again? Was it that I was tired? Did I even have a reason?

Frowny face.

I grab the whiteboard and launch it across the room.

On Danny's beach, things have changed. There's a wooden hut with a palm-leaf roof. Danny's sitting in a chair in front of the hut, leaning back with his legs crossed. He smiles when he sees me, gestures at the empty chair next to him, motions for me to sit.

"Welcome back. It's good to see you."

"You have a…where did that hut come from?"

"I built it. It started raining and I didn't know what to do, so I went into the forest and cut down some trees and built this."

"It started raining?"

"Surprise, right?"

"You cut down trees?"

"I know what you're thinking, but it's okay. New ones grow back just as soon as the old ones fall down. It's really an amazing place here. I'm settling in. It's nice to have a bed now, and a table. I don't really use them, but I like having them anyway. I put a coconut on the table because I didn't know what else to do. You could go inside and look at it if you want."

He looks so young, so unconcerned. Maybe the way he did a long time ago, only back then I wasn't paying attention.

"I worry about us, Danny."

"Are you thinking of leaving again?"

"I don't know where I would go."

"You could have this place. I could leave and you could stay here. Take the bed and the table and the coconut. Let the waves come in at night and wash your feet. I did buy it for you, after all."

"It seems lonely."

"It's not. I can't explain it."

"Can you tell me about Dora?"

"You wouldn't like that story. It's sad. It ends with her falling off a roof."

"Falling or jumping? Or being pushed?"

"Any of those. They're all sad."

"Is it true that she was with Lee that night? That you didn't know her?"

He doesn't speak, just looks out at the ocean, as if the answer to my questions was the rock he threw back into the water, and the only way I'll ever find it is to dive in and swim along the ocean floor, holding my breath, for another million years.

"There's something I'm not getting, isn't there?"

He blinks at me like he doesn't understand the question. "I always thought you were smart. The kids take after you. Those pictures they tape up to the walls, it's nothing I would ever do."

"Do they really want to go all those places, or is it just an exercise in dreaming? I don't know."

"I don't know either."

"I should be keeping better track."

"Don't be hard on yourself."

"I thought there would be another…something else. But it never came. Somehow we ended up here instead."

"Paradise."

"Why is it so depressing here?"

"You're not looking at it the right way. You keep expecting this place to give you something that doesn't exist on its own. You have to approach it like an artist would. You have to single out the colors and shapes. The lines. The *composition*. Make it the most remarkable thing you know how to make. It takes effort and passion and desire. You put these into it and you get a reward in return. The formula is not complicated."

"You sound like Evan."

"He's not wrong. A secret path to joy. Such a simple concept, really. We divide the world into two categories: the ones who are skeptical and the ones who believe, who commit to the search. Which kind of person is going to find it? I mean, the answer is pretty obvious, right?"

"But, listen to how you sound—"

"All I know is I see paradise, okay? I don't know what you see, but if it's not this, then…" He shrugs.

How long would it take to swim across the ocean? To find a different beach with a different sort of sand and a different horizon line? If I start now, will I make it to the other side before I'm dead?

I get up in the middle of the night and turn on the computer, thinking I'll go through every file if I need to. Between the hours of two and five a.m. the need to know hits me like a swarm. What is Danny writing? Finding this out is urgent, deathly important, the secret to my survival.

The computer asks me for a password. I try Evan. I try Penelope. I try Cassandra. I try full names, middle names, names plus birthdates. None of them work. I try Dora, Dora MacIntosh, DannyIrvingliar63. None of them work.

With a flashlight in my hand, I sneak back into the bedroom, tiptoe into the closet, lift up the board. It half-scrapes, half-bangs against the wall, loud enough for Danny to hear. Loud enough to wake him? Maybe. I shine the light into the hole and confirm that it's empty, then let it fall back into place and turn off the flashlight. It's too dark in the bedroom to tell whether Danny's eyes are open, but what does it matter? When I crawl back into bed, he is still. Too still, maybe? I turn over onto my side and stare into the darkness, letting my eyes slowly readjust.

This could go on forever.

Dora's brother Gerry calls me at the bakery, apologizes for bothering me, says he needs to talk to me again. His voice is thin and stretched out, like an old cassette tape recording. We agree that there won't be any walking this time. We'll meet at the coffee shop around the corner instead. What could he want to talk about? Uneasily, I consider the possibilities. *We went through Dora's house and we found out some new information. She knew your husband. He's the reason she's dead.* And then what will I say to him? *No, it was me.* I'm *the reason she's dead.*

Gerry looks the same. The same navy blue pea coat and black knit cap. The same hulking figure, which seems reduced, somehow, from its original robustness. There is something about the tentative way he moves, his labored breathing, that makes it seem like a small, old man resides within him, manipulating this younger man's

body. He winces as he sits down, as though his legs are not meant
to be bent. Maybe this is the reason we walked the last time. He's
a nomad. He walks and stands, sleeps standing up; this is just how
he was created.

"Thanks for talking with me again." He removes his gloves slowly, exposing huge, dark hands. The left one is disfigured by an irregular mass of white scar tissue. I glance at it quickly, then look away,
pretending not to notice the way he rubs at it with his other hand.

"Danny still isn't talking," I offer.

Gerry nods like he understands. "It's been a hard couple months
for a lot of us. Sometimes this happens. People close off. Their
brains try to process a traumatic event by re-sorting and re-align-
ing, but somehow they flip the wrong switch. It's not the pain that
gets turned off, but speech. I don't understand how it happens. I
just know it does."

"I think he's faking."

I expect surprise, but Gerry is measured, unphased. His mouth
turns up the slightest bit, in what seems to be the beginnings of a
smile, and stops there.

"Danny was always hard to read. I mean, that's part of his thing,
right? Why all the girls were attracted to him? It's the mystery.
You're always wondering a little bit what he's thinking, whether
he approves, whether he finds the things you say interesting. Even
when he's talking it seems almost like he isn't."

I hold my breath. "Wait…why are you talking about Danny like
you know him?"

He stares down the table, opens his mouth, then closes it again.
Finally, he raises his head and speaks. "I almost told you last time,
but then I thought maybe it was none of my business what you
know and what you find out. And not just that, but there was…it's
hard to explain. Just the way you didn't know anything. The fact
that you had no idea. So peaceful. Like if there was a way I could
have traded places with you I would have."

"It hasn't been peaceful at all. More like torture."

"How would knowing help you? That's the way I rationalized
it. I mean, it would still be up to Danny to tell you what happened
that night. I could tell you how everyone knows each other, but I
don't know how Dora and Danny ended up on the roof that night,

why she jumped or fell."

"Or was pushed."

Gerry cringes. "What I'm saying is I could tell you *why* she's dead, but not how it happened."

"Tell me then. Why is she dead?"

He closes his eyes, and it seems like he might die right there. Life might seep out of his body, leaving me waiting to hear the answer from a corpse. I can feel my heart pounding in my chest, the urgency of its beating.

"We were all cursed," says Gerry finally. "Me, Dora, Katy, Suzie. All of us. We're all dead." He locks his fingers together and places his hands in front of his mouth. It seems like he might start weeping. Or praying.

"What?" A shadow approaches; a terrible, monstrous shape looming on the horizon that I should have seen earlier. I haven't been paying enough attention. To colors and shapes. Composition. My artistic eye is dead and now I'm here, pretending to want to drink coffee with Gerry MacIntosh.

"We were young. We weren't thinking. We let it happen."

"But you're not..." Except that he is, isn't he? The labored breathing, the stoop, the body that only seems to be functioning because of its largeness. Some improbable sickness is eating away at him, slowly, from the inside.

"It's a matter of weeks, maybe months if I'm lucky. But what's the point in counting?"

"I don't know what to say. I'm so sorry."

"All of us before forty. Katy before twenty-five. At first you think it's just run-of the mill tragedy, but then you understand that it was your own bad ideas, your own selfishness."

"But...I don't think I understand."

"Stitch is next. He has to know that. He has to be wondering when it will happen. Every day, walking down the street looking up, looking down. Afraid to trip, for some kind of fluke accident to happen. Afraid to drive. Stroke. Heart attack. House fire."

An unwelcome thought flutters in, then nestles in my stomach.

"What about Danny?"

Gerry shrugs. "It's hard to say. You'd think it would be all of us, but Danny kind of stayed back. He—"

"Stayed back from what?" I try to picture Danny standing in a group of people, these names that Gerry has listed that I've never heard before. But I can't summon an image of where they would be, what they would be doing that would cause Danny to back away from them slowly, tell them he's not participating.

Gerry is silent. He appears to be rolling on waves in a tiny lifeboat, fighting to keep himself from throwing up. All he really wants to do is curl up in the corner and close his eyes, but instead he's stuck in this never-ending conversation with me.

"This is like, what? Witchcraft?" I imagine an altar in a field somewhere. Crowns made out of thorns and vines woven into garland, Gerry in a cape slitting the throat of a baby cow, a baby lamb. Blood pouring out, being collected into some ceremonial vessel. "Tell me."

"Danny should tell you."

"He's not talking. He hasn't even admitted to me that he knew Dora, but he did, didn't he?"

"Well, Stitch should, then."

"Stitch? Is that...someone? A person?"

Gerry winces again, breathes in sharply. The movement is almost imperceptible. Not a shudder or a spasm, but a slower, more insidious force passing between his organs and inside his veins. I don't want to consider it, the idea of a curse, of Danny and some friends drunkenly opening a portal to hell. It's the stuff of movies, all of this.

The movement passes and Gerry breathes again, straightens up as much as he can.

"Evan. Stitch. Same person. That's what we called him back then."

Evan? This has to make sense. Once I process it for long enough, it will. No wonder all the crying. No wonder the secret path to joy.

"What are you talking about? Are you making this up?"

"None of it's good, Cassie. It hasn't been good for ten years."

For a while, we sit quietly, surrounded by the busy din of the coffee shop. Gerry was right. Why did I let myself know this? I don't want it. I want to shove it back into whatever dark hole has been keeping it hidden for the past decade.

Gerry hasn't touched his coffee. He opens the lid and looks down at the brown liquid, then lets the lid drop to the table. "I should clarify that I'm not Dora's brother. I can at least tell you that. I met Dora the same time I met your husband. Fifteen years ago. We all went up to a cabin for a week. It was at the end of the longest dirt road any of us had ever seen."

And then he tells me a story—the beginning of a story—about a hot week in July at a cabin with no electricity or running water. Danny, Evan, Dora, Katy, Suzie, and Gerry, whose name isn't Gerry at all but Taz. They carved their names on a wooden post in one of the closets. He labors over the descriptions, trying to get them right, even though I'm not paying attention. What I'm hearing is Danny loved Dora. The woman who died. Taz never gets to the curse, which in the end doesn't even matter. It's just one of a million other secrets. Danny loved Dora. Somehow, this is what matters most.

# CHAPTER 18

A storm has come through recently. The ocean has a roughed-up appearance: frothy, muddy, and strewn with all of the thousand lost items that you never knew were there. Danny is lying on his side, his knees slightly bent, with both arms stretched out between them.

"You look tired."

"It got a bit windy. It was hard to stand up."

"Is that my fault?"

"That question is complicated, but no, I don't think you control the wind."

"Do you still like it here?"

"The thing is, I wanted *you* to like it. I bought it for *you*."

"I imagined it differently. That's all."

"What do you want me to fix? I'll do what I can, but you know there's only so much. At some point we run out of scenarios."

I watch him survey the wreckage, running through all his various plans, deciding which ones are workable and then realizing that none of them are.

"The first time I came here," I say, "I thought we were going to solve all of our problems. Didn't it feel like that? Conversation by conversation. You were so perfect. I felt like an intruder and I thought you would make me feel at home. This was the scenario that I pictured. But we never got there. I couldn't get us there."

He sighs. "You want too much. You let everything disappoint you."

"But Dora, Danny. The curse. What am I supposed to do with any of that?"

There's more I want to explain, but a huge wave appears, mesmerizing and beautiful like a slow-moving animal, folding onto itself. It rises over us, silver and mystifying, then crashes down, knocking me over and pulling us in.

We're underwater, breathing somehow, communicating without

talking, discussing which direction will lead us back to land.

Danny swims and I follow. We're fast and strong, as though we've evolved to do this. We could swim forever. But weren't we supposed to head back to shore? I call out to Danny, suggest that we come up for air and check where we are, but Danny tells me to keep going. It's best to stay underwater, avoid the vertigo. I don't understand what he means.

"If you come upon a school of sharks, you have to avoid their faces. Swim around them."

How far are we going?

"It might be sea turtles instead. They're gorgeous."

It should be dark under water, but it's lit up, shimmering in misplaced greens and pinks. Danny tells me that we need to look for the cave; once we get there we can stop. I grab his shoulder and close my eyes, letting myself float behind him. Each time I breathe, I expect to fight for oxygen, to feel the panic of suffocation, but instead air passes into my lungs freely.

At last we stop. Danny closes a door behind us and the water vanishes. We're in a living room, grand and beautiful. Just one of hundreds of rooms, Danny tells me; it will take years to explore them all. We'll bring the kids here. We'll all live down here together.

"I can't decide. I might like the beach better."

"I really wish you would make up your mind."

"I think you meant to take Dora here."

"She died, in one of the rooms. I still haven't found her, but I'm guessing we will eventually. We could just chuck the body out the door, release it to the sea."

"Danny..."

When I inform Danny that the kids are spending the night with their grandparents, he doesn't question it. His expression is cool and still, like a winter sky. On the way home from dropping them off, I begin to make a list, words I'll use to extract the truth, sentences I'll build out of these words. But by the time I've parked the car and I'm walking up the stairs to the apartment, all that runs through my head is this: Daniel Francis Irving is a big fat liar.

The living room is dark. Danny is sitting in the corner, lit up by a small desktop lamp and the light from his computer.

"Danny."

He leans forward, then stands up, a sheet of paper falling off his lap and onto the floor. He's smiling slightly, in the manner of a parking attendant or a waiter. Someone who's told to stand at the X and be pleasant.

*Daniel Francis Irving is a big fat liar.*

"I talked to your friend Taz yesterday. He told me about Dora MacIntosh. That you knew her."

I look for a reaction—surprise or anger or any emotion at all, a change in his shoulders and jawline—but Danny is calm as he makes his way to the couch and sits down.

"Dora," I repeat. "You knew her, but you told me..."

He shakes his head, closes his eyes, and presses three fingertips against his forehead.

"Lee's roommate told the police that she came out of Lee's bedroom that night, but it never happened that way, did it?"

He keeps his eyes closed, the fingers pressing in, as though he's waiting to receive a telepathic message.

"What else? What am I missing? Did you push her off the roof?"

He shakes his head again.

"What happened?"

He sighs and looks up at me, his eyes soft this time. His face. Something is gone; some hardness. It's the beard, I realize. How is it that I'm only just noticing? Did he shave it in the morning? Just a few minutes ago while I was dropping off the kids? Is it possible that it's been gone for days and I haven't noticed?

He pulls a dry erase marker from behind his ear and writes:

I WANTED TO COME UP WITH A
PLAN BEFORE YOU FOUND OUT

He approaches, rests a hand on my shoulder, lifts my chin with the other one so that I'm forced to look up at him.

"What plan?"

As Danny leads me to the computer, I notice that the tabletop is strangely neat, devoid of what seems like a dozen items that should be there, although I can't name any of them. Danny gives the mouse a shake and the monitor revives from darkness. A box asks for a password, the same box that has denied me so many times. He types something in quickly, moves the mouse, clicks. The screen fills with white space, and near the top, a few lines of text.

```
The cabin slept six, with room for another
couple on the couches, a dozen on the floor
in sleeping bags.

I should have turned back after we started up
that dirt road. That was my mistake.

Cassie, I've been trying to figure out how to
tell you everything. I wanted to write it all
down so you could read it and so the police
would have a complete version of the story,
but I ended up deleting it all.

The End
```

When I turn toward Danny, he smiles, faintly, without looking at me. From his mouth, a strange croaking sound emerges. He clears his throat.

"It took me a while to work something out. I really wish you had a little more patience, Cas."

# CHAPTER 19

## (DANNY)

I always told myself that they weren't my bodies to report. I hadn't seen them. I didn't know what they looked like, how to explain where they were located, except somewhere in the forest, west of the ridge we hiked up. Once I knew nobody else was going to report them, I should have done it. That's on me, not doing it.

It was almost like we could believe they didn't exist. Katy and Taz had made them up so they'd have a better story to tell us. It just didn't feel like anyone was missing. It's not logical, but at the same time it makes sense. What are two people out of billions? You think if you stay quiet the world won't miss them.

I assumed one of us would eventually figure out the right thing to do. But when it should have been my turn, I kept waiting. Time passed. With every year that went by, the bodies became less relevant to the world we all inhabited.

And then we started dying. Not long after Katy we lost Suzie, during childbirth. It wasn't supposed to happen in the modern era, but sometimes there were complications. A hospital bed stained with blood and in the middle of it a baby crying for a mother she would never meet.

Did it make us nervous? I can't remember. I only remember feeling sad, the hard weight of processing another inexplicable death, the breathless wince as I thought of Suzie padding across the kitchen in her bare feet, wrapped in that towel, wringing her hair out onto the floor. So much life in that moment, but now…nothing.

Another phone call from Dora. Another funeral. Evan told me he had to go, that Dora needed him there. "She's like a ghost, Danny. She doesn't know how to deal with this."

What was I supposed to do? I warned him that it wasn't the right thing to do, thinking maybe if he spent a night or two mulling it over, he'd come to the same conclusion, but instead he took off without telling me, called me from the road in the middle of the night. "I think I was her first love. I have a responsibility. As a decent human, I need to do this." I hung up the phone thinking he and Dora were going to the police, finally. I thought this was what he meant.

After the funeral, Evan was quieter than I'd ever known him to be. We sat across a table from each other for what seemed like hours while I tried and failed to come up with words that would land right in the silence. "You don't like to be the only one talking, do you?" His voice I hardly recognized. It was Dora, somehow, speaking through him.

They talked for forty hours straight, he told me. They hadn't planned it this way. It was just a matter of saying everything they needed to say to one another, and when they were finally done he looked down at his watch and whispered *holy shit*. Forty hours, almost to the minute. For a split second, he felt the sensation of his heart stopping in his chest.

I don't think you can talk for forty hours. Nobody could do that. Not even Evan and Dora, although I could see them getting pretty far along; all those side roads and meanders they'd take together. All the trivial bits they'd cover, thinking it was important. Retreading the same stories again and again: Katy and Suzie Q. Katy and Suzie Q.

"I finally checked into life, Danny. I'm here, now, at last."

The expression on his face—I don't know. It was like nothing I'd seen before.

"I got hit by a lightning bolt," he said. "There's no other way to describe it. I see it clearly now. We all fit in—there is a specific place where each of us belongs—but the problem is figuring out where. All this time I've been in the wrong slot, but how would I know? Without anything to compare it to? Like would you know, Danny, if you belonged somewhere else? Probably not. The only reason *I* know is because of what happened to me on the way back from Dora's.

"I stopped at this hamburger place to get something to eat, and as I was waiting in line, I felt a presence behind me—I don't even know how to explain it—like a low hum on some other frequency that I was suddenly tuned in to. So I turned around and there was this guy there. I couldn't even describe him if you asked me to. All he was doing was looking up at the menu, but he had some quality in him that made me pause. Just one of those things, you know? Like I knew I *needed* to talk to him, except I wasn't sure why or even what I would say. Eventually, he lowered his eyes from the menu board, and what I noticed—immediately—were the clearest, most shining eyes I'd ever seen. I can't even describe it to you. Just that this guy was a magnet. And there I was, thinking he was about to get mad at me for staring at him, start making the wrong assumptions about me or whatever, but instead his face opened up into a smile. It was like he knew exactly what I was seeing, like it happened to him all the time. He had gemstones for eyes and teeth made out of pearls. Honestly, I think I would have done anything this guy told me to; I would have gone anywhere with him. That's the power of what he had to show me. That's what I'm ready to tap into. I'm telling you, it would blow your mind."

I didn't understand him, the words he was using, what he was trying to tell me. In the past fifteen years we'd been through a lot, but never anything like this. I mean, suddenly he seems two inches taller and his hair looks darker and he's got this urgency about him that I've never seen before. He's certain. Every word, he's sure what it means and that it's right, even as he speaks sentence after sentence that doesn't make any sense. He told me I just had to go to one meeting and I'd be able to see it too: the extraordinary beauty of ordinary objects. The colors in my rainbow would become more vibrant. What in God's name does that even mean? Just one meeting, he told me, and I would understand the way I was meant to be living.

A few days later he quit his job. He was going to work full time recruiting members for JoyPath. I remember wondering if his real job would take him back in a few weeks once he realized his mistake. He and Jill had three kids by this time, the youngest one an infant, and suddenly the family didn't have any health care, but he said it didn't matter because they were all going to be great. They were going to be a great family. Life was going to be spectacular. Great people found other great people, the ones who *understood*.

"You know who isn't great?" he said. "Those two people who

jumped out of the helicopter that day. They never deserved to have the ivory in the first place."

According to Evan, this was the problem. The *only* problem.

Dora herded us all together for another reunion. Ten years. She said we couldn't let it go by unacknowledged, even though this was exactly what I wanted to do. If we'd all just been okay with not keeping in touch, we could have imagined Taz and Katy traveling to the ends of the earth together, Suzie off living some exciting life, rich and happy and surrounded by kindness. Instead, they were gone. Not just missing from our lives but missing from the earth. Thinking about it brought me down, made my brain dance around wondering about goodness and justice and whether there was anyone out there keeping score. Why did we need to get together to talk about it more? Why did I even go?

None of us were up for driving all the way to the cabin again, so we met at Taz's house, a huge, sprawling thing deep in the suburbs that seemed empty even though it had everything you needed to live. Except Katy, of course. Taz said it was too big, but he'd never be able to sell it because every room reminded him of her. *She liked paint. She liked carpeting.*

"You have to look forward," said Evan, "Not back into the past."

"Fuck you. Your wife didn't die. You have the *option* of ruining your marriage and letting yours walk away."

For a minute I thought Evan was going to punch him. I saw the twitch under his left eye, but then watched the impulse pass across his face and vanish. What did it become? It had to become something, right? He set his hand on Taz's arm. "You're right. I'm sorry. I deserved that."

I don't know what we thought we were doing, what was supposed to happen.

Dora kept going on about Katy and Suzie, how they were some of the best friends she'd ever had, how Suzie's laugh was the most delightful sound she'd ever heard, and how Katy had taught her so much about being present in life and being confident and belonging. How there's just something about being a teenager, the

friendships that form when you're young that occupy a deep place
in your heart, and even though you worry about forgetting them
it's impossible because the heart is still forming—it's expanding—
and it hasn't been broken yet and this is why early friendships stay
special forever. I wondered if these were statements a doctor should
be making, but I let her keep talking because what else was I going
to do?

It was almost okay. For the first hour or so, nobody mentioned
the tusk and I thought this was all it would be—a memorial at Taz's
house followed by all of us leaving quietly, getting on with our lives
and hopefully this time leaving the bad memories behind for good.

All afternoon it seemed like we were waiting for the others to
arrive so the main event could start. But it was only us and there
was no other event. Just the four of us sitting around and talking
for the sake of filling up the silence that would otherwise be too
much to bear.

I guess it was bound to happen with all that time to kill and
the rooms so empty and our brains being what they were. If Evan
hadn't said it, someone else would have.

"Hey, did anyone figure out who dug up the tusk? Whatever
happened to that thing?"

Taz cringed a little. I thought about him lugging a tusk through
the woods for Katy, being the kind of guy who would love a girl so
much he'd do anything for her. How messed up was the world when
a guy like Taz Ferris was the one to lose his wife so young?

"I'll be honest, Taz," said Dora. "I thought it was you and Katy—
and I promise I'm not mad about this and won't ever be mad about
it. I thought you guys made up that story to throw us off, I mean
about coming back to dig it up and not finding it."

Taz shook his head. "It wasn't us. I swear it wasn't."

Dora rested her hand on his forearm and spoke to him quietly.
"It's fine. I don't need to know. We've all moved on, haven't we?"

"Of course," said Evan. "Nobody cares anymore."

"Seriously, though. It wasn't us."

Evan turned to Dora. "And it wasn't you, either?" I wondered why
he was asking her when he must have already known the answer.

"I swear on my life. It wasn't me."

It was like slow motion after that. One by one, they all turned to look at me.

"What do I want with that fucking thing?"

"You're not answering the question."

"No. I don't have it. Okay? On my honor, I don't have the tusk."

The silence we'd been avoiding arrived after that. Just the four of us staring down at the floor, pretending we were so lost in thought that we didn't notice the quiet creeping in from parts of the house we hadn't even seen. Nobody dared to look up. For the longest time, we just sat there.

At some point the doorbell rang and Taz went to answer it, then came back a minute later with an armful of pizzas. We didn't understand why he ordered so many pizzas for just four of us, but we all ate a couple slices without saying much. Taz, though; I don't think he ate anything. It seemed to me like he was just holding it together. He was a faded sign on an abandoned building, hanging on but no longer serving a useful purpose.

"Did you hear that Suzie's daughter is three already?" Dora asked.

We let the question linger, unanswered. I grabbed Dora's hand and squeezed it and watched her close her eyes to keep from crying. It was never her success in life that impressed me but moments like this, when her heart was so huge it consumed her.

I wiped my mouth and cleared my throat. "So…what happened? With those two people in the woods? Did anyone ever figure out who they were?"

I guess you could say that this was just me being a dick, but the truth was it bothered me being there, talking about every other topic but ignoring the most important one.

"It's too late, Danny," said Evan.

"Too late for what?"

"They've been out there for ten years. They're probably just… bones strewn about the forest now. We wouldn't be able to tell anybody where they are, even if we knew who to tell."

"I'm just asking if anybody ever figured out who they were."

Taz's voice seemed to come from a different part of the room. "I tried. I've searched up and down the internet for those two and never found any leads. I've searched missing persons databases, looked at photographs, tried to match faces that look nothing alike, just to come up with an answer. But I couldn't. You can't. There's nothing out there."

"What about the pilot of the helicopter?" I asked. "Why wouldn't he have come forward?"

"Maybe what he did is manslaughter."

"Honestly," said Evan, "it just makes me wonder whether we're even remembering what happened correctly. I mean, did we really see anything? Weren't we all high that day?"

"I wasn't," said Taz. "Plus, Katy and I hiked out there and—"

"Wait," Evan held up a hand. "Let me just work through this for a second. What I'm saying is what if there were no people falling from the sky that day. No helicopter noise to get our attention, no parachutes opening too late. Nobody hitting the ground at all. Just unbroken blue sky? What about that?"

"Evan..."

"I saw them," said Taz. "Remember?"

"But maybe you're just seeing what your mind's eye is telling—"

"I saw her face! She had freckles. She was sunburned. There were little bits of skin peeling off of her nose. That's how close I got. When I bent down to listen for a heartbeat, her hair was draped across her neck. It was brown, wavy, lightened at the tips. Her shirt was blue and it had some kind of a picture on it—words, which I read except my brain was so messed up I couldn't make sense of them."

"Oh my God," said Dora softly.

"Okay," said Evan, "I get it."

The afternoon passed into evening. We piled the mostly full pizza boxes on top of one another and the gathering limped to an end. I watched Dora walk up to Evan and whisper in his ear, then take him by the arm and lead him off toward the kitchen. Probably it wouldn't be forty hours this time but I decided not to wait. I shook Taz's hand and started to say a polite goodbye, but he stopped me before I could get through it.

"You understand it's a curse, right? You get this?"

His face was pale, almost see-through. A shiver rolled through my body, the same heart-stopping kind of cold that assaults you right after jumping into a swimming pool.

"I don't believe in—"

"It's my turn next. The doctors say it's treatable, if I'm lucky it'll turn out fine." He shook his head and I could feel the intensity of his eyes, their dry, piercing heat that made it seem like it was impossible for him to ever cry again. "But we know I'm not lucky, right?"

"Man, I'm sorry. Jesus."

"Did you touch it, Danny?"

"Touch what?"

"The tusk. That day at the cabin when Katy... Before we buried it."

It was hard to think about that day, to acknowledge its existence in my memory banks. But I could still picture them, a bunch of dumb teenagers stroking and caressing the thing like it was going to give them all superpowers or something. I'd stayed away, although I couldn't tell you why.

I shook my head.

"Maybe you'll be okay, then." Taz clapped a hand against my shoulder, and I thought there would be more, but in the next instant he was gone, done, disappeared into some other empty wing of the house.

And that was it. Our last reunion. I got into my car and drove home.

It got to be a pattern with Dora. She vanished and reappeared and vanished and reappeared, and each time she reappeared it was to tell us about something terrible that had happened. I should have known when she turned up without any bad news to deliver, that this time it would be one of us.

That night on the roof. We're getting there.

Evan had been seeing Dora when he could. A few times a month, he'd meet her halfway to Mapleville for a night, a few hours. Somehow, she made the time for him. They weren't dating; it was an arrangement. I didn't get it, but why did I need to? They were two adults—let them do whatever the hell they wanted to.

We'd talk, late at night. Evan was focused on my happiness, on what JoyPath could do for me. It would straighten out my life, and then I could share what I learned with others. Together, we would change the human outlook. It was a crock of shit but he believed in it, so why not let him have it?

Evan always got me to talk. I don't know how he did it, but before I knew what was happening, I told him about Cas, how she wasn't sleeping, how I would wake up in the middle of the night and find her walking around the house, cleaning up or making a sandwich. Things that I used to do as a kid whenever I was nervous but didn't know why. Somehow, this made Evan angry.

"Either you guys do it differently or you don't do it at all. Your life doesn't right itself for you; that's up to you."

I didn't know why I was letting him talk to me, why I would listen to anything he said. Probably there was something comforting about it, about him. How large he was. How absurd.

"Sometimes I'll see a girl and she'll turn her head and smile, and I'll just think…"

Evan shook his head. "It's not like that. It shouldn't be like that."

"But it happened to you. With Jill. All the time."

"She wasn't the right one for me. That's why. We weren't complete together. When you took what was best between us and added it up, you didn't even get a whole person. That's how incomplete we were. That's why I had to let her go."

"But your kids…"

"They'll stay my kids. Whatever time I'm missing with them now, I'll make it up later."

He would say garbage like this all the time, and afterward I'd get mad at myself for thinking that parts of it made sense.

"You either have to commit one hundred percent or you let her go."

I remember going home and trying to be the best husband I could be. Doing nice things for Cas and smiling at her and ignoring whatever it was that was annoying me, telling myself *this is the woman I'm in love with, this is the woman I'm in love with*, like a Positivity Loop in my brain. I thought if I tried hard enough, paid close enough attention, I'd feel the explosion that I remembered from before. It never came, but I tried not to read too much into it. My stepfather likes to say that there are really only four or five decisions that you make in life; the others are made for you. It just didn't seem like there was a decision that I needed to make. It seemed like this was life, period; the minutes and seconds that were going to add up to the rest of time, with me inside of it until I was dead.

To be clear: I didn't ask Evan to follow her. I never would have done that. It was all him, the way he operated. With no real job, he had the time to cruise around the city, starting up conversations, looking for people to help. This was his *profession* now, he said: being a human among other humans, recognizing greatness in a world where it was lacking.

Somehow, I became one of his projects. He followed Cassie to help me.

He trailed her to the parking lot of some bar he'd never heard of before, in a part of town he didn't know existed. He watched her, sitting in her car, talking on her phone, checking her hair and face in the mirror. And just like that, it hit him: Cassie was a heartbreakingly incomplete person. Something about the way she walked toward the bar, the way her face was, the identity of her; it was impossible to describe in any other way. Evan deliberated going in after her, acting surprised to run into her, spending the evening with her and her friends, taking notes. Instead, he stayed in his car and waited.

Hours later, when Cassie left the bar, Evan focused on the crucial details: the length of her stride, the quickness of her walk, the way she tucked a piece of hair behind her ear, her head tipped forward and a secret smile on her face. Eight, nine, ten, steps across the parking lot, to a blue van off in the corner, the key in her hand sliding quickly into the lock and the door open and her gone, the parking lot empty and eerie behind her. He thought she would drive off; it seemed to him that he was witnessing the very act of leaving. These were the words he used, the observations he made. I imagined Evan with his chin on his fist, staring at some unfamiliar vehicle and picturing what Cas might be doing inside of it; what *he* should do, as an observer on the outside of it, whether there was anything at all to be done. *For five or ten minutes that van was the only thing in my thoughts. And then* he *walked over—that…man.*

Some people just give you the wrong feeling, Evan explained. You get so you can tell, and as soon as he saw this guy he knew. The way he seemed to cut through space when he walked. You could almost make out the sharp edges of his soul. He was tall, messy, too put-upon by life to care about it. *He just didn't value what was meant to be valued. That was obvious.* The man's face had no expression on it whatsoever. There was no thought behind his existence. No contemplation. No *love.*

Evan watched the man disappear into the blue van in the same way that Cassie had. Afterward, the wind picked up. Loose garbage danced across the parking lot like tumbleweeds. A nighttime symphony, he called it. The music in his head was pure melancholy.

*Time passed like this. I stayed inside the car, following all the hidden cues that surrounded me. How long? Long enough.*

Eventually, the van door opened and the man stepped out. Evan watched him fiddle with the hem of his sleeve, briefly, before slinking away across the parking lot. The night appeared to rush in around him, welcoming him, taking him.

*It took everything I had to not run up behind him and throw him to the ground. It was utter restraint, to a degree that I have never known before.*

I held my breath, waiting to hear the rest, to know whether Cas got out of the van okay, wanting her to be okay. It was like I didn't know the ending, that there was a possibility she might not have made it home.

*What I have to tell you is that I saw every emotion on her face; ten thousand experiences coming to the surface. I don't know how to explain it except to say that it felt like a battle, like she would take all of this… noise home with her and sort through it while she slept with clenched teeth.*

Evan waited for Cassie to get into her car and drive away. He followed her home, made sure she got back to the apartment safely, then turned around and headed straight back to the bar to find the loveless man and figure out what to do about him. The bartender, it so happened. Evan sat down and let the man serve him a Coke, then spent the rest of the night watching the guy, piecing together what he had just seen and what it meant for me, his best friend. He chewed on the situation, ruminating about human traits and human imperfections and human responsibilities. The illusion of human completeness. Ten times, a hundred times, he went over this. Then, when he was as certain as he was going to be, he followed the bartender home.

Hearing that Dora had a fiancé—that part is news. I don't know how you hide a fiancé, how you carry on with someone like Evan without a fiancé knowing about it. It doesn't seem possible. It doesn't seem like Dora. Where did she tell the guy she was going when she came up to see Evan that weekend?

It was the first time Evan didn't meet her halfway. Is this part important? I mean, when you consider what happened later?

I didn't know she was coming. When she rang my doorbell, I didn't even recognize her at first. I couldn't see the girl from the cabin anywhere in her face. Her eyes—they just…I don't know how to explain it. Time had passed. Sure. Yeah, I guess that was it.

"I waited out in the car until they left. Your wife and kids. I want you to know that. I'm not just storming your home or anything."

It was her, but also not her. She looked like a Barbie doll that someone had dressed up all wrong. The red dress she was wearing wasn't the right color, the right length, the right weight for the weather. Doctor MacIntosh, I thought. How is this what a Doctor MacIntosh wears? Her face was thinner than I remembered, the red from her dress reflecting off it in an unflattering way. And her hair. That fucked up hair. Stick-straight like the tail of a horse and so dark it was almost black, a short fringe of bangs chopped in a harsh line across her forehead.

Those drooping shoulders. The way she tilted her head. I expected her to collapse and start crying, tell me that she was going through a nervous breakdown. Instead, she laughed, her tight mouth relaxing and opening, pressing her eyes closed.

"You hate my hair." She laughed again, then ran her fingers through the black straw, pulling it upward, letting it slide off into her hands. Without the wig, her face was nothing but eyes. Her head was smooth with the soft down of new, virgin hair.

"I shaved it!" she announced. As if it wasn't obvious. "Well, almost. I left a little." She ran her hand along the curve of her skull and smiled like a kid. "I just wanted to know what it would feel like. Evan helped me."

I wondered what their "arrangement" was, if she had been naked in his bathroom at the time, letting the hair fall to the floor around her, laughing, unashamed, as he ran the clippers over her head.

"I don't know what to say."

"Can I come in? It won't be very long. Just a few minutes."

I stepped to the side and let her duck under my arm.

"I like your place," she said, barely glancing at anything.

"Fuck you."

Dora pretended to pout. "I never *got* that. Danny is hard. Danny is angry. It just seems so..." She twirled around in a circle and then collapsed onto the couch. "...tiring."

I sat in a chair about five or six feet away from her, trying not to stare at her shaved head, at the way her red dress was bunched up around her thighs.

"It's hot in here, isn't it?" I half expected the dress to come off next, that it was all part of the disguise and the next thing I knew she would be back in her blue bikini with some dumb little pop song playing and the sound of trees rustling at our backs. "I never pay attention to the weather anymore." She let her head drop back onto the couch and let out a big sigh. "I'm so unprepared always."

"Do you want some water?"

She waved a hand. "Don't bother."

I leaned forward, resting my forearms on my legs. "So. You and Evan..."

She raised both arms above her head, then let them flop back down on the couch. "He's compassionate. An idealist."

"Did you buy a copy of that book he's hawking?"

Her eyes were focused on the nothingness above her. "I wanted to hate it, but he convinced me otherwise. Who am I to judge? If he says he's found joy then why don't we let him have that?"

"It's a pyramid scheme."

"What do I care what it is? As long as he's not all the way at the bottom of it, right?"

"I guess."

She sighed, then closed her eyes. Her body was so still that I thought she was going to fall asleep, or already had. But then her eyes popped open and a serious expression worked its way onto her face.

"We talk. We help each other. But I don't love him."

"I don't need to know this."

"He told me. About your wife and that bartender. That's why I'm here."

I looked at my feet. It was too much. The dress, the hair, the eyes.

"He said you're not talking through it with him, but he can tell you're ripped up inside about it. His words, not mine."

"I don't want to have this conversation with you."

"You're so kind. So warm. So...big. The core of you. You make me think of a fireplace. You're the center of everything and we all just try to get close enough to warm our hands and feet."

"My God."

"I'm serious, Danny. I want to kill her for what she did."

I stood up. "You have to go now."

She stared at me, a frown settling between her eyes. A doctor reading test results, I thought. Doctor MacIntosh in her hideous red dress. "The thing is, I should have been more careful with you." She stood up and smoothed the front of her dress. Something about the way she did this confirmed that I was right. It was covering up some other outfit, one I wouldn't get to see.

"You were fine, and I'm not a fucking fireplace."

"Read between the lines, Danny." She moved in closer, pressing her shoulder against mine. A hand touched my cheek and directed my face toward hers. "I should have been more careful," she whispered, then kissed me slowly. It went on longer than it should have, the room spinning and spinning, the taste of lemons mixed with spice, my hand moving to her waist and then quickly back to my side again.

"You have to go."

Listen. I'm not the kind to have other people solve my problems.

I don't want anyone to think I wanted Evan's help, or Dora's, for that matter, but somehow the three of us ended up at that apartment anyway.

That night, we all met up at Evan's place. We were supposed to go out and have a little fun somewhere, which was probably a bad idea, but I'd let them talk me into it anyway. We ordered takeout, talked about a lot of dumb shit. Mostly about Dora. She had this bag of wigs and was trying them all on for us: black, brown, red, blonde, electric blue. I wanted to love her in them, but I missed the long brown hair, the tendrils spilling softly across her shoulders.

What do you call it? An intervention? Maybe that's what it was, because every time I mentioned going out, one of them would change the subject. I don't even know how we got there, how they led me there. To Cassie and that bartender.

"Here's what we'll do," said Dora. "We'll go talk to him. No posturing. No threatening. Just give him the message: what are your intentions with my wife? Why would you have intentions with someone else's wife?"

She looked at me playfully, as if it was all a joke and the only way to enjoy the rest of the evening was to be in on it with her. Then she tilted her head back and laughed. "What am I even saying?" She touched my forearm, gently, with a cold hand. "I'm sorry, Danny. You have to forgive me. I tend to have an unusual way of handling strife."

I didn't like the words she used, the way she spoke them. Evan punched her arm, for no reason I could tell, and she laughed again. They seemed stoned; like a couple of sixteen-year-olds trying to piece together a plan out of ideas that were way short on logic. I felt my hands tightening into fists, then counted backwards from ten and let a silent scream fill my brain.

"I think the two of you used to be perfect," said Evan. "You and Cas. I always thought that."

"What were they like?" asked Dora.

"Just...like a painting. Like colors on a canvas that stretched out for miles."

"No, Stop! That's enough, okay? A painting? Just stop talking. Can you do that? For five minutes?"

I walked across the room, as far as I could go before the wall stopped me. It was cool against my forehead, pleasant even. The rage seemed to drip out through my fingertips. Behind me, I could hear Evan's voice.

"Sorry, man. I…Sorry."

At that moment, I still didn't think it would lead anywhere. Expectations were meant to be put to rest. What was life anyway but a series of lowered expectations? And then at the end of it, heart disease or cancer, or hours in a wheelchair staring at people whose names you don't remember, creating a new life in your head at the end of the old one, except no matter how far back you go, that one ends in exactly the same way. I could find a girl, I supposed, to get even; go off and screw her and come back home and never mention it. Maybe it would even go on like this for years, until eventually we both got too old to care anymore.

"Seriously, though." It was Dora talking again. She was supposed to be a buried memory but now she was a shaved head and a bag of terrible wigs and a laugh that was starting to feel like abrasions up and down my arms. "I was joking about going to talk to him. I don't think you should do that."

"No, he should. Talk to *her* first, and then afterward talk to him. Make peace. Find the path to forgiveness."

"Why?" asked Dora. "Why does everyone need to forgive all the time? Aren't some things unforgiveable?"

"Hey buddy. Are you still with us?"

I turned and slid to the floor. You would think that eventually they'd have to change the subject, but it was starting to seem like the two of them could talk about this one thing for forty hours, with me trapped in the middle of it. They took turns with the advice, telling me I needed objectivity, a light hand, a list of what was most important to me.

"The thing is," Evan explained, "joy and tragedy are so closely integrated. The wall between them is blurry. I like to think of them as interlaced fingers." He laced his own fingers together and held them out to illustrate what he meant.

Dora rolled her eyes. "So dramatic, this one." She was wearing the electric blue wig by this time. I don't know what the point of this was supposed to be. I never knew with her. It made me so tired. Each thing made me tired; hundreds of things, every day.

"When you go to see the bartender, I think you just offer your hand to the guy. Start it off with a friendly overture."

"He's a person, you're a person."

"Exactly," said Dora. "Two people. Don't forget it."

"You have to view it not as a confrontation, but as an investigation. You have an open mind. You're finding out information, you're relaying information. You're keeping the Big Emotions out of it. For now."

Dora shrugged. "Maybe. But if they come knocking, I think you let them in."

Their voices made me dizzy, the way they buzzed around from idea to idea without ever landing on anything substantial. It was absurd: seeing the two of them together, listening to them talk, thinking maybe they deserved each other after all and then realizing I didn't care. Instead, I thought of Cassie, the conversation we would have when I got home that night, the way we would talk it through and fix ourselves because that's the kind of couple we were. I never expected the night to end up where it did. That fucking roof. Why did they insist we go find the bartender that night? Why did I go along with it?

Dora went into the bedroom with her bag and reemerged a couple minutes later wearing the worst wig of the bunch. It was half bleached blonde and half black and made her look hideous. Why would you wear this to go talk to a bartender who was screwing your friend's wife? I should have asked, but it was easier to just follow them out of the apartment. To get in the back seat of the car and leave them up front to drive.

We parked next to a high curb. It seemed twice the height of a regular curb, at least. The apartment buildings continued up and down the block: red brick, blonde brick, red brick, blonde brick, each one with the same single step up to the entry door. I didn't know the neighborhood, the people. It seemed hard, stark, washed out and trampled on repeatedly, but when I tried to pinpoint the difference between this block and the one where we lived, I couldn't come up with anything. I tried to imagine Cassie inside the building we were looking at; an old couch, an old mattress. A dirty plastic cup to drink from. A dirty window to look out of. Cassie lying on her back, staring at the ceiling, talking to some stranger about her dad, telling him the same story she had told me, about seeing her mom kneeling on the floor with her eyes wide and her hand pressed against her head, and the silence that took over the room, wanting to run to her but afraid to move, afraid of what had just happened, of what was happening, of the potential for worse. She'd told me this story so many times it got so I couldn't listen to it anymore. *I don't know the significance of it, because we all just moved on. My mom got up and we ate dinner and eventually things got so they seemed normal again and none of us ever talked about it. Now sometimes it feels like I only dreamed it.* Would she tell him this, lying in his musty sheets? *One terrible day, and every other day was more or less normal. But how do you ever let go of the terrible day?*

We sat in the car for hours. I closed my eyes and listened to Dora's voice, Evan's voice, Dora's voice. Evan started telling a story about a talk he'd given at a conference, about a woman in a black and white dress who fainted, and how they had to call the paramedics and whisk her away. Dora speculated about possible causes, contributing factors. She talked about patients she'd seen, the strange illnesses she'd encountered, how her relationship to the human body had changed, and not necessarily for the better. *It's all clinical now. There isn't any magic.*

As I dozed off, their voices stayed with me: the rising and falling syllables, the quiet chuckles, the urgent pauses, the sound of their bodies shifting; a hand rubbing or scratching. It was peaceful to listen, to imagine myself somewhere else, rowing a boat across a lake with their voices in my head but not needing to respond. I thought maybe this was the heart of friendship, somehow, but when I tried to follow the idea further it turned out to be not much of anything at all.

What time was it when I opened my eyes and sat up, aware of the long stretch of silence that had just passed? The night was pure black around us, broken by the cool white of a streetlight, which distorted the buildings and sidewalks. Dora and Evan's conversation had come to an end. They leaned back into their seats like a couple of travelers waiting out the last hours of a red-eye flight. A thought occurred to me, one that seemed to weave all the bits and pieces together: past and present and a momentarily clear future. We were...we were...there was a place. We were going there. We would find it. The glare of the streetlight reflecting off the sidewalk was so harsh it made me squint. I waited for the thought to fall into place, but it never did.

"What time is it?" My voice was hoarse.

Slowly, Evan powered back up again. He ran his fingers through his hair, rested his forearm on his head. "It looks like 2:30. 3:00, maybe."

I wondered what Cas and the kids were doing, then remembered they would all be asleep. I imagined the almost-silence of the apartment, the occasional creaks and thumps whose origins I could never identify. What would happen if Cas woke up and noticed I'd never come home? Instinctively, I pulled my phone from my pocket, as if it might ring at that very second. No messages. Nothing.

If I never went back—what would she do then? I tried to think of places I could be instead of home, but I didn't have the imagination for it, to make up some alternate future for myself.

"It's strange, being up this late," said Dora. "The sensory experience—it's completely different."

Evan exhaled deeply, resettling himself into his seat. I watched him grab Dora's hand, pull it in close to his stomach. "Danny." His eyes found me in the rear-view mirror. "I'm thinking of moving. Down to Mapleville."

Dora sat up, her body suddenly rigid. "We said we were going to talk about this more."

Evan lifted her hand and kissed it. "It's completely clear to me right now. Sitting here. It seems ridiculous to even discuss it. The answer is so big and obvious."

"Not now...please. Let's just..."

"But you're leaving tomorrow."

Dora slid her hand out from his and made a show of bending forward to scratch her ankle, adjust her shoe. She sat up and hugged herself, rubbing her shoulders. "I don't see how we fit together,

Evan. Not now but indefinitely."

"I'm not saying we move in together right away. I can find a studio or something."

"What about your kids?"

"A one bedroom, then."

"That isn't what I meant." She shook her head. "Anyway, I work all the time. I wouldn't have much more time to see you. And you…"

"I work all the time too." He smiled at her, one of his brilliant smiles that reminded me of afternoons in high school, the plans we made, the ideas he got. "I love you Dora."

"Not now."

"It's not time-specific." He laughed. "It transcends time."

Dora hugged herself tighter. I wanted to remind them that I was there, but what do you say in a situation like this?

"We have a saying at JoyPath, which is 'stop hiding behind *Later*.' So many of us cede our whole lives to Later. Inaction strips us of our potential. Success and joy are about acting. And doing."

Dora pressed a palm against her forehead. "I can't listen to that right now." Her eyes were shut tight, like a child playing hide and seek. "I'm sorry."

Evan studied her face, lifted a piece of her wig between his fingers as if it was truly attached to her scalp, a part of her.

"Anyway," she continued. "Tonight we're here for Danny. This is about him."

It was hard to see Evan's face with all the angles and shadows, but I knew his tendencies, how to read his feelings from the position of his shoulders and neck. He was my best friend, after all. I knew when the anger was rising, when the acid was traveling through his bones.

"He's barely even here," Evan said coldly. "He never wanted to do this."

I waited for him to find me in the rearview mirror but his eyes were locked on Dora. You can't put three humans together in a parked car for this long. Not at night. This is the truth of the situation. We forgot to account for our own stupidity.

It was about time for me to do something, so I scooted across my seat and pushed open the door handle. There was a loud scraping noise as the bottom of the door caught on the curb. I stumbled out of the car and nearly fell over. Both of my feet were asleep. Dora called after me, or at least I imagined she did.

I remember most of it, what happened next, the strangeness and improbability of it. There is a story, a chronology, starting not long after I got out of the car and ending when the gun was fired. There was a flash, yes, but...

The thing is, sometimes after you see the flash and events come back to you in pieces, you understand, too slowly, that this is because they are actually broken. You try to reassemble them, or at least to extract the truth from them. This is your duty, more or less. But isn't it also your duty to protect your family, to finally make good on promises, to get things back under control again?

I think it is. So you leave out a few parts. Small details. Without them, the story still feels complete. It's huge already and doesn't need to be any bigger.

In fact, the smaller the better. Rearrange a few things. Add a few things, and delete a whole lot. No dead bodies, no tusk, no discussions about a curse. Just some old friends who once stayed at a cabin together where not much happened. Young people being stupid and somehow making lifelong friendships out of this. Nothing too much out of the ordinary, except a few tragic deaths along the way. Which aren't that out of the ordinary, really. These are the happenings in life, that sometimes lead, by whatever twisted route, to a bigger tragedy: an unfortunate night when a woman falls. When a woman is pushed.

Three old friends decide to confront a bartender. They knock on his door late at night and his roommate tells them to take their disagreements out of the apartment, so they head up to the roof. They don't expect, as they walk up the stairs in single file, that they are headed to an execution. They look for humanity, which they presume is always present, but on this particular night, in this particular person, they can't find it. They reason, they argue, they try to remain calm when the bartender produces a gun from nowhere and tells them that he has had enough and it's time to be afraid. They stand near the edge—too close to the edge. He makes them line up on a lip of bricks and tell him what they see. They look down, over the tops of streetlights, and look for the best place to land if they are forced to jump. The woman turns back, angry, and reaches for the bartender's arm. As effortlessly as if he were shrugging off a jacket, he lowers his shoulder and presses his body into hers. She falls. The two remaining friends are too shocked to speak. One of them runs for the stairs, in search of the fallen woman. The other one begins to follow, but stops near the center of the roof and turns around. In the darkness, all he can make out is the bartender's gray shape, an approximation of where his head and arms and legs must be.

"You killed her."

The bartender's voice is chillingly calm. "No, she jumped. Don't do anything. Stop your friend."

The man takes a step toward the bartender and there is a flash. The explosion, the white, the silence, the dark.

# CHAPTER 20
## (CASSIE)

We're not Dwell on the Past People. We're not Dwell on the Fifty Pages that Danny Wrote but Then Deleted People. He meant for me to read it, but now he's changed his mind and instead tells me, with his newfound voice, what happened. It was valuable, necessary—the act of writing it down to get his facts in order—but now his mind is clear. He will tell the police the parts they need to hear—about the bartender and me and some version of what happened on the roof—and afterward it will be time to move on. On Danny's face, I see this. His relief and what is supposed to be a reflection of my relief. But I keep imagining the pages he wrote, wondering how many times her name appeared. Dora. Dora. Dora Dora Dora Dora Dora. After everything I've caused, I'm not supposed to care, but I do.

Danny's voice wavers in a way that it never did before. I guess it would happen to anyone after not speaking for months.

"I hope you understand why I have to do this. I've wrestled with it for weeks now. Quietly, in my own head, you know? Call it soul searching if you want to. I've gone over all the options again and again, and this is the only one that isn't…messy. Do you understand, Cas? If I come forward now and say that Evan was up there with me? It raises too many questions."

"Of course it does. Why wouldn't he have been there when the police arrived? I don't understand how Lee just goes back into his apartment and pretends nothing happened, where Evan goes."

"Real life isn't that neat. Maybe you don't realize this. When situations happen, you don't respond the way you might think. Evan was in shock. He didn't know yet that I'd been shot. Once he realized Dora was dead, he went back into the building to find me. He found the bartender instead. He was afraid."

I try to imagine Lee with wild eyes, an animal look, a gun point-ed at Evan's head. Is that how he would do it? I can't picture it. What Lee could have said to Evan to make him stay quiet, to convince him to leave. That Evan would be this frightened of a person. Is it possible that some people are simply unknowable madmen, that good people fall for madmen, plan their lives out with villains?

"What about Dora?"

I already know what Danny is going to say. The story he plans to tell the police will match the one Lee's roommate told me. *Tell your husband we're good. I got everything. Tell him not to come back.*

"She was at the building already. Someone the bartender knew. This protects both of us."

"And what happens when they find out that you and Dora used to...when someone that she knows remembers you?"

Danny shakes his head. "Dora never introduced me to anyone. It wasn't like that. And all the people who knew about us are dead. Well, except for Evan. And Taz, of course. I never expected he would show up, and now we've put him in this position. I feel bad about it, but..." Danny shrugs.

"You were thinking he would be dead already. You were hoping. Then you wouldn't have had to tell me about Dora at all. What else are you leaving out? Why did Taz tell me about a curse? He wouldn't finish the story and now you won't either."

"Cassie, please. This isn't a normal situation. I'm just barely keeping the balance here. I don't know why Evan did what he did, but it's better if we leave him out of this. Either way, the police get the right guy. It's tied up in a water-tight bow. There's a bartender with a motive. A doctor living a secret life with a hundred wigs, an apartment nobody knew about. She came up to the city and hung out with the lowlife on South Jefferson. Dora doesn't deserve this ending but it was the best I could do, given the situation."

Danny crosses his arms, looks off to the side, up at the ceiling.

A bright light rushes at me, and I blink it away. It comes back and I blink again. Again and again, until it's not very bright and hardly a light at all. I want to be furious, except how can I be from all the way at the bottom of the pile—me and my bad decisions with everyone else on top cleaning up my messes, undoing all that I've made terrible. The rest is kids at a cabin, a summer a long time ago, blue skies and forests and sex. Danny loved Dora, even if he tells me he didn't. Evan loved Dora but she didn't love him. She jumped off the roof.

No.

Lee pushed her.

Do I believe this? That Lee could push someone off a roof, that he could shoot into darkness, knowing that a living person was inside of it? And then a couple of days later hand me a drink at the Silver Whistle like nothing had happened?

"And what if the police come and talk to me again? Do I pretend you never told me any of this?"

Danny nods and closes his eyes, as if my question makes him weary. "I value honesty; you know this, Cas. But it's too late now. This is the story we have to stick with. But I don't want you to worry. Why would the police need to talk to you?"

"Because they're not idiots."

He puts his hands on my shoulders and waits for my eyes to find his. "You don't need to worry about this, Cas. I fixed everything."

"If they find out Evan and Dora were dating it's all going to come apart."

"Shhh. Listen. Dating's not even the right word for what it was. It's fine. It's all worked out. The police want to close cases. This is a gift. Promise me you'll stop worrying."

As he pulls my face into his chest, I try to think of a couple embracing, the way they look in profile as her cheek hits a button on his shirt and his arms cross over her shoulder blades. I make room for this singular thought, which I consider giving some fancy name like "living in the moment," and wonder if my mother did the same that morning after my dad swung a dictionary in the name of being fearless and we watched her drop to her knees. That morning when we all sat down and ate breakfast together and the makeup almost covered her bruise but not quite, and my mother said she needed to buy groceries and my dad said he could take her—he had to go to the hardware store anyway for more caulk—and I watched the way they rested their hands on the table in between sips of coffee, lonely fingers finding others to touch.

Evan appears, in a tan corduroy blazer and crisp, dark jeans.

He and Danny hug. They linger there, like survivors of some war who are thankful for one another's lives.

Evan turns to me, his eyes misted over with affection. "Oh, Cas. I'm so glad we're finally *here*. I'm so glad we could get this far."

"I wish one of you would have told me sooner. We could have been here weeks ago."

He closes his eyes, shakes his head, draws me in for a smothering embrace. He smells different. A new deodorant or aftershave. Piece by piece, he's remodeling. "We had to let things unfold, aerate, settle. I know you get this."

When he steps back, the mistiness has cleared. No weeping today. Instead, he smooths back his hair and straightens his jacket.

I imagine a table set for dinner. The plates are brown, variations on stone, with tan napkins folded up next to them, matching forks and knives. Empty glasses. Nice but not too nice. Danny and me with all our pieces assembled at last. Somewhere beneath us, the ground trembles in the same way it always has: the ceaseless reshaping of rocks as the earth shifts its bones, underground caverns that I've never known about, collapsing, stories deep.

"Cas, I just want you to know. About that bartender..."

I turn away.

"No, listen to me. Not everyone is a good judge of character, not all the time. You picked the worst one, and I know that hurts, but you have to remember that you also picked the best one. He's the one who's still here."

*I've always wanted to live in a farmhouse. Drink water that I knew was clean. What about one of those houses built into a hill? Or is that too silly?*

I should have known.

"In an average life," Evan continues, "the laws of averages apply. This is the truth."

I should have known I should have known I should have known.

Danny steps forward. He looks nervous, like he did the night he proposed. He takes my hands in the same way he did then, shaking them from side to side the tiniest bit before he begins speaking. "I forgive you."

I picture the brown place setting again. The plates and bowls that from far away look solid, but up close they're sprinkled with tiny flecks of color. This is good. It's exactly what I want.

Evan rests a hand on Danny's shoulder but says nothing.

"You bought me an island," I say.

Danny laughs; the sound radiates off of him in waves.

"Not yet," says Danny, and Evan laughs too.

Taped to the wall, past Danny's head and off to the left, are the kids' pictures. The Wall of Dreams. We need to start now. Save up the money, try harder, work to earn happiness. Finally, I get it. Dora's not here. Dora's not here! We're standing together, our feet planted for balance, our hearts open and ready for more.

Everything is fixed. In the morning, Danny will go to the police and tell them he has his voice back, his memories, all of it. He'll make a statement about what happened on the roof. A version of events that matches what Lee's roommate told them. Case closed. Right?

Dora is gone. Lee is gone. It's just us again. Evan has a job for Danny; a speaking engagement that pays five hundred dollars. The first of many, he assures us.

So what if Evan has dragged Danny into his bullshit pyramid scheme?

So what if we've all just decided to lie to the police?

So what if Evan keeps preaching about finding our truths, when it's obvious there are still a million secrets Danny is keeping from me?

So what?

# Part II

# CHAPTER 21

## (DANNY AND CURT)

The cabin slept six. It was off in the middle of nowhere, at the end of a long dirt road that tended to wash out in the spring. You needed a truck with good clearance to get up there, so Danny rented the one with the fattest tires he could find and brought a lot of cash for gas. It was a good hundred and fifty miles to pick up Curt, and then an even longer drive up to the cabin.

"I'll pay you back," Curt promised, "when I work something out."

It had been four years, already, of trying to work something out, and they both knew that four years could easily turn into forty, and at that point how likely was it that Curt would even still be alive? At that point what would any of this matter?

But you had to try. You had to do what you could.

In the truck, they barely talked. Curt's hands were shoved into his sweatshirt pockets, and after a while Danny wondered what was wrong with them, what his brother might be holding that he didn't want Danny to see. The longer they drove, the more it burned him, all that was lacking between them. No hands, no trust; Curt must have known this. But whenever Danny looked over, ready to stitch together the void with the right couple of words, he saw a dirty sweatshirt with a rigid body inside, a man who sat without occupying his seat, eyes wide and focused on nothing but road. Danny settled on the wrong couple of words.

"So, how long were you living there? In that tent?"

"It was okay. I don't really want to talk about it."

"This place is nicer at least. It has a wood-burning stove."

Curt chuckled to himself for no reason that Danny could fathom.

"I move around."

"Mom wonders if you're dead."

"She wishes I was."

"No."

"Fuck her."

"Okay. Yeah, I get it."

More silence. The miles passed. Danny caught himself remembering that night with their father, Curt's wild eyes and shaking hands and the heat that rose from his body. He'd handed Danny his driver's license and instructed him to tell everyone he was headed west, to Reno or Sacramento or Danny could pick some other city if he felt like it. Then he'd packed a duffle bag and taken off, leaving Danny confused, still holding the license, not sure what to do next. Danny remembered creeping down to the basement and seeing his father slumped into an unconscious heap next to the washing machine, then going back upstairs, sliding the license between the pages of a school textbook, giving Curt a twenty-minute head start, and calling 911.

They found Curt's car a week later, three hundred miles to the north, burned up and pushed into a small lake. But they didn't find Curt. Nobody heard from him. He was gone for months, for years. They convinced Danny that his disappearance was permanent, which he'd believed until the day a letter arrived for him in the mail.

I'm sorry about what happened, about how I left things. Could you call me? I need help.

Danny went over the list of instructions at least ten times: the stove, the tool shed, the lanterns, the creek and the water buckets, the importance of the water purifier. Curt couldn't tell whether he was nervous or distracted. He couldn't tell much anymore. His surroundings and the people inside them blended and blurred together. Yes, he'd managed to lose his glasses, but that was only part of the problem. It was his brain, the whole of it. Once his head was right, once everything was *clean* again, he'd regain his focus. It was a longer process, though, than he'd anticipated. In fact, he was dirtier now than he'd ever been. His hands looked like they'd been petrified and pulled out of the earth, and he couldn't stand to look at them. Sometimes he dreamed of dipping them in a bucket full of acid to strip away the top layers of skin and start over.

Curt wanted to explain why he'd run away, but at the same time what was the point? Instead, he listened politely as Danny talked. He tried to be thankful, to remember what thankful people said. He felt his mind running in circles as he considered the words *thankful* and *grateful*, whether they meant the same thing or were slightly different. Which one would be better to use now? Thankful? Grateful? He didn't have anyone to ask, any means of looking it up. In the end, neither meant anything. They fell in the heap with all the other useless words he'd considered trying out over the last twenty-four hours.

"You won't get any phone reception up here," Danny was explaining. "I won't be able to check on you, but I'll come see you. I'll bring you more food when I can. Give me a list of what you want."

The truth was, it didn't matter what he ate, where he slept, but he wrote down a list to be nice. Things he thought someone might want to eat.

All he needed was a warm and quiet place, a bed to lie in where he could finally work things out, figure out what to do next. A week of undisturbed thinking, when he wouldn't have to worry about being found or stabbed or swallowed up by the earth, about giving up and letting the oblivion take over. A cabin in the middle of nowhere sounded nice. It was the stuff of movies.

Brotherly love brotherly love brotherly love. Was it real, or just an expression? They'd been brothers, but it seemed like probably they weren't anymore. Why would Curt feel this way? Danny was helping him, being generous, and he couldn't manage to be grateful. Thankful. Brotherly love.

"I don't think anyone will come here for a while. When we left a couple days ago, Dora told me she was closing it up for the summer. Nobody else in her family uses it much anymore. But if someone does come, hmm, maybe we should pick a spot in the woods—"

"It's fine. I'll be fine."

"But I don't want you to—"

"Stop worrying about it. This is great." *This is greatful. I'm grateful*. It still wasn't quite right.

Danny hesitated next to the truck. It was starting to get dark and he had a long drive home and then work in the morning. He probably wouldn't get much sleep. Curt remembered when they were kids, the way he woke up sometimes and saw the bedroom door cracked open and knew that Danny was up and wandering around the house. When he finally slid back into the room, he did it so quietly you could hardly tell he was there. He wanted to ask Danny about it now, whether it had been sleepwalking or something else, but it wasn't the time. It would never, probably, be the time.

Danny sighed. "I'll try to come back next weekend. I can't promise."

"You already brought me a ton of food. I don't need anything else."

"Maybe in a couple weeks. Next month for sure. It shouldn't get cold for a while."

"If I'm not here don't worry about me."

Danny drove away without saying anything more, but Curt understood that he understood, and maybe that was what brotherly love was once you chipped away at it and reduced it down to its core. He'd mull this over for the next few days, work it out along with all the rest there was to be worked out. A mental housekeeping. Had he finally earned this?

Curt went back into the cabin and walked through each room, looking in closets and cupboards and the medicine cabinet, behind furniture, under the mattresses, inside the refrigerator that someone had lugged all the way up there even though there was no electricity to run it. He put away the bags of food that Danny had brought. Some of it in the kitchen cupboards and pantry, but some of it in the closets upstairs, under extra blankets. The packages that could be chewed through by mice he put in the refrigerator or the plastic bins. Then he folded up the empty paper bags and walked outside and set them next to the fire pit.

He circled the cabin four or five times, tracing out a slightly larger radius on each circuit, until he was well into the woods. He tried out the key to the shed that Danny had shown him, then shined a flashlight inside, taking inventory. Next to the shed was a small stack of firewood that wouldn't last long; no more than a few days.

He'd forgotten to ask Danny about the girl whose family owned the cabin. He couldn't remember her name, and he didn't really care, but it seemed like something a person should ask. *What did you do up here with your friends?* He saw the evidence: bottle caps lying in the dirt, a pair of swim trunks spread over a tree branch, a headlamp sitting on the porch rail. While Curt was huddled up in a damp sleeping bag, Danny was partying with his friends, getting up whenever he felt like it, taking naps in the sunshine. Curt felt twinges, a painful stabbing that was whatever the opposite of brotherly love was. He swatted it away, picking up the bottle caps and the swim trunks and tossing them into a garbage bag. Then he followed a well-worn path into the woods and looked around. The light was getting dim, but Curt could tell that the landscape didn't look right. There was a low mound of bare dirt that had recently been packed down, and next to it, like a mangled tombstone, a rock covered in smears of what may or may not have been blood. Curt pictured some drunken forest rite and felt twinges again. The anger he was okay with, but the jealousy he fought against as fiercely as he knew how until it was gone, reduced to a muffled cry deep at the bottom of a hole. Curt stared again at the stained rock. In the morning he'd come back and sort it all out.

Curt built a fire and filled a large pot with water. While he waited for it to heat up, he stripped off his clothes and fed them, piece by piece, into the fire, watching the flames crackle and send blue smoke into the sky. Danny had bought him new clothes, shampoo, shaving cream and a razor. Danny had done everything for him. In the old days, Curt might have known how to thank him, but then again he never would have needed the help. He back-tracked as far as he could, trying to remember their last conversation, the last place they had gone together. But the scene he ended on was one in which his mom stood in front of him with her hands on her hips, telling him that he was missing a heartbeat or two. Slowly, the water became warm. Curt dipped a washcloth into the pot, then rubbed a bar of soap on it until it was covered in suds, and brought it to his face.

# CHAPTER 22
## (ANTON AND CURT)

The problem was that Anton didn't have a plan.

There had been a plan, once, but it was Emmaline's plan and now she was dead. He'd watched her plummeting toward the ground, but instead of pulling her rip cord, she'd closed her eyes and continued to fall.

He'd called out to her, but his voice had been erased by the wind. He'd considered following her headlong into the earth, but released his parachute at the last second instead, skittering past some tree branches before slamming into the ground, the parachute tangling in the canopy above him.

He'd expected Emmaline to find him. If anyone could have cheated death, it would have been her. He tried shouting her name, but discovered he'd lost the ability to open his mouth, to make sounds at all. For a long while after impact, he felt his body continue to spin. He couldn't remember where Emmaline had landed, which direction the helicopter had come from, where the supplies would be relative to his current location.

Eventually, the sensation of movement ceased. In the still forest, Anton focused on the smell of leaf litter, the insect frass that fell like irregular raindrops, the chipping, crackling sound of nearby animal movement that reminded him of the gerbils he'd had as a kid. This was it—the peace that he and Emmaline had been searching for. They'd found it. Only now…

There were choices to make, decisions about what would happen next.

For a while, the parachute had been stuck, billowing out and then settling. Billowing and settling, billowing and settling, before finally coming to rest on top of him. He was aware of time passing, the need to find Emmaline intensifying with each lost hour.

His body, it seemed, had been shattered in the fall. Only molecular memory held it together. If he sat up, he would collapse into a pile of once-human pieces. The smarter choice was to close his eyes again and hope that it wouldn't be for the last time. He'd dreamt of heat, of fever, of races run on four legs. He'd thought he'd heard voices, people coming for him, the sound of footfall, the sound of confusion.

Night fell. The parachute grew damp with condensation. Erasure or recovery—those seemed like the only two options. He dreamed of wild animals pulling at the parachute with their teeth, planted forelegs and shaking heads, of holding on and fighting back for it: his only blanket. Day eventually came, and he would have been content to let it pass away again into nightfall if not for the intensity with which he began to desire something to drink.

Dehydration. Of course.

He'd managed to force himself onto two legs, and after a wobbly several minutes he'd staggered off, wrapped in the parachute, uncertain where Emmaline might be, where the supplies might have landed. He'd tried again to call her, but her name emerged from his mouth as little more than a rough-edged whisper. He waited, expecting her. Any minute, she would appear to him, in her angel form, in her bird form, a majestic being of power and light.

He called her name again. No answer.

Eventually he'd found her. No miracles had occurred, but as he considered the tragedy of her body, she seemed like a miracle nonetheless. Her arms were open, the tusk nowhere to be found. Had she discovered a way to take it with her into the afterlife, to reunite it with its former owner? This he could imagine: Emmaline resting among the elephants in a better world, one without misery. Hadn't it been foolish to believe they could change this one? Wasn't it far beyond hope already?

Anton set up a tent and camped out, like they'd planned. He ate tasteless packets of food, and considered setting a snare trap like

they'd been taught in their survival class, but the thought of killing and skinning an animal made his stomach turn. What was the
plan now? How long would he stay there with Emmaline's body so
close? He'd wrapped it up tightly in the parachute. Eventually, he
would have to bury it.

You could see the cabin on the aerial imagery. They'd known it
was there and thought that if they were lucky it would be empty.
Anton wasn't certain why he chose the cabin instead of heading
back to civilization. Instinct, perhaps. The pain he felt was other-
worldly. It came from sources and in forms that he couldn't identify.
Legions of internal injuries, starting with his heart and radiating
outwards from there. Probably he needed a hospital, but it seemed
like if he kept walking all the parts that had been jostled and bruised
by the fall would settle back into place and begin to heal.

Hours later, when Anton reached the cabin, he set down his pack
and stared at the case of beer on the porch, wondering if it was real.
He dug his fingernails into his palms, thinking of the childhood friend
who had dared him to do this once, how surprised he'd been by how
difficult it was to cut through the skin, and remembering the thrill
when he'd succeeded, smearing the blood around his palm with a fin-
gertip before wiping it on his pants.

Anton stared at the case of beer. Real or imagined? He walked
over and reached out for it, placed a hand on top of it.

"You can have one if you want. I think they're warm, though."

Anton spun around. The man standing in front of him was real:
life size, his eyes the color of mud and honey, somehow light and
dark all at once. He wore a shirt with sleeves that were a little too
short on him and held a wrench in one hand.

"I'm lost." Anton's hands were shaking. "I mean, I have a GPS,
but...Emmaline is dead."

The man set down the wrench. "Are you hungry?"

Curt had spent a couple days making a list of everything he wanted to work through in his head. He'd thought it would be a short list, but it became a long one and he decided to just keep going until he felt like it was complete. It had hurt his hands to write, and there were words he couldn't remember how to spell, although he wasn't certain he'd ever been much of a speller. School had happened so long ago, and he'd always been preoccupied there, making plans about which girl to ask out next instead of worrying about passing American History. Already, the list was too long to be useful, but there would be time to clean it up, get it right. In the meantime, there were other tasks that required his attention. Like digging up that fresh patch of earth in the woods to see what was buried there.

The tusk wasn't what he'd been expecting, but without any deliberation, he'd pulled it from the soil and wiped it off, then brought it back to the cabin and polished it, for a long while, with a T-shirt. He might have spent more time puzzling over its origin and the circumstances surrounding its burial, but Curt's brain wasn't really equipped for speculation. Ever since that afternoon with his father he'd been a man who reacted first and deliberated later, and now the way his brain was telling him to react was by wrapping the tusk in a towel and hiding it at the bottom of his backpack.

Later, the injured man wasn't what Curt was expecting either. The strange way he held his arms away from his body, as if he didn't understand that they were attached to him. The way he started sentences but didn't finish them. The way he spoke of the dead woman. Curt had been through his own shock, of course. He could almost remember how it went, the way days passed without fastening themselves to memory and the heat of instinct that took over when rationality and common sense left. This man was wild-eyed, unable to find the words to communicate what had happened to him.

So Curt decided to remain calm and wait, see where it would lead.

In time, Curt learned the man's name. He learned who Emmaline was and how she had died, listened to Anton's description of her defeated smile before she jumped, the moment when he knew that something was wrong. They were supposed to jump together,

Anton insisted. That was the plan.

Clearly, Anton was hurt. The way he winced and sometimes clutched his side. Broken ribs, maybe, and who knew what other internal damage. He complained that his spine wasn't straight, and wondered aloud if the vertebrae were starting to peel apart. Curt had seen a lot of guys in bad shape, though, and this one certainly wasn't the worst.

Anton spoke in a low, hoarse voice, his gaze always turned toward the floor. He went on about Emmaline's patient brown eyes, the kindness in her heart, the way she liked a little bit of danger in her life, which was why people sometimes compared her to her father, a man she hated, a thrill seeker who stole from the earth in the name of entertainment.

"She was so complex, so wonderful, but her father treated her like a possession. He wanted to marry her off, collect a worthy son-in-law. She had hundreds of promising suitors, but she picked me. I didn't get it; I never have. And now, after seeing...after watching her...I don't know. What if I wasn't anyone to her? What if she had some bigger plan that I missed and now it's too late because...

"Is it okay if I lie down on the couch for a while? Maybe if I rest for a few minutes it won't hurt as much."

Curt stood up. "It doesn't bother me." He went outside and sat on the porch, looked out at the woods and wondered what it would be like to live in the wilderness forever. Were there people already doing this? It seemed possible. Living and dying without anyone realizing. It didn't seem so bad.

The man staying in the cabin was generous—sharing his food and giving up his couch and listening whenever Anton wanted to talk. But there was a coolness about him that suggested he preferred solitude. He didn't say much. All Anton could get out of him was that he hadn't been staying there long, that the cabin belonged to a friend, and that he'd come up for a while to get his head together. His life back home was transitional, he said, although he failed to mention where back home was, what he was transitioning from or to.

Anton found himself talking too much, revealing too many details to a stranger. He would need to learn how to stay quiet, to stop saying her name. Once Randall Kincaid received the first few letters, he would start asking questions. He would start looking. Anton had assured Emmaline that her plan was magnificent. They would pretend they'd gone to Africa to embark on a life of activism. Emmaline's disappearance would grab the media's attention, which she would use to single-handedly shut down illegal elephant poaching. Anton was certain she could.

Dear Dad,

Every night I hear screams in my sleep. I wake up wondering about a horrible past that I'm unable to remember. Was it something you did, when I was younger? Did I have a different mother? Did I watch you kill her? The possibilities seem without limit. I can imagine them so vividly that they feel like real memories.

Anton imagined the look on Randall Kincaid's face when he read this, the clenching of his gut like he'd just been punched. His favorite daughter let loose in the wilds of Africa to make amends on his behalf. It had been so poetic.

Was it a brother or sister, unsuspecting and trusting? Could you have done this, if it felt necessary to you? I can imagine it just as easily.

*The thing is that I don't really believe in some terrible event that happened a long time ago. The screams are just there, in my head. You always like to say that we're the same, so I guess you hear the screams too. It would explain so much.*

As Anton lay on the couch and watched the room turn dusk-gray, he began to see the stupidity of Emmaline's plan. She was smarter than that. It had never been her intention to follow through.

*Do you really think that hearing more screams will cover up the ones that are already there? I don't think this is true. I think the only way to find silence is to jump straight into it.*

Anton's eyes burned. He couldn't remember it hurting this much to cry. How could he not have seen what Emmaline was going to do? She'd given him copies of the letters to bring with him, just in case. If he dug them out of his backpack and read through them again, would he discover more clues?

The idea had been that they would hide out in the woods long enough for Randall Kincaid to discover there was no record of his daughter traveling overseas. Likely, Randall would track down that woman in Tanzania they'd hired to send the letters, who would convince him of the truth: that she'd accepted a job from a stranger because it was easy pay, that she knew nothing of Emmaline's whereabouts. After that, the plan grew fuzzy. Eventually they'd hike out of the woods and let themselves be found. Cable news networks would interview them and Emmaline would use the spotlight to make her case, challenge her father to use his wealth and influence for good. Conservation. Justice. Humanity. Somehow, Emmaline would accomplish this. But now Anton wondered why they hadn't just gone to Africa to work with the organizations that were already fighting for these causes. Unless that part was never the point?

Listening wasn't difficult. Eventually, he would get tired of it, but for now hearing Anton talk about his girlfriend wasn't going to interfere much with Curt's goal of staying in one place for a while and doing nothing.

"She had plans, outlandish ideas that I was in love with. She wanted to go into space and find Earth's twin, then keep its discovery a secret. No industrial revolution, this time. No genocide. No plastic. She wanted to build a modern day Noah's ark, a covered, protected biome with its own air source, its own water source. She wanted to love everyone, almost as much as she wanted to kill everyone, to wipe the scourge of humankind off the earth."

Anton stared down at the empty metal cup he was holding as if he didn't understand how it had come to be there, then winced and closed his eyes. Curt knew this, the way it worked. The dull pain of forgetting and the sharp pain of remembering, followed by the crushing guilt of allowing yourself to forget.

"We can't leave the body there, right?"

Answers never came to Curt quickly. He needed time to consider the options. *Could* they leave the body there? Well certainly they could, but maybe that wasn't what Anton was asking.

"I don't know what to do," Anton said. "I can't go anywhere and pretend that...."

"They'll be looking for me too. Her father. If I go back and tell him that she's...I mean, how does that work? Is there a way for this to happen without everyone blaming me for Emmaline's death?"

Curt considered this carefully. "So what you're saying is you want to leave her there."

"I'm not sure if I'm saying that, no."

"You don't report the body?"

"Does it help anyone if we do?"

Curt knew it probably did, but he didn't answer. He, himself, wasn't in the business of reporting bodies, after all.

Anton began to weep. "She had the tusk with her, in her hands. I don't see why you would jump holding an object that weighs ten pounds, but she insisted. Afterward, I searched all over for it. I think I searched...it's hard to say. Maybe we could go back there together? I think I could get us there with my GPS. Do we...could we bury her? Out here, where she probably wanted to be, and then call it good?"

*A tusk*, thought Curt. *Interesting*.

# CHAPTER 23
## (CASSIE)

"The explosion happens first," says Danny. He's standing at the lectern, neat and handsome in a suit that I helped him pick out. I don't know where he got the money. I never know where it comes from, where it goes when it leaves.

"There's a burst of white that tears the color from your brain and flattens your surroundings into paper. You're standing inside an overexposed photograph, balancing in the aftermath, weightless, crackling, crumbling into human confetti. You're left with shadows, gradations of black."

Evan must have written this for him. These aren't Danny's words.

"The white is loud, but the black that follows it is flushed of sound. It feels like you've just been shot into space and this is the first truly frightening thing that has ever happened to you. Pure darkness. The intolerable quiet that makes you pray for colors to return."

We're not Stand in Front of an Audience and Tell Stories About Ourselves People.

We weren't this before, but now we are.

"The explosion happens first and then you wait. In the aftermath, you wonder whether anyone has died."

The people in the room are attentive and curious. Their chins are raised, their mouths slightly open, their eyes focused, concentrating on the words. Each speaker has been assigned a chapter of the *Secret Path to Joy*. Danny's is Commitment. Evan's is Self-Adjustment. They each earn five hundred dollars for this—turning a list of bullet points into a compelling talk—with the potential to earn more if they are picked to speak at the bigger conferences.

I add it up and don't see where a new suit comes from, but Evan has one too. A new jacket, anyway, startlingly purple-blue and shining like gasoline in a puddle.

Danny gives his talk like every sentence is one last thought he just happened to remember. *Oh, by the way, I was on a roof, left for dead, but then I came back. I saw my life ending but decided not to let it.* I don't even know if this is true. He's never mentioned seeing his life ending. I listen to him talk about how he had no memories, no voice, nothing to lead him out of the darkness, but he came back anyway, one agonizing step at a time. He uses words like *determination* and *fraught* and *resurrection*.

Danny goes on about finding himself, about finding me again, about a marriage that had dwindled down to nothing more than a threadbare swatch of fabric. He talks about wind, garbage, bruises, makes connections I don't quite follow. But then again I haven't read the book. What do I know?

"My wife tells me that after the accident we met on a beach in her dreams. While she slept, we talked in ways we never had before. What a gift, right? My dreams were darkness and hers were light, and somehow because of this we managed to find each other again. We forced open all the windows that had been painted shut and let the fresh air in. We made a commitment to our shared happy ending."

My legs feel numb, my arms, all the parts in between. A man standing next to me nods his head. His arms are crossed and his neck is tilted to the side. He purses his lips and starts moving his mouth. Maybe he has a wife at home who is slipping away. He's here for her, to better himself so that he can be better for her. It doesn't matter. As I watch his head, nodding away, I want to smack him. Why am I here, listening to this?

"I thought I was dead and my voice went away, but somehow I spoke to my wife. Think about this for a minute; how incredible it is."

He pauses, for what should seem like too long but is somehow just long enough.

"Here's the secret, the reason you all came here. It's as simple as this: make a commitment to a happy ending. Follow your path to joy. Even if you can't find it right away, know that it's there, and work your way toward it. *Trust* its existence and don't stop until you find it. It sounds simple, but you'd be surprised how many people give up within a month or two. I've never understood it, quitting before you even begin, refusing to believe in future possibility because of past disappointment. But let me tell you what I learned all those months when I couldn't talk, when I couldn't remember what happened to me. The path leading up to now doesn't matter. What matters is the path forward."

The applause builds slowly and then tapers off again, into expectant silence. Oh God. How did we become this?

"I'd like to talk about myself for a little while, to give you some context. When I was fourteen, my father became an addict. Pain killers. None of us saw it coming. He was in an accident, the doctors prescribed the typical round of opioids for him, and within a few days it was the start of the end. Just like that, without any warning. A switch flipping.

"In less than a year, my father was dead, and my brother was on the run. We knew it was self-defense and probably an accident. We understood this. My brother was trying to save himself from a desperate animal who had begun to prey on his own family, his children. My father would sneak into our bedroom and look through our belongings, take our cash, whatever he could sell. In the end he didn't even look like my father anymore. The shell was there, but everything else..."

The room is silent as Danny trails off.

"I'm thirty-five years old now. My brother has been gone for twenty years."

A woman near me gasps and covers her mouth with her hand, shakes her head.

"I don't know whether he's still alive. But at the same time, why would I give up on him? What good does this do me? So I place him in multiple locations along my path to joy. I give myself the *opportunity* to look for him and find him as I move forward, but I don't dwell on the process. I don't dwell on *his* path or where he's been and how things will be if we ever...*when* I find him again. I just see his face. I imagine embracing him, letting him know that the family forgives him, that there is nothing to forgive, that the path forward is the only path."

He's telling the nodding strangers details he's never told me. Later, if I ask him to talk about it, he'll pull me close and press his face into my hair and tell me that he can't. The speeches are his job but they exhaust him emotionally. When the day ends he wants to come home and retreat to a safe space, one where silence is allowed and appreciated. This is me: Danny's safe space.

There's a strange taste in my mouth, a vaguely metallic sensation. What are they piping into the room through the vents? You never know. The way things are orchestrated. And yet I'm standing here. Somehow, this is where I ended up.

We visit Taz in the hospital. He's in his final days now. Hours. It's hard to say. Danny and Evan sit by his side and tell stories. They fill in each other's blanks so seamlessly that you wonder if it's rehearsed. Whenever one of them stops talking, the other one picks up the thread.

"We were making those drinks, with vodka and—I don't know what it was. Kool Aid or something."

"Dora and Suzie Q kept adding food coloring to everything. Do you remember that? All of our tongues were purple."

"They took all those pictures, but I never saw any of them later."

"Taz had pictures, I think. From Katy's camera."

They turn to look at Taz, at the unimposing shape of his body on the bed. His eyes are closed, and behind them he's stepping backwards, into the unknown. I think of a thin membrane, a drip in an empty room, smallness inside largeness, receding and receding and receding.

"The thing is even if we knew how it would all turn out, I don't think we would have done anything different that week."

"No. Why would we? Every idea we had was perfect. Do you remember?" Evan directs the question at Taz's still form. "You and Katy made up that card game. Find the Nines."

"Find the Nines. The rules kept changing. Why was it so funny? I don't think I've laughed that hard since."

"Dora knew the words to every song."

"Dora was in love with everything."

"It seemed like it. She wanted to be."

Their voices are different, but they sound the same. The

inflections, the high points and low points. The way they pause and breathe and hang in the air and somehow make you hang there with them, anticipating the next word. The soft but confident voices of men who belong.

Evan slides his hand under Taz's and gently lifts it off the bed. He rubs his finger along the faded patch of scar tissue. Danny looks at me. Our eyes meet. We exchange tiny smiles of acknowledgement. We're not infinite. We're receding too. Our greatest moments have already happened, even though Danny tells me the opposite every night before we go to sleep. The best parts are coming, he says; it's all about patience. Life is this promise.

Evan holds Taz's hand like he's estimating its weight. "I never understood why you did this, with the rock."

"He told me it was to remind himself."

"Of what?"

Danny shrugs. He tilts his head toward me and smiles, as if to say, *we made it. It's too late for a deathbed confession from Taz.*

I look away, protecting my own secret: a few weeks ago, Taz already confessed. I think he confessed. I'm not sure to what.

After Dora's death, Taz moved into an apartment in town. Danny and Evan were confused about why he was there, why he would sell the house he once claimed he could never leave and go to a random city to die. Danny said Taz had always been unpredictable; he'd always had a few cards up his sleeve. Evan would glance over at me and then back at Danny, concern consuming his face. They'd wait until I was distracted with the kids, until I'd left the room, and then later I'd find them whispering, Evan with an arm on Danny's shoulder, filling his ears with supportive words.

We started visiting. Danny and Evan would go over and play cards. I guess this was what they thought they were supposed to do. But you could tell. I mean you would have to be stupid not to see it. The glances, the low voices in dark rooms. They were worried.

There was a woman taking care of him who introduced herself as Miss Sherril. Taz called her his nurse, but she seemed more like a girlfriend, the way she touched him, the tenderness in her face,

the way her voice always sounded a bit like a lullaby. I didn't understand it, but it didn't seem like a situation you would need to
understand. She was beautiful. Her nails were perfect. Her hands.
The door always made a tidy click when she walked through it and
closed it behind her. They laughed quietly together, at things that
didn't seem like jokes.

During one of our visits, Taz said there was a book he wanted me
to read. It was a strange request, but I guess the sick are allowed,
so I followed him to an extra bedroom, thinking about that first
cold night we met. His fisherman's outfit. A conversation I couldn't
quite remember. The bedroom walls were lined in bookshelves, the
books arranged by color. The only piece of furniture was an over-
sized chair with soft cushions, next to a lamp, near the center of
the room.

"As you can imagine," he explained, "I read a lot these days. I
have a list."

"How many..."

"Are left? It's okay. You can ask."

I shook my head, reached out for a yellow-spined book, flipped
through its pages.

"Listen," Taz said. "Danny is decent."

"Of course he is."

"I even knew it back then. Evan, on the other hand..." he
shrugged.

"They both mean well," I said. "They do what they think is right."

Taz closed his eyes and placed a hand on his forehead. I wanted
to be the kind of person who could comfort a dying man.

"You still don't know," he said, finally.

"No." Whatever it was, the answer couldn't be yes.

"I get it, though. Why he wouldn't tell you. It's hard to come to
terms with it. I've had fifteen years, more or less." He rested a hand
on my arm. "But the thing is. Like I was saying, Danny is decent.
Sometimes you don't know early on. Sometimes it takes a while to
settle in."

His breaths were shallow. I thought maybe it was a struggle for
him to speak and that if I was decent myself I would make him
stop. I'd fill in the rest for him, say something lively and witty to
make us both laugh, then lead him away, back to the living room.

"I believe in extenuating circumstances," Taz continued. "Extraordinary circumstances. It would be hypocritical if I didn't. So I think what you need to do, Cassie, is just go with whatever Danny says. I think you'll be fine."

I nodded, not sure what he was saying. "Okay."

"I'm not trying to drag you into anything. Please believe me."

"Okay."

"Danny promised me he'd figure out a way to make everything right again. This is what he does, right? Figure things out?"

Was this true? I couldn't decide.

"I'll make sure he does."

"No, it's not that." His hand slid off my arm and he shuffled toward the chair, let his body drop onto the cushioned seat. I watched him grimace and rest his head. His breathing softened and he seemed to fade into sleep. When he spoke again, his voice was a murmur.

"Sometimes I can't remember. Too many versions going around in my head. They collide and split apart. Some of them I remember from dreams. I've had so many dreams. In the ones where I'm a hero, I wake up disappointed in myself, but even when I'm not the hero I wake up just as disappointed. Lately I've been giving myself more leeway. Being decent—it takes a while to settle in sometimes. Did I say that already?"

I cleared my throat. "Yes, you did."

He seemed to hear me and not hear me. "I don't want to drag you into this, but I need to tell someone. Later, maybe, you'll understand."

I nodded, even though he couldn't see me. "What is it?"

"We only ever saw one of them. The woman."

Was this even meant for me? I imagined a face behind his closed eyelids, a person who wasn't me that he'd summoned near to listen.

"We told everyone we found both bodies but we didn't. I mean, we saw the one and just assumed...at the time we couldn't think what to do. But you don't use logic. The adrenaline comes in, along with all these bizarre feelings and urges. Before I knew what was happening, Katy was running away. She was lifting that thing off the ground and running with super-human speed, unburdened by the extra weight in her arms. Nothing was normal. Nothing was the way we would have done it if it was all laid out on paper and we had time to think about it.

"I don't understand how the brain works. It seemed logical at the time. Either the second person was already dead or they weren't. And if not dead then alive and this was somehow nothing to worry about. Either way, it was okay to pretend we'd never been there.

"Later we looked at the news, searched the Web. We wanted proof that everything had worked itself out, but we never found it. After a while, you know, the grim possibilities are all that's left. We had to consider them. What if the second person had been alive but injured? What if they needed our help?"

I didn't understand any of it. He sounded like a person trapped on the edge of consciousness, his brain tortured by chemicals and haunted by sickbed dreams.

"It was up to us to do something. We finally realized this, but when we went back for the tusk, it wasn't there. I swear this is true. It was gone. And what's more, the *body* wasn't there anymore. I don't know how to explain this. I've tried. Is the woman a ghost or is she not a ghost? Is she the one who's been killing all of us? Was she never dead to begin with? Did we imagine the whole thing?"

His breath was shallow and quick, his eyelids nearly translucent. Did he say tusk? Body? Ghost? Time passed. Too much time. I glanced at the doorway, wondering if it would be better to leave.

"He might have pushed her. I don't know if Evan even..."

As he trailed off, I heard Evan's voice erupting from the living room. Danny's laughter. At last Miss Sherril appeared. She smiled at Taz's sleeping figure, kneeled in front of him, checked his pulse, rearranged his arms, covered him with a blanket. "My sleeping prince," she said, and kissed him on the forehead.

When they moved Taz to the hospital, Miss Sherril disappeared. As Danny and Evan tell their bedside stories, I wonder what new tragedy she's moved on to, what new prince. I stand back, looking at Taz's graying face, imagining what dream he might be having now, hoping it's one where he's the hero. His confession sticks with me, even though I've been trying to release it, willing it to grow wings and flutter away.

*He might have pushed her.*

In the car on the way home, Danny smiles. He pats my leg, looks up at my face.

"I know it's hard," he says. It's a drive that usually makes him impatient, but tonight Danny takes his time. He stops for a jay-walker, slows down at two yellow lights, hums quietly the whole way home.

*Is the woman a ghost or is she not a ghost? Is she the one who's been killing all of us?*

Would Danny know what this means? Would he tell me if he did?

On a Wednesday after the bakery closes, I go to the Silver Whistle for the first time in months. I half expect to see it boarded up and empty, but when I arrive it's unchanged. The same neon signs. The same cars. The same dirty garbage can with a cracked red lid.

I pull into a parking spot and send a text to Cherie and Lori, Annette and Julia.

> Help! At the Silver Whistle. Come save me.

These days, Danny likes to point out how hectic life is, how good it feels after all those months of sitting still after the accident, when time slowed down and the world was quiet but it felt like life was passing him by. Now he's in the thick of it. Almost daily, he reminds me of this. We've become In The Thick of it People. We're attentive to ourselves and our family, we enjoy one another, we breathe, consciously, always in the moment.

In the moment, I wonder why I'm here, what I'm looking for. The best idea would be to leave, but I've already texted the ladies and it seems appropriate to have a drink in memory of Taz. Even if he wasn't really my friend and I don't really drink anymore.

Inside, there's a man sitting at the bar. I remember him from before: his plaid work shirts and the way he sits alone, resting his elbows on the bar and sometimes watching the TV, moving his head now and then, but never turning around until he's finished his last beer and it's time to go. As I approach the bar, I notice the way his hair tucks into the back of his collar and the sprinkling of sawdust on his sleeves.

The new bartender tracks me with his eyes. He has an over-grown beard and a furrowed brow, eyes that seem lost in his face. He seems to consider the possibility that he might recognize me before turning away.

When I reach the man in plaid, I brush the sawdust from his sleeve. We both watch it fall to the floor. Slowly, he turns his head toward me, then back to the nothingness in front of him. I sit on the stool to his right.

The bartender drops a coaster in front of me.

"What can I get for you?"

"I guess a beer. Whatever's good. Something on tap."

The man in the plaid shirt turns his head again. "All this time I've never seen you order a beer. Not even once."

"What?"

"That other bartender used to bring you mixed drinks all the time. That's all I'm saying." He curves his hand loosely around the base of his glass. It feels like I should explain myself to him—why I would go into a van at midnight and wait for a madman, how I could wrap myself in his blankets but still not know his character. There is so much to explain. When someone does finally ask me "how could you?" I can draw a map of all the crisscrossing lines that diagram out the complexity of it: the nervousness and hope and heartbreak and disbelief. The way they shift into rage sometimes, without warning, as I catch myself following these lines backward and forward, trying to come up with a way to make them disappear, to go back far enough in time to erase all the vodka tonics and late nights and bad decisions.

The bartender sets a glass of amber liquid on the coaster in front of me, topped in a thin layer of foam. Something is supposed to happen next, but I don't know what. It must be that I drink the beer. That seems right. The bartender stares as I lift the glass. He isn't quite right. His eyes. They're burned-out holes.

"This here is Cassie," says the man in plaid.

"Cassie," repeats the bartender. He nods. "Oh, you're the one who..." He trails off.

"What?"

"Nothing. I think I know someone who knows your husband is all."

"My husband? Who knows my husband?"

He waves his hand in front of him like he's swatting a fly away. "Ah, never mind. I'm just your bartender, okay?" He offers me his hand. "I go by Lee."

I feel the moment snap in two. This is not what happens next.

"What kind of a joke is that? Fuck you."

The man in plaid laughs and shakes his head. "Get a load of that. It's in the job title. Bartender Lee."

"No. I'm not doing this." I step back from the bar, looking for truth in the bartender's face. How does this sad stranger know me?

The man in the plaid shirt laughs again. "Don't you get it? One Lee leaves, another one takes his place. It's like that clown, on TV."

"Wait," says the bartender. "Sorry. This isn't what I do. I'm an activist first. This job is just so I can eat, pay the rent. It's better for me this way, having a pseudonym. Usually I take the name of who-ever had the job before me. It feels meaningful. I don't know why."

The man in plaid can't stop laughing. "An activist, you say? What do you activate?" He has a loud, crackling guffaw that rumbles through his throat before spilling from his mouth.

Why did I come here? What was I supposed to do? There's a checklist I'm supposed to follow in situations like this, one that Danny made for me. There's a checklist, now, for every situation. They are a crucial part of our commitment to the happy ending. A way to protect ourselves so that others won't derail us.

"You can't use your real name because you're an activist?"

"Sometimes it's better to be anonymous. Especially if you're not..." He trails off, a look of discomfort on his face, like he has burns all over his body that haven't quite healed. I imagine him running through fires, trying to move fast enough to escape the flames. The image nauseates me. I don't know where it has come from, why anyone would picture this.

"Okay. I get it. I understand." Except that I don't.

The bartender pats the bar next to my glass. "Come on," he says quietly. "Sit down. That one's on the house." The man in the plaid shirt is still asking him what he activates, laughing at this joke, which seems to be the funniest thing he's said in decades. I sit down again and take another sip of my beer, trying to think of Taz, to send him off properly, but instead I think about Lee—the first Lee—and the way he told me once that some people are like slivers that fit into the spots in between, how there's nothing structural offered, but when you step back and look at the whole picture, they make it more complete. I don't understand how the man who says this and the man who shot Danny could be the same person.

Eventually the man in the plaid shirt runs out of things to laugh about and leaves. The ladies never show up, but I hear my phone vibrating with their texts. The bartender works, cleans, stares off into space, circles back to me to see whether I need another beer.

"What did you do?" I ask.

"I don't know what you mean."

"The one before you shot someone. I don't know if you heard. I'm wondering what you did. Did you blow up a corporate…something? An oil rig? Are you with that group that set fire to those refineries? Revenge Gaia?"

He rubs his forehead with wet fingers. "I get these headaches. A long time ago I got a concussion and…I guess you never really heal."

"Oh. I'm sorry."

"It's like an alarm sounding, you know? Every time one hits I remember what I'm supposed to be doing. Instead of just accepting the world for what it is and going to bed at night thinking it's okay to wake up in the morning with nothing changed. Every day that goes by is another chance wasted."

It's like he's winding up a ball of twine, ordering and compressing his thoughts so he can shove them back into his pocket.

"I always thought change was gradual."

He presses a whole palm against his forehead now, closes his eyes and waits for something to pass. "I didn't do anything. That was my problem. I failed to act. I walked passively into a trap that I'd set for myself. Years ago. And I can't blame the concussion for that."

When he drops his hand, I can see the deep lines in his brow, the tired smears of sweat. "You get complacent thinking change happens slowly," he says. "But think back as far as you can remember. It's the big moments—the sudden ones—that startle us so much we can't process them right away."

"Assassinations. Terrorist attacks."

"Uprisings."

"Do they have those anymore?"

"They must, somewhere."

"Viral videos."

"Yes, the internet." He looks disappointed as he says this.

"You're not a Lee. You're a...I don't know."

He offers me his hand, for a second time. "I'm Anton. You can call me Anton."

I don't have the stomach to finish my beer, but I stay anyway, occasionally sipping so it looks like I have a reason to be there. The bartender who isn't Lee and might not even be Anton is tapping the bar nervously with his index finger, like he's waiting for something—possibly for *me* to do something. Maybe it's just the tapping sound in my head and the beer-wash taste in my mouth, but I feel it too. It's about time I do something.

# CHAPTER 24
## (CURT)

You can't predict what your talent will be. Curt's was that he could write the letters. The process of typing them was slow and unnatural, but he took his time with them, looked up the words he wasn't certain how to spell, and read them out loud to make sure they didn't sound off. They sounded, more or less, like the letters he'd wished he could send to his own father, the ones he sometimes worked out in his head when he'd run out of other things to think about.

Dear Dad,

I've spent the last six months working at a bus station, cleaning the bathrooms, mostly. The floors. I'm on the night shift, so there aren't many buses coming through. It's fine. Usually it's quiet. Sometimes the drivers come in and say hello but there's never much talk beyond that. You can tell their minds are somewhere else. I understand this. I'm not so far off myself. Eventually, though, after you spend enough time looking through the schedule, you break down and buy a ticket. The name of another town sounds better than the name of the one you're in, and maybe this will finally be the place for you. I know you think your world is big, but mine is even bigger. Put a dot on a map and maybe that's where I am now. Until the next time,

*Emmaline*

It turned out he wasn't too bad at forgery, either. He'd read and then re-read the photocopied letters he'd taken from Anton's backpack, studying her handwriting, imagining writing them himself. Before he understood what he was doing, he'd practiced her signature for hours. Page after page, covered in her name—Emmaline Emmaline Emmaline—until he'd gotten it exactly right.

The tusk traveled with him. It was too heavy, too bulky, took up too much room in his backpack, but he accepted the burden. Sometimes he took photographs, carefully, when nobody else was around. The tusk on a playground swing, the tusk in a booth at a fast food restaurant, the tusk on a park bench, surrounded by pigeons. He'd print them out at the library and save them up until he was ready to move on, then mail off the one or two he thought were the best, along with the letter to Randall Kincaid. Her father, his father—what was the difference when all you were trying to do was strategically break someone's heart? By the time Randall Kincaid received the letter, Curt and Emmaline would have already moved on.

For years, he sent them; one every few months, every six months, every year. Always, it felt like he was headed toward a conclusion, that eventually he would come to the end of a page and sign Emmaline's name and know that it was the last time. He never suspected that after a few years he would still have more to say. If you wanted to make a case for ghosts, maybe this was it.

```
Dear Dad
```

he would start, and the words would come out as effortlessly as cereal being shaken from a box.

The final words; he knew what they would be.

```
I am already dead.
```

But he couldn't convince Emmaline to write them. She turned out to be weaker than she'd believed. The early letters promised no chance of forgiveness, but in later ones she allowed herself to consider it.

```
Maybe  one  day  we'll  understand  each  other
better. People can change. It happens.
```

For several years, Curt lost track of Anton. They parted ways as friends, more or less. Curt gave Anton a key to the cabin, just in case, and Anton promised to send letters from Africa. There was no chance he would make it there, but Curt looked for him anyway. On the news. On the internet. Whenever he had access to these luxuries. Curt understood the process, the cycle. You disappeared, you came up for air, and then you went under again. You never stayed in one place long enough to lose your vigilance. At least Anton could contact his family, let them know he was okay. He could lead a reasonably normal life, for short stretches of time, until the paranoia hit, the sensation that he'd gone for too long with too much complacency and not enough vigilance. When they did cross paths again, Anton was still talking about her—Emmaline. In his mind, he hadn't landed yet. The parachute continued to fall, the ground beneath him but just out of reach. Curt understood. She wasn't the kind of person you could forget.

Over the years, they more or less stayed in touch. Whenever Anton reappeared, Curt considered telling him about the letters he'd been sending, the tusk he'd been carrying around with him, but couldn't endure the thought of trying to explain himself. He kept his mouth shut, like you were supposed to.

He traveled. Hitchhiking, finding work where they didn't ask questions, then leaving whenever it got too comfortable.

```
The  thing  about  the  nomadic  life,  Dad,  is
that  whenever  it  starts  feeling  like  may-
be  you  could  call  this  place  home,  the  next
day  you're  up  early  making  plans,  pacing  the
room,  enraged  at  yourself  for  accepting  the
circumstances and making do.
```

At least once a year, he'd wind up back at the cabin. Danny would stay the weekend, and they'd spend quiet nights by the fire, watching the flames but never saying much. Curt never mentioned the letters, Anton and his eternally broken heart, the body wrapped in a parachute that they'd carried for miles, then buried together. Curt wondered what Danny knew about the tusk, whether he and his friends had been the ones to bury it, but he never asked. On Sunday afternoon, Danny would press some money into his hand, give him a stiff hug and drive off. They were brothers, still, and they behaved in the best way brothers knew how.

It seemed like just a few years, but all of a sudden it was fifteen of them. Danny got married, had a couple kids. He told Curt he couldn't afford to keep giving him money, but he did anyway. They got older. Curt had a harder time finding places to fit in. Danny insisted that he could come "home," that nobody would be looking for him after so many years. Curt didn't bother reminding Danny that accident or not, a man was still dead because of him, and it was about fifteen years too late to tell his side of the story, that nobody wanted to hear from the guy who'd run away. The divide between Curt and Danny was inevitable with time. When you live under a System, like Danny did, it doesn't matter who you once were. Eventually you believe in the System. You find yourself doing math problems that you never considered back when you were a kid. He could see Danny working it out in his head, understanding that even if Curt had ended up in jail, he would have served his time already, that the alternative Curt had chosen could never be the better option.

```
I don't have many possessions. I leave the
tusk in lockers for months at a time, hoping
that someone will steal it, but nobody does.
I try not to think of it as a burden, but
an object that will one day liberate me, al-
though I don't know how. At night, I hear it
scream. The anguish is ever present. To si-
lence it, I write in my journal, unload every
terrible thought I have until my heart rate
drops back down to normal. It's the story of
my childhood. About you and me, then and now.
```

I keep wondering who will read it. When I'm
done, what will happen to it? It excites me
and scares me at the same time.

Danny and his math. Sure, a person could learn to add and sub-
tract and extrapolate, but it never led to an answer. It was all just
statistics. *You're thirty-seven, Curt. You've been alive for thirty-seven
years and I've been alive for thirty-five. Think of all that time, all the
things we should have had worked out by now.* Hearing it made him
feel like a train derailing. Mile Post 37. Except that the train, the
tracks, they didn't exist. If you stop counting, you might be twenty
or you might be fifty or you might be eighty, and in varying stages
of used up-ness. It just *felt* less scary if you were filed into a particular slot. The outcome never changed. A man can become a monster at thirty-five. A girl might die at twenty-four. An older brother
might become a younger brother or vice versa. Time was inevitable
but not dependable, not in the way it mapped itself out.

There was the gratitude to focus on, the intangibles. Sentences
repeated over and over again until they settled in like warm glue.
*Thank you. You're a life saver. Thank you. I don't know where I would
be. I can't thank you enough. I can't say it like I mean it, but I do.* After
a while they were little more than a buzzing in his ears.

"Cassie is cheating on me," Danny told him. "And apart from
that she's angry most of the time."

Curt waited for the rest, whatever that might be.

"I guess there's a cause and effect there," Danny continued.
"Wouldn't you say?"

"You want me to try to connect them? Those two things?"

"I haven't been the way I wanted to be. I had ideas, but then..."

Curt counted backwards from ten, slowly. It helped, sometimes,
when a situation seemed flipped over and switched around, when
the words he was hearing didn't make the right kind of sense. *I had
ideas.* Ideas. Ideas. There was something there, but Curt couldn't
quite flip it back so that it pointed in the right direction.

"I'm thinking she wonders where all of your money goes. Where
you get to when you skip town for the night. I'm betting she looks
at your odometer, does her own math."

Danny shrugged, looked away. "I guess."

They'd never talked like this when they were kids. For so many years he'd pretended Danny wasn't around, imagined having a big, messy room to himself, with a low bed and an expensive stereo, where he could bring giggling girls at night and undress them in the lamplight. So maybe it had turned out the right way, all things considering, now that they were real brothers, the kind who helped each other out.

"So, what now? Do you want me to go rough him up a little? This guy who's fucking Cassie?"

# CHAPTER 25
## (DANNY)

His wife had secrets. There were places she went, papers in her purse, things she hid from him. A drawer with a lock on it. There was a flavor of inevitability to it: busting the lock open with a hammer, only to find the drawer empty except for the copy of the book he'd given her. *The Secret Path to Joy.*

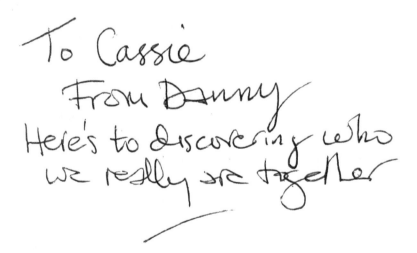

To Cassie
From Danny
Here's to discovering who
we really are together

The binding pristine. Never even opened.

Evan handed down instructions like he was qualified to give them. *You have to decide whether you still love her. You have to decide whether the hourglass is empty. Sometimes this happens. It's natural.*

It was the same Evan who brought women back to his apartment, one after another, a different face each time although after a while they all began to look a little bit the same. Was this a type? Evan's type? Or just the way eagerness looked, if eagerness *had* a look. Girls who turned up at JoyPath events ready to attach themselves to anyone who saw their *true potential.* Evan said they were the best recruits, the most malleable, the most open-minded. They had the imagination for it, whatever that meant. He could go through them like this, in the manner of an assembly line. He hadn't seen his kids in months, years. What felt like forever.

They didn't talk about Dora anymore. It was better this way, even though the past sometimes still nagged at him, in the way of an unfinished sentence.

*Everyone dies but us. This is what happens.*

As far as Cassie, he didn't understand this concept of deciding whether you still loved a person. It wasn't a decision, was it? More like a state of being.

She told him she was at the library doing research.

"But you don't study anything," he said, knowing it was the wrong response even before she shrugged her shoulders and turned away, smiling about her secret plans.

Most of the time it felt like Danny was out there alone, walking the path for both of them. He did what he could to inspire Cassie to join him, broaching the important topics carefully, dutifully.

"I've been thinking about your father lately. Ways you could fix things with him."

"There's nothing to fix."

"I don't understand grudges. I like a clean slate."

"It's not a grudge."

"What, then?"

She shrugged. "I made an adjustment. We all adjusted ourselves."

"But your parents..."

She looked at him in that way, with the same weary expression she used with the kids after a particularly bad day.

"There are things that happen that you never see." Her voice was even, without inflection. "They happen without happening. Sometimes they're more important than the events people measure."

He didn't understand the gray areas she was always inhabiting. Places that held her down and stopped her from moving forward.

"I'm just saying. We should clean all of our slates. You and me. Start from there." There was no good way to explain what he meant, that every person had to allow every other person their one mistake. The reciprocity. His mistake, her mistake. Because otherwise you spent your life digging out of it, which was exhausting and debilitating. Just look at the proof.

So many conversations, just like this. Small and quick, and over before they had hardly begun. They were followed by what felt like hours of silence, broken by the whispers and gasps of sex. He paid close attention to her face, watched her wanting what he was able to give her. Afterward he would take note of her body next to his, the way she fixed her eyes on the line where the wall met the ceiling, with a slight frown. He imagined her trying to solve a problem with no answer. Each night the same problem, but never a solution.

"What are you thinking about?"

"I don't understand people, what they do."

Was she talking about him? He thought of ways to respond, questions he could ask, but instead of asking them he drifted off to sleep, and in the morning there were the kids and getting ready and trying to remember where everything went, where everyone had to be, and when.

Every day, they kissed goodbye. She told him she would miss him. Her smile was a place he remembered, a favorite spot. He wondered whether she really went to the library on Saturday afternoons, whether she was being honest about the papers she hid from him when she said they were drafts of poetry that she couldn't share with him yet. There was something about the way she laughed afterward, as if she didn't expect him to believe her. Danny laughed too, and this was okay. It counted. It went—almost all of it—in the happy column.

Steps forward. Slow steps forward.

Danny had a plan; he was going to smooth out the knots and make it all tolerable again, for everyone. He'd get Curt back into the family, figure out a way for all of this to be okay. They were going to be brothers again. Bottom bunk, top bunk, ceiling, whatever the equivalent of that might be—Danny would figure it out.

He'd been ready to move forward, finally. Work on fixing all of the past damage. Work on his wife, his kids, his family.

He hadn't expected it to turn out like this with Curt. He hadn't imagined that it could get this out of control.

When he'd woken up in the hospital bed and understood that he'd lost a few days, Danny had wondered about Curt: where he was, whether he was in trouble, what parts of the story he was forgetting. He tried calling the number to Curt's newest prepaid phone, but it was no longer in service. Danny didn't hear from him for weeks, long enough to wonder whether he'd run again. Was he re-disappeared or had something even worse happened this time?

Possibly Curt had left clues that Danny hadn't picked up on at the time. Emergency procedures to follow in a situation like this: a night on a roof that erased time in a flash. Curt had talked before about bus stations and diners and seedy grocery stores with stale cereal, flour infested with moths. The idea of Curt going back to these places was impossible to accept. Curt deserved better and Danny would help him—of course he would. He didn't always understand Curt, but he tried to listen. *Gratitude, Danny. I keep getting stuck on it. Something about it doesn't feel quite right. It's barbed. It keeps pulling me back. I understand how it's supposed to go—be thankful, be grateful. But there's another piece isn't there? That's the problem.*

They'd been making progress, filling in that ugly void. Danny could see the structure they were building together and the space it would one day inhabit. But then Dora had happened, that night on the roof, and Danny had gotten sidetracked holding all the pieces together. The patience, the silence, the careful planning and surprisingly successful execution, because he'd never expected it to work like it did. He hadn't expected that the roommate, for the right price, would stick to his story and be so convincing when he did. He hadn't expected the bartender to leave so easily, as if all he'd been waiting for was instructions to go. He hadn't expected that not a single person on South Jefferson Street would come forward with information about what they'd heard or seen. And then afterward, with perfect timing, Taz's death and the secrets that went with him. Add to all of this his new opportunity with JoyPath and it was starting to look like his plans might actually pay off this time. Danny hadn't expected to be one of those people. But sometimes you just close your eyes and when you open them, this is who you are.

And yet.

Their debt had gotten out of control. He'd paid the bartender's roommate too much. He'd given Curt too much over the years. His medical bills after the accident were more than he knew how to manage. Somehow he'd succeeded in keeping the worst of it from Cassie, but he wouldn't be able to for much longer. It infuriated Danny that she still had to work two jobs: mornings at the bakery, weekend evenings at the restaurant, extra shifts when she could get them. The JoyPath speaking engagements didn't pay enough, fast enough. Money wasn't coming in from the new recruits like they'd said it would. *Be patient*, they told him. It was about waiting, deserving, earning what you were worth.

Evan's message never changed. *You have to decide whether you still love her.* Evan, clutching a coffee cup in one hand and running the other one through his now gel-spiky hair, his eyes red-rimmed and bloodshot, his clothes slightly rumpled and damp, like they had spent the night on the floor of some basement apartment. *You have to decide whether you still love her.* Maybe this had started out being about Cassie, but after the first hundred times it was clear that it was something else. This was Evan talking to nobody, about no one. No one that they discussed any longer, anyway.

Daily, he offered up his unsolicited advice, his enlightened perspective on the world.

"What you have to remember is that wealth comes in different forms. You don't always recognize it at first."

"Only the money kind feels like freedom."

"Oh come on, Danny. You know that's not true."

Evan carried folded up pieces of paper in his pocket. He'd taken to drawing as he talked. Writing down words, circling them and drawing lines between them. Flow charts that simplified life's most important processes into basic diagrams.

"Here you have money, and here you have self-fulfillment. In between them is a river."

He drew two circles with a wavy line in between.

Money ⌇⌇ S-f

"The focus is here. On getting across. Maybe money helps you, but what you have to remember is that it's not your only asset. It might not even be an important one."

He wrote several more words.

Perseverance. Passion. Talent. Open-mindedness. Big-heartedness. _Sex_

He underlined "sex" three times before circling it. Danny looked away. Sometimes he forgot that none of this had any meaning.

The women probably would have lined up for Danny too. They slipped him their phone numbers and told him that all they wanted was a few hours alone somewhere to talk. They wore loose, sleeveless dresses that fluttered out around their knees, stacks of bracelets, long necklaces, rings. They carried around copies of *The Secret Path to Joy*, with Post-it notes marking their favorite pages, pencil notes inside. The one who looked like she couldn't have been more than twenty with a tattoo of a house on her wrist, covering up a scar that she called "ancient" from a dark time in her past—*a place for it to rest peacefully.*

This is truth.
Yes, this.
Definitely this.

They told him they knew pain. They were willing to share. They were willing to listen. They approached him with their heads tilted forward, their eyes focused on the line of buttons on his shirt, tripping over their words. With each one, Danny imagined lifting up her chin, forcing her eyes to meet his, righting the balance somehow, although he didn't know how to do that, what he would say or do, whether it was even possible. He'd look at them and wonder if these were the same women with the damp basement apartments, Evan's clothes in a pile on the floor as he shared his pain with them. Danny wanted to drive away, find a place so remote that nobody could hear for miles, and yell at the trees until the trapped feeling was gone.

"What I'm thinking," said Evan, "is maybe you and me could write our own book. Like a sequel, except that this would be its own thing. Set up our own conferences, maybe. Do this whole thing better."

"Didn't we sign something?"

"I was talking to an attorney the other night. She thinks if we named our venture a certain way, did the business license right, it wouldn't be an issue."

Danny nodded.

"We need to focus on *innovation*, you and me."

Danny nodded again.

He never quite got it, why anyone would listen to Evan, why anyone would try to write a book just because Evan told them too, but here he was, doing just that. Staring at a computer screen again while wondering where his wife was, sensing the change in the lighting of the room as the hours fell away, taking breaks for the kids, for dinner, to talk to Cassie or at least sit in the same room as her, next to her, while they thought about different things. Maybe she really was writing poetry. Maybe that's all it was.

He spent days recounting the story of the night Curt and his father went to war, trying to describe the way his body shook, the terror in Curt's eyes as he handed Danny his driver's license. Each draft was days of work, at least, each read-through a disappointment.

How many times would he start over before he accepted there was no book to be written, no way to tell the story correctly?

Curt called, eventually, from a new number.

"I'm sorry I ran. The whole thing spooked me."

"You shouldn't have been there. It would have been my fault if something happened to you."

There was a long pause. Danny heard a faint sound, wetly labored breathing that made him wonder whether Curt was crying, whether this was even something Curt might do.

"Are you still there?"

More labored breathing. The sound of a truck passing by.

"Listen, Danny. I didn't know you knew anything about that body, that elephant tusk."

"What?"

"Do you really think it cursed you to touch it? Because if it did, then...I don't know. I guess that means I'm fucked."

Danny closed his eyes. How could this be happening?

Emmaline Kincaid.

Finally, Danny learned her name. She was somebody. *A* body. They had watched her die.

According to Curt, the other person had lived. The other parachute. A man had needed help but they'd gone home instead. The man's first name was Anton. Curt had never had reason to learn his last name.

Danny stared at the wall as Curt went over all of it: burying her body, the letters he wrote to Emmaline's father, what it was that compelled him to, how it all went back to where a person's brain was, the ways you sorted through your emotions and how, at the right time, the letters might work their way in, a silver thread cross-knit with the black and gray and rusty red. You never knew what you might do, why you might start confusing yourself with the woman who jumped. It sounded impossible, but it wasn't. This could happen. It *did* happen.

Danny remained calm and started in on a new set of calculations. Curt was writing letters to the dead woman's father, pretending to be her. *He* was the reason she'd never been reported as missing. What kind of a person was his brother, to do this? How much could be unknowable within someone?

"Where is the tusk now?"

There was noise on the other end, the whooshing of cars, or possibly wind. Danny imagined the phone resting on a sidewalk, that he would wait for Curt to come back on the line until the battery ran out. Where did he go when he left? Was there a destination, or did he just start walking in whatever direction was convenient until he got somewhere?

Thirty seconds, forty seconds, forty-five seconds before Curt's voice returned. "I think I just need to deal with it."

"We should meet up and figure this out."

"No, I think…let me just take care of this one."

"Curt." His brother had the tusk. How was that possible?

"The thing is, Danny, that I'm so grateful to you. You've been…"

"Let's meet," said Danny. "We'll come up with something."

"Nah, let me take care of it, okay? I got it."

"It's not even anything to take care of. Everything's fine."

"So, what I figure is it's my fault dad died—I mean, I'm the one who pushed him down those stairs so hard he…What I'm saying is what I did is about a million times worse than not telling someone you think you might have seen someone die, so—this is like one of your mathematical equations, right? I have the bigger number so I absorb yours and then you absorb someone else's and then we keep on going down the line until we don't quite get to zero. It has to do with infinity. I never really got all that stuff."

"Infinity."

"Yeah."

"I can't let you."

"Well, too bad."

"Call me tomorrow. Let's talk about this tomorrow."

"Yeah, okay."

Randall Kincaid lived in Boulder Hill Park. You could see pictures of his estate from above. Crisp aerial photography that probably wasn't available fifteen years ago. Not just one pool but three: bright blue rectangles that seemed to hold the heart of everything. Cool water, clean and smooth. Maybe this was what Danny had wanted all along.

Danny waited for Curt to call, but he never did. He waited for the money to start coming in, for Cassie to write him a love poem, for tragedy to mend itself. Every morning the kids woke up and they seemed small enough, like there was still time. But the problem with waiting was there was always a breaking point you couldn't see coming.

Because what if Curt never came back? What if this was it and he was going to spend another fifteen years waiting around?

Dear Mr. Kincaid,

We have never met, but I have some information you might find interesting. It is regarding your daughter Emmaline who disappeared about fifteen years ago. I understand how difficult it must be to go all this time without knowing what happened to her. I wish I had some good news to give you, but I don't. However, I understand that closure can help, so I would like to tell you what I know.

# CHAPTER 26
## (CASSIE)

I drop the kids off for play dates, for lessons after school. I watch Nel at her ballet classes at the community center, and something about seeing her in a leotard with her hands raised above her head makes my heart die a little. Her body falls limp as she bends at the waist, like a marionette released from its strings, and I feel myself going limp too, the air slowly leaving my lungs.

E goes to chess club with his best friend, Myron. Danny tells me that E doesn't actually like playing, isn't interested in chess; he only joined because of Myron. He presents this like a problem and then waits for me to solve it. Myron is a lively, emphatic kid with a million stories and hardly any of them true. His mother speaks sentences made up of words I've never tried using before. *Concurrently, we're determining the feasibility of this proposition. On paper, it's quite promising.* His father I've never seen. He travels for work. He's in Bangladesh this month, the Philippines next month. His work is important, but I can never quite bring it into focus. The mother, though; her makeup is understated but perfect, and her eyes are like marbles, shining and huge.

"I think you should be doing karate instead of chess," Danny tells E. "They're really the same thing. You use your mind, you come up with a strategy to defeat an opponent. Except only one of them is practical. What do you think?"

E chews on the inside of his lip and says that he agrees. He always agrees with Danny.

Nel twirls around in a pink tutu, spinning as fast as she can and then stumbling drunkenly around the room, until she collapses and yells, "everything is spinning. Spinning. Spinning."

E practices holding his breath for as long as he can. He asks me if I can see him starting to turn blue, asks me to take a video of him so he can watch his technique. I try to imagine what he and Myron do on their play dates, but there's just emptiness, a room with nothing in it. "They're inquisitive boys," offers the mother. "Their personalities are well-suited to one another." We have these conversations. This is how time moves forward.

The few days I am able to pick up the kids from school, I watch Nel on the playground, surrounded by a group of girls that look oddly like her, like they could have all come from the same womb. I overhear her talking.

"My dad is famous. He writes books and tells stories on a stage. He has an aw-dee-ance." The girls bring their heads forward until they are almost touching. Later, Nel is smiling, a happy, perfect creature. "Did you see all my friends, Mommy?"

Day ends, night comes. A day, a night. A day, a night. A day, a night.

On one of these nights, after the kids are asleep, Danny and I sit in the living room with the lights off and the windows open, listening to distant thunder, the room a pleasant mix of warm and cool and the smell of wet grass, wet sidewalk, catalpa trees. I think it's love; something about it is love, but I wouldn't know how to describe it if anyone asked, and the only way to keep it is to be still, to commit ourselves to never moving again.

The breeze pushes the curtains up and out, billowing fabric lit up by the streetlight outside. It reminds me of an old movie, a show I watched when I was a kid that would have seemed scary in a way I couldn't explain. A sudden gust hits, sending the curtains so far into the room that they fly almost parallel to the floor. Then, just as suddenly, they fall. We hold our breath, waiting to see what happens next.

Danny starts talking, then stops again. *I was thinking. It's weird. I just.*

My mother used to tell me that a person's most desirable qualities were also their most undesirable qualities, which meant that the opposite also had to be true. The logic always seemed off, but I accepted it as a daughter accepts any other gift from her mother, and carried it with me, unsure of what I would eventually do with it. Do I start trying to apply it to Danny, or is that a pointless exercise?

At last he works out what he wants to say.

"You're lucky you never had a terrible life."

"That is lucky."

"You almost did, and then you didn't. That blows my mind."

"Why would it?"

"It's just so fortunate. All these things we can be thankful for. The extra strength I have after going through so much with my father and Curt. The fact that you were on the edge of something horrible, but then your dad got it together. He made his one mistake and then moved on. Everyone gets to fuck up once, you know? All of us."

He looks at me and waits. I'm not sure for what.

"Your dad found his path. He saw a better future and took control."

*Found his path.* I don't understand this, the way everyone finds their way. We don't have permission to be lost anymore. All of our destinations have to be drawn out and marked with a pin, surrounded by thick black arrows so there's no way we'll miss.

"I've been thinking," he continues, "that the best thing probably doesn't look like anything special. It's simplicity, being decent, doing normal things. You don't have to be great. Our kids don't have to be great. In fact, maybe it's better not to be."

I close my eyes and wonder if the breeze will return. You can never predict which dance of the curtains will be the last, when the wind will quiet for good.

"Please stop talking."

He pauses, then says my name, as if trying it out for the first time. "Cassie."

I brace myself for more, but there isn't any.

The new bartender and I are friends. "Anton." He introduces me to people, other activists, who passionately explain to me that we are losing the earth, piece by piece. Picture humankind standing on a cliff, looking into an abyss. Picture this, they say, and then tell me it's not our responsibility to take action.

Did you know that sea levels are rising by three millimeters a year? That polar bears are starving to death and the coral reefs are being bleached white?

Did you know that there are a hundred tons of garbage in the Pacific Ocean?

Did you know that if global temperatures increase by three to four degrees Celsius, twenty to thirty percent of all plant and animal species alive today will likely go extinct?

I didn't know. Each new fact I learn is almost too much to bear. Someone hands me a bumper sticker that says *LIVE GENTLY*, a list of phone numbers to start calling: my congress-people and senators.

They are quick to point out, when I ask, that they don't condone ecoterrorism under any circumstance. Not only do groups like Revenge Gaia use morally unconscionable methods, but they turn public opinion against legitimate conservation groups. *Stay away from the fringe* is the message I hear. Be angry and passionate, but also be respectful and kind.

Passionate and kind. This is what I try to be.

There is a young woman with jet black hair and stack of bracelets traveling up her arm, an older woman in a braid with oversize sweaters and a soft expression, a man who walks around shirtless, with bumper stickers plastered to his chest and across his back, a widower with a voice like a rusty scalpel who keeps saying that he's outraged, outraged, outraged. I stand next to them on the courthouse steps, I march with them down First Street, listening to the car horns and the people yelling, until the police funnel us back toward the sidewalk. At all of these events, Anton wears a mask. Each one is the face of an animal: a tiger, a cheetah, an elephant, a rhinoceros. They're huge and magnificent, pieces of art. Even when it's above ninety degrees and oppressively humid, he places one over his head and becomes a different being. There is something ominous in the way he marches, his slow footsteps and silence, the way he turns to stare at bystanders but never speaks.

We are a single unit, a unifying idea. The thrill of change. The responsibility to it. When we chant together our voices have weight.

Even mine. Especially mine. We paint banners to hang off buildings and billboards, choreograph human blockades, order bags of manure and have them delivered to a CEO's house. We storm the civic center plaza, our bodies atingle, ready to channel lightning.

We meet up in basements, dining rooms, backyards. We share food. I bring in desserts and listen to the angry widower tell me that he always thought his wife made the best apple crumble until he tasted mine. Somehow I'm back here, at the intersection of anger and grief.

A day, a night. A day, a night.

Sometimes it's remarkable how many hours one night can contain. At two a.m. the sidewalk outside is empty and white-lit, stark against the alien patterns of shadows cast by the trees. The bark is gray and roughened, like sculpted clay. Welcome to the hour of inspiration. Or so they say. I sit at the kitchen table with pen and paper, chiseling phrases from the creaking stillness.

Clouds from below.
Safe spaces.
Lost days.
Compassion. Compassionate.
People who are like slivers.
Silver. Shivers.

The only way to succeed is to not get ahead of yourself. Start with the smallest pieces and build outward from there.

It's my grandmother's old table, with a faded Formica top and metal legs that wobble and squeak when you wipe it down in the evening. The corners are rimmed in ancient, greasy blackness; this is how it's always been—this kitchen, this table. Did I expect that we'd still be using it after this many years, or did I imagine a smooth wooden tabletop by now? Drawers beneath the counter that glide closed, a set of new chairs, one of those rolltop things that you put bread in.

My father told me to be fearless, and somehow it feels the same. What he meant, what he wasn't able to say. This is the closest I've been to it.

The table isn't enough. The paper on top of it.

*He said he bought me an island.*

*But really what it was*

*Was a different kind of roof.*

I don't know why I can't tell Danny or the kids about my activist friends, why I can't follow through on the simple gesture of putting a *LIVE GENTLY* bumper sticker on my car.

Repeatedly, Anton brings up the name Randall Kincaid. An amoral, inhuman demon. An enemy of the earth. The Furniture King; that's how we know him. Exotic wood sources, unsustainably harvested, questionable working conditions in his factories, exotic big game hunts for sport.

"No," says Anton. "It's so much more than that."

We're online every day, posting the truth. We give the R. K. Kincaid Corporation an F rating and encourage others to boycott. We track down pictures of Randall Kincaid posing with a dead lion and the gun he used to slaughter it. We post them wherever we can, instruct our followers to do the same, trying our hardest to make them go viral. #conservation #endangered #deforestation #notrophyhunt.

For Anton, this is not enough to bring down evil.

"Sometimes I wish we were more like Revenge Gaia, that we could be if the situation warranted. Because if anyone deserved to have…to be…"

A woman named Maureen steps forward and places her hand on his arm. "We don't want to lose you. Talk to us. Let it out."

"Just knowing that he's out there, that there might be others like him who call themselves human…it makes me want to tear things apart with my hands. Him. I would, if I had the chance." Anton's face is red. His eyes are alive.

Maureen leads him to a chair. "Tell us. Whatever is burning in your heart, release it. We're here to listen." She kneels at his feet and takes his hand. In my periphery, I see movement toward the floor, a kneeling body, another kneeling body, until we're all on the floor, waiting for Anton to speak.

There are no details at first. Just a woman alive and then a woman dead, and for years afterward a man tormented by his past decisions. Every day, Anton tries to undo them, but after a certain point this is hopeless. The love is trapped behind glass; you have it, but you don't, but still you hope to find it again, to find her, even though you know this is impossible.

"Her name was Emmaline Kincaid," Anton admits, finally. He rubs his face, then threads his fingers together and places his hands awkwardly on his lap. "*His* daughter. Randall Kincaid's. And when I lost her, I lost everything."

We kneel. We try to process the information we're receiving. Randall Kincaid's daughter?

"Emmaline was the greatest woman who ever lived. I know this to be true. But she hated her father, and sometimes despised herself because she'd catch herself loving him. I think this is what drove her to end her life. I really do. How does good come from evil? How do we *accept* that this can happen?"

When Anton looks up, his eyes meet mine. Are we friends now? Am I supposed to know how to answer questions like these?

"She said her father was…that there was a tendency some people had. She remembered seeing some of the items in his collection even as a little girl. A tiger's head on the wall in the basement. A rug of shining black fur on her parents' bedroom floor.

"Later it was the ivory carvings. He would talk about the artistry, the intricacy. He assured her that that he was only interested as an appreciator of art. Once the animal was dead there wasn't much you could do for it, except to honor it and allow it to experience immortality in this way. It was important to know your history, to understand its difficulties and complexities. There was a time, not that long ago, when the only way to survive was to slaughter the beast who sought to slaughter you. *As humans we should all be thankful that we no longer have the need.*

"For her sixteenth birthday it was a set of hairpins. He told her she'd be the only one at school with them. Carved out of a rhino's horn.

"She remembered holding a weapon with a curved handle, her father beaming at her. All vintage pieces, he promised her. All harvested long before anyone understood the long-term ramifications. Man is naïve, and then we learn. There was a paper trail, a certification process to keep the collectors in line. A market that functioned independent of modern-day poaching. For years, Emmaline allowed herself to believe him."

Anton presses his hands over his eyes, rubs his face again, with shaking hands.

"There was an elephant tusk. She was carrying it with her when she died. This was the part that…"

In the quiet of the room, I hear one of us swallow.

"Her father gave it to her, of course. This was years later, when he'd finally stopped trying to sell the lies. He thought she would want it, that she was old enough to finally grasp…I don't know. This was what horrified her. That he might think this, that she might have said or done something to let on that she would want it. Or that secretly she *did* want it.

"God. The story he told her, about the hunt he'd been on. That if you paid the right people this was something you could do. The whole premise seemed improbable, like a fiction created by his dark brain.

"They threatened to shoot him if he didn't follow their

instructions. It wasn't safe. Poachers were killed on sight; no arrests made, no questions asked. Wherever they were, they must have been trespassing. They walked for what seemed like hours, his guides occasionally whispering amongst themselves. He thought that they might end up shooting him instead, that he would be dead within hours, but instead luck intervened and they came upon a herd of elephants. Part of a herd? Six or seven of them, including a young one. He used the word 'mercy,' explained that since the adults would soon be dead, they had to kill the young one too.

"This story she told me—she could barely repeat it. Her father described the details to her, thinking she wanted to hear them. That you shoot them with a single bullet to the head. That when one goes down the others in the group start screaming—an incredible vibrating sound that he couldn't even describe in words. They start moving, trying to defend one another. They think it's possible that they won't all die.

"Within minutes, they all go down and you just want a moment—some time to reflect—but instead the guides are moving you along, warning you that you have to be quick or you'll be dead too, shot with no hesitation. This was part of the thrill, which he thought Emmaline, of all people, would understand. The men took up their axes and began hacking away at the faces of what had moments before been living beings, separating ivory from flesh. One of the men handed Randall an axe and gestured toward the juvenile. It was exceptionally hard work. Exceptionally messy.

"Can you imagine being her? Having to listen to this, to the reasons he used to justify it? We're living in the era of extinction, he told her, dealing with species that won't survive another twenty-five years. It's a matter of getting there first, claiming the trophies while you still can. Not over-sentimentalizing it. You do what you need to. The villagers leave out poisoned pumpkins for the elephants to eat. This is just reality. Every living thing on the planet is a resource, and if it wasn't the humans exploiting them, some other being would have come along and done it by now."

Anton leans sideways in his chair, like he might slump over at any moment.

"She just...I mean, we'd go out searching for these places. We'd track them down, clutching our cameras but afraid to take pictures because of how impossible they seemed. Baked and bleached rocks, cliffs at the edge of an ocean, a giant forest, screeching with life and swollen with mist, where you expected to run into a dinosaur at any moment. I'd try to tell her that these places were proof of...I didn't quite know what, but it didn't matter because Emmaline would chime in before I got around to finishing the sentence. What good were these miniscule fragments when everything in between them was torn up? They only served as reminders of a wilderness that had been carved into so many times there was no way to fill it back in."

Anton begins weeping into his hand. I hear bodies shifting uncomfortably. Legs unaccustomed to kneeling.

A woman named Dominique breaks the silence.

"Anton. I'm so sorry. I never knew. Of course Randall Kincaid would be important to you. Let us help. Let us do what we can." She places a hand on Anton's left knee. Maureen puts a hand on his right knee.

"We had a plan once," says Anton suddenly. "Only Emmaline's parachute never opened."

---

A day, a night. A day, a night. Waking up to darkness and the twitch of agitation, unspecified, unclassified. The low blue flames of a simmering panic.

*The women jump and the men run.*
*He bought me an island*
*On top of a roof*
*And there were underwater caves*
*twenty stories deep.*

The words that come out are never the right ones, so I crawl back into bed and tell myself to sleep, start over again in the morning. There are no more dreams about paradise. Instead I see a body, an airplane, a parachute, a tusk. A body. A tusk. I've heard this before, haven't I? I pull it in, coax it to come near, then lose my grasp and watch it fall away. A daytime sky, a nighttime sky, hundreds of stories. It feels like…nothing…nothing. The sound of an alarm jerks me awake and I'm in bed, staring at the line where the ceiling meets the wall. The same line, every day. Wall, ceiling, Danny.

At what point do I sense that there is a direction in which all of this is headed? Not a path forward, but a path backward. No way to tell the two apart.

# CHAPTER 27

Danny thinks I should see Dora's cabin, that our journey is meant to take us there. I watch him fidget with his hands as he explains, in a quiet voice, how this will bring closure.

"I don't want to stay there, in the same bed that—"

"We're not going to *stay* there. I just want you to see it. I think this is important."

So we take a family trip up north. We rent a cottage by a lake, close to town, but with spotty cell phone reception. Danny promises to teach E how to row a boat, promises to buy Nel an inflatable raft that looks like an octopus. His parents tag along, in a second car, so we'll have someone to watch the kids when we make our pilgrimage to the cabin.

On the first afternoon, we sit on the porch and stare at the lake. It's the green-blue of water and the blue-blue of the sky reflected off its surface. Danny puts an arm around my shoulder and pulls me in, kissing my head. "We don't do this enough."

The kids play and the adults laugh and Bill tells stories about his daughters when they were young. But Danny is distracted by his phone, annoyed by the periodic lapses in coverage. He checks it at odd times and in odd places, with a nervousness that I observe with an unsteady stomach. He holds the phone in one hand and rubs my back with the other.

"Can't you put that away?"

"Sorry." He slides the phone into his pocket, but ten minutes later he's out on the front steps, staring at it again.

When the call he's been waiting for finally comes in, it's late, dark. Danny grabs his phone and wanders away, the jaunty ringtone fading as he disappears down the road. When he returns fifteen minutes later, he has a familiar look on his face: a mixture of resolve and resignation. The look of the family decision maker doing his job, knowing what's best for us.

The next morning Danny consults a book and picks out a family hike. He wants to find the perfect vista, the most picturesque and unforgettable view of the hills off to the west. A gift from him to us.

He's rented an SUV, a silver Chevrolet with huge tires. You need them, Danny explains, because with some of the roads you never know what to expect, and sometimes they're impassable otherwise. He talks like someone who knows the area well, like he's been up here every summer since he was a kid. I don't understand how it's a gift, how finally showing your family what you've kept hidden from them is giving them anything at all.

We park at the side of the road and head up a narrow trail. Danny consults his book quietly, then throws it into his backpack. "Does everyone have their water?"

"How long is it?" asks E.

"Not long, buddy. Not long."

"I'm going to fly when we get to the top," says Nel. Everything she says breaks my heart.

We trudge upward, Nel holding Danny's hand and E staring at his feet, counting out steps to the top. Eventually, somehow, we get there. By this time, Nel is riding on Danny's shoulders. He sets her down, gently, and warns her to stay back from the edge.

"Forty-five thousand, eight hundred seventy-six," announces E. "Just a guess, though. I stopped counting."

When I look up, my breath catches. The sky is clear, postcard blue, the trees stretching out forever, forming a blanket of greenery that undulates with the rolling hills. Ten different shades of green, interspersed in haphazard perfection. The simple beauty of it arrests me, the luck of coming upon this hidden landscape. Understanding that I'm only here by accident, because hundreds of billions of molecules happened to arrange themselves into the shape of me, to give me legs that work, to put whatever sequence of thoughts into my brain were needed for me to make the decisions that have led me here. Maybe, just for a moment, I understand why Emmaline jumped.

"What's wrong with you, Mommy?" asks Nel.

Danny and E turn to look at me.

"What—you're crying? Cas…"

E laughs. "God, mom."

Danny studies my face, thoughtfully.

"What?"

"Nothing. I'm just glad we did this. That's all."

The next day, after we say goodbye to the kids, I hop into our ridiculous SUV and wait while Danny walks up the road with his phone and makes a call. After a few minutes, he returns, smiling and full of energy. "You ready?"

He's already warned me that the road is long, so long that it seems endless, but you have to stick with it. Once we get there, it will be a quick visit. We'll look at the cabin together and when Danny drives away from it for the last time, I'll be at his side. Somehow, this will be our resolution.

Time slows down, then speeds up.

The road isn't endless after all. Twenty minutes in, we're stopped by a tree lying on its side, the road disappearing beneath a mess of branches and dried-up needles. It's massive, alarmingly tall, even in its fallen state. I look for a beginning and an end, a top and a bottom, but can't find them.

"Shit." Danny jumps out of the vehicle, walks from one side of the road to the other and then back again. He tries his phone, returns it to his pocket, walks toward my open window, then turns back to consider the tree again.

"It's fine," I say. "It doesn't matter. I didn't need to see the cabin."

"Cas." He places his hands above my window, stretches out his arms, looks at the ground.

"Come on. It's fine. Let's just go back."

"No. We have to wait. I don't know if he'll…"

"Who? What is it, Danny?"

Time slows down, then speeds up.

Danny leads me out of the vehicle, directs me to a half-decayed log that cracks and crunches under our weight as we sit. He puts his arm around me, pulls me toward him. That classic Danny maneuver. It feels like an ending, a place to stop time and dissolve into darkness.

"I guess I need to tell you something."

I close my eyes. "It's almost like someone put that tree there, isn't it?"

"Just listen for a minute. It's going to be okay. We're heading in the right direction."

"Like they didn't want the road to be endless anymore."

"I always hated this fucking road. No one ever took care of it."

"They didn't want you up there."

"Maybe not."

You could say that Danny lays everything on me all at once, but the truth is that as he talks, I understand that it's been seeping in, slowly, for weeks. If only I'd paid more attention. Taz's confession and Anton's heartbreak. The same sky, the same bodies falling, the same parachute that never opened. Emmaline Kincaid.

It's not just the forest that seems to stretch out forever; it's this too. When you're in it, you don't see how interconnected it all is. But once you go up to the highest vantage point, you understand how it loops together. Two people jump out of a helicopter. The parachute that opens is blue. Danny and his friends watch from a ridge top, confused at first and then, later, terrified, once it hits them. What they've done.

Emmaline's missing tusk: they stole it. They left Anton for dead. They went home and kept their mouths shut and then, one by one, they started dying. Danny assures me that there are nuances, exceptions to be made for youth and naivety, or call it stupidity if you want. Later you live with the guilt, you let it pull you apart again and again, until you're certain that the remorse is there, that it's *genuine*. It's not a ball in the pit of your stomach like they always say, but the pit itself, the hole cut into you that makes you feel every day like you're spilling out onto the floor. It's the urgency of keeping yourself intact, of remembering what makes you human.

Whenever Danny pauses, I hear the sound of wind blowing through the canopy, trying to lift the leaves and carry them away.

Danny's been in touch with Curt, he explains. For years. I try to swallow, to focus on the sound of the leaves hanging on and fighting back. As he talks, Danny looks down at his hands, at my hands inside of his, the palms and fingers and wrists that represent us. It was never the right time to tell me about Curt. Surely, I understand this. It was the circumstances, the situation. Impossible.

Curt stayed at Dora's cabin for a while, but only because the timing was right. Anton found Curt or Curt found Anton, but however their meeting transpired, Curt helped Anton and later Anton helped Curt, and the moral of the story isn't related to what anyone didn't do, but what they *did* do. Regular people who stumble upon misfortune and make mistakes, but ultimately do their best to help one another. *It's people helping people out*, Danny keeps saying.

Curt was supposed to be gone forever, but instead, somehow, he came back. He brought Anton to the Silver Whistle, told him about a job opening he knew about. All the players know each other. Their secrets link up, they spill out and unfurl, and together we head toward a single, tragic ending. What was it that Lee's roommate called me? A bouncing dot that pulls everyone else toward the center? Maybe he was right.

*It's people helping people out.*

After Taz died, Danny hoped life would return to normal. Most things work themselves out on their own, with time, but this was different. This was...

"The curse," I say.

Danny doesn't look up, doesn't seem surprised to hear this. "No. Not a curse." His face is hard, his jaw set. Rockface. I see it now. "Believing that is like giving everything you have away. This is just life. Sometimes life is shit, and it's up to you to deal with it. *Me*, I should say. I'm the one dealing with everyone else's messes."

He turns to me, finally. There's a startling intimacy in his expression. "What if at the end of all this, we realize the tusk made our lives better, not worse? What if that's what ends up happening?"

I'm aware of a thumping sound, my blood pulsing through the

forest, burrowing up from the ground and pushing through the leaf litter, as the forest tries to claim my body. Danny is watchful, waiting for me to respond. He's lit up by the sun just like I remember. When was that? We were on the beach. He bought me an island. It was so many years ago it hardly seems like it happened. Danny is golden and perfect, like a statue. His mouth turns up into the slightest suggestion of a smile.

The end, I think. Make this the end.

But no. It's not the end. Danny waits until we hear another vehicle coming up the road to tell me why it can't be.

We're meeting Randall Kincaid. He's here to finally see his daughter's body. Danny is making amends.

The Furniture King arrives in some kind of off-road vehicle in electric green with two rows of seats and net-like fabric where doors should be. He rides with a driver and another man, both of them impossibly large and ice-eyed, rifles strapped across their bodies. Randall has snow-white hair and the face of an old man, but he leaps out of the vehicle with surprising agility. He's done it before with his own rifle, flushed with purpose, ready to take down another beast and make it his. He turns toward Danny and me, a pair of sunglasses hiding his eyes.

Danny rises from the log, tapping me lightly on the elbow which I guess means I'm supposed to stand too. The armed men move between him and Randall. They pat him down on his back, around the waist, around the ankles. Then they come up to me and do the same.

"Easy," says Danny. "Watch those hands."

The men circle our vehicle, reach up into each wheel well, feel along the undersides of the bumpers, searching all the places a person might think of to hide something, if there was something to be hidden. One of them slides on his back and vanishes underneath the vehicle. We wait in silence until he reemerges.

"I apologize for all the drama," Randall says. "But seeing as how we're in the middle of nowhere."

"I get it," says Danny.

I hold my breath as Danny and Randall shake hands, and imagine the sun burning away the air above us. It seems possible that Randall and his henchmen are made of fire, that in a few minutes we all will be.

"Mrs. Irving? A pleasure." I lift my hand, as if to wave, and stare into the dark planes of his sunglasses. The armed men have moved on from the SUV and are investigating the fallen tree. They walk the length of it, from one side of the road to the other, then push into the forest and disappear.

"I reckon they'll find a way around it." Randall seems to be staring at me, although I can't tell for certain. "You remind me a little bit of my daughter."

From all directions, heat presses in on us. It's a miracle we're all still here, that the ground hasn't liquefied beneath us yet.

They start talking about Emmaline. Danny speaks slowly, calmly, about her body, how he came to find out where it was.

"This guy—look—I don't really know him. He's a friend of a guy someone I worked with knows. We all ended up drinking together one night. You know how it is. You meet people one night and never see them again. One minute we're all talking about whether any of us are sober enough to drive home and the next minute he starts getting all worked up, telling us a story about some girl he dated, how the two of them jumped from a helicopter into a forest years ago and her parachute didn't open. He was afraid someone would come looking for him, so he buried her and then disappeared."

Wisps of Randall's fine white hair rise in the breeze. He has that way of standing, the posture, the solid footing. I try to imagine him lifting an axe, bringing it down and burying it in the hide of the animal that has toppled to the ground and might still be alive. The same sunglasses, the same neat khaki pants and off-white linen shirt. The same brown vest.

"At first, I didn't believe the guy, but he swore up and down that it was true. He pulled up the aerial imagery on his phone, showed me right where it happened, pointed out this endless road and the cabin at the end of it, how he hid there for a while to recuperate.

How he went back and found her and somehow had the strength to carry the body for miles to give her a proper burial. It's been eating away at him ever since, making him sick."

"So it was a confession, then." Randall pauses. "At a bar with strangers."

"Alcohol does that sometimes."

"And was it the alcohol that also made you decide to come looking for...her? A couple weeks ago, was it?" His head shifts toward the tree that's blocking the road. My eyes follow along with its movements: toward the tree, slowly, and then back again.

Danny shrugs. "It seemed to me like it was the right thing to do. I understand you don't know anything about me, but I have a set of rules that—"

"Do you think we'd be standing here if I didn't know anything about you?"

"I guess not. I guess that makes two of us." Randall nods slightly, and Danny responds with the same gesture. I want to step back and sit on the log again, but I'm afraid to move. Fifteen minutes ago, we were so close to something. If only I could interrupt and remind Danny of this, tell him how ironic it is—can't he see?—that the secret path to joy turned out to be a dirt road blocked by a tree.

Danny resumes his story. "The cabin wasn't all that hard to find, once I got on the right road. The guy told me he marked the grave with a big rock, and I found that too. It's a little ways back in the woods. I drew a map, in case it helps."

He pulls something out of his back pocket. Paper, folded. A photograph of Anton nestled into the crease. The sight of him offering these items to Randall is incomprehensible. One of the armed men takes them, flips them upside down, holds them up to the light, sniffs them, then passes them on to his boss.

Randall handles the photograph like it's a priceless artifact. "Where'd you get this?"

Danny shrugs. "People were taking pictures that night."

"I'd recognize the son of a bitch anywhere. That's *him*. My God, it really is."

This time I do step back. The men look up at me, possibly readying their guns, although who can be sure anymore whether any of this is real?

"Danny." I feel myself teetering, the heat taking me at last.

He whips his head around. On his face I see surprise, frustration, more surprise. "Jesus, Cas. Why don't you go sit over there in the shade?"

I find the shade, the log, the forest that has fallen silent, as if aware that an enemy is here. Randall is already strategizing how they'll cut into it to get around the tree, so they can drive up the road and dig up her body. Exhume. Is that the word? The men have machetes, now, in addition to their rifles. They hack away at tree branches and shrubs with long slicing motions. Danny and Randall stand side by side with their arms crossed until the men return to the vehicle. Danny starts to climb in after them, but the hand of a giant stops him, fingers spread out over Danny's chest. "Not you."

Randall pauses before climbing into the vehicle. "We'll take it from here. I'll be in touch."

They roar and crush and snap their way around the fallen tree, until they've torn a hole through the forest.

"I don't understand what you just did."

Danny doesn't look at me. "Come on," he says, heading toward the SUV.

"Danny."

"I don't want to talk about it right now. It's too fucking hot out."

He holds my door open and waits for me to get in.

"But why would you give him that picture?"

He closes his eyes and sighs. "Just get in the car. Please."

"They'll go after him."

"It was just a photograph. He wouldn't have believed me otherwise."

"You made that story up. It never happened."

"It doesn't change anything, Cas. Just, I wish you would look at the big picture sometimes."

"It just feels like—"

"You can't have it both ways. Either you want me to fix this or you don't. How do we know Anton is even telling the truth? All we know is the daughter's parachute never opened. Maybe he tampered with it. Maybe he wanted her gone and made it look like suicide."

"Come on. The way he talks about her? He still hasn't gotten over her. It's like—what?"

Something is wrong with Danny's face. His eyes. They're wild. So angry they could slice me into pieces.

"The way he *talks* about her? What are you saying? You and Anton have...*conversations?*"

"He's an activist, Danny. There's a group of us."

"No. Tell me this isn't happening. Tell me you're not mixed up with them too. That ecoterrorist group. Please. I know you're smarter than this."

"Revenge Gaia? Of course not. We're peaceful. We use our voices. We want to protect...things." I hold out my hand in the direction of nothing in particular. "This."

Danny puts his hands on my shoulders and holds them square, tilts his head down so that his face is all I can see.

"I don't think you understand—"

"You're wrong. I do understand."

"—how hard it is to hold all of this together. This is what I'm talking about. Dora, Curt, you. You keep ruining all my plans." His eyes are still wild, but his voice is calm. "I don't know why I keep trying so hard."

"*What* are you holding together, exactly? You keep saying this, but then..."

Danny closes his eyes. "Listen to me. Let me tell you what's at stake here, how delicate it is. If Kincaid's people do some poking around and he finds out about this—there's no way to explain it. I can't even comprehend this. Another bartender?" He releases my shoulders, walks around to his side of the vehicle, and climbs inside.

"There's nothing to find out about. It's not just him, but a whole community of us. These are good people. We're trying to make a difference, do work that matters."

"I need you to help *me*, okay? Can you do that, please? By getting in the car?"

"After everything that just happened, this is what you're mad about? My volunteer work?"

"I can't have this discussion right now. We need to go. Either get in the car or I'm leaving without you."

Danny starts the ignition. His jaw is clenched into stone. Rockface. I can't think of him as anything else now.

Somehow, I force my feet to move, open the door, climb into the seat. "I knew you wouldn't get it."

Danny grips the steering wheel and reverses too fast, turns too fast, nearly drives off the road. "Stop talking. I need to think."

There are miles of silence. The road feels longer on the way back. How many times did Danny drive it to see Dora? To visit Curt? Was there ever a time when we weren't Keep Secrets from Each Other People? It seems like there was. Back in the old days, when we were on that deserted island together.

Back at the cottage, Danny's parents look at us and know not to ask how it was. Danny storms off to the bedroom and closes the door. Deb looks up at me quizzically and I shrug my shoulders. "It's hot," I offer.

The kids want to know why Dad is so mad, whether there is still time to go out on the rowboat before dinner. Nel shows me the stuffed bear she bought in town, tells me about the movie they're watching. "Do you want to watch with us?"

My children. How do I lift them up out of the mud and keep them there? I sit between them on the couch and stare at the TV screen. What was it like to be Nel's age, or E's age, and wonder what my future would be like? Did I ever do this? Because it doesn't seem like you can. There's no way to predict, to prepare, to decide you want something different and make the choices to get you there. There is no secret path to joy.

I want to stand up in front of them and start making promises, assure them of all the things I will do to make them good human beings and secure people.

*I hereby swear that I will feed you healthy foods.*

*I hereby swear that I will play games with you and help you with your homework and be at home more.*

*I hereby swear that I will stop being an activist, or at least that I won't get arrested doing it.*

*I hereby swear—*

A door bangs. Danny comes rushing out of the bedroom and blazes through the living room. "I have to go into town for a few minutes," he announces.

As I follow him out of the house, I hear Nel whining about the lake, E calling out a question I can't decipher.

"Don't come with me. Stay here."

"Did they find her?"

"Of course they found her."

"Where are you going now?"

"I'm serious. Stay here with the kids."

Bill appears in the doorway. "Is everything okay?"

"We'll be back soon," I say, and follow Danny into the SUV.

We meet Randall and his silent henchmen in front of a boarded-up building in town.

"I'm not sure what to say," offers Danny. "My condolences."

I wonder how much of her would be left after all this time, how Randall would know for certain that the dead woman is his daughter, but there doesn't seem to be any question about her identity. Somehow he can tell just by looking at her bones.

Randall makes a strange noise, then removes his sunglasses and presses his fingers between his eyes, as if double-checking that his tear ducts are sealed shut. "I mean, of course, after so many years, we all suspected."

Danny places a hand on his shoulder. "I'm so sorry. I can't imagine."

"No, you can't." A change comes over Randall's face as he covers Danny's hand with his own. His shoulders straighten. His eyes are coldwater blue.

"I need you to help me find him. Tell me what you know."

Danny shakes his head. "I don't think I can help. I only talked to him once."

Randall slaps the top of Danny's hand. "I know, I know. I get it, but listen." He glances in my direction. "Listen," he repeats, placing a palm on Danny's back and turning him away from me. His voice is low. *Your wife looks like she...*what? What do I look like?

Please, Danny. Don't.

They walk a few steps before stopping, just out of earshot. As they talk, Danny's shoulders fall. There's a piece of paper, a pen.

Danny writing. Randall pocketing the paper. Afterward, they walk toward Randall's vehicle. Randall reaches inside, pulls out a plastic shopping bag, and hands it to Danny. It's light gray with green lettering, spelling out a word I can't decipher.

They shake hands.

Time speeds up.

If I was going to do something, how would that begin? Would it be with me noticing the keys to the rental vehicle in the tray between the seats? Would it be with me climbing into the driver's seat and adjusting it so that my feet rest comfortably on the pedals? Danny stands with a still back, nodding as Randall talks. It's two men chatting on a street corner as the afternoon touches the evening. It's a plastic shopping bag, hanging from Danny's fingers, and the thousand words that this transaction somehow requires. When I press the ignition button, Danny jerks his head toward the sound of an engine roaring to life, and in the few confusing seconds before he thinks to run toward me, I pull those huge tires out onto the road and find out what they can do. Just like that I'm a small monster inside of a bigger monster, letting my husband fade in the rearview mirror, tearing across the road, ignoring speed limits, looking for a town to flatten as I figure out what to do next.

Which is what?

Text Anton. Call him. Warn him. Any of these things. My right hand pats my pockets, hovers over the seat next to me, searches for the object that I already know is missing.

My phone. Back at the cottage.

There is math I could be doing if I was more level-headed. How long before Randall finds Anton? Will he head straight to the Silver Whistle? Is there a private plane involved, a private helicopter? The math, I'm sure, would tell me that there isn't enough time.

It's alarming that a person's heart can beat this hard for this long. It feels like it could explode, whatever the heart version of that is. Of course: heart attack. I pray that I won't have one at the wheel, that I won't hit a deer, that I won't at any moment see an electric green vehicle approaching in my rearview mirror. When the cottage comes into view, I pull into the driveway with a whoosh and will myself to be calm. To look calm. To at least stop shaking.

Bill is standing on the porch with his arms crossed, his face crunched into a frown. He's got those blue rocket eyes, ready to launch. "Danny just called me and asked me to pick him up in town. I thought the two of you were together."

"Uh, yeah. He had something he needed to do and I realized I forgot my phone. My wallet."

Bill is one of those men who stare and never waver. He's the kind who can spot a racing heartbeat from six feet away.

"So I decided to come here and get it, then head back." I try to smile. *Silly me.*

"What's that, now?"

"I was thinking the kids might like to come along this time. Are they still watching that movie?" As I move toward the door, Bill positions his body in front of mine.

"We'll get ice cream," I offer.

Bill grabs my arm, firmly, just below the shoulder. "Tell me what's going on. Is Danny in trouble again? I can never tell with him."

"I can't tell either."

He stares. He doesn't waver. I think we must be wondering the same things—about me and what I've just said—although I can't quite keep it straight in my mind. There's too much urgency, pushing out in all directions. Dire. The word loops on repeat, like a tornado warning. Dirediredire.

It would be easy to let it go, watch it float away and become someone else's garbage, let Bill lead me back into the cottage and give me permission to sleep.

But diredirediredirediredire Anton. That was it. Anton. I have to call him. How much time is left?

I change my answer. "I don't think Danny's in trouble."

"Why don't you let me take care of this? I'll go get him."

Bill releases my arm and holds the door open, gestures for me to head inside. "We can all talk about this when I get back." As we stand in the doorway, I see the blur of time in my periphery, racing by. Dire.

The kids seem both happy and unhappy to see me.

"Where's Daddy?" Nel asks.

"He'll be back soon." I scan the kitchen for my purse, the bedroom, the family room. Deb watches me, wearing a black swimsuit, a towel wrapped around her waist.

"Is everything okay?"

"Everything's fine. I just…there was a phone call I was supposed to make and I forgot my phone. Oh and Bill went into town. He just left."

I spot a strap of brown next to E's legs, nudge his body forward with shaky hands, and grab my purse.

"You and Dad didn't look too happy this afternoon," he says.

This afternoon? I try to remember it: the tree blocking the road, the men patting me down, everything that should have happened but didn't or maybe the opposite of that entirely. It's hard to keep it straight.

"We're okay," I say, before spinning around and heading outside, looking for a spot where my phone has enough bars to place a call. I listen to a series of rings that ends with Anton's voice, telling me he'll get back to me when he can.

I text:

> Randall Kincaid is coming for you. Leave town. NOW

Does it sound like a joke? Could someone interpret it that way?

> Call me as soon as you get this.
>
> Delivered

Off to the west, the sun is setting. The day is falling away from me. When I walk back to the cottage, Nel is waiting for me on the front steps. "Can I help you, Mommy?"

I stare at her tiny, beautiful face, the messy curls of her hair. It's hard to believe that Danny and I could have made a person this perfect, this easy to ruin.

"Go get E," I whisper. "Go get your bear."

"Okay."

"But do it quietly."

How long before Danny returns with Bill? And then what?

Seconds pass, drips that puddle into minutes. I check my bars, recheck my bars, send another text:

> He has men. They have guns

The clock says 6:22. What do these numbers mean? 6:22 6:22 6:23. How much time is left?

> They found her

At last Nel returns, her brother at her side. "What are we doing? Where's dad?"

I try to smile. "Do you guys want some ice cream?" Light-hearted and sing-song is what I'm going for.

They tilt their heads, eye me warily. Nel's brow furrows.

"But we didn't eat dinner yet."

"Well, we'll do that too, then. How about it?"

"I'm not wearing any shoes," says E. He starts back toward the house, but I catch him by the arm, press him toward the back seat.

"We're on vacation. Who needs shoes?"

I help them both with their seatbelts, ignoring E's skeptical glare. "Where is dad? Is he meeting us there?"

Deb steps out onto the porch as I'm climbing into the driver's seat. Behind the cottage, the sun is falling, second into second into second.

"Where are you off to now?"

"Ice cream!" yells Nel.

"We just took them for ice cream a few hours ago. They don't need more." Deb approaches the vehicle. "Where'd you say Bill went? You better let me call him. They might want you to stay here."

I point at the sky for no reason at all, smiling as brightly as I can. "Don't worry about it. We'll be back soon."

"But...wait!" yells Deb, but we're already backing out of the driveway, already gone. I wonder how I must look to her, what she'll say about me when Danny returns. *She just took the kids and drove away.*

As we speed toward the highway, I work out the least damaging way to tell the kids that their vacation is over, that there's no time for dinner. *I'm sorry, but I have a friend I need to help.*

Anton still hasn't called. What other choice do I have?

# CHAPTER 28

## (EMMALINE)

When your father is Randall Kincaid, what do you do? Do you do anything? Maybe not, but she heard herself telling Anton that she needed to do something and him telling her of course she did, that they could change the world, the two of them. She wanted to love him. She supposed that maybe she even did, but when she was a young girl she'd gotten confused somewhere along the way about what it was going to feel like when it happened. She had imagined bright colors and clean edges, but instead there was this. Stories about elephants screaming.

The idea of parachuting into the forest and living off the land, pretending to be missing. It had seemed so solid before. But now, up in the helicopter and ready to jump, she understood that it was all wrong. But the thing of it is, once a plan is in motion, especially one this big, halting it is like devastation. You can't keep unwinding and rewinding, unwinding and rewinding. At some point you have to let go of both ends, watch them stream away from you, and be proud of what you have accomplished.

Emmaline checked the supply pack one final time. What possessed her to take out the tusk? It was impractical to jump with it, but when had this ever been about being practical? Anton eyed her quizzically, but said nothing. She re-secured the pack and checked her own parachute, inched her way closer to the door. Anton slid in beside her. In a few seconds, they would be free. Beneath her, the forest was magnificent. It was right, jumping into this.

They dropped the pack of supplies and watched it float away. There was no time to reconsider. She wrapped one arm around the tusk and took a moment to appreciate the unadulterated blueness of the sky. She would try to think of a name for it as she fell, this most brilliant of colors she had ever seen.

Would it matter if nobody found them? As the trees rushed toward her, she could feel the tusk slipping. It was time to pull the cord, but Emmaline hesitated, knowing that if she moved her arms the tusk would fall. It was either the tusk or the parachute, and only one of these choices was sane. Details of the land came into view, the banks of a river cutting through the trees. Above her, a hawk floated by, its only purpose in that moment to remind her that she could never be as majestic. Just look at it—the pattern of its feathers and the angle of its flight. She and her kind would never be the answer. Emmaline didn't look for Anton. Instead she closed her eyes. All that mattered was what was right. It was clear. It was peaceful. It was—

Dear Dad,

Sometimes, the world gets so loud. I feel like everyone is yelling. I don't understand why we do this. Shouldn't we focus on listening, on loving and being kind? Maybe we don't know how. Maybe this is what evolution is: we lose the ability to hear noise, and we don't know where the silence is. Sometimes it seems like the only way to find it is to jump straight into it and trust it will be there.

Emmaline

# CHAPTER 29
## (CASSIE)

There are hours of driving, a highway that goes on and on and on. It baffles me, how we've managed to build so many roads, connect so many places together. How many places are there? What enormous number? The thought of it is breathtaking. I glance at my children's unsmiling faces and wonder how to begin explaining it to them. We could go somewhere. We should. After everything back home is fixed, I could put them in the car and we could find our favorite place and live there, and… would Danny be there too? I don't know I don't know I don't know.

He calls, again and again. The conversations end before they've even started. He tries to explain. He tells me that I don't understand, I need to listen, but as much as he explains, I don't come any closer to understanding. He talks about finally getting ahead, about me finally going to baking school, all of us remembering our dreams. He assures me we had them, that we've always been Follow a Dream People.

*All I told him is the name of the bar. That's it. You have to trust me. It will all turn out fine. Just stay away from it. Don't go there. Promise me, Cas.*

The kids are worried. Nel is crying. They keep asking me where we're going, why we didn't bring our suitcases with us, why E couldn't even have his shoes. They want to talk to their father. They're hungry. Everything they ask for, I refuse. *Bricks of soft clay. Please don't break.*

My list of promises grows, then shrinks down to one: *I hereby swear to keep you safe.* Mile marker after mile marker, I repeat this one sentence, a silent chant in my head to keep us all going, past Marshall, past Greenfield, past Panhandle. At some point, my thoughts drift to Lee and the in-between spaces he used to talk about, how you can go your whole life without noticing them, but once you start looking they're everywhere. You can see the light shining through them, pinpoints and slivers of white, like sunshine through old floorboards. This is what I focus on as we barrel forward: the negative space, illuminated by a light nobody was expecting.

The tires spin. The fuel tank goes empty. We stop for gas and three bags of sunflower seeds. The sky turns dark. Finally, we make it back inside the city limits and find our way to Cherie's place, where I drop off the kids for dinner. *A half hour*, I promise them. *I'll see you soon.* Her dogs run in circles, looking for bodies to jump on and faces to lick. Larry comes in the room with a gigantic bag of cheese puffs. For the first time in hours, my children are smiling. I pull Cherie to the side.

"Thank you. I owe you for this."

"What happened? You're shivering."

"Don't let them call Danny. Please. No matter how much they beg."

"Oh shit. What did he do this time?"

How do you make a plan? How do you decide what to do?

The truth is that I didn't do the first bad thing, or the worst bad thing, and possibly what I've done isn't bad at all. Maybe this is the first time I've ever pulled into the parking lot of a bar called the Silver Whistle in a crappy little strip mall on the southwest side of town. It could take me years to arrange events in the right chronological order. Some things we lose before we even have them and others we have without understanding how we got them. Why else would it happen like this: the parking lot empty and darker than usual, the air smelling of smoke and ash, damp wood, burned wood. A barricade in front of the bar, too small to be called a fence. A sign taped to a window:

Is it the past? The future? Both?

The building looks mostly intact, at least from the front, but the windows are blackened, the neon signs emptied of their color. A martini glass that used to be pink, an olive that used to be blue. Should I remember a fire? Did I hear about it on the news?

It doesn't seem possible that Randall's men could have gotten here fast enough to do this much damage. Unless I got lost somewhere along the way? As I try to make sense of what has happened, the dark edges of doom begin to flutter down around me. Someone has been here and erased all the people. What other explanation is there?

This would be the right time to turn around and drive away, but I've already been by Anton's empty apartment and I don't know where else to go. As I step down out of the SUV and begin walking toward the bar, it seems possible that I may be erased too.

Part of me expects magic. When I open the door, there will be light and color, the murmur of voices overhead, a stairway that leads up, up, up, into the clouds. Nel and E will be laughing, making new friends. *Can this be our home now, Mommy?*

*Of course it can. We can all stay here.*

Behind me, I hear the sound of an engine, wheels on asphalt, the slow passage of a car through the parking lot. When I push on the door, it pushes back. Even with my shoulder engaged—a whole-body heave from the knees—the door refuses to yield. How can I save a man if every door is locked?

I consider the situation for another few seconds, then turn around. A car is parked next to the SUV. An old-looking maroon sedan with a square of gray primer near one of the rear wheels. Is it familiar? Do I know it? A door swings open. A person steps out. A dark figure. A man-shaped person in a dark, hooded sweatshirt.

Is running an option? Maybe he wouldn't catch me. Maybe I would pick the right direction and end up somewhere that isn't here and throw myself into the arms of a stranger ready to help. They tell you it's instinct, that you'll make the right decisions when you need to, but sometimes there is just this: a locked door or nothing.

The man turns toward me, rests his arm on the hood of the sedan, and waits.

He isn't familiar. The way he stands, the way he turns his head, the way he shifts from one leg to the other. From a distance, his hands appear to be empty. I consider the odds of what happens next. Is there a way that this ends with me walking back to that ridiculous silver SUV and simply driving away?

It's not a long walk. I've done it before. Too many times. It always seemed like if I didn't, there would be less of me left in the world. Those nights in the van. The way something about the shape of it reminded me of the bookshelves in my bedroom as a kid: the pile of acorns I collected and the glass swan with its clear feathers swirled in blue and a vase of dried flowers my mother gave me with no other explanation than that she thought they were pretty. The bedroom light was warm, incandescent. I remembered lying on the floor looking up at it. Why would I be lying on the floor? Why would I be in a van waiting for Lee, my head spinning with the thought of going home but deciding not to? I didn't love the glass swan, but I collected more of them anyway, hoping that with the thrill of numbers my feelings would change. They crowded out the things I did love, the things I must have loved but forgot.

How do you explain this to another person?

I fix my eyes on the driver's side door of the SUV, avoiding the dark figure who, I'm certain, can only be waiting for me. I count out the steps out in my head. One, two, three, four, five, six, seven.

"Cassie."

The softness in his voice catches me off guard. It's this part that makes me curious enough to turn my head.

I don't think immediately that it's Danny, or even that he resembles Danny. It's more Deb that I see—Danny's mother's face on a man I've never met before. Now that I'm up close, I remember the sedan. Danny said he was borrowing it from a friend until he could get his own car fixed. A few days or maybe a few weeks later it was gone and Danny's car was back. How many other details like this are there?

"We've never met," he offers.

I try to recollect the face on the driver's license, the one Danny slid out of my hand years ago. Curt as a teenager, before he disappeared.

"Danny doesn't really talk about you. I recognize that car, though."

He looks down and considers the hood of the sedan for several seconds. Ten. Twenty. I lose count. When he raises his head again, his eyes flash awake, like he's just remembered why he's here.

"We already warned Anton. He knows what happened. I mean up at the cabin."

"Danny gave him a photograph. I don't even...I don't think..." The sobs rise up quickly, as the pieces start to fall into place. What must have happened at the Silver Whistle while I was gone. What might still happen. Even if Curt is telling me the truth—even if they've warned Anton—what difference does it make? The fire will happen. The fire has happened. If they haven't already, Randall's people will find him.

Why did I think I would be able to save him?

Curt raises a hand in my direction, as if to touch my shoulder despite the car and the distance between us. "Oh, hey. It's okay. Don't worry. We figured everything out."

I try calling Anton again. It's the same empty ringing that I've heard a hundred times already, but this time I'm aware of music, muffled but near: lively percussion and high-pitched bells. Brazilian Carnival music, Anton explained to me once. The happiest ringtone he could find.

Where is he now? Shoved in the trunk? Kidnapped? Hiding?

"It's in there." Curt gestures toward the car window. In the darkness I can just make out the shape of a phone on the passenger seat.

"Where is Anton? What happened to the Silver Whistle?"

The man I'm talking to, I realize, is a person who killed his own father. A terrible accident, Danny called it. But still, Curt ran.

"He's in the belly of the beast now. That group—what are they called?—has him hidden. Revenge Gaia. I don't really get that name."

I'm shaking my head, thinking about the refinery fires, the people who died. "No. That's not right. Anton didn't agree with what they did. He wouldn't have let himself be…What are you saying? They took him?"

"It's a shade of gray type thing, Cassie. Anton agreed with them enough. Given what happened. They'll take care of him. They wouldn't have started this fire otherwise."

"What? I don't understand. Is that a metaphor, or…?"

"You didn't hear it from me, of course."

"But…" I sift through the pieces, try to put them in order, identify a starting point behind which they all line up. Anton mute inside his elaborate animal masks. The quiet, the kindness, the pledge of non-violence. I thought the layers were finally settling, that you could see the lines between them clearly, but now they're shaken up again.

It occurs to me that Danny must be on his way. That's why we're here, talking in a parking lot that smells like a bonfire gone wrong.

Curt's voice is low and steady. It has the same placid quality as water lapping at the bottom of a rowboat. "All this is nothing, really. It seems worse than it is. Say I die, or Danny dies. That's not terrible. I mean overall. I mean to the millions of people who don't know us, what does it matter? Anton dies. Randall Kincaid dies. It'll happen eventually. The last elephant dies. The last polar bear dies." He shrugs. "I guess probably. I guess this is worse, but I've never even seen either one in my life, so…

"My point is that you don't know. None of us have the ability. In the meantime, we just, we see things. We try to love things but we hate a lot of things anyway. We let things ruin us. We believe in curses, we don't believe in curses—I don't know."

Curt rubs his hands together. His shoulders are hunched forward and his neck is bent, as if from a lifetime of trying to make himself smaller.

"Stop crying, Cassie. It's okay. It'll be okay. We've got it all planned out."

"But why would they set this place on fire?"

"Isn't that what they do, though? It's how they make a statement, how they start a war."

"But…what war?"

"You need to get people's attention. You need pictures of a burning building with Randall Kincaid's name underneath. Bring up the trophy hunts, the conditions in his factories overseas, his missing daughter. Randall Kincaid, fire. Randall Kincaid, fire. A detailed account of the elephant hunt. Pictures of his daughter. Excerpts from her diaries. Her own words and her own signature, or close to it anyway. Too close to tell the difference. Anton's letters about fear and exile. Being in hiding. It doesn't even need to be true. When he signed Emmaline's name; he made them hers. You just need to push it along until the collective opinion turns against Randall Kincaid, and after that it's a matter of keeping it going as long as people will listen, or until the tide turns the other way, but who knows where all of us will be by that time." Curt laughs, as if he finds this statement funny.

"Tomorrow morning, Cassie. Go online and type in the words 'Randall Kincaid.' You'll see what I mean."

It doesn't seem like there will be a tomorrow, that we will ever make it that far.

I wonder if the kids are asleep, if Danny somehow found them and took them home, if this conversation with Curt was all another part of the plan. But then another thought pushes its way through, past all the confusion, and settles in. The gap it fills has been there for years. "All that money Danny saved up, that went away. That was you."

Curt smiles shyly and rubs his face. "I asked him to stop, but he wouldn't. He's hard-headed. You know this. He goes on with the family stuff, the brothers stuff. I appreciate him, though. I really do."

My throat hurts. It feels like I've been yelling all day, but when I think back on it, it seems like most of the last twelve hours have been silence. There was never anyone to save. This is what Curt is communicating to me. All those miles of driving, hurrying to get here. For what? Nothing, I guess. This, whatever it is.

"What would have happened if..." The tears return, the sentence dies.

"I'm sorry. Really. I mean, basically all of this is me. Whatever is going wrong in your life, I did it to you. You don't think about day to day. You just kind of do what you can, try to make things right, and all it does is blow up on you, over and over, like one of those fireworks. You think it's done and how can there possibly be any more to it, but it just keeps going, twinkling, falling down to the water.

"So I don't know. I guess maybe I'll just go to the police and turn myself in. Let them know they can stop looking for me. While I'm at it, I can let them know I was the one who shot Danny, maybe even hand over the—"

"Wait a minute."

"What?"

"*You* shot Danny?"

"It was an accident, of course." Curt stares at me over the top of his car. He taps the hood with a finger. "He used to keep secrets from me too, if that makes you feel better. We just sort of understood each other. You know what I mean, don't you?"

Curt continues talking. There are sentences I don't hear. I'm too dizzy to think. We're not meant to travel in time. We're not meant to keep working the same spot over and over, shaping it into something different.

I'm not sure what happens next. Do I fall? Does Curt lift me off the ground and put me inside his car? At some point I'm aware of being stretched out on a back seat. Curt is talking, I guess on the phone. *I found her. She's here.* What happens next? Does Curt take me back to Danny and set me back on that long, arduous path to joy? Thinking about it makes my stomach churn. The nausea comes in waves. I slide my head past the edge of the seat and turn toward the floor, ready to throw up if that's what it comes to. A blue towel with a frayed edge is shoved underneath the passenger's seat. If I concentrate on each separate thread, the churning stops. I follow the threads as far as I can, until they're lost in the weave of the towel. One of these threads must be me. I grab one and pull, feel it catch and hold. The towel is surprisingly heavy. It's wrapped around something solid—a weapon, I assume, trying to feel the shape of it with my fingers. It's smooth and curved, and...

Oh.

*It's cursed*, I tell myself. *Let go*. But it's already out of the towel and in my hands, milky white and honey brown with streaks of gray, polished to a shine. The gentle curve, the rounded tip. Centuries of time. I know the story, that it's only been around for a couple decades, but the tusk seems ancient. Worshipped and buried and worshipped and buried and dug up to be worshipped again. The heft of it: hard and heavy yet somehow fragile, too. Ready to be sliced into with a knife. A million dead elephants and only their tusks left behind. Human-carved stories in ivory, displayed on shelves. Somehow, I remember this, the reason for it that dates back to a time when the earth seemed so vast we thought it had no end.

I smell the fire again, try to remember what has burned.

Outside, I hear voices, Danny and Curt talking. Do they sound like brothers? I guess it doesn't matter. The tusk is on my lap, in my hands, cradled in my arms. There's a story that goes with it, one that I finally understand. Randall Kincaid with a gun. Randall Kincaid with an axe. Randall Kincaid with a daughter he adored, giving her gifts he couldn't explain but hoped she would understand. I see it in perfect focus: the wide, low browns of the African savannah broken by the occasional flat-topped tree, wisps of clouds stretching out overhead, the slow plodding of gigantic feet, the trunk implausible, the ears implausible, the tusks the most implausible of all. How did such a creature come into existence? I see a baby being born, the herd roaming together and then being torn apart and the anger building, the drum beating, the internet and the drones and the guns, people being shot and beaten and pushed and falling falling falling falling. If I dig deeper I'll understand the rest: the scar on Taz's hand and the X on Lee's chest, and the reason he left even though he didn't shoot Danny, the earthy mushroom smell on his clothes. The line down my mother's face that separates what's hard from what's soft. Evan's triumphant star-filled sky. I can almost, finally, put all of it into words.

I open the door and step out of the car.

# CHAPTER 30

## (DANNY)

There was getting to be too much to keep track of. It was like trying to control a wild animal; every time you think it's stopped growing and you finally almost have it tamed, the thing puts on another ten pounds and grows a sharper set of teeth. Danny kept thinking *keep it simple*, but in reality nothing was. He sometimes considered starting over from scratch, with a smooth surface he could tuck in around the edges and build up just the way he wanted. Sometimes he thought about leaving with the kids, taking them on a speaking tour so he could show them different cities and different people, all the ways there were to look and talk and live. He didn't quite know what Cas would do, but he would try his hardest to fit her in. He always tried. Of course he did.

He'd more or less convinced Curt to turn himself in. It seemed like he had, although with Curt you could never tell for sure. They'd talked about what had begun to seem inevitable, that sometimes you just have to make amends the way society expects you to, to seek forgiveness via the formal avenues. Curt kept saying that he was tired, that he felt like a piece of rubber stretched across a crater, so thin that he was hardly there anymore, nothing left of him but the feeling of being pulled apart. When it gets that bad, sometimes you just have to let go.

The fire, on the other, hand, had been out of his control. That ecoterrorist group, Anton, all of it. They were unpredictable, and the smartest thing to do was maintain his distance, make sure Cas stayed away too. He'd use the money from Randall Kincaid to send her to school, start her baking again. Then the speaking engagements would take off. There would be money that was theirs and not a loan from his parents or her parents. If they wanted to, they could move. They could find a place, open a bakery, give it a cute name, let the kids help with the menus. They would do catering, weddings, JoyPath events. And then—who knows? The kids would see how you build a dream into a life; small to big but never so big that you forget to love. There would be money for college, space to soar. All you had to do was find your path, start moving forward.

Curt met him at the car, gave him a quick hug like he always did.

"I think she's tired. Maybe a little sick. Possibly shock? I don't know. She's in the back seat."

"What did you tell her? Because I said—"

"Danny, come on."

Sometimes Danny forgot that Curt was the older brother, that when they were kids Curt would barely even let Danny talk to him. The way his mom explained it, Curt's emotions didn't fall into the right slots all the time, and she knew it wasn't his fault but she also knew there probably wasn't any way to fix it. Some people were just broken this way. Danny thought maybe it was better now. Maybe being broken in certain ways had allowed him to heal in others.

"Did Kincaid's people come through here?"

"I think so. I was parked a little way from here, but I did see a car earlier. A man got out and walked around for a little while, tried the bar's front door. He could've been anyone, I guess. I don't know."

Danny nodded. He was certain he'd get a phone call soon, if not a visit, from one of Kincaid's men. It would all look suspicious, the timing of it. He'd have to try to convince Kincaid that his conversation with Anton that night hadn't been a coincidence. Now that Revenge Gaia was involved, it made more sense that Anton had told a group of strangers about Emmaline because he was hoping she would be found. He'd set in motion a plan and Danny was an unwitting pawn. Could he make Kincaid believe this? Danny was persuasive. He was reasonable. He'd proven that. As long as Kincaid didn't poke around any deeper and somehow trace the ownership of the cabin back to the MacIntosh family, didn't find Dora's obituary, didn't read about an incident on a roof last October: a man injured and a woman dead.

It was all there, so close to the surface. You wouldn't have to dig far at all. Ten minutes, maybe…

A headache pulsed between Danny's eyes. He would have to work it out later. There were ways around every land mine. You just had to be creative. Right now what he had to do was get his wife and his brother away from this burned-up bar. Find the kids. Make sure they were safe.

A car door opened. Cassie emerged slowly, her brown hair pulled back into a messy ponytail, her upper body tilted forward and her shoulders tight. Danny watched her turn her head from side to side, as if confused about where she was. Her gaze lingered on the burned-out building, like she was seeing it for the first time. She was carrying—what was it? Something white, in her arms, something heavy, something—

"Oh my God, Cassie. No."

It took some time before her eyes found him. They were miniature lanterns, exploding in the night. He'd seen this look before, the same worn-out, half-crazed expression on Katy's face that day at the cabin, when she'd held the tusk just like Cassie was holding it now: arms out and palms up, like something she almost couldn't bear to touch.

"Oh shit." Curt took a step toward her.

"I think I figured it out," said Cassie. "Almost. I'm working on it."

It wasn't supposed to happen like this.

# CHAPTER 31
## (CASSIE)

The thing is, we're not Believe in a Curse People. Danny knows this. His problem is that he doesn't have the imagination. He can't see anything but a car, a parking lot, a roof, a tusk. With him, it's the same idea, over and over, until he's convinced it's a fact: that he's always done the best he could and that this is what life is, for all of us to do the best we can. But he's wrong. It's up to me now to explain, to be patient, to make *him* better.

"You said it yourself, Danny. Remember? 'Believing that is like giving everything you have away.'"

He shakes his head. "Cas, don't."

"It's not a path at all. Some parts of it you skip over, because they don't happen until later. And you're not always walking. Sometimes you jump, you swim, you fall."

"We should go." Danny looks around nervously. I can see his brain working, building out his Danny equations and then trying to solve them.

"What will you do with the money Randall Kincaid gave you? Will you buy me an island?"

His mouth opens, but no words come out. It's okay, though. We're Figure It Out Quietly People. We've always been like this: me holding the tusk and him holding the...I don't remember what it was. But he's clever; he knows. We can find our way back.

"We have to go," Danny says.

"Where?"

"Home. Let's get the kids. They must be scared. Exhausted. Where did you leave them?"

"Tell me the plan first. What is it?"

Danny's phone rings. Curt lifts his head, checks the darkness behind him.

It must be Randall Kincaid calling, with his cloud-white hair and khaki pants, wanting to know why Danny sent him to look for Anton in a burned-out bar. Has he been on the internet? Has the war already started?

The phone rings again, a square of light that Danny swipes with his thumb, making it go dark.

"He'll come for you. He's an amoral, inhumane demon."

"No, he's just a man. I'll figure it out."

"They just leave them in place when they're done, their faces cut to pieces. This is what he does. As a hobby."

"I'm not happy about it either, Cas, but right now—"

"It's funny, isn't it? You'd think it was supposed to be a weapon, the way it looks. But evolution wasn't expecting us. Our guns and our axes."

"Let's get the kids. We can stay with my parents."

"Do you still have that bag of money with you?"

"We can talk about it later."

"I'm wondering, what if there's a tracking device in there? Like what if someone could follow you? What if he's tracked you here and those men from earlier are off somewhere in the shadows."

Danny looks off to the north, to the east, past the edges of the parking lot.

"You're being dramatic. We don't have time for this." As Danny approaches, I raise the tusk over my head.

He stops, wraps each of his hands around an invisible object, and squeezes.

"It feels like you could do some damage with this if you wanted to, though. Just an observation."

Danny listens. He thinks. He breathes.

"You told Randall Kincaid you went up there with Anton's map two weeks ago. But that tree—the one that stopped us—it's been down for more than two weeks. Wasn't that obvious?"

He surveys the parking lot again, end to end. I wish I could grant him a wish, the kind that erases time.

"He'll find us, Danny, even if he's not tracking the money."

"Is that what this is about? The money?"

"You're not listening to me."

"Fine." He walks toward Bill's Toyota. I don't know what

happened to Bill, where Danny dropped him off along the way, what explanation he offered before taking off again. Curt watches Danny with a thoughtful expression. He is tall, calm. All these years, Danny kept this person a secret from me.

"I know places he can go," Curt tells me, quietly. "I can help."

Our eyes meet, briefly, before Curt looks away.

A car door slams. Danny is carrying a gray plastic shopping bag with green lettering. He has a long stride, a rock face. He holds out the bag, lets it fall to the ground, a couple feet away from me. "I didn't count it, but that seems more or less like half."

"Why do we want this? You need to give it back. Just...leave it for him somewhere."

"Wait," says Curt. "We could get pretty far with that."

Danny shakes his head, slowly at first and then more quickly. "You guys are turning this into—my God, it's like you think he won't even talk to me first. I can fix this."

Curt stares at the bag. "If you don't want to run, we could go to the police. I'll turn myself in. We'll tell them what really happened on the roof."

Danny covers his face with both hands, mutters something unintelligible into his palms.

"But if we are going to leave, we should do it before morning."

The truth hovers nearby, a wisp-like, wind-lifted creature that drifts and drifts until finally it is within reach.

"Did you push her? Dora MacIntosh. Did you kill her?"

I look at the backs of Danny's hands. I imagine that they are shaking, that he must be shaking as much as I am. Maybe I don't need to see his eyes.

"It was an accident. I swear it was."

Is it a cold night? I can't tell. There was a fire here; it should be warm. I let Danny's words sift between the cracks and settle. I parse out their meanings, translate and then retranslate.

"You pushed Dora."

"I can't explain it. It wouldn't make sense to you. But the thing is that she *wanted* to jump. She wanted me to push her. I'm sure of it."

# CHAPTER 32
## (DANNY)

There was a flash, yes, but it didn't erase as much as it should have. I keep watching it, a movie inside my head, looping on repeat: the sidewalk, the apartment building, the roof. The sidewalk, the apartment building, the roof. The sidewalk. The man. Curt.

We were there for hours that night, in Evan's car, waiting for nothing. I started texting with Curt, a long, pointless back-and-forth that made me miss all the years I didn't have a brother to do this with.

> What neighborhood does he live in? What street are you on? Can you just get out and walk home?

I fell asleep and when I woke up it seemed like hours had gone by. I listened to Evan declaring his love for Dora, asking her to move in with him, her hesitation, her rejection. I wanted to tell Evan to let her go, that it wasn't worth the fight. This was her, the way she was. You couldn't let yourself get wrapped up in her.

> You still there?

Yup
Delivered

> I'm coming to pick you up. What's the address?

It wasn't instantaneous. I didn't stumble onto the sidewalk and see him heading in my direction. Time passed. I'm not sure how much. A few minutes, maybe, of me drifting, surveying the unfamiliar block, wondering where to be, now that I'd decided to not be in the car anymore. The inexplicably high curbs, the planting squares between the sidewalk and the street. An urban renewal project? I puzzled over the dead trees inside of them, winter skeletons lining the block, the mulch around their bases so fresh that you had to wonder whether they'd been planted this way, their branches without buds, dry and brittle. Had anyone noticed? The trees were as lifeless as the buildings and streetlight poles. Did anyone care? These thoughts could have taken thirty seconds or thirty minutes; your guess is as good as mine. But eventually there he was on the sidewalk, finally getting home from work.

Even before I heard Evan calling my name, I knew it was him. I tried working out what I would say, how this would go down. *You're the lowlife who's fucking my wife.* Do you even start the conversation with words? Or do you start it with a nice punch to the face instead?

He was a little taller than me, maybe a little thinner, a little older. He was wearing some retro-grunge outfit: a flannel shirt with the sleeves rolled up and faded jeans. Hiking boots. There was a tattoo on the inside of his left arm—a knife or something equally stupid—and black lettering on his right arm that started somewhere past his sleeve and continued to the edge of his palm. You could tell, just by looking at him, what he wanted to be but wasn't.

*You're fucking my wife.*

Jesus. Why him? Why not some slick investment banker who could take her out on a boat and give her jewelry, promises he never meant to keep?

When there was about twenty feet of sidewalk between us, we both stopped walking. His eyes dropped quickly to my hands, my pockets, my stomach. "Do I know you?"

"You're the bartender."

"Who wants to know?"

*You're fucking my wife.* What was I supposed to do, now that we were here? What options did I have, except to beat the shit out of him or turn around and head back to the car?

He turned up the short walkway toward the apartment building. I could hear Evan coming up behind me, his deep voice, calling out. "Wait! Please—we just want to talk."

The bartender turned around in front of the door, crossed his arms, jutted his chin toward Evan. "I remember you. You were in the bar that one night. You looked like a pedophile."

Evan offered his hand. Jesus Christ. He wasn't kidding. "Evan Conway. Lee, isn't it?"

"Whatever you're selling, I'm not interested."

"Easy," said Evan. He looked ridiculous in his blazer. "We can all be gentlemen, can't we? We're just here to chat. To exchange some information. A few minutes, huh?"

"It's three o'clock in the fucking morning."

I was staring at his face—those eyes and those cheekbones and that mouth—wondering what Cas saw when she looked at him, which one of them had started the flirting, which one had pushed it to escalate into something more.

"This is important." Evan wasn't going to let up. "I promise you we wouldn't be here if it wasn't."

I pictured the bartender rushing at Evan and knocking him down, smashing his head against the sidewalk, the freakishly high curb. He seemed like the kind who would. One of those rail-thin types who are also as tough as rails. Sure, there were two of us and only one of him, but what if he had friends, neighbors, people who were already watching us, wondering when the right time to get involved would be? What then?

"Fuck off." He pushed the door open with his back and stepped inside. Without understanding why, I followed him, not expecting the door to be as heavy as it was when it hit my arm and nearly pushed me back outside.

"Leave him, Danny. Let's go."

I opened my mouth to say something. What was it going to be? I honestly don't know. The bartender grabbed me by the shirt and pulled me inside the foyer, then threw me up against the wall, his arm a metal beam against my throat. I couldn't move, couldn't breathe. Through a window I saw Evan's face, Dora's hideous wig.

The bartender was standing in a lunge with his face about three inches from mine and one leg stretched out behind him, his heel pressed up against the door. He had this wild-animal look, like he was a jackal ready to bite, although I'd never seen one before, wasn't even really sure what one would look like.

"What do you want?" he barked, then eased off my windpipe just enough for me to breathe.

"Cassie," I coughed.

I watched him figuring out what to do with this piece of information, the way it banged around in his head for a minute before clicking into place. He looked at the floor like he wasn't sure what to do next. He looked at my feet, my clothes, the spot where his arm pressed against my neck. Behind him, Evan and Dora were banging on the glass, saying God only knows what. "So I guess you're the husband." He shook his head, like he wanted me to lie about it. Maybe that was why I didn't respond.

"And you came here to do what? You're going to teach me a lesson, now? Is that it?"

I should have said something, I guess. Except what do you say? All those hours in the car and I still hadn't come up with anything. Instead, I turned toward the door and watched Evan yelling on the other side of the glass. Dora had one hand up, her fingertips touching the window, her head tilted slightly, with a puzzling smile on her face. Was that a smile? That fucked-up wig. That fucked-up smile. She'd made me into a cliché is what she'd done. The jealous husband. She was watching it play out, amused, delighted—I don't even know. Her face wasn't familiar anymore; there was nothing in it that I remembered.

"Who is she?" the bartender asked.

I exhaled and closed my eyes. "Why do people like you think this is okay? That's what I don't get."

He pressed his arm into my throat again. I looked at him and wondered if he was a decent man, if he thought this about himself, if this is what Cassie thought. It seemed like I used to be able to read her mind—this was the kind of couple we were—but now...I mean, I wanted her to not be an idiot.

"You need to get over your... whatever it is and take it up with her. Understand? This isn't my problem."

It felt, for a while, like the best option would just be to let the guy keep crushing my windpipe. There was a commotion off to my right, an interior door crashing open and a man running through. A face. A gun. A hissing voice. Evan's ridiculous blazer. Dora's terrible, selfish smile. It seemed okay to end the night there, just fade to black and wake up somewhere else. I guess this is what ended up happening, what sort of happened.

The man who marched us up onto the roof had a chipped tooth, black hair slicked into a wet-looking ponytail. He waved the gun around like it was a toy, pointing us in the direction of the stairs, commanding us to start walking.

The bartender seemed to sigh, angrily, then pushed me down the hallway toward the stairs. "Go."

"I'm not going onto anyone's roof."

"Listen to him. If he wants us on the roof, we're going on the roof." He sported a look of resignation, like this wasn't his first trip up the stairs, like he wanted to be there even less than we did.

The dark-haired man had a weasel-like grin. One eye drooped and the other one was wide and alert, like a spotlight. He put an arm around Dora, then leaned forward and pressed his nose into the top of her head. "That doesn't smell like real hair to me."

Dora looked like she was about ready to cry. "We want to leave, okay? Just let us go."

"Oh, sweetheart. Don't be afraid. I'm just particular, is all. I like things to be where I want them to be."

"We shouldn't have come here," said Evan. "We were wrong. We apologize. Do you hear what I'm saying? We'll leave."

The weasel leveled the gun at him. "Stick around," he ordered. Then, to Dora: "There's a nice view up top. I promise you'll like it."

The bartender pushed me again, and this time I started walking up, up, up around the creaky stairwell. The light in the hallway was dim, the carpeting worn down to the wood along the edge of each stair. I heard the others behind me, marching up in single file: the bartender, Evan, Dora. The weasel bringing up the rear.

The roof was unimpressive. Low and flat and tar-covered, with a narrow brick edge poking up all the way around it. We stood in a loose circle around two plastic chairs and a low table, covered in empty beer cans. Scattered around us there was garbage, broken glass, more cans. Dora looked cold and nervous. Evan wrapped an arm around her shoulder.

"We asked for a roof garden, but they wouldn't put one in for us. Someone left us these chairs, though. They put a busted lock on the door, along with a sign that says No Roof Access, just in case anything happens up here." He turned to Dora. "Which nothing ever does.

"I like to talk on the phone up here. Do my business. Especially at night in the summer, when there's a nice breeze. It's a little cool tonight, but not too bad, considering how late in the year it is."

I wondered if the bartender had ever brought Cassie up here, if they'd sat in these same plastic chairs, drinking beer and trading stories.

"You all need to relax," said the weasel. "You." He gestured the hand with the gun toward me. "You don't want to talk. Why is that?"

"I don't have much to say."

"I get it." He turned to Evan. "Is that your girlfriend?" This time he waved at Dora.

"She's…yes. The most important person in my life."

The weasel seemed surprised by this response. He pulled a keychain out of his pocket and shone a beam of light into Dora's face. She scrunched her eyes and turned away. "And is *he* the most important person in your life? This is true?"

"That's private."

The weasel laughed. "Do you know that I got into law school? I wanted to be a moderator. An arbitrator. Whatever you call them. Do you feel me? I'm good with disputes. Slow down the pace. Take it up on the roof. Put people under the open sky and everyone starts to calm down."

"That makes sense," said Evan, inexplicably.

The weasel turned toward Evan. "I don't understand the sport coat. I don't understand those pants and those shoes with that sport coat. You need different shoes. Something that shines a little more. I'm not really a fan of suede." Evan looked down at his feet. It felt like he was falling for a practical joke; for a series of jokes, one after the other.

"Can we get on with this?" barked the bartender. "I'm tired."

"Fine." The weasel sat in one of the chairs and rested the gun in his lap. "Would you like to sit down, my dear?" he asked Dora, gesturing at the chair next to him.

"No." Evan pulled Dora close, his arm tight around her.

He shrugged. "Suit yourself. Anyone else?"

I stepped into the circle and sat in the empty chair. My throat was hurting, but also my legs, although I wasn't sure why. Plus I'm a little bit afraid of heights, and something about the weakness in my knees and the darkness and the fact that I hadn't eaten anything since breakfast and now felt like I'd never be able to swallow again—it didn't seem like I could stand up for much longer.

"Lee." The weasel looked up at the bartender, who I didn't think looked anything like a Lee. "Tell me what's going on here."

"Nothing. We have a friend in common. That's all."

It seemed like the night was never going to end. I looked off in the direction that I thought was the east and tried to find the first blue beginnings of morning, but there was no horizon line in the distance yet, just more of the same black sky.

"He was fucking my wife. Is. Basically that's the situation."

The weasel considered my statement for a short while. "Yeah, you kind of strike me as the possessive type. The silent demeanor. The rock face. The short fuse, ready to blow." He paused. "I guess I wouldn't be happy about that either. But you know what they say."

"Can we go now?" asked Dora.

"Not yet. I want to hear more from Rockface over here first. So your wife..." He broke off as a look of understanding crossed his face. "Oh, wait a minute. I know who you're talking about. Don't I, Lee? She was the one who came here that night. With the shoes."

Lee only shrugged.

"Of course I remember her. She was so drunk she could barely stand. A delightful little mess, really, with that dress and everything."

"Stop."

"Nice legs, though. Just an all-around pleasing shape to her. Good skin tone. I notice details like that."

The bartender's face cringed as he listened to the weasel talk about Cassie. It was evidence that he cared about her, I guess. Did I want this or the opposite? I couldn't decide. Both ideas made me feel sick.

Evan was talking. Muttering, under his breath at first and then slightly louder.

"This is the curse. This is the curse. This is—"

"Shut up about the curse."

"What curse?" asked the weasel.

"No," said Evan. "Listen to me. Taz was right. We might only have five or ten minutes left; it might end for us tonight. And if not tonight then soon. It's all headed that way. It's all...leaving."

The bartender looked at me. It seemed, strangely, like we had something in common, like he wasn't such a bad guy even though I knew it was my duty to hate him. "What's he talking about?"

The weasel leaned forward in his chair. "Now this is something I find interesting. Who's cursed?"

"Nobody. There is no curse."

"We all are, Danny. We made the wrong choices and I thought maybe we could make up for it along the way but I was stupid. In the past it's been hazy, but now it's peacefully clear. We have to be honest, and make amends. Right now."

Dora was crying into his chest, but I couldn't figure out why. She reminded me of a bird, somehow. She always had. A bird that sings to try to please you but then flies away when you get close. I didn't want Evan to have her. It shouldn't have mattered, but somehow it did.

At some point the bartender and his roommate stopped talking. We had become a beautiful, tragic spectacle. There was a moment of cool silence, a brief period when it seemed like we all just wanted to sit and feel the edges of fall in the air. But then Evan started up again; he kept at it.

"Danny, you're like my brother, but sometimes I hated you. I liked you best when you were unhappy, because it made me feel better about myself. Sometimes I would have these thoughts...like...I don't even want to repeat them here. I can't say them out loud. It's so painful for me to even tell you this. These are the petty emotions that people feel; the ones that ruin us. But all of us—we're the best person and we're also the worst person. The daily struggle is sending the darkest parts back down to the bottom and letting the good stuff rise to the surface."

Then it was Dora's turn. As she spoke, my throat burned. "I always wanted you and Cassie to break up. Without even meeting her, I decided she couldn't improve you. She made you harder, helped you put a shell around all the good parts you used to have. Do you even remember how you were before? Don't you ever miss that?" Her crying turned into sobbing. "You always pretend not to remember! That note you wrote to me. How could you not remember it later?"

"Oh my God," said Evan. "Dora. What...?"

He dropped his arm. Their bodies separated. "No," Dora continued. "You're not getting it. Nobody ever gets it. Do you remember the cabin? There wasn't anyone else; just us. The road was too long; we were so far away. We settled in together so fast. Carrying those buckets of water up from the creek. Making toast on the campfire grate. The way it didn't rain that whole week. The way you could hear the creek if it was quiet enough. You guys would stand around throwing rocks into the water and somehow this was enough. I said I wanted to make a time capsule and you thought I meant it literally. I was here and you were all somewhere over there."

I saw her arm stretch out, off to the side, to mark whatever fictitious "there" she was referencing. I looked off in that direction, squinting, hoping for insight but finding nothing. Out of all the things to miss, it seemed like this one was the most important.

"And then people started falling out of the sky. It was a message to us, because it was so impossible. We should have listened but we didn't.

"*You* were impossible, Danny. That's what I can't get over."

She stepped back, disappearing from view. Everything Dora said confused me. She had always been like this. You'd put the effort into trying, almost work it enough so that it started to make sense and then the whole thing would collapse in on itself.

Evan came toward me and crouched down at my side. "Just imagine we fixed everything. We came up here and all the stars were out and we all looked up and joined arms and...I can't even come up with an ending to that. But just imagine it. Make up your own ending."

The door to the roof opened with a metallic scraping noise. The weasel spun around and pointed the gun into the darkness. Evan and the bartender turned their heads.

"Danny?"

I turned to see my brother stepping out of the shadows, a man returning from the dead.

"I heard people up here. Is that you?" He looked from face to face, until he found mine. "Is everything okay?"

The weasel stood up and blocked Curt midstride, pointing the gun at his chest. "Who's this?"

I rose from my chair, still dizzy and maybe not yet quite able to stand. I didn't understand how the night could get any more impossible to believe, how many friends of mine could make their way onto this one desolate roof. They all seemed to move at once, in eerie slow motion, toward Curt: Evan, the bartender, his roommate.

"Danny. What's going on?"

I forced the words out. "I'm fine, Curt. It's fine."

Curt held up his hands and addressed the weasel. "I'm just here for Danny. You can put that down."

The weasel laughed, a loud, cackling cry that spun out into the night. I imagined it traveling, echoing, rousing children from sleep up and down the block, the next block over, down the street from room to room. It sliced into the air like a knife, and before I could warn him, Curt stepped through, into the opening.

It's hard to say exactly what happened next. I remember seeing Evan walk up to Curt, put a hand on his shoulder and feel along his arm to his wrist and then back up again. "Holy shit. You're Danny's brother? Where did you come from?" The weasel was laughing. They were standing around, having a meet and greet, while Dora was...where was she?

I backed away from Curt and the others, toward the edge of the roof. "Dora."

"Why'd you let him bring us up here, Danny? Did you know this was going to happen?"

She was taller than me somehow, which seemed impossible until I noticed that she was standing on the lip of bricks that wound around the edge of the roof, her wig off and dangling from one hand.

"*We* could have been the ones who fell." Her voice was far away. "But we weren't. Because we were born as us instead of them."

"Things happen the way they do. You could spend a million years trying to come up with a reason for it."

"Close your eyes and listen to the sounds of life. When you open them again..." She let the wig drop from her hand, down, to whatever was below her.

I heard voices behind me. The bartender's roommate talking much louder than the night could tolerate. "You were *missing* for fifteen years? My God, that's a revelation, isn't it? And are you part of the curse too?" The murmurs of Curt's voice, Evan's voice.

In front of me, Dora swayed, arms out to her sides. "Do you remember how it ended? Your note?"

"Come on, Dora. Just get down, okay? Why does it always have to be a performance with you?"

"When you open them again *I'll be gone*. That's what you wrote to me. What an asshole you were."

"It was stupid. The whole thing was stupid."

"How is it that none of us ever told anyone what we saw that day? That's what I want to know."

"It doesn't matter, Dora."

"We all watch two people die and not a single one of us tells anybody about it? Of course it matters." I took a step closer, let her rest her right hand on my shoulder. "The curse isn't the tusk, it's us."

"There's no curse. It's just bad luck."

"Same thing." Slowly, she nudged her head forward, looked down at the four stories of early-fall night between her and the ground. I put my hand on her waist, tried to get as tight of a grasp on her dress as I could.

I could feel the building vibrating, my head pounding.

"Dora."

"We have to tell somebody. Tomorrow. Let's do it tomorrow. Come with me."

"We can't do that."

"Why not?"

"Because then..." I didn't have the words to explain it, how there was still a chance of escaping it if we just gave it enough time. We didn't do anything wrong. We didn't do anything wrong.

"It could have been you and me jumping. *We* could have been the ones who fell." Her fingers closed around my shoulder. I felt her pulling. "Come on, Danny."

It sure seemed like she was going to jump. If you had been there, this is what you would have thought too. The way she was talking, the way she was pulling at me, the way I was pulling back.

"We have to tell somebody," she pleaded.

"No, it's too late."

"We have to."

The more she pulled, the more I pulled back, and I don't know why I didn't just yell out for help, but I guess maybe I forgot the others were even there. After a while she was tugging so hard that if I didn't fight it we would have both gone over the edge.

"Let's just go. We'll tell someone. We'll be sorry about it. We'll get on with life. I'll let Evan down gently and marry a nice accountant, and you can convince Cassie not to sleep around on you anymore and it'll be happily ever after for all of us. Somersaults and lawn mowers and hot dogs out on the grill. Right?"

"Dora, that's not—"

"Or how about this? You tell Cassie that you're never taking her back, that you never wanted to be with her anyway, but you settled for her because you couldn't have me. Does that sound better?"

"Stop."

"But you still think about me all the time. You try not to, but you can't help it because—"

"You need to stop talking. Now."

I don't really know if you can reduce what came next to this happened or that happened. It was like an eye blinking, a finger twitching. A hand slipping.

I remember Dora pulling, as if with super-human strength. That might be an exaggeration, I guess. The look on her face. Hideous and selfish. I remember letting go of her dress, opening my hand, lifting my arm and turning my shoulder so that her hand slipped off. I remember watching her teeter, trying to regain her balance.

I remember thinking that there was an easy way and there was a hard way, the sensation of my mind snapping in two. From behind me that loud, cackling laughter again. An easy way and a hard way.

I remember reaching out, pressing my palm against Dora's waist. Pushing. The way her body spun around as she fell. The look on her face: the not-surprise, as if she had known all along that this would happen.

After that, it was a blur, a rush of bodies, a salty, city-night taste in my mouth as voices called out Dora's name, then stopped as we all listened for a response that never came. I wanted to run too, but where would I go? My head was pounding, the echo of Dora's voice crashing around inside of it.

"What just happened? Where is she?"

The desperation in Evan's face. It made me feel sick.

"She just...jumped."

"What do you mean? Danny... What did you do to her?"

Evan's blazer flapped out behind him as he ran at me. I remember thinking, as he approached, that maybe he'd been right after all: the three of us, taken out that very night. In another instant, it would happen.

A flash, yes. Darkness, a flash, and then darkness again.

# CHAPTER 33
## (CURT)

They ended up on a roof. All six of them: Danny, Evan, Dora, Curt, the bartender, his roommate. It felt like a place Curt had been before; maybe not that roof exactly but one more or less like it. He remembered a hot night, a girl in a white dress and sandals, her arms and legs dark and smooth. She liked to look at him over one shoulder, to turn around and catch him staring at her. He'd promised her something, as soon as the sun went down, but he couldn't remember what anymore, or even her face. Just the white dress, with spaghetti straps resting on her shoulders. He couldn't remember the roof either, but what did it matter when they were all more or less the same?

The night was a mess, dressed up in so many confusing layers. Curt didn't understand how he had come to be there, standing next to a person who was talking about a tusk—*his* tusk—convinced that it was a cursed object. He didn't understand how the gun ended up in his hand, how the woman ended up on the sidewalk. Danny said later it was her family who owned the cabin. It all seemed impossible. And yet, these things had happened, as naturally as breathing, which was what startled him.

He remembered the one with the gun laughing, a paralyzing and mirthless sound that came from a hole somewhere in his skull, and the other one saying *oh my God she went over the side*, as if it weren't a building at all but a boat. Evan rushing toward Danny, coming forward like a wave, like human panic. *What did you do to her?* The light was dim, but Curt could imagine the look in his eyes, that wild animal turmoil, the adrenaline rush and the super strength, the ability to injure without pausing to deliberate first.

"I tried to stop her. I swear."

"How could you let her do that? What kind of a fucking person are you?"

Curt reached for the gun, pulling it from the man's hand without pausing to think first. It was easy to come upon a weapon, to have one in your hands. The desire to act overcame him, and he raised the gun, hesitated. Seeing Danny's head turn toward him, but not quite finding his eyes. Not knowing, but at the same time knowing. There was fear and rage, and only Curt could feel it. *This person wants to hurt you, Danny*, he thought, wondering if it was dark enough for Danny to read his thoughts. *Stay there. Don't move.* Except that Danny did move, pushing Evan out of the way, just as Curt wished that he could undo the entire night. Suck the bullet back into the gun, and then the one before that, hand the gun back to the man with the black ponytail and head down the stairs and back into the evening.

Why did he fire two shots? He'd never know. He watched Danny slump over and realized what he'd done. Evan ran away, down the stairs. The man with the ponytail ran to the other side of the roof and disappeared. Curt watched the other man—the kind one— kneel down next to Danny. Curt wanted to help but it was time for him to run again. There was never going to be redemption, forgiveness, an end to the running.

The kneeling man had his head next to Danny's mouth as if he was listening to a secret. Curt didn't know whether to stand or kneel himself. How could it possibly be that he would kill his father *and* his brother? What kind of a person did that make him?

"It was an accident. I thought…"

"I think we're supposed to press down on the wounds? Is that what we do? Try to stop the bleeding?"

"I don't know. I'm sorry."

"Shit. What do we do?"

"Is he alive?"

"Yeah, but. I mean…"

Curt dropped his phone next to Danny and asked the kneeling man to call 911, certain that Danny wouldn't live until morning. He couldn't stick around and wait for the inevitable. He didn't know how to do this.

"I can't stay," he announced, realizing how bad it sounded. The man looked up.

"Take the gun with you."

"What?"

"Get rid of it. Make sure nobody finds it."

He paused, thinking he should try to explain himself, his actions, all of them for the past twenty years. Why was it that when it mattered there was never enough time? Curt stepped toward the edge and looked down on the sidewalk below. He could make out the woman's shaved head, one of her arms stretched out to the side as if reaching for an object, a person. Evan kneeling next to her, palm pressed against the side of his head, staring, frozen in place. It seemed like maybe the building wasn't so tall, that a human being could survive a fall from this high up. Just a couple broken legs, maybe. But looking at the shape of her body, of Evan's kneeling body, Curt understood that she was dead.

"I should call for the ambulance now. You should leave. If you go that way"—the man pointed in the direction the other one had gone, toward the rear of the building—"you can jump down onto the fire escape."

He held Curt's phone, waited. "If anyone asks, I didn't see anything."

Curt wanted to say something, to express his appreciation, but instead he ran. This, he knew how to do.

# CHAPTER 34
## (CASSIE)

The truth takes time to unravel. The night on the roof. Danny pushing Dora. Curt shooting Danny. Evan running, Curt running. Lee staying behind to help.

---

We mapped it all out, what we would do in the morning, where we would go. An apartment in the city, a house in the country. Cool water from a well and fruit trees: apples and pears and peaches. Avocados. Olives. We'd raise animals, ride horses, create art and sell it at a gallery in town. We'd write poetry, lyrics to our own songs.

*When does all of this happen?*

*As soon as the sun rises we're on our way.*

Him laughing. Me laughing. Not knowing what time it was, safe in the dark.

*Look out there. It may never rise.*

*You know it will eventually. It always does.*

Promises that weren't promises. A plan between strangers. An impossible story, like you might read in a book.

He was a madman and then he wasn't.

---

I don't know anymore, what to do. The things that people do. The decisions that they make. They are part of a world that doesn't include me.

I sit in Bill's car with the bag of money on the seat next to me and the tusk on the floor. Time has passed since I watched Danny drive away, but I don't know how long. Before he left, he promised me he'd figure everything out, that we'd move on from this, that we were the kind of people who could. A few minutes later, Curt followed him, getting as far as the parking lot exit before turning around, driving back and rolling down his window as he pulled up next to me. He offered me the frayed blue towel with no explanation, held it for me while I wrapped the tusk in it, watched me shift the bundle to my left arm in the same way I used to hold my children when they were babies.

There were a few sentences, pieces of sentences, ideas that never led anywhere, and after a few minutes we both gave up.

*I thought when we finally met it would be...you know.*

*I don't know if it matters but...what I mean is I don't want to pick a side.*

*I just keep thinking about the kids...your kids...what would happen if their dad was gone.*

When he drove away it was like a hole had been blown open in the night. Darkness opening up into more darkness, and Danny and Curt taking the blackest path through it.

Am I supposed to make a decision now? Is that what happens next?

I wake to the sound of knocking, knuckles on glass, a stranger's face glaring at me through the driver's side window.

I lower the window four or five inches, maybe more. Far enough for the man to insert his hand through the opening. The gun he's holding is black and dull. He offers me a view of it head on, its small, round entry to blackness more or less even with my eyes. What is the smaller circle underneath that one for? Does it have a purpose or is it just there for balance?

"Get out of the car," the man orders. His face is large and oval and a few days unshaven. He's wearing diamond stud earrings in both ears, an ornate gold ring with a blue stone on his finger. I try to imagine his life outside of work, what his house looks like, what color towels he has, what he tells people he does for a living.

In his other hand he's holding a phone, up to his ear. "Yeah, I found the wife in the parking lot at the bar." Is he one of the henchmen from earlier? I try to match his face up with one I've already seen, but it isn't familiar.

"Get out of the car," he repeats, knocking the gun against the window frame. "She's not listening…come on. Out."

"Is that Randall Kincaid on the phone?"

"Does it look to you like I'm playing around here? I want you out of the car and standing over there." His voice tightens into a fist. He gestures behind him, at nothing in particular, continues to talk to me and the person on the phone in turns. "No, I don't see anyone else here. Yeah, well it doesn't make sense to me either. Hey. Do you not understand English? Out."

"You can have the money." I nod toward the plastic bag. "If that's what you came for."

He leans in closer. I can see a faint dimple in his left cheek. "Where is your husband?"

I'm supposed to be frightened, but instead what I feel is tired. This might be the ending. I might not have to make any more decisions, or see another morning.

I can hear Randall on the other end of the phone, issuing instructions in smooth-edged syllables.

"Could I talk to him?" I raise my voice: "Mr. Kincaid! Tell him to hand me the phone!"

The man pauses, listening. "Yeah, okay. Okay. Yeah. Fine." He pushes the phone through the open window and it drops into my lap. I try to make myself feel more afraid, to inhabit the same space as this man and his gun. *He might kill me*, I tell myself, but how come my hands aren't shaking? Why is my heart not racing? It seems possible that I'm already dead. I have the tusk now; isn't that a clue? Did I die in the fire? In a car crash on the way home?

I pick up the phone and press it to my ear. "Randall Kincaid?"

"Where's your husband, Mrs. Irving?"

"I don't know. They left. He gave me half the money, not that I wanted it. You can have it back."

There's silence on the other end, as if the line has gone dead, then Randall's voice emerges from the same black hole that Danny and Curt drove through earlier. "The money is yours as long as I get Anton Low in return. It's the same thing I told your husband."

"What are you going to do once you find him?"

"That's none of your concern. This is personal business."

I try to picture his face as we talk, but the image that flashes into my head is of my father, from years ago. My mom is the young woman standing next to him. He reaches out for her hand as she steps onto a boat. I follow her, wearing a stiff orange life vest. We motor out onto the lake and drink sodas out of a cooler. My mom's hair becomes tangled up in the breeze. The motor makes it too loud for us to speak, so we turn our faces to the wind and let it press them into smiles. As we pass another boat, my mom lifts her hand and waves. The memory confuses me. Am I falling asleep?

I focus on the car, the phone, the voice on the other end of the line.

"Your daughter jumped. This was her decision. Not to open her parachute."

"You didn't know her. This is just what someone wanted you to believe."

"I don't understand what the revenge is for. You both lost the same person. He watched her die. What would you add on top of that that would make you feel better?"

"It's not about feeling better. You're missing the point entirely."

"Settling scores, then."

"He sent me letters. He wanted me to think she was alive. It was calculated. There were pictures..."

Randall's voice vanishes into the darkness again. I reach over and grab the plastic bag from the passenger seat. How much money is in it? I never looked, never counted it, never even guessed. I fold the plastic over onto itself until it becomes a parcel small enough to push through five inches of open window. The man with the oval face watches it hit the ground, but doesn't move.

"Mr. Kincaid? Are you still there? I just returned the money. However much was in there. It's on the ground in front of your... friend. I honestly don't know where Danny went. I never know. We're not like that."

"You realize that there's no difference between me and your husband, don't you? If he was in my position he would do exactly what I'm doing."

I see my dad's face again. My mom's face. There were cabins on the lake. A bar with open windows, music pouring out. The clothes we were wearing, my mom in a peach-colored sundress, her arms tan. There must be something special about this memory, but I can't figure it out. It's just a place where we were once, where I remember being.

"Emmaline was worried she was like you. That's why she did it."

*She would have learned*, I think as I press the End Call button, *how to live with herself.*

# CHAPTER 35

From the east, the sky begins to lighten, gradually at first and then all at once. I expect it to be magnificent but instead it feels routine. Black becomes saturated with blue and purple. A white-orange glow breaks through and pushes the darkness up from below. I dared the sun to rise, and it did.

*You know it will eventually. It always does.*

In the light of morning, the Silver Whistle looks like it's been abandoned for decades, fallen into disrepair and gutted by vandals. Smoky windows with ancient burned-out neon signs reminding anyone who might happen by that it was once a place where people gathered and drank too much on Wednesday nights, forgot who they were or pretended to forget, got caught up in the lights reflecting off the liquor bottles, sprinkles of joy, moments that should have passed quietly but instead came to rest and then grew, into questionable decisions, turmoil, tragedy, fire. So long ago, all of it. Mostly just rumors now.

It's 7:16 when I turn on my phone. Almost immediately, it rings. It's Annette, calling to tell me she's heard I left Danny and there's plenty of room at her place if I need to crash there for a while. *It's not like that*, I explain, even though I'm not certain what it is like, how I'll describe it when it's a story with a past tense.

Lori calls and offers to watch the kids if Cherie can't. She'll take the day off work if she needs to. She'll make lunch for them, wants to know if they have any allergies, what kind of foods they like, what they won't eat.

Cherie calls to yell at me for not answering my phone, for not coming back last night, for making her worry that I was dead. Then she breaks into tears and tells me how relieved she is that I'm okay.

"The kids are sleeping. We stayed up late waiting for you. Should I wake them up?"

"No that's okay. I'll be there soon. I'm sorry."

"I'm supposed to be at work in an hour. Let me know if you need me to call in."

"I'll be there in a half hour."

I listen to her hesitate. "A half hour again, huh? Are you going to tell me what happened?"

"Danny...I don't know. He might be leaving. I'm not sure."

"He was trying to take the kids, wasn't he?"

"No, nothing like that."

"Because he came here looking for them."

"He did?" I try to put together the hours after he left, where Danny might have gone while I was here, in this car, waiting for... what is it exactly? Did a man with a gun come and threaten me? Did I talk to Randall Kincaid on the phone, or was that a dream?

"It was early. Five-thirty, maybe. I told him to fuck off. That I hadn't heard from you in a week. Larry got out the baseball bat, just in case."

Was he going to take them, or was it a visit to say goodbye? What did we decide before he headed off into his dark hole? Was there anything we *could* decide?

"You need to tell us what he did, Cas. So we can help."

"I don't think I can explain."

"You two got married so young. It shouldn't matter but sometimes it does. You became different people. It doesn't mean you failed at anything."

"Everything happened out of order. I keep trying to reorganize it, but I lose the thread."

"Where are you right now?"

"At my mom's." The lie is effortless, necessary even. "Did you know there was a fire at the Silver Whistle?"

"It's about time that goddamn place burned down."

"Hey, do you know those houses built into the side of the hill?"

"Which ones? What hill are you talking about?"

"I don't know. I can't even remember where I saw them. Geo-something, I think they're called."

"You sound delirious. Go to sleep. Let me call in to work."

"Really, though. What do you think it would be like to live in a house like that? On a hillside?"

"Are you serious? A bedroom underground without any windows? It would be like being buried alive."

"Maybe you're right." I take up the thread again, follow it as far back as I can, and start over. "Do you ever have moments when you remember something that happened a long time ago, like being in a place, and it seems like it's crucial to who you are, but in the end it's not anything? It's just an event, from the past?"

"Can I bring the kids to you now? At your mom's? I'm worried about you. I'll feel better when I see you."

"Give me a half hour. Forty-five minutes at the most."

I lift the bundle from the floor of the car, set it in my lap, unwrap the tusk. It's milky white, streaked with honey and caramel. I run my hand along its shining surface. What do they do to it to make it so smooth? I press the cool ivory against my face. I pull on the thread, let it unravel. What do I do when I get to the end?

Without their father, what would Nel and E do? Would they always look back, remembering that it used to be different and wondering why it changed? I can hear myself talking to them, choosing words carefully, trying to explain without explaining. *Your father isn't bad, he just went too far trying to fix things for us. He was unlucky. He got mixed up. We're all allowed to make one mistake.*

Danny will tell them about the Secret Path to Joy, he'll make them believe in it. We'll pack up the car and move, from town to town. He'll tell me the next place will be better, the next one will be for us and we'll stop and open up our bakery and nobody will remember the names Randall Kincaid, Emmaline Kincaid, Dora MacIntosh. We'll get by, we'll manage. We'll never tell the children what really happened, and eventually they'll grow up. Life will leap forward. We'll erase the past the best that we can. We'll grow old, we'll die. In the best reality, this is what will happen.

Once upon a time, there was a man who killed a woman that he used to love. It was an accident but also it wasn't. It's hard to explain. And once upon a time there was a different man, a madman who parked his van in a parking lot and kept company with married women late at night. These are the kind of men that deserve to be blamed for murder, and when they run, to be hunted down.

---

That peach sundress my mom used to wear. I'm certain she doesn't have it anymore. What was on her feet? White sandals, maybe? How do I have a memory of these clothes, these people? The man, the woman, the girl. I don't know them. We're not them.

# CHAPTER 36

## (TREASURES)

After they killed the beast, it didn't stop screaming. They could hear its cries as they sawed off the bloodied, jagged edges, estimated how much the tusks weighed, what they were worth.

*Sometimes it takes a while*, they said. They covered their ears and waited.

And waited.

And then watched, as the ground rumbled and tumbled and opened up and swallowed the beasts and all of the treasures that the men had taken.

It had to be magic. Sorcery.

Because one by one, the humans died.

They looked for rooftops so that they could jump.

They looked for islands so that the sea might rise and swallow them up.

And the ones who made plans that failed—they discovered that there were no more beasts left to kill, so they made more weapons and killed one another instead.

They burned down buildings and drove away in cars and when they reached the land where all roads end, they climbed into rocket ships and shot themselves into space, in search of silence.

# CHAPTER 37
## (CASSIE)

I'm a bouncing dot. I'm nothing but trouble.

I've ruined a family, Evan says, a legacy. Danny clawed himself out of a disaster for us, but I was too short-sighted to understand his vision, too impatient to let it unfold the way it was supposed to. *He never would have gone to the police like you did.* Evan's hair is longer, parted in the middle and tucked behind his ears. There's a young woman with a sprawling house and an empty life who he's wellness coaching and possibly dating, a new business enterprise in the works, the book he still intends to write with Danny after all the dust settles. When he hands me one of his business cards, it occurs to me that we might never speak again.

Bill has released his rockets, straight into my chest, but somehow I've survived. He tells me he's been talking to good lawyers, getting good advice. If it comes to it, nobody will take my word over Danny's. We need to think about the kids, what's in their best interest. He's decided they should stay with him and Deb for the time being. *They need a stable home right now.* I hang up and block his number, too exhausted to fight.

My mom shows up at my apartment with a suitcase, says she'll help out as long as I need her. She wakes up early and makes breakfast, watches the kids while I'm at work. Out of the hard side of her face, she tells me she always knew Danny was trouble. She sounds like my father, uses words that he would use. Then she clutches her neck and goes back to being herself. "There are people who can help after events like these. People you can call." I see it in her eyes. The regret she works so hard to hide. So one night I ask her about the summer we rented a cabin and a boat, when we motored out to the middle of the lake with fishing poles and a cooler full of sandwiches and drinks. This time I see a flash of joy. "Oh, that was so long ago. I can barely remember." The soft side of her mouth trembles. She touches it with her fingers and her eyes grow wide.

Danny is nowhere. Or he is nearby. Or he is miles away, to the west, to the south, in a place I can only dream of. When he calls, I let him talk to the kids on speaker phone. I listen as he tells them how much he misses them and tries to explain why he's gone. *Life gets wobbly sometimes but you have to ride it out the best you can.* One night he calls and the two of us talk past midnight. It'll only be a few days, he says, a few weeks. However long it takes to figure out the Kincaid situation and the Curt situation. He promises me we're not My Word Against Your Word People; he just has to work through it in his head first: how the truth will sound in his voice, how to file down the sharp points of it so they won't hurt as much. I have nothing to promise in return, so instead I tell him that the apartment reminds me of an empty classroom, a place someone forgot to board up. I can't explain, but Danny says he understands. Our voices are low as we discuss how much of the past to erase, how people find new homes.

The kids and I talk about where we want to live. We make plans after dinner, on Sunday mornings as we cuddle up in my bed to-gether. We talk. We cry. We give up and then start over. They don't want to leave. I don't want to leave. We decide to stay. School starts and we surrender ourselves to routine. The chaotic mornings, the homework, the Boys and Girls Club, rushed dinners and even more rushed bedtimes. Some evenings E goes quiet without warning, his face darkens, he walks away and closes his bedroom door and doesn't reemerge until morning. It all feels normal. Within the realm of normal. We're adjusting. This is what adjustment feels like. The way people glance at us sometimes, never quite managing to smile. The way we hold our breath without knowing it as we wait for a difficult moment to pass. The things we want to say but don't. The way Nel cries quietly at bedtime and whispers to her stuffed bear. It will all pass. Won't it?

Eventually, we make real plans, the kind that stick. Lori's cousin lives in Vermont, in a land of rolling hills and good schools, where people love baked goods, where bakeries abound. She has a mother-in-law apartment on her property that we can rent. It's too small for the three of us but we pretend not to notice. The October weekend we go to visit, the place is filled with tourists who've come for the fall color. How strange that the leaves are so vibrant right as they are dying. We head in the same direction as all the other cars: up into the hills. I find myself wondering what is hidden in the woods, what tragedies lie settled beneath the leaf litter.

On the way back into town, we happen across a field where a hot air balloon hovers above the ground, a young couple in the basket, nervous and giggling. He must have a ring in his pocket. He's planned this out for months. We sit and watch as the balloon sails into the sky. In our imaginations, we consider the possibility of being happy.

The movers come, they pack up what is left of our belongings into a small truck. In one of the boxes there's a fraying towel with an ill-gotten trophy swaddled inside. There's a story told and re-told, an ending that isn't mine. I'll steward it along, though, until it's my turn to let it go.

Nel writes a note that says

The Irvings used to live here and then they moved-away. Nel, Evan, Mommy, and Daddy.

Before we leave, I place it in Danny's secret hiding spot in the closet. Nel's fairy wings are invisible, but sometimes when she turns, I can almost see their shimmering outlines. There was a room, once, with velvet curtains, where I tried to leave her. A place that was better than wherever I was headed. Is that what happened? I don't know anymore. It might have been a dream, a distant past cross-knit with a future that never happened. Our lives have been so much out of order for so long.

This part, though, is now. It happens on a morning in November. The sky is gray mixed with pockets of back-lit white. We pile into the car, bundled up in sweaters, our winter coats heaped up between the kids. Pillows, sleeping bags, stuffed animals. Crackers and juice boxes. A printed out map with our route traced in yellow. So many roads out there that we've never thought might be ours. Finally, it's time.

We drive.

We look east, we look north.

Out of the cracks, like slivers of light.

We drive.

CPSIA information can be obtained
at www.ICGtesting.com
Printed in the USA
JSHW011748301122
34019JS00003B/3

9 781948 585712